WHITE LINE WARRIORS

WHITE LINE WARRIORS

Driver reveals the personal side of life she and her husband shared earning a living driving truck while at the same time giving credit to all the other thousands of truckers out there hauling freight 24/7!

Written By

BILLIE A. KENNEDY

Library of Congress Control Number:		2013901270
ISBN:	Hardcover	978-1-4797-8247-5
	Softcover	978-1-4797-8246-8
	Ebook	978-1-4797-8248-2

This book was printed in the United States of America.

To order additional copies of this book, contact:
Xlibris Corporation
1-888-795-4274
www.Xlibris.com
Orders@Xlibris.com
99833

For my mother Anne, my husband Ron, my three wonderful children
Kim, Kellie and Jason
My grandson's Jake and Sam and future grandchildren

Billie A. Kennedy

To All the Men and Women Who Drive Big Rigs
You Are the Nation's

White Line Warriors!

And

For all those who read my book, I hope you learn from it, enjoy reading it and walk away with a new appreciation for all of the many thousands of truckers out there carrying the load for you!

Billie A. Kennedy

ABOUT THE AUTHOR

Billie A. Dana (Kennedy) was born in Sumas, Washington, a small town located near the Canadian border. She is one of five siblings having two older sisters and two younger brothers. She grew up in Bellingham, Washington being raised solely by her mother. Times were tough back then and she learned early in life that if she wanted something beyond what her mother could afford, she would have to work for it. Her first experience in writing was during junior high school where she actively participated in publishing their monthly school newsletter. Later on in life she accepted the entire task of creating a "first "company employee newsletter for her boss and she continued that responsibility for several more years. Writing has always been her interest, but having a job and earning an income obviously took priority. She and her husband raised three children. All of them graduated from college, something she is very proud of and was never able to accomplish herself.

She spent most of her working career as a hospital Patient Account Manager. Having only a high school diploma, she entered hospital administration hired on as an entry level file clerk. In time she ultimately advanced to the position of "Director of Patient Administrative Services". In between her busy job at the hospital she also ran a tight ship with her children at home and found time to help her husband with his business.

After retirement she decided to pack a suitcase and ride along with her truck driver husband delivering freight up and down the west coast. It wasn't long though before she got tired of being a passenger and decided to learn how to drive truck herself. Billie kept a journal of the life that the two of them shared out on the road (with the intent to pass it on to her children), but as time went by, it became more apparent to her that she must share this personal trucking experience with others as well.

CONTENTS

INTRODUCTION

WELCOME TO LONG HAUL TRUCKING

For the past several years I have been doing long haul trucking with my husband Ron along with our big yellow cat "Diesel". We have driven in almost every state within the United States, and it wasn't until June, 2008 that we decided to park the truck and take our own leave of absence. This was partially due to high fuel prices, the desire to get our ten acres fenced and to take care of Ron's elderly mother. She has Dementia, (which is common with ageing), and it's progressively gotten worse. She needs someone to be with her 24 hours a day.

Now I find myself with hours to spare, the house is clean, the weather has changed and frankly, I'm bored having this much time on my hands. I have worked since I was old enough to pick strawberries for my school clothes. Spare time does not sit well with me, so this is a perfect opportunity to get started on my book sharing with you what life is "really" like out there on the road for the truckers who drive the "Big Rigs"! (My book reveals "our" own personal first-hand experience!)

Before I begin, not every driver you see inside a big rig got their "first" job driving an 18-wheeler and then stuck with that profession for 20 years or more. Many of us, if not most, had other careers before we signed on to "white line fever!" Take myself for example; the majority of my working years were spent in a hospital setting as a Patient Account Manager. It was quite a switch for me to give up a five-day a week job with my own office space, kicking off the high heels for tennis shoes, leaving the makeup behind, putting on jeans, a T-shirt, plus a few extra changes of clothes and then climb inside the cab! I was like a little kid with wild expectations; eagerly spinning my wheels to get going and be off on a new and exciting adventure! I loved it and couldn't wait for Ron to start the engine!

When I look back, I never once in my wildest dreams ever envisioned that I would have enough courage or desire to get behind the wheel of our truck and then actually learn how to drive it! This thought would have probably scared me to death! My initial plan was to ride along with Ron and enjoy the scenery. However, it's never too late or uncommon, especially if you're a woman, to change your mind without much notice and announce that you now want to learn how to drive truck yourself!

I love to travel and it seemed to me driving truck cross country with my husband would be like a paid vacation. Whoopee! How wonderful I thought, the two of us together, enjoying all the scenery and while at the same time, we would be getting PAID for it! What a great way to earn a living! No doubt we both imagined it to be the best of both worlds! There were so many states that neither of us had ever seen. Most of my travel in the past was by air and this job offered sight-seeing at its best! I was 57 year old when I told my husband about my desire to learn how to drive a big rig. Jokingly, I told Ron I wanted to "RUN with the BIG DOGS"! He laughed, but he also took me at my word and appeared enthusiastic about the idea knowing as a team we would make much more money. But however, he also was quick to tell me about the downside!

You basically live out of a suitcase! The lifestyle is tough and takes some time adjusting to the confinement of living each day inside your home on wheels. In the beginning, even trying to sleep at night with all the noise surrounding you takes some getting used to. Some drivers on their maiden run have been known to quit way before or shortly after delivering their first load! The stress a new driver may endure along the way, like relentless heavy traffic, weather conditions, slowdowns through construction zones, driving through unfamiliar towns and cities, and watching for highway directional signs, can sometimes end up being way too much for them to handle. After enduring several hours of driving, some rookies stress level simply gets maxed out! This is so understandable when you consider the rookie, for the very first time, is running alone out on the interstate. He must drive without the help and encouragement he previously received from having an instructor sitting in the passenger seat beside him. Suddenly finding themselves in this situation immediately takes them out of their comfort zone! The reality of knowing it's now their "sole" responsibility to safely get the load delivered, constantly eats away on their mind, and for some drivers; it puts them over the edge! They end up parking their truck, throwing in the towel and taking a bus back home! Fortunately this scenario applies only to a very small percent of rookies; most of them make it!

From day one, I started out keeping a journal. It was not because I planned to eventually write a book. I actually wanted to keep a record of what our day to day life was like living out of a truck. My vision was that one day I would eventually share our around the clock trucking experience, with my three children, Kim, Kellie and Jason. I wanted to give them the "inside scoop" on what life is really like for long haul drivers. Since then, I totally changed my mind; I felt a stronger need, almost as if it were my duty, to educate others as well about our trucking experience.

What really got me thinking that I should share my journal with everyone is the constant encouragement that I received from others. Anytime we were home and around friends or relatives they would listen to me tell one or more of my trucking stories, then beg for more! All of the stories were true of course and for my audience, that made it even more intriguing. Some of my experiences were funny, others were frightening or sad. It didn't matter what I revealed to others about our personal life out on the road, people listened with fascination and wanted to know more! Our conversations always ended with "Billie you should write a book!" From all this encouragement, it finally dawned on me that most people are ignorant about the truck driving industry (through no fault of their own), but they really don't have a clue about the inner world of trucking. Once I realized all this, I suddenly had an overwhelming desire to educate the world; like a mother hen watching over her chicks, I wanted to speak up and speak out in defense of all the great men and women out there driving big rigs! I was firmly convinced! "All that I have learned in the past several years running team with Ron, I now must pass on to others as well; not just my kids!"

What I hope to achieve from all those who will eventually read my book, is the satisfaction that they will come out with a better understanding, appreciation, and respect for all the truckers they once took for granted! The men and women who keep America going, the ones they use to cuss out, flip off, honk at, and pass by every day driving their four wheelers on our highways throughout the nation!

These working men and women deserve so much more recognition and admiration, but the truth of the matter is that most of them are

NOT getting it; at least as often as they should! Many don't even get an "atta-boy" from their own employer or even much less from the customers they serve! I could even go so far as to include some of the trucker's families as well but will be quick to say, it's not the public's fault! After all they're not out here living the hard life. I myself at one time could not even imagine the work Ron had ahead of him every time he pulled out of our driveway. I was happy about the money he was making, but had no clue how hard he had to work for it!

I'll never forget a story told to us by one team driver. The driver Matt tired and just getting off the road, said he went into his home office and told management he was so proud of the total miles driven between him and his wife. (As I recall, over 24 thousand miles in one month, all delivery's were on time and accident free). Now, take my word for it, that's putting the ol' peddle to the metal! When you're running that hard, you never stop! There is no time for showers or nice warm dinners in a restaurant. In fact, most likely the truck is probably still running while fueling and the other driver is inside the truck stop filling a thermos and picking up pre made sandwiches. Matt continued by telling us he suggested to the manager that it would be nice if the company gave them one of their jackets for their exceptional efforts. Much to his surprise, the response he got was very deflating and depressing. The answer was "you get a pay check don't you? That's your reward!" Needless to say, to not even get a "thank you" hurts!

We all want to be appreciated, especially when we go the extra mile to make the company money. I'm sure this is part of the reason why we often hear about some companies having so much trouble in maintaining their driver retention. People are human and will perform to higher expectations when the company they work for acknowledges their efforts. Even a simple "thank you" or "good job" from the boss or customer makes a driver feel good! When a driver gets his belly full of being treated like a number instead of an asset to the company they work for, he or she will most likely quit at that point and find another job promising better treatment.

"If you bought it, a truck brought it!" This is not an original statement and I'm sure many people have seen this message posted on the back of a big rig. But, it's a fact! None of us would be able to enjoy all the things we take for granted, if it were not for the thousands of dedicated truck drivers delivering goods to us each and every day of the year; not only in the United States but Canada as well! Yes, every day, none stop!

There is no such thing as weekends or holidays off in the long haul trucking business. You live the job 24/7! Americans need and depend on truck drivers to keep them supplied with everything imaginable; like fuel for their auto, food on their table and even the toilet paper they use in their bathroom! Sure, there are other modes of hauling freight, like trains, airplanes and ocean freighters, but they can only go so far with it and then must rely on truckers to come in, take over and get their freight delivered! Truck drivers not only move freight for thousands of shippers, they are also called upon to help out during times of weather related disasters such as tornados, hurricanes or earthquakes. For just these reasons alone, I wonder how many Americans would survive without the enormous contribution that truckers make in insuring that their every wants and needs are met!

Many people, (like myself at one time), viewed a big rig as a "monster" a huge obstacle hogging the lane in front of us, and when it comes to driving up behind one, four wheelers quickly become annoyed as hell! The slower 18 wheeler forces them to slow down and remain stuck driving behind it for possibly several more miles, (depending on traffic)! Their automatic response is to immediately look for the first chance to escape, pass and get around it! What four wheelers need to understand is that the drivers of big rigs don't like to drive below the speed limit either. They would prefer to maintain keeping with the flow of traffic. But, when you're climbing a hill or hauling heavy freight the slow speed is unavoidable.

Admittedly, before learning to drive an 18 wheeler, I never once thought about the "driver behind the wheel"! It didn't even cross my mind what he or she might be hauling, if they were married or not, do they have kids, how many days have they been away from home, does the driver have health issues, could he/she be on drugs, tired, fatigued, or are they new to the job? I also neglected to give thought as to whether the driver was a "rookie" or a seasoned "old timer". Actually, like so many others, I didn't really care! I was caught up in my own life and not remotely interested in another person's way of earning a living.

How about the driver's feelings? Most people in reverse never consider how much misery they, "four wheelers" cause drivers of the big rigs! They pass on the RIGHT, follow too close, or pass a truck then quickly dart back in front it! These maneuvers put truckers in a continual defensive driving mode and sadly, many individuals have lost their lives doing it! Big rigs cannot stop on a dime! Under these circumstances an

18 wheeler could become a lethal weapon should it become involved in an accident caused by a careless four wheeler!

Drivers are of all ages and they come in all shapes, sizes, male, female, and from all races. When you look up at the driver sitting behind the wheel of a big rig, DON'T ever take for granted that he/she is just some dumb bunny that has no brains and the only job they could get was driving truck! Far be it from that! There are *many* people from other professions that got tired of what they were doing for a living and chose for their own personal reasons to drive truck; including the men and women who have served in our military! There are also many other drivers out there that finished up one career and started a new one driving truck; like a couple school teachers we saw in passing. They made their previous employment known by painting a message on their truck that read "Two Retired School Teachers". No, the men and women you see driving a big rig are not all the so called labeled "red necks"!

In all fairness, I will be the first to admit there are some inconsiderate jerks driving truck on the interstate! But, for the most part, you can be assured the rest of us are responsible professional drivers simply doing what we're being paid to do; haul freight! The bad apples don't last long and sooner or later they quit or get fired from the company they work for.

Sitting at a truck stop restaurant having dinner one night, I met a driver who previously earned his living as a dentist. He said he just got burned out from all the paperwork, patient complaints, crying kids and emergency calls on his days off. He said the independence and the freedom truck driving offered was exactly what he needed. On the other hand, I had a conversation with another driver that told me he's been behind a steering wheel since he started out with his first peddle car. Driving truck was the only life he knew. No, he was not a college graduate, but in my opinion, that man with his many years experience, was a true professional in his own right, regardless of what level of education he may have received. He proudly told me he has been driving 18-wheelers for more than 30 years, and then added jokingly, he was still married to the same woman! (It is a common fact that the divorce rate is high in the trucking industry.) When I asked what he attributed to his long marriage, he said "my wife nags too much, I love her dearly, but we get along great only seeing each other every few weeks". "She gets my paycheck and I get to do what makes me happy!"

There are many other drivers out there, and for "their" own reasons, chose the trucking industry as a way to earn a living. The face you see behind the wheel is a very real person and they deserve all the respect we can give them. Did you know that many of these drivers are away from home for weeks, or months at a time? As a matter of fact, for some drivers, the truck they drive is their home! They don't always get to share Christmas, Thanksgiving or other holidays with their family. During these times, a driver's participation only amounts to a phone call.

When a driver begins his day he already knows he's going to be constantly dealing with the ongoing pressure of safely navigating his rig through a never ending flow of traffic. He is also prepared to handle any other pop up surprise that may challenge his driving skills as well. Most often his day will end without problems, but then there are other days when the life of a driver turns upside down! For instance, you never want to get yourself in a painful situation by making a bad turn that instantly puts you out of route! This type of error will become one of your worst nightmares, especially if you're in a big city and end up on the wrong side of town! A simple decision to take an unfamiliar exit off the interstate could be costly and lead you into harm's way! It creates enormous stress when you don't know where you're at or how to find a way out! Not to mention loss of driving time and in some cases, it could possibly cost the driver his life plus the freight he's hauling! Believe me, although this doesn't happen frequently; it could! Most often predicaments like this can be avoided with good pre trip planning. Every day presents a new challenge for a driver and even after good trip planning, you always need to be prepared to expect the unexpected! Welcome to the world of trucking!

Constantly keeping your eye on the road, watching for "bears" (State Patrol Officers), "coops" (weigh stations), state highway signs, weather conditions, pedestrians or critters crossing the highway, debris such as "gators" (pieces of blown tires), motorcycles, (some are in groups of over a thousand when you go through South Dakota during Sturgis Bike Week), hitch hikers, tail wagging trailers pulled by four wheelers, slow moving rental vehicles, motor homes, accidents, disabled vehicles, stretches of road construction, monitoring gages on the dash, frequent mirror checks, stops to make sure the load is still secure, communicating with dispatchers, and planning allowable driving hours to make an "on time" delivery is all in a days' work for a driver. If this isn't enough to keep that trucker's mind busy, in addition to all this, I'll throw in a few more things that might be going on with the driver behind the wheel! What if he/she is not feeling very well? Maybe the food last night was bad. What if the driver has personal problems going on like pending divorce or a sick family member, or maybe he is in debt over his head!

These are all very real things that a driver could be thinking about, and yet, he is expected to remain alert and focused on his driving; never allowing his mind to drift off throwing him into a state of complacency. This isn't always easy to do, but the driver knows he is responsible for a safe delivery from the minute he accepts the load to the time he delivers it. I cannot count the times I have overheard driver conversations where there was a sick child, death in the family, girlfriend problems, talk of divorce or financial problems thus leaving the driver frustrated and helpless because he is unable to immediately do anything to resolve these issues. He must keep on driving looking forward to when he will be able to shut down for the night. When that time comes, he will have the opportunity to address all the problems he was unable to deal with earlier.

Finding a parking spot for an 18-wheeler is a real pain no matter where you are within the United States! Most truck stops are packed by 4 p.m., or what few tight spaces are left, you really don't want! Not every driver backs up straight into a parking stall and often when they do their wheels are over the painted line! Because of the tightness, backing into a spot like this puts you at risk of hitting someone else's rig, or worse yet, them hitting you when they pull out! Looking for a place to park is a challenge to say the least. It could be at a rest area, off/on ramp, closed scale house, or if you're lucky, you might get to a truck stop early enough to find a spot. Some of these places only allow temporary parking, like rest stops that have posted limited hours for parking. In some states, if you are parked on one of the interstate on/off ramps, a trooper will pull up, hammer on your door, wake you up, and tell you to move or he'll give you a ticket!

I remember one year we found ourselves in an ice storm that started the other side of Albuquerque, NM. We continued to drive as the highway became worse with every mile. When it flat out became too dangerous to drive, we decided to find somewhere to pull off and call it a day! We both kept our eyes out for a place to park. Other drivers ahead of us of course had the same idea and the places we spotted were already full of trucks. We had to continue on looking for a place, ANY place to park at this point, but there were none to be found! Every time we passed a truck stop we could see they were jammed packed, in fact drivers "created" spots to help other drivers squeeze in! All of the lots were nothing but a sea of trucks, looking just like the hundreds of boats we have all observed tightly clustered together inside a harbor!! The on/off ramps, every one of them, were solid bumper to bumper with parked 18-wheelers with no doubt a very relieved driver inside!

We continued to drive in freezing rain making our current predicament even more miserable. Not only do you have poor visibility, the highway becomes glare ice, the wipers cake up smearing the windshield, antenna's take a beating, your tires feel like mush, (no grip) and you better hope your defrost works! At this point all of the traffic out on the interstate got down to a VERY slow crawl!

We caught up with other trucks ahead of us and were quickly down to the speed of a slug! As we drove along in the caravan we witnessed several slide offs of big trucks and four wheelers. Mostly fender benders, but all of them were stuck and we knew they would remain there for several hours before a wrecker would arrive. Driving is treacherous and no doubt wreckers have more vehicle accidents and slide offs than they can possibly handle.

We finally made it to Amarillo, TX and to no surprise you couldn't even buy a place to park! We ended up driving along the side streets and much to our surprise, low and behold; we spotted a church parking lot that had been plowed! Bingo! Boy was that a welcome site! Ron quickly pulled in and just hoped that we wouldn't be asked to move before morning. You cannot imagine the relief you feel knowing that you didn't get into an accident, you're still hooked to the trailer, the freight is in tack, and you're off that icy miserable highway! We could finally start to unwind and only hope by morning that the roads will be safe to drive on.

Getting back to the life of the truckers out here; all of us want to look forward to a hot meal when the day is done, make a few phone calls, do some reading, watch a little TV, listen to music, talk to other drivers over the CB, do laundry or maybe even squeeze in a shower. (Not necessarily in that order!) The other thing we all like to do once in a while is deliberately strike up a conversation with other drivers over the course of dinner. Swapping stories none stop is to be expected! I'm sure many of the stories we heard were made up or exaggerated. It's sort of like who can out do who; so the more you sit there and listen, the bigger and better the story gets! One of the hot topics of conversation for a driver is bad mouthing their dispatcher! Every driver I swear has his own story about a crabby, insensitive dispatcher that lacked understanding of their particular situation. Sitting there, the person telling the story gets full support of every other driver because they too can easily relate having experienced the same treatment. Then there are other times that we prefer to sit quietly and eat dinner alone, however, if you've got ears you can't help but hear what's going on around you. Ron and I have been married for so long that we don't have to say anything to know what the other person is thinking. Many times while eating one of us will overhear something and will give each other that "did you just hear what I heard" look!

I witnessed one time a young driver trying to eat his dinner across from our table. His phone rings, he starts out real happy to get the call, and by the end of the call, he pushes his plate away and is obviously upset, clearly sick to his stomach. (Dealing with problems over the phone and trying to resolve them makes all of us feel so helpless.) With frustration in his face, he gets up, leaves the table and heads back to his truck. I can't be sure, but it appeared to me that he was talking to a wife or girlfriend who was accusing him of "having a good time."

(Yes, the rumor is correct; there are "hookers" at some truck stops! This could make a wife suspicious at home, but most drivers avoid them like the plague!)

I must admit, before I got out on the road I had a few phone conversations with Ron like the one I just heard. I feel bad now for the stress I previously caused my husband, but admittedly at the time, I felt insecure with his absence and was probably more jealous than anything else. I visualized his job to be "cushy", no pressure, imagining that all he had to do was drive and really, how hard could that be? I obviously felt resentful and sorry for myself because in my opinion, I was the one at home taking care of the house, mowing the lawn, taking out the garbage, paying bills and working at my regular job. I would then vision him having a good time, eating his meals in a restaurant, probably putting on his best smile for a waitress, occasionally staying in motels and enjoying the freedom of the open road!

When I overheard the conversation next to us I wanted so bad to have the trucker pass me the phone. I had the urge to help this guy and whoever he was talking to by describing the scene. (Let's just say I wanted to patch things up for him.) The restaurant was a "dive", the waitresses were not movie stars, service was poor and there were flies everywhere! I sat there and imagined if I were able to talk to the other person I would explain what it's "really" like out here! Whatever was being said ruined this trucker's dinner! Given the chance, I would also have pointed out to the caller that he was sitting alone in a corner booth by himself! When a driver intentionally picks a booth distancing him away from others, there's a good chance he's tired, worn out and wants to be left alone! This would be especially true if the guy had a hard day out on the road. The last thing he needed was to end his day by winding up in an argument! I felt sorry for him.

What you have read so far is a small glimpse, just a peek into the inside world of long haul trucking. There is much more to learn about the job itself and what it requires, including the not so pleasant lifestyle. The entire contents of "White Line Warriors" were taken from the many memories and notes that I had previously recorded in my journal. All of the trucking events, experiences and the day to day life conveyed in my book are solely an expression of my own personal perception of what took place. Although my writings are based upon a true story, I have changed some of the locations, names of fellow drivers, people we met along the way and omitted company names to protect their identity.

CHAPTER 1

STARTING OUT

My journey off into the world of long haul trucking goes back to the spring of 1999 and as I recall, it was April fool's Day! Not really, but it was the first part of April. When I think about it though, there were times I thought both of us were" fools" or just plain nuts for being out here driving truck, especially in the winter! As you travel along with us, I hope you will enjoy reading my personal documented entries, get to know us, not only as truckers, but as a couple with family holding on to love and concern for each other regardless of distance. This is our "first hand" experience!

We started out in debt by purchasing a brand new Volvo truck. What's the old saying? "You've got to spend money to make money!" Or maybe our thinking was another old saying, "No one ever made it BIG by thinking little!" Or here's another one, "Those who succeed are willing to take risk!" (I would love to give credit to whoever came out with these profound statements because I believe each and every word of them!) Whatever the reason to support our decision, we mutually agreed buying a truck was indeed the right thing to do! The Volvo was black with gray leather interior, heated seats, 13 speed, big windows, large sleeper, and had lots and lots of storage space inside.

We had a professional painter do the lettering, "KENNEDY TRUCKING", Spanaway, Washington, plus paid additional money for, (at that time), the required listing of our gross weight of 80,000lbs. Just to top it off we had the painter do a little pin stripping! What a beauty! Our painter even surprised us by putting each of our first names just below the windows on both doors! Lastly, before we even took off on our first run, we went into the truck stop and purchased a refrigerator/cooler along with a small television. We both felt great knowing we topped off the truck with these two final amenities, thus making our $145,000 house even more comfortable and "road ready"!

Most owner/operators take pride in their trucks no matter what they drive, especially if they have something to work with. Company drivers on the other hand unfortunately don't have that much of an option. They get whatever truck is assigned to them and as far as I know, they are not allowed to add personalized lettering, pin stripping, fancy paint jobs, extra air horns or additional chrome. In contrast, a driver owning his own truck and leased on to the same company under most circumstances can do whatever he wants to his rig as long as he has the money to pay for it and the D.O.T. (Department of Transportation) doesn't find a problem with the enhancement.

Speaking of the D.O.T, most officers are pretty decent, but once in a while you run into one with bunny rabbit brains and a huge authority ego! They will try to find something wrong with your truck or log book even if it takes them forever! I know this first hand and it's not fun! It causes you stress, time, and resentment especially when you feel the surprise inspection was unnecessary when they end up finding no errors in your log or any mechanical problems! Don't get me wrong, D.O.T. inspectors are necessary and provide a very important service monitoring truck and driver compliance, but like I say, once in a while you run into an inspector that seems to get a real boost to his/her inner ego by making a driver's day miserable!

So here we are into the first week of April as owner/operators and our dispatched assignment is to go pick up a load of paper from a mill in Montana. Our loading appointment is scheduled for 12:30 a.m. which means we need to eat dinner early, try to grab a few hours sleep, get up, get loaded and drive all night! Although I could have stayed sleeping, I got up with Ron at midnight and we drove over to the mill. When we arrived, another truck was backed up to the loading dock which left us no choice but to sit and wait until the driver pulled out. Ron was not very happy about this unexpected delay but about an hour and a half later our trailer was finally loaded and we now could be on our way. Ron went in and got the paperwork, documented "load time" on his driver log then proceeded to drive to a nearby truck stop to weigh. The scale ticket showed that our total weight was 77,833 lbs. which means that we've probably got about 42,000 lbs. riding in the trailer.

When you scale, you get a breakdown of your axel weights and if the weight is "over" 12,000 lbs. on the steers, 34,000 lbs. on the drives or 34,000 lbs. on the trailer axels, you've got a problem! In this case, you've got to get out, pull the slider release on the trailer, then slide your axels and adjust the weight in order to meet D.O.T. axel weight limitations. Sometimes this procedure is repeated several times until you get it right! The D.O.T. may pull you in if they see that you're overweight on "any" axel after driving over their scales. When this happens, chances are they will make you stay there in their parking lot, sliding your axels and reweigh until you're legal! Resolving this problem could even go so far as having another truck come in and take part of your load! The possibility of a costly fine, plus all of the lost driving time caused by the delay could result in a late delivery, not to mention the enormous stress it puts on a driver. In our case, we only had to slide the axels once!

Satisfied with the weight distribution, Ron got out on the interstate and drove about 600 miles before stopping! We ran into a pretty good snow storm just outside Salt Lake City, UT. In the midst of the storm, we witnessed a car lose control right in front of us, spin out and come to an abrupt stop in a snow bank! When we passed the stuck vehicle, the man driving was still holding on to the steering wheel and looked absolutely frozen to it! He had passed us earlier and at that time, Ron said that the guy was driving way too fast for icy road conditions! Now the jerk got what he needed and deserved; a "wake up call!" He obviously wasn't hurt and in no way were we about to feel sorry for him!

Stayed overnight in Nephi, UT and after a cup or two of strong black coffee we headed out early this morning traveling south on Interstate 15. With each mile I enjoyed the changes in scenery and even spotted an occasional deer grazing in someone's pasture along the way. Our route through Utah gave me an introduction to their gorgeous red rock country sides dotted with small prickly cactus along with lush patches of what appeared to be juniper trees. Much to my surprise though, after only driving a short distance into Arizona, the rolling landscape changed! Suddenly we found ourselves engulfed; shadowed by enormous, beautiful, towering mountain sides of bright red rock. We instantly became very small and frankly it felt a bit intimidating! Dropping down into the Virgin River Gorge I still could not believe my eyes as I observed the size of the mountains quickly increasing in height! They all were magnificent giant towers of solid red rock keeping us captured in their beauty. It would make anyone driving feel like an ant in a caravan about to be swallowed up by these monsters! This area truly is one of nature's gorgeous wonders! I also saw my first cactus; in fact I was able to identify four different varieties. From the Utah/Arizona line it is only 38 miles before you cross into Nevada, but the short drive offers 38 miles of spectacular scenery!

We're in Nevada now and all of a sudden we're up against driving through a very strong head wind! Ron said it's sucking the fuel right out of our exhaust pipes! I've never felt wind gusts so severe and as I look in the mirror, I can see our trailer swaying behind us like a dog wagging his tail! I'm afraid that the wind is going to blow us over! We're running ahead of schedule so I suggested to Ron that we stop for awhile thinking the wind might calm down. Ron agreed to give it a try. We are in the small town of Mesquite, Nevada and there are no truck stops. The only parking for big rigs is conveniently provided to truckers at the local casinos. Makes sense to me! A trucker's dollar spends the same as four wheelers; it's all revenue! We went into the casino but didn't stay long. I lost $32 and didn't like it one bit!

It was still windy when we walked back, but we had a load to deliver regardless and had already used up some our driving time. Ron started the truck and instantly a light came on telling us to "stop" low coolant! He got out, pulled the hood and quickly identified the problem. We have two gallons of drinking water on board and Ron had to use both of them in the radiator. While he was pouring the water, he spotted a slow leak and assured me it was nothing to worry about. He said we'll get the problem fixed at the next truck stop. I was relieved with his assessment; we don't need major expenses to take away from our earnings!

We are down for the night at a Pilot truck stop in Barstow, CA. and the wind has not let up! When we were coming into Barstow earlier, some wise guy dump truck driver almost side swiped us by merging too fast over into our lane! I thought for sure he was going to slam right into my door! Ron avoided the collision, but had a few choice words for the driver along with giving him the familiar hand gesture! I'm glad we're off the road because the whole day has been hectic. Sitting here in the parking lot we can see two semi trucks that haul for professional race car drivers. Their advertising is beautiful, and I swear both trucks and trailers are spit shinned! Not a speck of dust on them!

Today is the 3rd of May and we are in Kent, WA backed up to a dock getting several rolls of carpet unloaded. This completes our first trip and we are anxious to get home. We chose not to take Diesel, (our cat) for our first solo run because we knew she might become a problem, (like wanting to jump out the window)! Unfortunately, a cat is not like a dog and you'll waste your time if you even think that you can tell them what to do! Diesel is actually Ron's cat; I don't even like her that much. I just tolerate her and she knows it!

Currently we live only a short distance from where we dropped the trailer, but in the near future we plan to move to Eastern Washington. Ron's mom is getting up there in age and we know she could use our help. She lives alone on 5 acres and has a large yard with several flower beds. It's getting more apparent that the work required in maintaining the property has become way too much for her to handle. Eventually we'll be there to help out!

One night at home and we're off again. This time, the cat is on board, but not by choice! We put her in a pet travel carrier and she is driving us crazy with her loud, continuous me yew's! Her high pitched screeching is distracting and annoying to say the least! The cat knows how to get our attention! She doesn't like being locked inside the carrier and is making no bones about it! Ron said, "Too bad, she's going to stay put in there until we get out of traffic"!

Because it was late yesterday, we dropped the trailer at the receiving dock in Kent to be unloaded and bob tailed home. Now the trailer is empty and we're hooked back up to it waiting for dispatch to give us a load. In the meantime, we let Diesel out of her cage. Much to both of our surprise, after she did some extensive exploring, she settled right down! Now she is snuggled up to her big plush duck sound asleep. When we brought Diesel home from the pet store she was a tiny kitten. We thought she was too young to be taken away from her mother, so to make her feel better; we bought her a big plush duck. That did the trick! She cuddled right up to it and has slept with her duck ever since! I guess the plush animal provided a little extra comfort and security in the absence of her mother.

I called all three of our kids last night to let them know we were home, but no answer. I was anxious to tell them all about my first hand experience of delivering freight with Ron. I had also intended to mention that their dad has a soft spot; he's not always grumpy! When we went through Deer Lodge, MT. Ron spotted an old man that appeared to be enjoying the morning by sitting in his wheel chair and watching all the traffic whiz by on the interstate. (We think he was in a retirement center.) When the old man saw our truck he instantly raised both arms high in the air and waved them back and forth at us. Ron could not resist and blew out several big long blasts from our air horns along with a wave back at him. I know this made the little old man very happy! A trucker acknowledged his wave! (Who knows maybe the old man was once a driver himself!)

We eventually got a load out of Kent, but had to drive empty to Vancouver, WA to get it. Diesel has abandoned her travel carrier and has accepted the fact that riding in the truck is her new home away from home. She lays up on the dash and looks at oncoming traffic. It's funny to watch her if she spots those orange cones going through road construction. I swear she is trying to count every one as she moves her head quickly back and forth. This will probably be her only exercise for the day because her preference is to lay upside down, legs stretched out and fall asleep!

Today is the 8th of May and we have stopped for the night in Santa Nella, CA. Ron is writing a note to his mother in a card we bought her for Mother's Day. We will mail it on our way to dinner. I'm looking forward to trying out the advertised famous *pea soup* across the street from us. The weather is warm but very windy and I can feel it rocking the trailer.

Nothing eventful since my last entry and if there was, I forgot it. I get caught up every day enjoying the scenery all around us and forget to write in my journal. (Just for record, it is now the 17th of May.) We were home again last weekend, but just for one day which allowed enough time to get the mail, pay bills, do laundry, and buy supplies for the truck. This time dispatch gave us a pre loaded trailer full of fireworks to haul to Montana. When I saw the placards reading "EXPLOSIVES" on the sides and back of the trailer it made me nervous. Ron assured me we were safe, but I continued to worry until the load got delivered! From Montana they gave us a load with two drops in California; one in Fresno and the other in La Mirada. Today we are back in Kent, WA waiting to get unloaded. It makes me laugh when I think about the distances we continually travel. It's sort of like a little game! "Now you see us, now you don't!" Or, "Here today, gone tomorrow!" So far I like this trucking life! While sitting here, I made my usual phone calls to all three kids. Kellie said she took Jake and Sam, (our grandsons) to Andrew's Air force base to see an air show. I'm glad she does things with them that boys like to do!

It is hard to believe I don't have to go to work anymore. I don't like the word "retired", I'm too young. However, I have had moments when I feel non-productive and think that I should still be contributing to the work force. Fortunately, these thoughts are short lived when I'm distracted daily by the beauty of all that I see out the window of the truck. Admittedly, I did have one emotional day; complete with tears! It was when it dawned on me that I had no job for the first time in my life all because I quit the one I did have! At that particular moment reality set in and it hit me hard; like a ton of bricks! It gave me an overwhelming feeling of nausea. I even felt a little panicked knowing that I willingly chose to throw in the towel and give up earning my own money just to go trucking with Ron. It made me feel empty knowing I no longer had the security and financial reward of being employed. I did this to myself! I no longer had a resource to contribute to our income!

This thought was painfully hard for me to swallow after working for so many years! My wallet was empty; I had no money of my own.

Whenever we needed something from a truck stop Ron would reach into his wallet and send me in to buy either food or supplies while he was fueling. I would return handing him back his change. The more I thought about my dependency of asking him for money, the more I resented it. It finally got to me and I blurted out my feelings! Ron had no idea I was so upset and when I started crying, he really felt bad. He felt so bad that he gave me his wallet and said "you can take all the money, I don't need it, you are the one that runs in with the thermos and buys sandwiches." I couldn't live with that decision either, so we compromised and split the cash! I'm glad this issue is over between us and I can put it behind me.

I love observing wildlife and the array of different flowers in bloom as we travel along the highways. So far I have seen Mule Deer, elk, antelope, skunks, porcupine, muskrats, ducks and several birds to include pheasants and even a bald eagle. The wild flowers are everywhere. In California the red and orange poppies are in bloom as well as "The Lords Candle" or as I call them, giant yucca plants. In Washington and Oregon all the beautiful dogwood trees are in bloom. This is the "paid vacation" that I imagined it would be!

Getting back to trucking, the crew finished unloading us in Kent, (it was a partial drop) so we still have one more place to stop and then we will head home for a day and a half. Not only the two of us, but Diesel as well, will be glad to get out of the truck and enjoy a bit more freedom of movement. I planted a vegetable garden earlier. Ron keeps it watered with a timer so I'm sure I'll be greeted with a bunch of weeds to pull.

Some driver just came in on the CB radio and asked for a radio check. Ron usually is the one to respond but he is out of the truck so I did it. The CB radio is a life line for communicating with other drivers. Most of the time drivers use their CB radio to get directions, do radio checks (to see if their voice is being received loud and clear) or maybe they just want to swap information like, where they spotted a "bear", (state trooper) or if the next "coop" (scale house) is open or closed. This is a standard practice amongst truckers even if we don't know each other, especially when it comes to sharing information like I just mentioned. Sure, once in a while the conversations over the CB can become smutty when two drivers get into an argument and want to stop and duke it out on the road! (This to my knowledge, actually getting into a fist fight, rarely ever happens.) It's interesting though how listening to a heated conversation between two drivers can get your attention. You even find yourself taking sides and cheering for the good guy! What is not surprising, the driver that got the argument going in the first place, nine times out of ten, is some little guy with a big mouth! Most of the time Ron stays out of the argument, but once in awhile, along with other drivers, he cannot resist putting in his two bits! This is when the conversation becomes REAL interesting! All of them are trying to out shout, get their point across, want to get in the last jab, ending the conversation with a final smart remark! Sometimes we get bored listening to sarcastic exchanges on the CB and when that happens, we shut it off and listen to audio books.

May 23rd and we are parked at a truck stop called Fat Harvey's in Canyonville, OR. Ron drove his maximum allowable hours today pushing a little more than usual just to get us here. He told me the food would be really good and is served in large portions! I can tell you one thing, this place is not fancy, but I trust his judgment. We've all heard that "truck drivers" know all the best places to eat! Well, tonight I will find out for myself. Meanwhile, Ron is catching up on his log. We, along with all the other 18 wheelers parked here, are running our engines keeping the air on. The temperature is around 85 degrees outside. This run so far has been pretty nice, at least up until yesterday when we made the decision to stop for the night in Nephi, UT.

We were sitting in our truck visiting after returning from a nice dinner. I was up front looking across the parking lot when I spotted a "shady" looking man walking towards Ron's side of the truck. He looked very suspicious and I instantly felt fear! Sure enough, the man continued walking right up to our truck, climbed up on our steps and braced his self by holding on to the outside mirror. I yelled at Ron, "Don't open your window, ignore him!" Close up, he had missing teeth, he was dirty, hair was uncombed, skinny, and had a very hard sunburned looking face with squinty eyes. He reminded me of every bad guy we always see in the horror movies!

Against my wishes, Ron buzzed down his window half way. The guy proceeded to tell him that he needed money to buy fuel and wanted to earn it by polishing our chrome wheels. (I was throwing a fit in the background!) He proceeded to tell Ron that he and his nephew have not had a shower or food in the last three days. (I'll bet the "not having a shower" was longer than that!) He continued by saying that he had just finished serving five years in prison for growing and selling pot. There was no way I would trust this guy and I really didn't believe all that he was saying! Ron, for some reason unknown to me, and I still don't know why, negotiated with him for the cost of shinning our wheels. Ron got him down to $10. The guy actually agreed to this and said he would get his nephew to help.

A few minutes later he returned with his so called nephew. He was younger, poorly dressed and looked just about as evil as his partner! They both proceeded to polish our wheels while Ron kept an eye on them in our mirrors. In the meantime, Ron instructed me to pack them up some food, and with reluctance, I went ahead and did it. I visualized Ron's request to be an act of "self protection" you know, like when you're up against a mean dog and you throw them a bone to keep them at bay! I thought maybe Ron's additional act of kindness will be enough that they will move on and leave us alone after their done.

When they were finished, the older guy asked Ron to get out of the truck so he could inspect their polish job. I immediately didn't like that idea and told Ron "Don't do it, just give them the money through the window!" Ron ignored me and said "Give me the bag of food. I'll just be a minute, and they're not going to do anything, there are too many other trucks around us." He gave them the $10 and the bag of food. (They didn't look like they were starving to me.) We then watched as the two of them walked away, relieved that they were out of our lives! I gave Ron and ear full when they were out of sight. I felt they could not be trusted for one split second! Ron agreed both creeps were of questionable character, but didn't think they had ulterior motives; I did!

Now, wouldn't you know, the minute we start to relax, here comes the older guy AGAIN! This time his obvious ploy was to get Ron engaged into another conversation by offering to share his "special recipe"; the one he mixes up and uses to polish wheels. Ron patronized him by pretending to write down the instructions. The stranger continued to force a conversation with Ron even after he finished giving him all the ingredients. I could tell the guys presence was starting to make Ron uncomfortable. I think Ron even became more suspicious they might be up to something when the so called nephew reappeared and stood there with hands on hip looking up at us! At this point Ron had enough, interrupted him, started the truck engine and said we had to leave! The creep continued to hold on as the truck started to move forward and then he finally let go, started laughing and jumped down from our steps! They were evil! Although we had planned to spend the night, Ron said as we rolled away, "They ARE up to something, I'm not sure what, but we're not going to stick around and find out either!" I was so glad! This unexpected situation forced us to drive another 52 miles before we could find another place to park. By the way, Fat Harvey's food was great!

We are now back in Auburn, WA unloading a few pieces and then the rest of the load delivers in Kent. When the trailer is empty we'll be off for a couple days. We are looking forward to a night at home, enough time to take care of a few things and then we will be gone again. I miss family and wish we could at least visit Kim while we're home. She has a new little pond and waterfall installed in her backyard that she would love for us to see.

May 26th and we are rolling down the highway listening to country music. In fact, the song that is playing as I write is, "Roll on Big Momma!" It's a song about a truck driver who calls his truck Big Momma. The music and words are very upbeat, somewhat inspiring and a song any trucker can easily relate to. You can even hear long blasts from a trucker's air horn in the background music!

Before leaving home yesterday, Ron surprised me and casually said, "You can start learning how to drive our truck today, it's not that hard to learn and I want you to give it a try." With that comment I instantly felt fear race through my entire body! No way!! Absolutely not! I actually felt sick to my stomach with his bright idea! Forget what I said in the past! The truck that I had enjoyed riding in for so many miles suddenly became an enemy and I absolutely wanted no part of it! It was a MONSTER in my mind!! I had NO confidence in myself and the thought of driving scared me to death! Ron continued to, at least what I considered at the time, to put pressure on me by repeatedly saying "Billie, I know you can do it, you've driven a truck before! I want you to at least try it just one time!" Thoughts raced through my head. Yes, I've driven a truck before but it didn't have 13 gears! I remembered watching Ron when he would shift. He would double clutch with each gear that he went into. I couldn't believe that he actually thought that his wife was capable of doing the same. Then I thought about the fact there is "NO" rear window in our big truck! That lost vision in itself stressed me even further! I've always had a rear window and inside mirror to see what traffic is doing behind me. Now I would have to depend on using the big mirrors attached outside of the truck next to our side windows and the ones mounted on our fenders!

Eventually I conceded and he took me to a nice straight street with very little traffic. I wasn't real happy, but determined to prove to him he was asking the wrong woman to get behind the wheel! He got out of the truck and I took position behind the wheel. I sat there and listened while he went through every gage on the dash, explaining the function of each and every one of them. I thought I would never be able to remember ALL of this information. He then proceeded to explain how to double clutch when shifting and further suggested that in time I too would develop a nice smooth rhythm. Sure, I thought to myself, you bet I will! At this point he said put it in first, let the clutch out easy, clutch, shift, clutch, and put it into second gear. Easier said than done! The truck bucked like a wild horse at a rodeo! That scared the devil out of me and Ron did the wrong thing; he yelled at me! He said you're going to take the transmission out! This is when my eyes filled with tears. Ron calmed down realizing how upset he made me and we both just sat there without saying a word. I regrouped, looked at him and said o.k. I'll try it again, but don't yell at me! Now that I had laid out the "ground rules" I was pretty sure he wouldn't jump up and down in his seat when I tried it again. Wrong!! This time though, I didn't let his loud voice interfere with my lesson! I was determined to get it right!

We spent about a half hour stopping and starting and in all honesty, after repeated tries I only made it to second gear! I just could not get the "feel" of double clutching. The problem I had was that I wanted to push the clutch all the way to the floor. I have since learned you don't have to do that! You barely have to press down on the clutch when you shift. I always believe in life "with every negative there is a positive". In my case; I did not conquer the knack of shifting in my first lesson, but I did get the feel of being behind the wheel, steered straight and was able to actually see what was behind me in the mirrors! I felt pretty accomplished for my very first try. Besides, I thought, for ANY person to just have the courage to learn to drive a big rig is commendable. I've now decided that I'm not going to give up, especially when I remember seeing other women driving out here. I know one woman in particular that I admire, Cindy. I've observed her skill in backing up and she can turn her truck on a dime! I too will persevere until I master and win the ultimate challenge I just put upon myself!

We've stopped for the night in Phoenix, OR and much to my surprise, Diesel slept most of the way. Outside of Medford, OR today Ron got on the CB radio and said a few choice words to another driver! I won't mention the company he works for, but it's one of them that always get cussed out by other truckers out here. They are considered slow, hold up traffic and are always in the way! The rumor is that this particular company has installed "speed governors" in all their trucks. Having this additional piece of equipment mounted under the hood restricts the driver from going over a certain speed. This becomes a problem for the driver considering a few states already have speed limits up to 75 mph! I've also heard rumors that in the future limits may even go higher on certain stretches of highway. Way too fast in my opinion for any 18 wheeler!

Most drivers will tell you when you are traveling at a higher speed, getting behind any of these slow trucks doing 55 mph, becomes a VERY REAL HAZARD! In a situation like this what occurs is that all the 18 wheelers, as well as the four wheelers, must hit their brakes and slow down for the slow moving truck in front of them! This chain reaction creates a long slow moving caravan forcing the rest of the traffic to stay in line until it's safe to pass. Unfortunately, not every trucker, or for that matter, four wheelers are blessed with an abundance of patience! Sooner or later, tempers flare, nasty words are shouted over the CB at the slow truck ahead, and as I personally witnessed, poor judgment starts to overrule the impatient driver's thinking! These reckless chance takers, the gamblers, (this includes everyone); cars, pickups, buses, motor homes, motorcycles and so on, begin to lose patience and stick their nose over the center line to get a peek at oncoming traffic. The risk they take is high, especially on a busy highway. Many deadly head-on collisions that resulted in taking the lives of innocent people (including the driver) have been solely attributed to someone's careless dumb ass decision to pull out and pass another vehicle!

Now, back to why Ron got upset with the driver that I previously mentioned. It was because the driver didn't have enough "steam" to complete his pass! He kept hovering along side of us neck to neck, running side by side, and it seemed like it would never end! (When you get two big rigs traveling next to each other blocking both lanes on the interstate, it instantly forces a slowdown of all other traffic.) Ultimately, Ron lost his patience and could no longer allow the problem to continue further. He backed off the accelerator giving the guy enough room to pull his rig over and get out of the hammer lane. When the driver merged into the lane in front of us he didn't allow enough space, cut it too short, and his trailer almost slammed into the hood of our truck! This is when Ron came unglued and wasted no time in getting on his air horn! He promptly gave the jerk several well deserved blasts! Ron wanted him to know he wasn't getting away with almost causing an accident and he was fed up with his sloppy driving!

Now you would expect that the driver learned a lesson from all this! You would also think he would turn tail under, be humiliated, embarrassed, and would stay in the right hand lane where he belonged! No he didn't! What actually happened was after the driver pulled his truck over in front of us, Ron was forced to slow down and reduce his speed. Ron continued to follow behind him for some time and then finally decided to pass so he could resume the speed he was originally driving. Ron no longer had completed his pass when in less than a minute I swear, the jerk pulled back out around us! He once again had his rig right out in the "hammer lane" hovering beside us nose to nose! This is when Ron stopped being "Mr. Nice Guy"! He grabbed the CB and without sparing any words, let the driver have it with both barrels! Unfortunately, chances are the driver of the other truck probably didn't even hear a word of what he was saying! Many drivers out here keep their CB's off just because they don't want to get yelled at! This is especially true for the ones that are driving a truck equipped with a governor. Nevertheless, I know it made Ron feel better to vent!

Here it is June 14th and we were only home a matter of hours and off again! "Love this trucking business!" We are on our way to Helena, MT, it is 80 degrees and I'm so glad we have air conditioning to keep us comfortable. Our route is taking us right through the city of Spokane. Unfortunately we won't have time to stop and see Ron's mother. However, just being close to the area where we met, married and raised our family is something we always look forward to. This trip we've got to keep rolling. We are under a load and on the push so we'll have to settle for viewing our familiar area looking out the windshield of our truck as we pass by.

Now we are in Montana, about five miles from the scale house and much to our surprise we just spotted a moose!! It was alongside the highway grazing on grass. We could hardly believe our eyes! On the subject of wildlife, I meant to mention earlier in my journal that going through Utah we saw three red fox. I consider this to be a rare sighting! I'm sure you don't get a chance to see red fox that often. Just went through the scale and I'm looking out the window at the world famous 50,000 Silver Dollars Restaurant and Bar. Ron took me in there once. The place is plastered with silver dollars everywhere on the walls, ceiling, tables and bar! They also have a gift shop with a huge variety of souvenirs including old coins. (I'm a coin collector, so I was in my height of glory!) We ate dinner in their restaurant, (prime rib), and the food was excellent! I would highly recommend to any trucker traveling I-90 that they take the time to stop. There is so much to see!

Our waitress was very friendly and she told us the story about a previous problem they had experienced a few years ago. She said "these big wild bears kept coming right up the steps and onto the long porch in front of their building; no doubt looking for food!" "People that were inside the restaurant stayed inside, and people that pulled up in their cars, didn't get out!" She claimed the bears were "grizzly" bears and were not common to the area. Her explanation for them even being there was that "the bears had to be relocated" for one reason or another. She continued by saying that the "locals" blamed "The Department of Fish and Game for not even warning the residents. She said "They just snuck them in on us!" Who knows? I was just glad they were gone!

Today we are in Montana and it's the 15th of June. We just got dispatched to pick up a load of talc and deliver it to Santa Anna, CA. Talc is very heavy and not a load either one of us wanted. (The heavier the load, the more fuel you burn and it takes forever to pull the load up long grades.) We just crawl!

I must mention that I have stopped even trying to put on makeup in the morning. As a matter of fact, I have not even worn any for a few months. Just imagine, me, going down the road, bouncing up and down and trying to put on mascara! I looked like a raccoon more than once! I decided to just give it up! As long as I don't pull the visor down and see myself, I hardly think about it anyway! Besides, Ron has not complained, so maybe I don't look that bad without it! The other thing I want share with all of you is that although I love what we are doing, there are some sacrifices we make for this wonderful life of independence! My family knows very well that Ron and I are, and always have been, very clean people. Now, things have changed and we do not get the luxury of a shower every day like we did at home. We carry water on board and are able to at least wash down at night. We also have these disposable moist wipes that we use throughout the day. Another thing I have to deal with is straight hair! I end up putting it in a pony tail because there's nothing else I can do with it. Going to the bathroom, especially during the night, is another problem for both of us. Ron is thinking about buying a porta potty. It gets real irritating when you have to get up, get dressed, and walk across the truck stop to go to the bathroom! Our bed I suppose would be considered "twin size" which barely allows room for the two of us. In fact, one of us has to sleep on our side. I always feel bad when I have to get up and climb over Ron disturbing his sleep. When it comes to brushing our teeth, the only way for us to do it is by pouring water into a cup then spit into a waste basket. This is a compromise, but when there is time, we take our toothbrush to the "trucker's only" bathroom and brush there!

One day I couldn't take it any longer because my hair is such a daily issue with me. I got my shampoo out of our travel bag, stuffed a hand towel in my jacket, and headed for the women's restroom! It was not easy washing my hair in a public sink, (much less tolerating the looks I got from other women) but that is exactly what I did and boy did I feel good after that!

What I am learning about living out of a truck, is that I cannot expect all the conveniences here that I took for granted and enjoyed at home. Sometimes you must be creative and make do with any alternative you can drum up. Both of us have come to deeply appreciate a nice hot shower in a motel, (which unfortunately, doesn't happen often enough!). Once in a while we are able to catch a quick shower at a truck stop. This is not our first choice, but it's better than not having one at all! We both think the showers at truck stops are dirty, even if they look clean. We even bought flip flops to wear in the shower to help protect our feet. The truck stops offer towels sometimes free and others charge for them. We prefer to use our own towels, washcloths, soap, and shampoo so we just bring them along with us. A couple times we have stayed overnight in a motel, but usually we're under so much pressure to get the load delivered, we don't have time to stop. Not all drivers are like mom and dad and it becomes quite visible by their appearance that they have gone several days without clean clothes and no doubt, without taking a shower. We all have choices, and I'll leave it at that!

June 16th and it won't be long and until we will be passing through Las Vegas. This has become a pretty regular route and I always enjoy seeing the massive sky scrapers with their flashy neon signs luring the public to come play at their casino. Their huge billboards advertise food,

top entertainment and "hottest slots "in town! I also have one spot that
I watch for going through this stretch on I-15 and it is just before you
really get into the heavy "Vegas" traffic. It's about as close as you can
get to the city itself without being there. You go under an overpass, and
that is where I always watch for a group of eight or ten homeless people.
They are always there and it seems they have made the shelter of the
underpass and nearby trees their home. I've seen make shift tents made
out of cardboard or miscellaneous other items used to create their own
private little space from one another. I have often wondered why the
city doesn't make them move, because even though I'm fascinated by
staring at these individuals, I'm sure to others, their presence appears to
be more of an eye sore!

I also ponder what their life was like and what made them end up
living here! I visualize their lives to be a "curve". They all started out
as an infant, and at this stage, someone had to be feeding and taking
care of them. I also think the care continued for some years after that.
BUT, somewhere along the way, something must have happened that
made them want to detach themselves from society. Whatever events in
life they experienced, whether it was bad parents, choosing the wrong
friends or getting hooked on drugs and alcohol, the results of their
actions put them in this position and no doubt, each blamed their past for
their predicament! The one thing they all share in common is the path
these individuals chose took a curve somewhere along the way and that
road eventually led them into homelessness. A life where they basically
must rely on begging for their daily food or look for it in a dumpster! I
wouldn't even be surprised if these same individuals, because they are
so close to the "Vegas" strip, just don't spend each day standing along
an off ramp holding up a sign up asking for help or walk down town
and beg for money from the tourists. I suppose I will never know the
answers to my curious thoughts each time we pass by, but I will continue
to watch for these poor souls and will always wonder WHY? How can
they appear so content with this self inflicted lifestyle?

Boy did I get side tracked! I was going to tell you about our brief
stop at the Moapa Indian truck stop. It's a few miles north of Las Vegas.
We knew it was hot and pulling some of the hills today Ron kept an eye
on all of the gages. We've seen too often trucks parked alongside the
highway because of overheating and we sure didn't want that to happen
to us. The truck stop was not that big but you could buy groceries,
fireworks, beverages, souvenirs or even play a few old slot machines. We

purchased a few snacks, dropped a couple quarters in the slot machines and headed back to our truck. When we were paying for our snacks I told the clerk waiting on us that when we got out of our truck it was like walking into a furnace! She said, "no doubt, the temperature outside here is 115 degrees!" Ron told me the Moapa's are a band of the Paiutes Tribe. (Now how did he know that?)

I'm doing pretty well lately remembering to add notes in my journal. Some days I guess I get too caught up in all that is going on inside and outside of the truck and then there are times when I'm just plain lazy! Anyway, it is the 17th of June and we are in Santa Anna, CA waiting to get unloaded. It's not as warm here as it was in Nevada yesterday, only 90 degrees. My skin has become sensitive to the sun and my arms are full of little red bumps. I remember this same rash happened to me last year after my first long exposure to the rays. No big deal and it will go away in a day or two. On the subject of weather, the one thing I don't like is that you can have beautiful sunny skies and when you get into certain areas of California, like Los Angeles, there are days when the sky darkens and turns to an ugly gray/amber color. Local people deny that the air is filled with smog, but I suspect that's probably what it is. Sometimes the air makes our eyes water and we both feel a burning sensation in them. On days like this we're always glad to get our load delivered, pick up another one and quickly head back to blue sky and sunshine!

It's been a week since my last entry. After hauling our load out of California and bringing it to Washington we were able to take three days off, not by choice, but what a treat! One of our air cans on the breaking system developed a leak and would not hold pressure. This is a very serious problem and we had to get it fixed. Running a truck in this condition is risky and would quickly be an automatic "out of service" violation from any D.O.T. officer. I'm glad we made it home safe and the truck is in the shop getting repaired.

I mentioned earlier that we planted a garden. Having three days off was perfect timing for harvesting some of the vegetables. We picked, washed and froze seven quarts of spinach. We also enjoyed fresh lettuce, radishes and green onions in a salad. There is nothing like "home grown" because you know what fertilizer has been used on it! Ron and I were born to work so you can just imagine how many more things we got done with the time off. Now we're all stocked up again inside the truck and waiting for workers to finish loading our trailer in Auburn. Just before we left this morning we got a phone call from our son, Jason. What a wonderful surprise! He will be getting discharged from the Air Force and will be home in two weeks. It's going to be so nice to have him back home!

I almost forgot to write this down and glad I just remembered what took place on our last trip. Ron was traveling on one of the Los Angeles freeways when he was suddenly cut off by two Hispanics driving recklessly in an old beat up truck. Ron hit the brakes HARD to avoid hitting them! Diesel flew off the top bunk, up in the air and landed smack in the waste basket! Bull's eye!! It scared the cat like you wouldn't believe! She jumped out of the waste basket just as quick as she got in it! Funniest thing I've ever seen! (I wonder if there is such a thing as seat belts for pets.) Needless to say, Ron did not take this incident lightly and promptly gave the Hispanics a big one finger wave. They acknowledged his gesture by giving Ron back a "double" wave! The driver and his passenger obviously didn't realize how close they came to getting run over by us! They appeared totally oblivious of the danger! Ron was very upset at their stupidity and shouted out some very strong words before he finally calmed down.

Another incident we came upon was a jack knifed rig right in front of us! It was a sunny day; the road was dry and straight for miles and miles ahead of us. We cannot be sure, but maybe the driver had a blow out on his *"steer"* tire. If this was the case, he most likely lost control and wasn't able to bring his rig to a safe stop. There were no apparent injuries, but I'll bet the driver wet his pants! It looked pretty ugly! "Knock on wood" we have never been in an accident but we've had some close calls. This driver that jack knifed his rig will have a long day of stress. Not just waiting for a wrecker, but the officer will go over his log, paperwork, climb inside the cab of his truck and go over it with a fine tooth comb, searching for possible drugs and alcohol. Pictures will be taken, (we all carry cameras), and he will have a lot of explaining to do when he calls his employer. This is a very bad day for the driver; wrecked truck and damaged trailer with freight inside of it that may not even be salvable! Now if this isn't enough problems for one trucker to handle, there's also the chance he'll end up losing a day's pay and quite possibly his job!

The law requires that "Driver Vehicle Inspections" be completed twice daily by every driver holding a Commercial Driver's License. Inspections are done prior to starting a trip and at the end of the work day. The results of the inspection are recorded in the driver's daily log. If any problems are found, they are also noted and the driver is expected to get them fixed. Unfortunately, I have heard many drivers complain that when they tell their company about a problem, they get brushed off. The usual answer is "next time you get to the terminal, bring it in and we'll take a look at it". I know buying truck tires is very costly, but when you do a V.I. (vehicle inspection), and the tires look like racing slicks, it's time for the company to bite the bullet and buy new ones! It is entirely possible that the jack knifed rig did have bad steer tires. I'll never know, but it does make me wonder. Funny and I don't mean funny ha, ha! If indeed the tires were bad, you can bet the "driver" is the one who's at "fault", and "not" the company he drives for!

June 27th and since my last entry, Ron has logged 2,753 miles and we still have another 120 miles to go to finish this trip into Oregon. On our way to California we ran into quite a lightning and thunder storm going through Idaho Falls, ID. This is the type of storm I don't like! The strikes were not pretty flashes that light up the whole sky, they were direct bolts hitting all around us! (I call them sizzlers!)

We came upon a BAD accident just past the exit into Lost Hills, CA. A small van had rolled over in the median and we heard on the CB radio that four people were air lifted to a nearby hospital. I was impressed with the compassion shown by truckers. One said "I hope there were no kids in there." Another trucker came on the CB and said "All we can do is pray".

Gave Jason a call and he said he will be coming home on the 22nd of July. He told us Kim (our daughter) is going to meet him in Sacramento, CA and then the two of them will "vacation" back to Washington State. It makes me feel good that our kids remain close even if they are all grown up and live apart. This thought also makes me wonder about all the other younger drivers out here on the road. I'm sure it must be very hard on them knowing the wife and kids he left behind will have to manage by themselves until he returns. Trucking is not a 9 to 5 job. Being away from home for lengthy periods of time is part of it! He won't be there to tuck his kids into bed or give his wife a goodnight kiss. This is the sacrifice, trade off, that must be considered by the driver before hiring on with a company.

We are now in Halsey, OR and parked for the night. Tomorrow we'll make our two drops, and then call dispatch to see if we can get a load home. We are running out of clean clothes, supplies and we both could use a shower. The constant confinement we share inside the cab is starting to wear on us both. Even though we stop at a truck stop each night, lately it's hard to get motivated enough to get out of the truck and walk around. Quite frankly, many truck stops reek of urine and it's enough to gag you! Unfortunately, "some" drivers are just plain too lazy to get out of their truck and walk the short distance to the restroom. Then there are others that decide to make their contribution right on the fuel island! My other reason for not getting out of the truck is that I don't like walking in front of the other drivers parked in the lot. You know you're being stared at! (Not that we don't do it ourselves!) As old as I am, I've been honked and whistled at and I just ignore it! I figure these are just some guys trying to have a little fun by getting someone's attention. After all, truck stops were built to accommodate truckers and many of them happen to be men! Truck stops are not a resort by any means; even if they include such amenities as barber shop, TV lounge, game room, restaurant, gift shop, laundry, showers, and access to the internet. Some even have movie theaters, chiropractors, dentists, basic medical services and a chapel to attend church on Sunday! This all might sound pretty nice, BUT in all reality, it still remains a TRUCK STOP!

Well we didn't get to go home like we wanted. Back to California! At least we are together and we did manage to have a shower and do some laundry, (although we don't like washing our clothes in machines used by the public). I'm getting a little annoyed with finding cat hair all over the truck. It's not the cat's fault, but I feel like it's unhealthy. I searched through Ron's tool box and found some duck tape. It seems to do the trick in lifting her bright orange hair off of the upholstery. If I ever get to a pet store I'll see if there is anything else I could try.

It is the 30th of June and we are sitting, just waiting for our turn to get loaded here in California. We are the 5th truck in line and so far we have sat here 3 ½ hours! It is very hot today and we are trying not to run the truck because it burns up fuel. When the heat becomes too unbearable, Ron starts the truck back up and turns on the air conditioning. Diesel likes warmth, but not this hot! She is lying on our bed upside down with all four legs stretched out. She looks funny in this position. She has a big fat cat belly, long legs and her head seems so small when compared to the rest of her body. I think she could care less what she looks like; it's her way of dealing with the heat!

Last night coming up the "grapevine" on I-5 there was a big brush fire still burning that covered several acres. We had already heard about it earlier on the CB radio and prepared for the delay. At one time the CHP, (California Highway Patrol) had to shut down the interstate to all traffic because of the thick black smoke and fire burning right up alongside the road. Shutting down the interstate creates a huge frustration for truckers knowing their load may end up being delivered late! There are three truck stops to pull into, but they all quickly become jammed packed with irritated drivers waiting it out until the interstate opens back up again. The steady stream of other drivers pulling in the truck stop only to discover all the spots have been taken must exit, get back on the highway and try to find a place to park on the shoulder. The CHP's decision to shut down the highway on the other hand creates a huge business for the truck stops! Their business "booms" with the increased revenue generated from grounded truckers and four wheelers! Observing "people behavior" under these circumstances is humorous and makes me wonder why instinctively, so many individuals, (like they were all programmed) after parking their vehicle, jump out and stampede like a bunch of wild cattle heading straight for the "snack bar!" Did they all get hungry at once?

It gets real crazy when word gets out that the highway is once again open. "Everyone" wants to leave at the same time! Congestion is unbelievable, people get impatient and once in a while I've even witnessed a little mild road rage going on. The four wheelers at this point have no tolerance with slow moving convoys of 18 wheelers. Even some of the drivers in the big rigs get irritated with each other! This is especially true for drivers when they find themselves behind a very slow moving truck! They lose momentum; have to grab a lower gear and stay put! A situation like this only fuels the flame and the driver's stress level gets even bigger. Even if the driver tries to get around the slow truck in front of him by turning on his signal, do you think a four wheeler would slow down and let the guy out so he could pass? NO! It's an exercise in futility. Not a chance! At this point, many heated words are exchanged between truckers over the CB radio. The venting, drivers telling other drivers how to drive their truck, continues, until you go up and over the grapevine! It makes it a bad day for everyone and the longer the interstate is shut down, congestion continues to build, the worse it becomes.

CHAPTER 2

ROOKIE IN TRAINING

We continue to sit waiting our turn to get loaded. I put my journal aside when Ron suggested for something to do he could show me how to fill out a daily log sheet. Ron doesn't have much patience and he expects you to retain instantly what he tells you. A couple times I found myself asking him the same question more than once. He didn't like it, but gave me the answer I was looking for. I'm sure with a little practice completing a log will become second nature to me and I won't need his help.

It's hard to keep occupied just sitting out here. We're parked in the middle of nowhere, staring out the window with only a huge warehouse in our view! There is basically nothing else to see or do. This particular company has a sign that tells drivers to stay inside their truck until notified that their load is ready. I would just once like to have one of them come out here and sit with us in the hot sun! They wouldn't like it either! Just to occupy my time, I made us both sandwiches. Thought about washing the inside windows, but physical exercise at this point just doesn't sound that appealing. I could knit, but who wants to get out the yarn and knit when it's 90+ degrees! Now I know I'm bored! I was looking at the grass and saw a snake slithering across the lawn. It's probably looking for water. Oh well, at least it's something to watch!

About two hours later, Ron, with sweat pouring off him, finally lost patience wanting to know how much longer we were going to have to continue sitting; got out of the truck and headed for the shipping office! When he returned, he had a big smile on his face. Our trailer was loaded and he got the o.k. to enter their parking area and hook up to it. Our load has two stops; one delivers in Aberdeen, and the other in

Monroe. Both of these locations are in Washington putting us very close to home. We are determined this time to hold our ground and not allow dispatch to turn us around and head us back to California after making our deliveries. We still have a house and yard to take care of along with numerous errands. By now our post office box is overflowing with mail and no doubt, the lawn needs to be mowed. None of these things will be taken care of if we don't insist on getting a couple days off.

We spent the night staying in Frazier Park at a Flying-J truck stop. As we were eating dinner, we were surprised by several "prisoners" being escorted into the dining area by officers of the law. There were so many, employees added extra tables in order to seat them all. The uniformed officers carried guns. At first, it was an uneasy feeling for me, but the more I observed them, I realized the prisoners were not as threatening as I initially thought. Later we learned that the prisoners were classified "minimum security" or "low risk". They were released from jail to help fight all the fires going on in the canyon. I studied their faces and watched them as they ate their dinner, hoping in turn, that they would not catch me looking. (I'm a people watcher.) I could not help but wonder what they did wrong to land up in jail? The whole bunch looked like ordinary young men and it was hard to imagine any of them breaking the law, which obviously they did. Anyway, I found myself instead of being afraid of them, I felt a bit sad knowing that through poor judgment they got themselves into this situation. All the freedom they once had was taken away and now their every movement was sharply watched continuously by officers of the law. Ron even said when he went to the restroom, an officer was standing inside and told him, "prisoners are in here and don't talk to them." When we left, I could only hope that each one of these young men will learn from their experience, do their time, and never break the law again.

Got up with Ron at 3:30 a.m., this is a killer for me! I managed to stagger half asleep into the truck stop to get our thermos filled with coffee. I also picked up a couple doughnuts and a carton of milk for us to have later. We, Ron actually, put the "peddle to the metal" today! He drove several hundred miles pushing his hours to the limit! Now we're parked in Oregon for the night and I know he's glad the long day of driving is finally over. I kept busy most of the trip studying for my CDL, (Commercial Driver's License). I'm looking forward to the time when I will be able to relieve Ron of some of the hours he's driving. He just told me he wants to get up at 3 a.m. in order to make the first drop in Aberdeen. I guess I had better put this journal away, pull drapes, set out clean clothes for morning and go to bed. Believe it or not, I'm pretty tired myself which is simply attributed to getting up early and sitting basically in one position for hours on end. The good news is; we checked with dispatch and they will get us a load home. Our timing is great because it's almost the fourth of July and we'll get an extra day off!

I have learned to appreciate what I used to take for granted. The majority of people have five day a week jobs and some only work four. They leave work, go home, relax, have a nice dinner and look forward to a couple days off. Long haul trucking does not allow this type of luxury. Our days extend far beyond the usual worker's 8 or 10 hour shift. Sometimes we have been known to skip dinner and go straight to bed just because we're too tired to eat! This is especially true after spending hours and hours out on the highway. Now, we're happy if we get to come home and relax every three or four weeks! I have even had some moments when I feel envious of others that live the normal life. While all of them are sound asleep with a full belly, truckers are running back and forth across the nation delivering goods to supply their every need. I wish people would realize how important truck drivers are to their "personal" survival! If they knew what the job of driving truck entails, most people no doubt would come out with a whole new appreciation! I'll just bet you, not one person shopping questions the can on the shelf in a grocery store and what it took to get it there, much less all the other things they buy like electronics, furniture, hardware, boats, automobiles; my list could go on forever!

July 10th and we're back in California waiting for our trailer to get loaded with carpet. It is very hot and humid. We've been laid over here for two days and Diesel is having a hard time with the heat. Up until today, I haven't had too much to complain about with her being in the truck with us. She pretty much has stuck to a routine. She wakes up in the morning, and if we're not up, she walks all over us until we do get up. From that point she gets fed, does her duty in the litter box, jumps up on the dash, watches a little traffic, enjoys the scenery for a few more minutes and then sleeps all day. When we shut down for the night, Ron buzzes his window down and she likes to lay on the edge of the window frame, (I don't know how she fits her fat body there) and amuses herself by looking at all the action going on around her. She really gets happy if another truck parks beside us with a dog inside it! When the dog spots her, the dog does what would be expected. It starts barking its head off, clawing at the window and wants to go after her! The more excited the dog gets the better our cat likes it! I swear that cat is smart because she knows the dog can't get to her and she will deliberately swish her tail or stand up and stretch just to antagonize the dog even further! Cats are hard to figure out because they definitely have a mind of their own. Just when we think we can trust her she does the unexpected! After all these trips, wouldn't you know she pulled a good one on us when we least expected it. She jumped right out of the truck and ran under a trailer! Fortunately, Diesel instantly knew she had put herself in very unfamiliar territory. She crouched down in a frozen position, afraid to go further and remained there until Ron was able to crawl underneath the trailer and get her. We all learned a lesson from this episode and we know Diesel was very glad to be back in the truck!

Today we stopped at a rest stop in Grants Pass, OR. I swear I have never in my life seen so many squirrels! You know, one squirrel is cute to watch, but when you see them by the hundreds they become rodents!! These squirrels were constantly on the move running all over the place and I quickly noticed that they were not afraid of humans. People on the sidewalks headed for restrooms were dodging them right and left! It was if they were on the attack!! I told Ron; forget it, "I'm not getting out of this truck!" Ron said, oh yes you are, we are not going to stop again! I continued to state my case, but I eventually gave in with his assurance he would walk beside me and chase them away.

Ron met me outside the restroom and when I walked out, I instantly saw that the squirrels had not disappeared; they were still all around us! At this point I asked Ron to give me a piggy back ride back to the truck. I didn't want those squirrels running across my feet! Ron brushed me off by laughing and saying I had nothing to fear. I thought sure, speak for yourself. We made it back to the truck and I was so glad to be inside and away from these fast moving little critters! Ron on the other hand was enjoying seeing so many squirrels at once. He told me to pass him my bag of sunflower seeds because he wanted to feed them. I handed him the bag and said "go for it", I'll watch! I took Ron's picture as the squirrels swarmed around his feet because I knew no one would believe how many there were and would probably say I was exaggerating. Watching from the truck, they looked like a sea of raging rats, not squirrels, rapidly converging upon Ron! All of them were frantically grabbing seeds away from each other selfishly stuffing them into their greedy little mouths! I flat out told Ron "Don't even think that I'll ever want to stop here again, not a chance!" He thought it was funny, obviously, I didn't!

Don't know where the year has gone, but we're halfway through it already. We are in Montana not knowing where our next load will take us. It gets a bit frustrating when you hurry up and deliver your fright and then to have to sit and wait. We did our usual check-in with the dispatcher after the trailer was empty and thought that another load would be all lined up for us. Wrong! You would think that a dispatcher, knowing two days in advance, (which seems like plenty of time), would have found us another load by now. What we heard instead was "Call me back in one hour. I'm working on some possibilities". This is so typical, and basically you're grounded at this point! You end up calling dispatch on the hour until they finally come up with a load. These phone calls may continue back and forth for several hours or even worse, one or more days! Idle time does not sit well with either of us. It wears on your nerves and the longer you have to wait; the more frustrating it gets! "If the wheels aren't turn'n, we're not earn'n!"

Driving in Montana along the river last night we got into thousands of flying ants, (at least that's what we think they were) and they totally plastered our windshield with their body parts! To top that off, a bird flew into the windshield! I'm surprised the bird didn't break the glass! Once in a while Ron has to come out with, what I call "his dry sense of humor!" After the bird hit the window he quickly said, "The last thing that bird saw was his ass!" I guess that's the difference between men and women. I felt sorry for the bird!

Throughout these past months I have been studying everything I need to know to take the written exam for my Commercial Driver License, (which is only part one of the requirement). At the end of each chapter there are test questions and Ron gives them to me. He then tells me if I answered right or wrong. I'm pretty confident I have learned what I need to know, so next time home I'm going to go down and take the exam. On the other hand, I've got a long way to go before I'll be ready to take the required driving portion! One of the problems I have is finding the time to get behind the wheel and practice. Getting a load delivered on time always takes priority.

Finally, we received a call from the dispatcher telling us to hook up to an empty trailer and drive to another small town in Montana to pick up a load of talc. Talc is a very heavy product to haul, but in this case, we were just glad to be rolling again! Now we are sitting here in Dillon in a staging area waiting for our turn to get loaded. Looking out the window I noticed a pretty little stream in walking distance. We both love to fish! I wish I had my fishing pole, but in reality, even if I caught one, what would I do with it? I've watched fishing experts on television and I could not do what they do. If I catch a fish it's mine! I would never go for the old "catch and release" that I've seen all those other fishermen doing.

It's now 5:30 p.m. and a guy came up to our truck and told Ron to go around to the back of the plant where they can load us. What a hell hole this turned out to be! White talc powder is flying through the air all around us! Our shinny black truck is now turning white and in the distance I can see a couple employees standing there laughing. They might think its funny, but I don't! The air is filled with this white stuff! There is also a man running a big loader that I've been watching. He scoops up a big bucket of talc and dumps it into this giant crusher. Every time he makes the dump, he sends another huge cloud of talc up in the air! There is no getting away from it! The talc is so fine that we're getting it inside the truck as well. What a mess to clean up!

Once we were loaded, we drove a short distance on the property to a location where the company provides a scale for the drivers to weigh. The scale itself is not at ground level and if I had to guess I would say the ramp is raised about 2' higher. In order to weigh, you must drive your tractor and trailer up on it. Ron pulled a fast one on me by saying "You're going to have to drive up on the scale because I need to get out and get our axel weights!" I don't like surprises and felt he should have warned me in advance! Knowing Ron though, he probably knew what I would say. He got me into a position where I had no choice but to get behind the wheel and drive up on the scale! There was another truck right behind us waiting to scale so the pressure was on for me to get on and off of it as quickly as possible. I was so scared, but I did it!

My biggest fear was driving up the ramp. I was so afraid that if I didn't keep myself centered, the tires would drop off the narrow edge throwing me and the whole darn truck and trailer over on its side! I never felt so relieved when Ron waived me on. I was glad to get off and let the other driver weigh. Ron thanked me for my help and told me I did a good job. I too was very proud of my accomplishment. It gave me more confidence and if we come here again I'll be ready to do my part. After sliding axels we were on our way headed south.

It is the 16th of July and we managed to deliver the talc, or better put, get rid of it! What a miserable heavy load to pull. You crawl up every hill! We had no time to stop and wash the layers of talc off our truck until today. We pulled into a truck wash in Barstow, CA and after a lengthy scrub down, a little wheel polishing, and a whole lot of cleaning inside; we're back to normal. The truck is clean inside and out! That makes us both happy!

We're under a new load and traveling through Nevada last night we ran into a huge thunder storm. This is the second storm in a week and it has caused quite a bit of flooding throughout the area. The sandy desert soil could not absorb the large volume of heavy rain coming down. In a short period of time there were rivers of water running everywhere!

The load we're under now goes to Auburn, WA so this time when we are home I'm going down to the Department of Licensing to take the Commercial Driver's exam. I've studied their book so much that the pages are falling out! No joke! I figure if I don't get all nervous and maintain the same confidence I have now, I should be able to pass it without much problem. I've heard from other drivers that it is tough to pass all four endorsements. We'll see!

Here today, gone tomorrow as the old saying goes! Today is the 22nd of July and we are back in California and as usual, waiting for our trailer to get loaded. This time we're going to haul office supplies instead of the usual carpet. It will be much lighter and I know we won't have to slide the axels! The GOOD NEWS is that when I was home, I "PASSED" the entire written exam and walked away with "all" endorsements!! I could hardly believe it when I was told the results of my test. There were other people there taking the exam and unfortunately for some of them, they didn't pass and will have to come back. I remember one young guy that sat beside me. He told me it was his fourth try and although he passed a couple sections, he was having a terrible time answering "hazmat" questions. I hope the next time he tries he will get the questions right. I must say that when Ron came and picked me up after the test I could tell by the look on his face that he wasn't so sure I had passed. When I told him, he reached over and planted a big fat kiss on my face! He was happy and probably at the same time relieved just knowing that he wouldn't have to put up with my whining for miles on end had I flunked! (I would have done just that!) My next challenge will be the driving test and I'm in no hurry!

This trip has been exceptional, no Diesel the cat on board! I'm enjoying every minute without her knowing I can open my door, buzz down my window, eat without being stared at, and I'm not getting walked on when I sleep! It's pretty nice to say the least. When it was time for us to leave from our last trip at home, Diesel got real smart! She now has figured out that if we start packing suitcases, to her, it can only mean she's going back in the truck! The thought was something she definitely had no interest in and absolutely had no intention of doing it! She was savoring her freedom, basking in the sun and thoroughly enjoying her mini vacation!

Our routine is to get everything loaded into the truck and then the very last thing we do is put the cat inside. Diesel sat right there in the living room watching our every move going in and out the door making several trips out to the truck with supplies. When we were done, the minute she saw Ron coming towards her, she ran! The chase was on! Ron is the one that has to pick her up and put her in the travel carrier because she is known to bite when she is mad at you. I refuse to take that chance! Now wouldn't you know, Ron finally won, but when we got to the terminal we were told the load would not be ready for 4 or 5 more hours so we turned around and came back home. When it came time to leave again, Diesel was nowhere to be found! We called her, looked all over inside and outside the house until we finally ran out of time. Ron was very frustrated and said "fine, she can just stay at home!" We called our neighbor Ken who happens to be retired, and he assured us he would make frequent checks on Diesel for us. He said if she was outside he would let her in so she could get to her food and water.

Thanks to the delay caused by Diesel we are now running behind schedule! We are picking up a load of grocery bags out of Port Townsend, WA and taking them to Mahlstrom Air Force Base in Great Falls, MT. Ron has a cousin Penny that lives in Great Falls but it is doubtful if we will have time to see her. I've never been there before so I'm looking forward to the trip.

Jason and Kim's trip home went without having any problems along the way. Kim said one time they even pulled into a casino where she saw several 18 wheelers parked on the chance the "parents" truck might be sitting there amongst them. Would have been great to see them both, but we were long gone! Now that Jason is out of the U.S. Air Force he'll be staying with her in Seattle until he returns to college. We're looking forward to seeing him a little more often. Plan to stay in Spokane, WA tonight and catch a quick visit with Ron's mother. We called her on the phone and she will drive down to the truck stop to meet us for dinner.

At times this is what a driver and family member must do if they want to see each other at all.

Made it to Great Falls, MT and are in the process of getting unloaded. Beautiful scenery all the way over and I enjoyed every mile. There were lots of trees, mountains, rivers and streams filled with wildlife to look at. The temperature outside the truck is 90 degrees and I don't need any more sun! Last time home I got sunburned on my legs and the top of my feet. I need to heal! Just got a call from dispatch and as soon as we are unloaded they want us to run empty over to Helena, MT for another load.

We got up at 3:30 a.m. because we were told we had a "hot load" that needed to get to Kootenai, ID ASAP! This is a "killer"! We only had about five hours sleep. This is when I am again reminded of all those people that have their cushy little 9 to 5 jobs with weekends off! Most people are sound asleep this early in the morning while we're out here hooking up to a trailer in the dark! Now we'll run our butts off to insure the delivery gets there on time! This is what's expected at times with the job.

We arrived on time and at least this same company has a load that we can take back to Montana. This is getting to be a long day already. Dispatch just told us that they have a load of paper that will not be ready to load until 10:30 p.m. tonight. (See what I mean about a long day.) There is no way Ron and I are going to get much sleep. When we pick up the load tonight we will be expected to drive for several more miles. Not fun! Besides having each other to talk to, the only other thing to break the silence of darkness is listening to the radio. Our life style does not affect the cat whatsoever! She sleeps regardless of what time frame we're on! I sound like I'm complaining, but every day is not as long as this one and I'm still enjoying all the freedom and independence that long haul trucking offers. Tonight we'll have dinner at the truck stop and I'm looking forward to sitting in the "drivers only" section. This is a place where truckers can enjoy having conversations with other truckers while eating dinner.

Well, once in a while we do get out of this truck and have some fun! It is July 31st and we stayed at Whiskey Pete's casino last night in Primm, NV. Ron won 350 quarters and gave them to me. There are actually two other casinos here that you can walk to or take their tram over the interstate to get to them. We tried all three, and by the time we got back I had lost most of his quarters! We topped the evening off by ordering steak and lobster for dinner. We had a good time to say the least. Just to get out of the truck and be around other people was refreshing. By the way, I want all my kids to know that your mother discovered some time ago that the slot machines, at least the nickel ones, have "old" coins in them. I have become a real coin collector. Many of the nickels I've found were minted back in the 40's and I have even found a few in the 30's! I bought myself some coin collector books to store them. I'm so into hunting for old coins that before we leave the casino, I buy rolls of nickels to look through while Ron drives down the road.

August 5th and we had two days off at home. Getting away from all the background noise that's always present with trucking, I was able to have nice phone conversations with each of the kids. It was fun to catch up on what they were doing. Kellie said she was having a combined birthday party for Jake and Sam because their birthdays are only a month apart. I suppose that's fine when they are so little, but I hope as they get older, Jake and Sam will be able to have their own special day to celebrate. Kellie sent us pictures and Ron is calling Sam "Little Sumo"!

Throughout these past months Ron has put me behind the wheel several times. I never wrote about each time he had me drive, mostly because I was too stressed after the lesson! The inside cab of the truck became pretty heated with either him or me shouting at each other! Not pretty for anyone's ears! Over these past months I have gained more confidence and not near as hesitant to get behind the wheel. Now, having said that, I can tell you I've missed more gears than I can count. I've been up the hill and down the hill, over bridges and long stretches of highway. More than once I pulled the truck over on the shoulder, put it in park and refused to drive any further. I didn't care if the load ever got delivered or if we sat there until the "cows came home"! When I've reached my max, I know it! I was not about to let Ron "bully" me into something I wanted no part of. The problem, at least one of them, was that all the experienced truckers would get right on my rear end and I didn't want to drive any faster than I already was going. Ron showed no mercy and would tell me "you've got to keep up with the traffic or you're going to get eaten alive"! I'm surprised that he didn't add to my misery any further by blurting out the old "If you can't run with the big dogs, stay on the porch!"

The other thing I absolutely freaked out about was when I knew there was a scale house ahead! The minute I spotted a sign, "scale house open" I would instantly panic and pull over on the shoulder! Ron would always get upset and try to persuade me to continue on; but I flat out refused! Stopping alongside the road, we both had to immediately show a required "driver's change" in our logs. Ron would then quickly trade places with me and drive to the scale. We were legal as far as my driver training goes. I had my permit, but I always felt intimidated about seeing these D.O.T officers in uniform each time we would pass over their scale. Maybe it's because they sit staring out the window at you. It's so obvious that they're not only checking out the truck and trailer; they're also taking a good look at the driver! I know the officers are only doing what they get paid to do but for me I found their presence to be intimidating. Their job is to make sure that the driver and whatever he is hauling is compliant and safe to continue back on to the interstate. This is my problem and I need to get over it!

Another challenge for me was trying to pull into a rest stop with angle parking. When you're pulling a 53' trailer it is not as easy as it looks, especially your first few tries. I found myself at times being envious of Ron when I observed his ease at maneuvering our rig precisely between the lines. I swear I could have gotten out with a measuring tape and the truck would be perfectly parked, exactly centered between the two parking stripes! It was almost like he was showing off! Believe me, at this point I refused to give him credit and build his male ego. Had I done that, we both would have quickly remembered and compared my last try. This would have caused frustration between the two of us. Silently though I couldn't help but be very impressed with his skills and wondered if I would ever be able to park like he does.

There were also times I actually thought I was crazy to even think I could drive an 18-wheeler! I've taken on a lot of challenges in my life that you wouldn't think a woman could do but I did! However, driving a big rig is a whole new ball game, especially when you're hauling as much as 80,000 pounds of weight flying down the highway! Your truck becomes a "lethal weapon!" and you better know what you're doing! This is an enormous responsibility for any driver and you, no way, can expect to maneuver your truck like you do when you drive your private automobile. You do not have the "turning power", much less quick acceleration and stopping action. Everything you do in a big truck is calculated by the driver and most of the time, everything is slow.

Ron has really been a good sport and has stuck with me on my continued effort to get a grip on driving our truck. I will say one thing, you're mother is not a quitter! When I see the need, and I do with Ron, I will persevere until I conquer the skills necessary to pass the required driving portion of the exam. I have witnessed Ron so tired that he refuses dinner, his legs cramping and his back in pain. I've witnessed him driving putting up with all this pain for miles and miles because the load had to be delivered on time. I know once I get my CDL, I will be able to give him a badly needed break. Maybe then he won't be so tired and worn out at the end of the day. When we were home this last time, Ron contacted a local truck driver training school. I went with him and signed up for lessons to the tune of $3,500! I start class on the 30th of this month. So far, I like the one instructor that I met and hope he will be the one to teach me the professional skills I need to pass the final portion.

Today is Wednesday, got up at 4 a.m. and we are on our way to Helena, MT. We saw several deer along the way and even one Bald Eagle! It's really a nice drive once you get out of all the coast traffic. We made a brief stop in Spokane to once again rendezvous with Ron's mother at the local truck stop. In a previous phone conversation with her I mentioned that Ron and I needed to learn to speak the Spanish language. (We have come to realize that so much of the populations we deal with in California are Hispanic people and although they speak English, at times, some of them are difficult for me to understand.) Much to our surprise, (it probably shouldn't have been, she is a retired school teacher), she greeted us with a bunch of "Learn to Speak Spanish" tapes and books! From one of our previous phone conversations, it never crossed my mind that she would then take it upon herself to see that we had the necessary tools to learn.

It's funny because we didn't consider our visit to become a gift exchange. But as it turned out, we also had a gift for her! Last time we were in California we came upon a mother with her son selling candles for his youth group. (Truck drivers are softies when it comes to kids!) We bought two of the fragrant candles and hoped they wouldn't melt inside the truck before we were able to deliver. I really admire my mother-in-law for being as old as she and still able to live by herself, handle her own affairs, and do all the things she likes to do like gardening or having fun visits with family and friends. I can only hope that her independence will last as she continues to age.

Today we are in Montana getting a load of talc. As always, we don't like getting heavy loads, but this plant seems much more organized. There is no talc flying through the air! We'll never get over our previous experience with talc all over our truck. This stuff is all bagged up and it's just a matter of having the guy on the fork lift put these giant bags in our trailer Boy, the miles we cover are incredible! Since my last entry we've been home for a very brief stay, in fact, Ron didn't get a day off at all because we arrived too late to deliver the load. The next morning Ron had to get up and go deliver it while I remained at home doing the laundry and running errands to pick up accumulated mail and purchase supplies at the grocery store. We both felt cheated by not getting any real time off.

August 6th and we're headed south cruising down the road listening to "old" country music on the radio. Yesterday I counted 21 strikes of lightening going over Monida Pass which is on the Montana, Idaho boarder. The lightning strikes were all direct hits putting on quite a show for us to see! When we got to Fort Hall Indian Reservation in Idaho, Ron stopped so I could mail a couple letters and buy a few supplies at their store. We also took time, just for fun to look at their gift store. There were several craft items for sale like beaded jewelry, carvings, and pottery along with plenty of souvenirs as well. I like to pick up gifts once in a while for family and while we were in the store I bought a little piggy bank for my sister-in-law, Sue, (she collects them) and I also purchased some berry jam for my mother-in-law for her birthday this month. What I like about stopping here is that there is plenty of truck parking. Having a grocery store is another big incentive for a driver to stop. Produce is hard for truckers to find because many of the big stores do not allow space for a big rig, so unless you "bob tail" to a store, you're out of luck! Many of our meals I fix right inside the cab and there's nothing like having a fresh salad with dinner!

Tonight we are parked in Santa Nella, CA and we're looking forward to seeing "Andy". He works at the restaurant across from the truck stop. We usually are able to stop and eat at his restaurant at least once a month and as a result we have become good friends. Andy was born in Mexico and still has family living there. We love to hear about how much better off he and is family are living in the United States. He has told us stories of the poverty in Mexico and what families must do to survive. One time I got into a conversation with Andy and I asked him "do Hispanic people really eat goats?" He laughed very hard at my question and gave me a look as if to say "where have you been all your life!" He went on to explain why, and then insisted some day when we have time he will cook us goat for dinner; assuring me that I would not know the difference between it and another piece of beef! He was probably right, but as of this date I have yet to try eating goat in any prepared form! The restaurant also has a gift shop so while we were there I bought a couple cook books and a coffee mug for my brother, John.

Now we are in Medford, OR for the night. We are getting our truck serviced so this gives me some time to make another entry in this journal. Actually when I think about it, there isn't much to say. The day was pretty uneventful; no bad accidents, construction delays or nasty weather to deal with. We should be home tomorrow and I know Diesel will be glad to see us. We left her home this last trip to give her a break as well as ourselves.

We got home late on Monday and Diesel was just fine. Today is the 11th of August and it is Jake's birthday. He is two years old. I sent him birthday presents and I hope they arrived on time. The garden is doing great, thanks to Ron setting up a timer so the vegetables get watered in our absence. Jason came out to visit with us in the afternoon. We took him to dinner at the "Hanger Inn" (It is a restaurant situated at a small airport where he worked and earned money to pay for flying lessons.) While waiting for our dinner to be served, I purchased a few "pull tabs". I told Jason if I won anything he could have it! Jason was very doubtful; he's not a gambler like his mother. He watched intently as I carefully opened each one and every time I opened a loser, he would say "I told you so!" I was beginning to wonder if maybe he was right. BUT! Just when neither of us expected it, I opened a tab and it said $300.00 winner! Now, I had to keep my word! It was a bit painful to hand over the money to him, but I was quickly rewarded with the huge smile on his face!

Friday the 13th and it is supposed to be a bad day but it isn't. The hours we keep are unreal! We both got up at 4:30 this morning and delivered a load in Torrance, CA. After that, we drove to another company and picked up a load of freight that delivers in Kent, WA. Again, no time for showers or a hot meal, we just keep rolling, rolling, rolling.

I've been telling Ron I'm getting tired of these same routes and we should ask for loads that go to other states. He quickly told me that the "long runs" dispatchers will only give to "teams" and WE are not a team Billie! O.K. Ron I get it! I didn't like his answer, but for me it's one more reason why I need to get my CDL. Besides, right now, I don't think Ron is even that interested in running some of the other states. It would put him in unfamiliar territory and out of his comfort zone. Not me, and I know Ron would do just fine, but until I get approved to drive with him, I guess I'll have to be satisfied with running up and down the coast.

Our day is not over and Ron wants us to at least make it to Santa Nella tonight before stopping. When he gets us out of LA traffic, I'll take over and drive the San Joaquin Valley giving him a much needed break. I'm a bit apprehensive about taking over the wheel knowing I will have my own challenge of dealing with the congestion on the interstate. I'll try not to get intimidated by all the "four wheelers" and big rigs. There are always a few jerks exceeding the speed limit, compelled to hang right on my back bumper until they can pass around me! I was told by an instructor to "Never let another driver "drive" your truck and don't allow yourself to be intimidated by their actions." I try to remember this little piece of advice when I'm driving, but sometimes you cannot help but feel pressured!

One thing for sure that I haven't mention in the past about this particular stretch of I-5 is the darn California tomato trucks! (More commonly know by truckers as "tomato freighters!) I know tomatoes are good for us, but geez, we get sprayed in the face every time we get behind one of those tomato haulers! In season, there are trucks after trucks, too many to count, hauling fresh tomatoes in their open trailers. You can bet every single one of them is going to "douse" you with tomato spray! The longer you're stuck driving behind one of them, the worse it gets! In seconds our windshield turns bright red. It gets so bad that we continually have to turn on the wipers and use our washer fluid to clean off the red spray! I don't know how many thousands of tomatoes it takes to fill their long trailers or how much it all might weigh, but it's quite evident; the tomatoes on the bottom are getting squished!

Sometimes the conversation between two drivers can get pretty heated over the CB radio especially when they suddenly find themselves following behind a trailer loaded full of ruby reds! The driver instantly reacts by getting on the CB and gives the other driver a piece of his mind; sparing no words of course! It's laughable listening to the sarcastic dialog going on between the two of them.

First of all, I know in my heart, these guys understand English, especially when they are getting cussed out! What "routinely" takes place is the driver getting sprayed gets on the CB radio. He then proceeds to tell the driver in front of him about the mess he's making by spraying red tomato juice all over his truck and the interstate! The driver's complaint is quickly ignored by the other. This lack of response irritates the hell out of him! He again gets on the CB radio, only this time he steps it up a notch by adding a few choice cuss words! A couple more miles down the road the driver spraying tomato juice decides to respond! He says something like "Shove it man, like, we're just trying to earn a living like you!" "You need to back off man, smoke a cigarette or something!" His response only makes the other driver even more irritated and determined to win the argument!

There are many tomato freighter drivers out here, caravans of them. When they hear one of their buddies getting yelled at over the CB by another driver, the others will jump in and come to his rescue. They all stick together and to irritate the complaining driver further, they all start speaking their native language to each other! I'm sure this is deliberate on their part and no doubt are having a good old time excluding the complaining driver from their personal conversation! There may be a few more exchanges of smart remarks, but eventually the frustrated driver following behind turns off his CB, pulls out, passes and goes on his way.

August 15th and we stayed in Oregon last night. This is a truck stop that I have mentioned before where we take the time to go inside the restaurant and eat. The building, along with big rig parking, is located on a hillside. It's not the best position to be in when you're trying to lay down and go to sleep! Depending on where you park, you're head is either going to be facing down hill (giving a feeling like you're stuck going belly down on a slide) or your facing up hill, climbing a mountain all night! In either case, it's an uncomfortable position when you're trying to sleep! Plus when it's hot, we crack the vents for air at night, but in doing so, we also have to put up with and endure the strong smell of urine! In the heat of summer the smell is relentless! All I can say is "Bless all the drivers that routinely have to put up with uncomfortable sleeping conditions at truck stops!" You have to be a hardy individual. The lifestyle is not a match for wimpy, whiney people. They wouldn't last five minutes in our world!

It's the 18th of August and the trip home wasn't too bad except for the fog. Fall is in the air and I could already notice some of the leaves on the trees are just starting to turn fall colors. Jason came out to visit and while he was there I asked him to take one of my big yellow sun flowers home for Kim. When I handed it to him several earwigs (ugly bugs) started falling out of the petals onto the ground. He instantly handed it back to me saying "I don't want the bugs in my car they'll be crawling all over the place"!" I proceeded to shake the flower until I was sure the earwigs were gone and then handed it back to him. At that point he reluctantly agreed to deliver the sun flower for me. Later that evening I got a phone call from Kim thanking me for the pretty flower. She then told me it was full of bugs and she had to put it outside in a vase!" Guess I won't be sending her any more flowers from my garden!

In our line of work visits with relatives or friends are few and far between. I have to be satisfied with phone calls like the one I got from Kellie today letting Jake and Sam say hello. It makes me feel sad at times because we're missing out on so many relationships that others take for granted. Just like today, I made a phone call to Ron's mother. I told her we would be passing through town and could she meet us at the truck stop for a cup of coffee. She of course agreed, but surprised me by adding that Ron's sister and her two kids were there for a visit and they would also be coming along to see us. Ron's sister lives in California and chances for them to see each other are rare. Her kids loved the truck. We let them climb inside and explore the interior. Ron topped it off by giving them a couple loud blasts out of the air horn. A brief visit, but nice, and then off again to deliver our load in Post Falls, ID. This is what I've come to expect driving truck. It would have been nice to have the time for a planned get together but that's not the reality of driving long haul.

Upon our arrival, Ron was instantly irritated when he found out he was the only one expected to unload our entire trailer! They supplied him with a pallet jack, walked off, and left the rest of the job up to him! Each pallet weighed 1,500 pounds (magazines) and there were 25 of them! We had to load these same pallets in Seattle and at that time I tried as much as I could to help him. The rules changed here and I had no choice but to stay out of the way. When Ron finished I couldn't help but feel sorry for him. He looked like he just climbed out of a shower; soaked with sweat running down his face and pouring off his body! He looked absolutely exhausted! Ron was so drenched with sweat that I gave him a clean shirt and a towel to dry his hair. He put on some deodorant, updated his log and got back behind the wheel heading for Montana. What I've shared is true. It's a misconception if you think all a trucker has to do is hook to a trailer, drive several miles and then bump a dock to have it unloaded. It's not uncommon for a driver to assist unloading and then there are times like today when the driver does it all!

August 20th and we are at a Sunshine Truck Stop in Parowan, UT. It is POURING rain with no relief in sight. Ron has been driving in rain for the past 650 miles and now I know he's had it! His back is hurting again. His eyes are watering, sore and red. He's complaining of having blurred vision while trying to complete his daily log. I'm an eye witness to what most people unfortunately never get to see; the toll it takes on a trucker after a long day of stressful driving conditions. For tonight I'll probably just make do with what we have on board for dinner, if Ron will eat at all! He's already telling me we have to get up early and I know what that means, three or four in the morning. The pressure never ends when you're under a load to get it delivered on time!

Before we left Montana we had our truck serviced in a shop where we have become friends with several of their employees. We've used these mechanics before and have total confidence in their work. While doing a preventive maintenance the mechanic informed Ron that our transmission cap was ruined and told him it needed to be replaced. He explained to Ron that whoever did our last service created the damage. He said the guy was either too lazy to correct the mistake or didn't know how! The mechanic was just as sure whoever ruined the cap was aware of it! Of course the previous mechanic didn't tell us about the problem at the time; he just smiled and took our money! Apparently the jerk used a power wrench to take the cap off and stripped all the threads off. His screw up costs us another $150 to get it fixed!

There is another drawback when you have mechanical problems out on the road. Some independent repair shops know you're not "local" and they don't have to worry about customer satisfaction because you'll be long gone; probably several states away after collecting a healthy chunk of money from your wallet. This puts a driver in a very vulnerable position and unfortunately, leaves him no choice but to accept the work and pay whatever it costs! Fact is, drivers are at their mercy and although not all the independent shops across the nation operate this way, I think there are plenty others that do! I've heard so many stories from other drivers that not only had to fork out big bucks due to an unexpected breakdown, but they also ended up with a lousy repair job! Anyway, while we were there, we also purchased a new CB radio. The one we had, the speaker went out, so that was another $125 we had to cough up. Not a profitable day!

We also took the time while in Montana to call the company we're leased on with in order to learn what their requirements are for me to get approved to drive with Ron. I did not like what I heard! They would expect me to spend 10 days there! TEN WHOLE DAYS ALONE! Ron would have to leave me there and continue trucking. I did not like that idea one single bit! That's too long to be away from Ron and confined with strangers. I got further stressed out when I was told I would be totally, (in my opinion) stranded, would have to stay in their dorm on site, sleep in a room with another female, someone I didn't even know, and then spend every single day doing time with instructors and attend daily sessions in a classroom. Poop on that! I told Ron, "You mean to tell me, I walk in with a bonafide CDL, with all the endorsements, licensed to drive in any state, and they still expect me to go through their entire orientation as well?" That's bull! I was pretty upset and felt it was totally unnecessary. I could only justify in my mind maybe spending a couple days. The first day I imagined completing their required paperwork and learning about company policies. The next day I would spend with an instructor starting out by performing a VI, (vehicle inspection) and then go for a test drive to confirm my ability to operate a big rig. But that's it! I felt they were asking too much, after all we were not "company" employees, we are "owner operators"; our truck, our fuel, our tires and we carry the insurance! Our insurance even covers their trailer and the freight inside of it! I felt they were crossing the line and expecting too much.

I have a tendency when I'm irritated and think I'm right, to continue to dwell on the problem for hours! Ron got tired of me complaining so finally said he would talk to the higher ups in the company next time he had a chance to see if maybe they would shorten the time I had to spend with them.

August 22nd and tomorrow is Ron's mother's birthday. We've picked up a few presents for her but won't be able to deliver them until we get a trip going through Spokane. I'll give her a call tomorrow like I always do on her birthday because that's the best I can do out here. It is very hot outside today, 109 degrees! We're sitting in the truck stop listening to country music and as I write, Ron is being entertained by watching the activity of other drivers. Some have their hoods up doing maintenance while others are polishing chrome or walking their pet. We should be doing some things ourselves, but it's too hot. I must say, looking out the window I have observed several overweight drivers, too much junk food no doubt! Sometimes I think that driver's eat food just for something to do!

August 23rd and today was the first time we didn't get the "green" light passing over the scale! It took me by surprise and I was so thankful I wasn't driving. The reader board in front of the truck lit up instructing the driver to pull around to the inspection area; door number four. This is so intimidating! A big bay door opened and a DOT officer motioned Ron to pull ahead into their building. I could see everything that was going on and wondered why Ron? They let all the other trucks continue through. What made them decide to pick us?

There isn't a driver on the road that welcomes the sight of a "coop" (scale house) and when they get pulled in, they have no idea what the DOT might possibly find wrong during an inspection. When you're red lighted, the world stops and you instantly are under their command! The eyes of the law are upon you! From here on out, it's yes sir and yes mam! Smart remarks will get a driver in trouble quicker than you can blink an eye! It's much better to go with the flow. (After all they're just doing their job.)

The DOT officer checked Ron's driver's license, medical card, registration on the truck, registration on the trailer, log book and then proceeded to check all around and under the truck. They also had him participate by checking all of the lights, brakes and air pressure. This all took place in Cottonwood, CA and we, after what seemed to be an eternity, passed with flying colors! Now we have a bright orange sticker on the windshield indicating that we have gone through and passed their inspection. Hopefully next time we roll over one of their scales they'll give us the green light instructing us to proceed back onto the interstate.

When I called Ron's mother to wish her happy birthday she was all upset. She could have cared less about her birthday. She was more interested in telling me about some paper she received in the mail claiming she hit a woman while turning into a driveway at a shopping center. (Funny she has never mentioned this incident to us before, but maybe she forgot or didn't think what occurred was that serious.) Continuing my conversation with her, I learned that the incident took place over a year ago! As usual, out here on the road we cannot do anything to help her until we get home and read for ourselves whatever papers she received. I told her not to worry. This is a good example of the frustration a driver goes through when someone at home depends on you for help. Her problem will stay on Ron's mind until he has the time off to take care of it.

We are in Eugene, OR tonight and about to go to bed. Driving over the passes today we counted seven direct hits of lightening that started fires. It's a bit frightening to see so many clouds of smoke billowing up through the trees. I hope the fires will quickly be contained and not get out of hand. We have to deliver this load in Kent, WA tomorrow so we'll be getting up about 2:30 a.m. and hitting the road. We already have the thermos filled and clothes set out for morning. It will be a short night!

Today is August 26th and we managed to get a measly 6 hours off at home before the phone rang and a dispatcher called us and said she has a load that goes to San Diego, CA. It was barely enough time to wash and dry clothes, pack suitcases, grocery shop and run to the post office. We didn't even have time to complain about our short stay! We were much too busy running around trying to get as much done as possible. (This is the kind of life to expect when you drive truck for a living.)

The temperature is in the low 100's today and we've been in smoke filled skies all the way from North Lake Shasta to Stockton, CA. which covers about 200 miles. There were 60 fires started by lightning strikes and the latest report is that there are still 47 fires burning. It must be awful for the fire crews to fight these fires when the temperature outside is so hot. I'll stick to the truck driving job where I can enjoy the air conditioned cab!

We saw a bad rollover this morning. A truck driver carrying a big load of lumber was completely turned over on its side. What a mess to clean up! Ron said no doubt the driver took the corner too fast, his load shifted and over he went! Accidents prompt an exchange of dialog between truckers over the CB radio. Today is no exception. Drivers got on the CB and gave each other their personal opinion on what might have caused the roll over, warned other truck drivers traveling in the opposite direction of the accident ahead, advised drivers where to watch for "bears" and other response vehicles near the scene; even giving the "mile marker" where the accident happened. It's not that drivers have anything against "bears" when they report seeing one. It's just a good way of keeping each other alert and compliant. Drivers may argue amongst themselves, but when it comes to serious information like an accident ahead, you can bet they will share it!

We made it to San Diego, CA and didn't have any problems finding the place to deliver our load. The not so good news is that there are four trucks ahead of us waiting to get unloaded! Ron had to start driving at 1:30 this morning so he's taking a nap. It's not just the long hours, but the California traffic will wear any driver down when you're stuck in it for mile after mile. If you talk to a trucker, they will tell you there is a short window of opportunity if you want to get through southern

California and avoid the massive traffic. This is usually between the hours of midnight and 3 a.m., after that, forget it!

While Ron is sleeping I got my driver's manual out and gave myself a quiz just to see how much information I'm retaining. Oh, well, it's something to do sitting here. When he wakes up I'm going to tell him about these cute little orange and green trolley cars hauling people around the city. I would like to ride in one, it looks like fun! It's too bad that we never get time off to enjoy some of the sites, explore the area and visit all the little tourists' shops we pass along the way. We have seen several interesting places we would like to stop at, but must continue on. We breathe a sigh, look at each other and say "someday"!

August 28th and what a morning! Just outside Toledo, WA approaching the Cowlitz River, we received several warnings from other truck drivers that a truck pulling two open trailers filled to the brim with cattle carcasses lost part of the load and it was spread all over the interstate! We were also warned that the smell is something like you have NEVER SMELLED BEFORE!! Passing drivers would tell us, you'll gag, you'll puke, and it will take your breath away, roll up your windows and plug your nose! Other driver's trying to describe the scene said it looks like "body parts" spread all over the place with a smell you'll never forget! It will knock you over!

When we were hearing all of these reports, we had no idea what we were in for! We actually laughed and said "It couldn't possibly be as bad as they are saying it is." OH WAS WE WRONG! Before we even got to the scene, the stench started filling the inside of our truck. The closer we got to the accident, the smell became more intense! These truckers knew what they were talking about. Neither of us had ever in our lifetime, smelled something that awful! I started getting the dry heaves, could hardly breathe and Ron was choking and gagging right along with me! The wind must have been blowing in our direction because we were getting the maximum dose! Passing by the mess, I could hardly look at the green slime, blood, guts and bones strewn all over the road! I pitied the cleanup crew that was already there. I'll bet they lose their appetite and won't eat for a week! We made it without actually vomiting, but we came darn close. It took us about another mile before we got away from the smell. This for sure, is one day neither of us will ever forget! We'll be home later today and on Monday, I will start my driving lessons.

Being self employed we cannot justify taking a month off. Ron solved the problem by making arrangements with a company that offers "one" on "one" driving lessons with a certified instructor. I will spend a week; 8 hours a day, covering all the things I need to know about the operation of a big rig; inside and out! I was told to meet the instructor in the morning, plan to do a complete vehicle inspection with him, and then the two of us will go out and drive. When the week is over I expect to have learned all the skills needed to pass the driving portion of the exam. I'm a bit apprehensive not knowing for sure what I'm up against, but I've gotten this far, and now I've got to follow through with my dream. I hope I don't scare the pants off the instructor during the process!

Well, the hardest week of my life is over! September 3, 1999 I took my driver's test with the examiner and PASSED! Now I have my own Commercial Driver's License. Whoopee!! My months and months of studying the manual, Ron spending time teaching me to drive out on the road and working with the driving instructor, finally paid off! I'll never have to go through this again! I feel proud to be amongst all the other men and women before me who had the will and desire to take on the challenge of learning to operate a big rig, not to mention learning all the required rules and regulations that go along with it! I'm very happy, but even after saying all that, the learning is not over, it's only just begun!

We're off to Arizona, but at least when we took the time off at home we were able to make a trip to Sumas, WA to see my dad. (That's where

I was born.) He will be 83 years old in a few months and sadly his age is catching up with him. It's not that often we get to visit with him and sometimes I feel guilty that we don't make more of an attempt. He is thrilled to see any of his five kids but it requires each of us to drive several miles for about a one or two hour visit. Seems like if Ron and I stay any longer than that, we run out of things to talk about or we get the feeling that he is tired and wants us to leave. We also were able to stop briefly along the way driving through Bellingham to see our son Jason. Like any mother, I always enjoy seeing his smiley little face!

The last day we were home, my brother John and his two boys stopped by for a surprise visit. Ron told them we were on our way to a big industrial area with plenty of room for me to practice driving our truck. John decided to follow along wanting to see his sister actually driving a big truck by herself. I took John, Adam and Brian for a short drive through the complex of warehouses. Missed a couple gears, but they had fun and I brought them back to where Ron was waiting. Standing there, I could tell Ron was beaming with pride. This was the first time I've driven off in our truck without Ron being inside.

Although I'm so relieved to have my CDL, it's not over yet. I still have to deal with the company we're leased on with and I'm not looking forward to that. After John left, Ron and I went for another spin. He tried teaching me to shift, passing a gear and going directly into fourth. I gave it a few tries; got frustrated and he did too, so we quit. This kind of shifting was never mentioned in driver training and I couldn't help but wonder in the future, what more bright ideas he might come up with. I hope none! It's all I can do to concentrate on what I do know!

We plan to stop tonight in Canyonville, OR and Ron has already told me that tomorrow he wants me to drive through the mountains. He said it will be a good experience for me. I'm a bit scared, but I'm not going to tell him that. I know there will be a whole lot of shifting gears, up and down. I've also heard too many stories about truckers missing gears or using their air brakes too much. In either of these cases, you can get yourself in a whole lot of trouble! That, I can do without!

Well, well, well, I didn't have to drive after all! Actually, I chickened out and convinced Ron I wasn't ready for this type of challenge and wanted more time practicing driving over rolling hills instead of mountains. I told him the smaller grades would help build my confidence. I knew that driving over hills I probably wouldn't have to work the gears as much and I was sure that if I missed any, I would be able to recover without panicking. He was a good sport and let me off the hook, at least for this time around.

The other thing that bugs me is that I still don't have the approval of the company to run as a team. They still consider me to be a student. I'm not sure if that matters to the DOT or not. I would think they would be more interested in knowing I have a valid CDL, required health card and my log is up to date. Nevertheless, this final approval is hanging over my head and I know I won't be happy until I get it taken care of. We are now stopped for the night at the truck stop in Lebec, CA. Another owner/operator leased on to this same company came over to our truck and is talking shop with Ron. I'm glad he has someone to visit with besides me for a change. I know it does him well because what guys have to talk about, I would probably find boring.

September 9th and we delivered our load in Glendale, AZ on the outskirts of Phoenix. It was hot and humid, over 100 degrees! We and I mean both of us, unloaded 270 pieces of furniture and all of it by hand! There wasn't even a pallet jack or a fork lift to make the job easier. Two nice young Hispanic employees, one spoke pretty good English and the other gave it a good try, helped us. After taking the first row of boxes off, Ron and I climbed into the trailer and proceeded to push every single boxed recliner forward until it reached the end of the trailer. The young men stood on the ground and carried off each box as we tipped them down in order for them to get a grip. (Back breaking to say the least!) This was taking forever and finally, Ron lost his patience, left me in the trailer to continue pushing boxes, and he jumped down and started helping the Hispanics. It seemed like we would never get the trailer unloaded and by the time we were finished we were exhausted, sweat pouring off both of us and we were flat worn out! We've got to drive back to Phoenix and then we're done for the day. As much as we don't like to use truck stop showers, tonight is an exception, this is an emergency! We've got to wash the sweat off!

One thing I spotted while we were unloading was what I called a lizard. Ron quickly corrected me and said it was a Gecko. Boy can they move fast! Also today was the first time I have ever seen the giant Saguaro cactus. I cannot believe how tall they are. Some of the cactuses are full of holes and Ron said the birds made them. I wouldn't be a bit surprised if in some of the holes, a big fat rattlesnake isn't curled up inside it! Let's just say I wouldn't want to find out by sticking my hand in there! One more thing I want to share is that it made me sick when

I saw beautiful Saguaro cactus sprayed with graffiti! We see graffiti plastered all over buildings, signs, overpasses, bridges, you name it, but it's just painful to see it sprayed on these magnificent products of nature. I find it hard to believe when all these punks have so many other places to spray their off the wall graffiti, why they would pick on a plant! Tomorrow we're off to Prescott, AZ, Lake Havasu City, and then on to Las Vegas, NV.

September 11th and today is our grandson Sam's very first birthday! I'll be sure to call Kellie later to see what she has planned for him. He is such a cutie! We had hoped to get a room for the night in Primm, NV at Whiskey Pete's casino, but none were available. They told us there is a big race going on for off road vehicles. Now we know why the air is so full of dust! We ended up sleeping in our truck, but before doing that, we walked up to the casino and had a delicious prime rib dinner. We are going to stop in Barstow, CA and get the truck washed. Our black truck looks brown!

Picked up a load late yesterday and then made it to Lebec, CA before calling it a night. We just did a driver change and guess who was driving, me! I drove 165 miles today! Must admit though when I started out, I was a little scared with all the traffic; having to merge and get right into it, but I did! It took me a few miles before I started to relax and then after that, I actually enjoyed giving Ron a break. I got right out there into the thick of it, changed lanes, passed other 18 wheelers, and ran with the big dogs! I felt pretty accomplished to say the least. I like it when Ron is proud of me and he told me so several times after he took over the wheel. My past vision of being able to help him out has now become reality. I know I still have a long way to go before my confidence level comes up, but each time I drive I feel like I'm making headway. Maybe someday after my grandchildren read my book they too will be inspired and not be afraid to take on any challenge put in front of them.

CHAPTER 3

RUNNING THE INTERSTATES

Stopped tonight just outside Klamath Falls, OR at a small roadside truck stop called the "18-Wheeler." This truck stop has been around awhile. It's the kind of place that's exclusively meant for truck drivers only! The building is small with a couple fuel islands, has a dirt parking lot and plenty of flies to greet you when you step out of your truck! Definitely not a place that would appeal to tourists, but frankly, the truckers like it that way! Nowadays most of the truck stops have diversified their business by catering to the "traveler". This change created higher revenue for them, but annoys the hell out of most truckers! Especially when they find a motor home parked in one of their spots or when they have to wait in long lines to pay a cashier! In fact, just to cater more to the traveler, several truck stops took out their restaurants and stocked the entire place with "grab and run" food! After hours on the road a driver looks forward to, and enjoys, getting out of the confinement of his truck and sitting down to a real dinner. Now they have no choice but to settle for a hot dog or pre made sandwich and go back and eat it in their truck. What money they get out of trucker's has lost its clout and now looked at as being just another dollar in their till! I must admit, this little truck stop cosmetically leaves a lot to be desired, but it's one of the few left where the waitress greets you with a smile and makes a driver feel at home!

As Ron and I sat eating dinner I told him years ago I actually lived in Klamath Falls. I was of preschool age but still for some reason I felt like I somewhat knew the area. My father Bill was in the logging industry not only employed as a driver, but also able to perform other logging related tasks as well. As a young man he decided to leave Washington for a job in Oregon. Along with that decision, he packed up his wife and four kids and moved them here. I suppose at the time, like many other young men with a family, he had visions of making "big money"! Obviously, that didn't happen and it wasn't long before we returned to Washington. Years later during conversations with him, he would always say our reason for leaving was because there were too many snakes! We also lived in Arcadia, CA for a while and he said the same thing only adding "California was full of timber rattlers"! He had no use for these critters and that's probably why I don't like them either! I use to think it was funny how he would raise his voice and say, "you get south, anywhere south and you run into too many snakes!" "I stay the hell away from them!"

It is the 19th of September and today is Kim's birthday. It would be nice to share it with her, but like too many other times before, sadly, it's not going to happen. Our stay at home on the 13th was another one of those "less than 24 hours" kind! It was barely enough time for the two of us to take care of everything needed in order to be "road ready". This is trucking! This is what to expect! Our job is hauling freight and we can't do it sitting in a recliner! Since leaving our driveway, we have already delivered a load to Helena, Montana, took another one to California and now we are on our way to Tigard, Oregon. I'm sure glad we packed additional clothes; it looks like we're going to be out here for a while. Freight has picked up and we are pretty much none stop!

September 27th and Wow! We just saw a herd of Elk run across the road in front of us! We are in the mountains, near La Pine, OR and what a sight to see! I never realized they were so big. We've got one drop in Bend, (7 pallets) and then will head for Salem for the second. Our route will take us over Santiam Pass which is a two lane highway, lots of ups and downs and curves to deal with. I'm glad that Ron is driving even if I know he'll probably cuss a few times when traffic gets backed up behind him. We crawl up the hills like a slow moving slug! It is inevitable that sooner or later we're going to irritate a whole bunch of four wheelers! No doubt, we'll get flipped off by some of them when they're finally able to pass and get around us. Ron will give the high sign right back! Our next stop was in Tigard, OR and we're going to be late! We were detained for more than two hours on highway 217 because of downed power lines caused by a big grass fire. Now we are running behind schedule and Ron is feeling pressured.

This is ending up to be a "not so fun day" for either of us! Unlike driving from point A to point B like most of the loads we get, this one had four stops; Tigard, Hillsboro, Mc Minnville and Milwaukee, Oregon. This is NOT what I vision "Long Haul Trucking" to be at all! What I haven't mentioned; at every single drop we both had to get out and help unload! (Even a robot's parts would wear out after doing all this physical work! I'm no spring chicken; this is hard back breaking labor for both of us!) When we arrived at our final drop in Milwaukee we were hit with another surprise! The area to maneuver was small and Ron knew it would be a difficult task for him to get his tractor and 53' trailer backed up against the dock! His driving skills were put to the test, but after a few "pull ups" and a couple "get out and looks" he finally bumped the dock! It was a tight squeeze putting it mildly! He did a great job!

While I was sitting there I sized up the next problem and frankly it appeared to be worse! I could see no way whatsoever he would be able to leave without possibly hitting something. He was going to have to back out from where we entered. Too many obstacles in the way! I got out of the truck and walked down the "alley" size driveway that we drove in on. It wasn't long and I discovered another way out. When Ron came back to the truck I showed him what I thought might work and he agreed. I could tell he was somewhat surprised that I had already checked out our next problem and found a solution. Now you would think at this point our day was over. It's supposed to be, but oh no, dispatch said as long as we're in the vicinity, we need to go to Jantzen Beach and pick up a partial load! It's incredible what they expect out of their drivers. What they're asking us to do exceeds the call of duty! We've already put in a full day; way beyond what's expected out of the average worker.

Dispatchers show no mercy! Their only interest is moving freight and it doesn't matter to them what a driver might think, just shut up and do it! We feel like two little kids getting punished at this point. We are not very happy, but we'll get the job done! Tonight we will stay at Jubitz Truck Stop. It accommodates several hundred big rigs, has a nice restaurant, plus a whole bunch of other amenities to meet any need of a driver. It's a very popular spot for truckers Traveling I-5 through Portland, OR.

When we got to Jubitz last night, Ron and I heard a "country music band" in their lounge. Before going to dinner we decided to go in and check it out. As tired as we both were, we actually got up when they played a slow song and danced. We stayed a while longer and enjoyed the music. It was so refreshing to be out of the truck and around others so full of life. Without realizing it, we have isolated ourselves by being alone so many days and weeks at a time. This was a reminder that socializing is healthy and a very much needed component in our lives.

It's a new day and we were so close to home while parked at Jubitz, but no luck! The wheels are once again rolling and they're sending us back south to Rialto, California with a bunch of store returns. Ron said he will drive to Redding and then I can take over and drive to Sacramento. I did my driving today but I guess I hit traffic wrong coming into to Sacramento. As I approached the city I was up to my eye balls with bumper to bumper congestion! All lanes were full of four wheelers darting in and out. I was doing just fine until I ran into this mess! Where did they all come from, don't they have jobs, is everyone out shopping? My blood pressure went up, my hands were sweating, and I told Ron "That does it! I'm not going to drive any further!" One thing for sure when you've been married as long as we have, Ron knew I meant every word and he wasn't about to argue or try to convince me otherwise! I pulled over to the shoulder, set the brakes and said "It's all yours, go for it!" He never said a word for the next few miles; he knew I needed to regroup and he wasn't about to get me riled up any further. From today's experience, it is obvious I have a long way to go before I don't allow myself to become so intimidated by heavy traffic situations. I'm not giving up; I'm just taking a break. Like a kid learning to ride a bike or a horse, if you fall or get bucked off, you get back on and ride! That's just what I intend on doing tomorrow.

Stayed in Santa Nella, CA last night and met a nice Canadian truck driver while out on the patio eating our dinner. Ron past experience of delivering several loads into Canada, made for interesting conversation between the two of them. We dropped our trailer in Rialto and found a place to park. Our load will be ready at 3 a.m. and this time Ron told me I don't need to get up with him. He would rather have me sleep so I can drive later.

Ron got up last night, hooked up to the trailer, did his VI and drove to the top of the "grapevine" before I even woke up. I can't believe I slept through all that noise, but I did. Not my turn to drive yet, but I will before our day is over. Our load has two drops and both of them are in Portland, Oregon. After the final delivery, we're done! The truck is headed home! It seems like we've been gone forever. The walls are closing in and the confinement of being cramped inside together for so many days is getting to us. We desperately need showers and a change of scenery. It's times like this when I start getting resentful; especially when I take note of all the other people living normal lives. I'll bet they all had a shower this morning, and I hope their water was cold! O.K. not really, but I can't help but be a bit jealous! It's times like this when I have to remind myself of the good we and other truckers do out here in order to make other people's lives comfortable. We, although taken for granted sometimes, are depended upon by millions of Americans to deliver their every want and need! Trucker's are indispensable when it comes to the general public's day to day survival. This thought alone makes me feel better!

Two days off at home and I know between the two of us we accomplish more work than the average human being. This time for example, we mowed the lawn, hoed the garden, pulled weeds in flower beds, picked fruit and vegetables, cleaned the interior and exterior of the truck, grocery shopped, ran errands, washed, folded and packed clothes, and then managed to BBQ a couple steaks! This is a lot to cram in with only a couple days off, but we did; the clock was ticking! Before running out of time, I managed to squeeze in a quick phone call to the kids and while I was doing that, Ron was on "countdown" closing windows and locking doors. His final chore was to find the cat and put her in the truck, (which is easier said than done!). Diesel is not the kind of cat that you can say "here kitty, kitty and she'll come right to you!" Not a chance! She wants to make sure you get a workout first before finding her! I try to ignore all the action going on around me, but eventually all the commotion gets to be too much and I'm compelled to stop what I'm doing and help him catch her!

September 29th and I must say if we ever get to retire this is probably the nicest time of year to travel. Traffic is much lighter when kids are back in school and vacations over. The highway gets down to truckers driving big rigs, a few snow birds headed for warmer weather, maybe a bus or two and then of course the usual share of four wheelers. Nevertheless, it makes you feel as though the whole world slows down. Leaves on trees are starting to turn their usual gold, red and orange colors. I love to watch them gently fluttering back and forth as they make their way to the ground. It also is my reminder to enjoy the brief beauty while it

lasts; its nature's prelude to winter! Even the air smells better when we
have not so warm days and cool evenings. I guess I just plain love this
time of year!

We are in Chandler, AZ, third in line and waiting to get unloaded.
I'm sitting up front looking out the window at what I think are lizards.
Boy do they move quickly! There seems to be quite a few of them and
they are dashing from one sage brush to another, probably trying to keep
in the shade. Its 96 degrees outside so no wonder they're "hot footing" it
across the sand! Diesel continues to sleep most of the time and today is
no exception. The only time you see any action out of our cat is when she
spots or hears a train. She does not like trains! Yesterday in California
we had to stop for a train that was about to cross over the road in front of
us. It was funny because she was up on the dash enjoying the sun while
keeping a close eye on the train as it slowly approached the crossing.
Diesel had no way of anticipating what was about to happen! When the
engineer let off several blasts from his air horn she jumped up on all
fours, grew wings and flew like a birdlike to the top bunk! Ron and I
couldn't stop laughing!

This is the thing I'm learning about cats, they give you the impression
that they are so lethargic, sleep eat and purr! They are masters of deception!
Before you know it they have you wrapped around their fingers, (paws)!
Oh have I learned! There is another side to their personality! Given
the right circumstance they can come on like a lion, fake sleeping and
charge like a bull! (I just described out cat!)

I'm continuing to drive without being signed on with the company
and it still bothers me. Ron said it shouldn't because we were approved
by them for me to drive with him sitting up front as a trainer. I'm just
not ready yet to sacrifice my time by spending 10 days going through
their lengthy orientation! Admittedly, I also know I still need more time
behind the wheel.

September 30th and after picking up a load in Phoenix, AZ this
morning we are now in Lebec, CA for the night. Last evening while
sitting in the truck stop, I was working on putting some coins that I had
found into my coin books. Ron was up front completing his daily log.
I just happened to glance out the window and I said to Ron "that guy is
coming up to our truck!" I swear truck stops are the "catch all" for free
loaders and beggars! We get hit up almost every time we park and I'm
not kidding! It's not only annoying, but it can be downright scary! The

guy approaching our truck was no exception. He looked pretty rough to me and not surprising, full of tattoos, dirty long hair and just plain skuzzy! So sure enough, just as I predicted, he came over, climbed up on our step and knocked on the side of Ron's window. Dam, I hate it when this happens to us!

Free loaders all have their unique story for begging, and believe me it's all phony! This guy's ploy I have to admit was a new one! He gave Ron a tale of woe with a little more creativity. He said in a "begging toned voice" (more accurately described), that he was "short" exactly, $4.16 from buying a new fan belt for his car. Quite frankly, I sized him up and I think he was giving Ron one big fat line of bull! He claimed to have walked over a mile just to get to the truck stop in hope of a driver helping him out. He even went so far as to say his wife and kids were waiting in the car for his return and he was sure they were all suffering from sitting in the hot sun. Get out the crying towel! His line of bull Ron either fell for or he just wanted to get rid of him. In either case, once he got the money out of Ron, ($5.00) he left. This is a prime example of how truck drivers get taken! The guy was shrewd. He played a hunch that if he asked for an "odd" amount in change, most drivers would probably not want to mess with finding 16 cents and would give him five bucks! Not too dumb! What a scam and it worked on Ron!

Sometimes I think Ron is too soft hearted. Just imagine if that same guy approached, (which I suspect he did) about 400 other trucks parked in the lot and let's just say "half" of them bought into his tale of woe. Let's also imagine the other drivers, like Ron, gave him $5.00 because they too didn't want to bother finding the exact amount of change. At the end of the day the "con" would walk away with $1,000 of tax free money! (Remember truck stops are around the clock operations so it allows the freeloaders plenty of time to beg!) Trucks come and go continuously giving the con a fresh supply of new drivers to hit on. Now, depending how "hard" these sleaze bags want to work their scam on innocent drivers, they could conceivably reap a nice little income of $30,000 a month!! The IRS needs to send their men with little brief cases out to the truck stops and nail these jerks! The bums need to get a job and pay taxes like the rest of us.

October 1st we got up at 3:30 a.m. delivered in Modesto, CA and now we are parked getting loaded with corn meal flour which we will take to Rancho Cucamonga. I'm absolutely enjoying the scenery. We are next to a pasture full of cows and bulls grazing in the field. There are several snow white birds feeding around the cattle. Every now and then one of the birds flies up and lands on the cows back. One flick of the cow's tail or a swish of its head sends the bird flying off! It's fun to sit and watch. I got my binoculars out and took a closer look at the birds and then located them in my North American bird's book. They are "Cattle Egrets" and are quite smaller than the "Snowy Egrets" that we see in the rice fields. Diesel herself enjoyed watching all the activity going on in the field laying up on the dash slowly swishing her tail and licking her chops! Her vision was opposite of mine. I was thinking about how much I enjoy watching nature and she was drooling thinking about "birdie dinner"! This for me is one of the benefits of driving truck. I never would have been able to see these egrets much less all the other wildlife I've seen had I stayed at home.

Ron has been keeping an eye on one of our steer tires for over a month now. We spotted a tire dealer on our way to pick up the corn meal so when we're done loading we will stop and get it checked. Of all the 18 tires that support the truck and trailer, you NEVER want one of your steer tires to blow out on you! I know if it happened to me, I would be in a horrible situation of trying to control the truck and trailer until I could safely come to a stop. In fact, I'm not so sure I could do it! For these reasons alone, I'm all for Ron stopping today. I have a hunch that after the dealer takes a look we will all agree it's time to buy a new set.

I called Kellie yesterday, the 5th of October to wish her happy birthday and enjoyed a nice conversation as well.

Today we delivered pasta and were surprised when we came up to the security shack and the guard stepped out and told us, (both of us) that we had to wear these gauze shower type caps before entering the plant. Not only did we both put on these caps, but Ron also had to wear a disposable beard protector! Boy, I'm telling you, he looked so funny and I was laughing my head off! Ron was laughing too only it was at me! He said "so you think I look funny, look at yourself in the mirror!" I did, and he was right, we both had the appearance of a doctor and nurse about to do surgery on someone! He didn't like it, but I could not pass up the opportunity! I got my camera, and took a picture of him. I guess on the more serious side, the company obviously had very strict rules on cleanliness and for that we are grateful! We also buy their products.

Since delivering the pasta, we went to Rialto, CA and now are headed for Oregon. We got off to a late start, but even at that, Ron's goal was to make it to a restaurant on top of Montgomery Pass located on the California/Nevada border. He warned me the place we would be stopping at was nothing to write home about, but has food and some old, old, slot machines that coughed out real coins. Being a coin collector, I am delighted at the thought of possibly finding some old coins out of the machines. By the time we got there they had closed the restaurant so there went any hopes of having a hot meal! The only food available was snacks like potato chips, peanuts and pop corn. (The pop corn was free but no telling how old it was!) The few customers inside were friendly and right out of the hills, including bib overalls and missing teeth! They starred at us both when we came through the door as if they were sizing us up to see if they liked us or not. Apparently we met with their approval and fit right in, (except for the bibs and missing teeth). The sizing up went both ways! I figured after looking them over that they no doubt were local folk and they all knew each other.

There were some pretty husky mountain boys inside playing pool, along with a few well fed women! I wouldn't want to tangle with any of them! I could tell that they were used to truck drivers stopping, and in all reality, they probably looked forward to their visits just to have fresh conversation. In short time Ron was invited into their conversation while I conveniently found a stool and sat down at a slot machine. What fun to actually have to pull a lever each time to spin the wheels! It wasn't long and clinkety clink nickels dropped down into the tray. I immediately went into my old coin searching mode, picked up every nickel checking the date and mint mark. I was really surprised to find six oldies! I suppose we were there a couple hours when Ron said "Billie, we've got to get up early and I'm starved!" On our way back to the truck I told Ron we were low on food supply but I would see what I could find. Not the best dinner in the world! We ended up eating cans of Beanie Weenies and topped them off with chocolate chip cookies! Tomorrow I've got to have a real meal with salad!

We delivered the last of our load in Richland, WA then got dispatched to Spokane for a load of pasta. Our trailer would not be loaded until morning so we parked it at their dock and bob tailed up to spend the night with Ron's mother. She put together a fantastic dinner for us which we both enjoyed and appreciated. There is nothing to compare with "home cooked" when you eat out every single day! She offered us a bedroom to sleep in but we declined and chose to sleep in the truck. We had to get up early anyway and we didn't want to bother her by thinking she had to get up and make us coffee.

Delivered the pasta load in Clackamus, OR and now we've been told by dispatch to stop at four different stores to pick up their returns and take them to Rialto, CA. This is not fun! You spend hours going from one store to another, back up to their dock and then sit until they load all their returns in the trailer. Believe me, store employees take their own sweet time loading with no consideration that the truck driver just might have a few other places to pick up at before he can even think about driving to Rialto! This is not what I imaged long haul trucking to be! I swear, once I'm approved for Ron and I to be a team, we are going to expand, I mean "really" expand and put some major miles under our belt! I'm already bored from repeatedly driving the I-5 corridor and there are plenty of other states out there that we would both love to see.

October 7th and I drove from Dunsmuir, CA to Westly which is a good 200 miles! Part of the I-5 run takes you through the Mt. Shasta canyon. This was my first 6% grade along with lots of up and downs and plenty of curves to maneuver around. I'm pretty proud of myself for all the down and up shifting it required and I didn't miss one gear!

October 8th and we're here at the Holiday Inn in Rancho Cucamunga, CA. Ron surprised me by saying "I've had it! We're not sleeping another night in this truck!" I have to admit we both feel, and probably look like, two homeless people you vision hitching a ride in a box car! We are absolutely grubby, probably smell, and are just desperate for showers, a nice dinner and the luxury of having a big bed to sleep in.

The temperature today is 97 degrees. We paid for a room and the first thing we did was have a shower! We were both worried about Diesel because the truck was parked in the sun and she was still inside. Ron said "I'll bet the truck is much hotter even with the vents open so we better walk out there and check on her. He was right! You cannot imagine how awful Ron and I felt when we climbed back in the truck. Inside the cab it was probably over 100 degrees! Poor Diesel! We both felt so sorry for her. I cannot believe how stupid we were! Diesel was panting with her tongue hanging out of her mouth keeping rhythm to her panting! There are not enough words to express how bad we felt or how worried we were for her. Ron immediately started the truck and turned on the air conditioning.

If the cat could talk, I'm sure she would have called us every name in the book! It's amazing, but it took about ten minutes and she was back to normal. We were pretty scared and I think we got back just in time to save her from having a heat stroke. I just glanced back at her and now I know she's back to normal. She is in her usual position of lying upside down on our bed with all "fours" stretched out; purring like a kitten! It's amazing how you get attached to an animal. As I told you before, I'm not into cats! Diesel is forcing me to like her! I think today, she won! The sun was going down and we stayed in the truck keeping the air conditioning on for about another half hour. At this point Ron shut the truck off and I climbed up on the top bunk and opened the windows and vents below. We both felt she would be just fine and we went back to the motel. We learned a lesson to say the least.

It is the 9th of October and we are picking up a load of office supplies. When we entered the plant, the guy inside the guard shack was telling us that yesterday there was a big snake out on the lawn. He thought it was a rattle snake but when animal control came out to investigate he found out it was only a harmless gopher snake. Doesn't matter, I don't like snakes and you can be darn sure if we get out of the truck I'm going to watch where I walk! Diesel is in a playful mood today. Ron gave her, of all things, a Q-tip and she is just going crazy batting it around. Our load is ready and we're headed home, well at least in that direction. You never know about a dispatcher! Just when you think you're going home they could call and send you somewhere else! It wouldn't be a major problem for us because we're together, but for a younger driver to get hit with a surprise like that, I'm sure would be a huge disappointment.

It's been a while since I've written in my journal and here we are already half way through the month of October. Today is the 16th and over the past week we've been to Washington, Montana, Utah, Arizona, and California. Today we are on our way to Salt Lake City after picking up a load of carpet and furniture in La Mirada, CA. Yesterday was very windy and today is no exception! We heard that some of the gusts were clocked at 60 mph! Our load is not all that heavy and the strong wind blowing against the side of our trailer makes it difficult to keep it on the road! We passed other drivers that obviously sized up the wind conditions and decided to pull off and park to avoid getting blown over. Ron said their trailers no doubt were empty making it even more risky for them to drive.

We saw the longest backup of traffic today and thank heaven we were traveling in the opposite direction! The line of four wheelers and semi trucks went on forever! There was no accident to blame for the backup, just road construction. Ron does not deal well with slowdowns and tends to do a whole lot of bitching, (which I have to listen to for as long as it lasts). I must admit, Ron is not the only one complaining. Other drivers, before you even reach the road construction are already on the CB radio voicing their personal irritations of having to slow their rig down to a crawl. Some of the driver comments are funny and then there are others that really make you want to plug your ears! Drivers can get real mouthy over the CB and that's probably because they know they can get away with it!

By the way, we are traveling down the highway today with two giant Halloween pumpkins wired onto our front bumper. They each have big happy faces. Ron wasn't too keen on the idea of putting them there, but I convinced him it would be fun to have a little "Halloween" decoration going down the road. It's getting real bumpy, too bumpy for me to write.

This morning we are in Clearfield, UT for a partial drop and then we'll do a final unload in Salt Lake City. Last week when we passed through Spokane we met Ron's mom at the truck stop. She greeted us with a bag of tomatoes. It's funny, because we picked tomatoes from our garden and had then on board to give to her! (Doesn't make much sense to me, but maybe not to hurt her feelings, we exchanged tomatoes!) I know she means well, but she also picked fresh catnip for Diesel. That's all we need is to have a wacky cat inside the truck stoned on catnip! I wanted to dump the catnip at the next rest stop but Ron said "no" we'll give it to her when we are parked. He won!

Ron drove hard today pushing his hours to the limit and he's visibly worn out! We are in Nephi, UT and shut down for the night. Traffic was relentless and we both are downright tired! Although I'm sitting up front and not driving; it still takes a toll on your body staying put for hours on end. We both sat and completed our daily logs. (I have to complete a log even if I don't drive, it's the law.) It's amazing, but when you are this tired, you don't have much of an appetite and sleep sounds better than food. However, I did manage to climb down out of the truck, walk across the parking lot and buy a couple slices of pizza. No telling how long the pizza had been sitting there under warming lights, but who cares, it was prime rib to us!

Got up this morning at 4:30 a.m. and we both feel much better. Today I'm going to send a post card to my dad and my brother Jerry. I want to thank Jerry and Carol for the BIG box of King crab legs, salmon, and halibut they sent to us last time we were at home. The box was huge and they told us they had their daughter Charley in Alaska air freight the fresh catch down to us. He also sent us a picture of a Caribou he bagged this year. What a wonderful brother and sister in law I have!

We are sitting in Selah, WA waiting for a load of apple juice which we will deliver to Rancho Cucamonga, CA. We're not too happy because filling a 53' trailer with all this juice creates a very heavy load to pull! We don't mind a heavy load once in a while, but when you get them back to back it cuts into our profit. (Remember we are owner operators and we pay for everything!) Heavy loads suck up the fuel and fuel is our biggest expense. We wanted to get a load home out of California, but the only thing they had was this one to Selah, WA, where we will unload, reload and then do a flip back to California. Ron said after we deliver the juice he is going to insist they dispatch us a load home; we'll see. Dispatchers in general could care less about the personal request of a driver. Sad but true, and I know some actually get irritated when it comes to a driver asking for time off because it reduces their resource in getting existing loads dispatched and off their backs.

Yesterday Ron took a little different route than the usual. We crossed over several mountain passes. I enjoyed looking at all the beautiful autumn colors of red, orange and gold leaves nestled amongst the dark green pine trees. However, the route he chose is another story and it ended up a real challenge for a big truck! He almost bit off more than he could chew! Uphill, downhill, hair pin curves, steep grades and deer popping out all over the place! (Not to mention the fact we were on a two lane road!) Talk about self inflicted pain! Some of those curves you could barely bend the trailer around. Ron's driving ability was tested to the max. Not only was the road two lane, but there were no paved shoulders! One slip of the duals off from the pavement and on to the soft dirt shoulders would probably tip us and the tractor trailer over on its side! What started out to be, what we thought would be, an enjoyable "new" route turned into a nightmare! It seems like it took us forever to get out of those mountains and down into the valley.

As a witness to Ron's driving, I must say I was very impressed how he was able to gage curves, grades and maneuver our 18 wheeler over several miles of hell! I didn't even complain when he burst out shouting a few choice words a couple times along the way. I'm sure in his mind he was madder at himself for picking such a terrible route! I know when to keep my mouth shut and today was one of those times! During these moments I continued to sit quietly and let him vent. (Actually one time during my silence, I was thinking he did it to himself; he created his own misery but in no way was I about to tell him that!) I don't mean to sound hard hearted but we've been married a long time, and like other wives, you come to know your husband's personality and under stressful conditions you learn to leave him alone!

Once we were down in the valley, essentially on flat ground, Ron started thinking about the route itself and began to question himself whether it was even legal for him to take the truck and trailer on that highway! Some routes are totally off limits to 18 wheelers. He was so right! Another trucker coming in the opposite direction got on his CB radio and told Ron 53' trailers were not allowed on this highway. The driver said it was restricted to only allowing a "set of joints" or a 48' foot trailer. Whoops!! Seems like in a situation like this you no sooner get out of stress and you're right back in it! Ron said "Billie, we are in deep trouble if a "bear" spots us!" So for the next few miles, we both watched for the "Johnny Law"! Finally, we made it to the interstate and knew we were home free! We were relieved to call it a day in Hermiston, OR but this was only after dropping off part of the load in Medford. This isn't the best truck stop we've ever stayed at, but at least we're off the road and now Ron will be able to unwind.

October 27, 1999 and in only a couple more months it will be the year 2000! There is so much hype on the news media about all the complications this will cause having a year that ends in zeros. I guess we'll just have to wait and see. We're in Portland, OR this morning and have one more stop then we will head for Kent, WA to final this load. Ron called dispatch and told them not to send us anywhere else because we need to take a few days off.

Today it is very overcast and rainy. It's supposed to rain all day today and tomorrow as well. I'm actually glad we're getting the moisture because the fire danger is so high. As usual this morning when we got up it was still dark outside. I did the usual and went inside the truck stop and filled our thermos. When I walked back to our truck I decided to check behind our trailer to see if there was a trash can for me to empty our waste basket. WRONG THING TO DO! I stepped in a squishy pile of dog poop! The instant aroma would gag the best of anyone! It was way too early in the morning for me to have to deal with cleaning dog poop off my shoe! I swear it took me forever to clean my tennis shoe before I could even consider getting back into the truck! This was not a good way to start my morning when you consider Ron and I don't even talk to each other for the first 50 miles! I need time to wake up! Now you think my day got off to a bad start, and it did; I also had another shocking surprise when I discovered Diesel took the liberty of peeing on our bed! What was she thinking! There was no way I was about to sleep in a litter box! Sometimes I think I can't take it anymore and I refuse to live in filth! Ron makes excuses for her and I don't! I think she did it on purpose!

November 5th and we did get to go home like we requested. As of today we've already been back out on the road for five days. We stayed in Jackpot, NV one night and I found a few more old coins. Last week when we were home we checked out all of our tire chains to make sure there were no broken links in case we need to use them. Ron said they were all in good shape. It's comforting to know we are prepared to comply with any chain requirements going over mountain passes. Diesel seems to be fine this trip out and mostly all she does is eat, sleep or lay up on the dash and watch traffic. Like always, when I'm home I managed to get a phone call in to Kim, Kellie and Jason. Kim said she was really looking forward to Thanksgiving when we all can be together. (I hope dispatch doesn't ruin our plans, but it could happen!)

Just when things are going good, wouldn't you know we developed a problem with the truck! This is the last thing any driver wants to happen when they're booking down the road! We all want to just flat out, get in the truck and drive without being bothered by any unexpected problems! Ron fortunately spotted a truck repair shop and by that time he had already diagnosed what was wrong. He has worked on engines his entire life because he always bought what I considered junk! The junk he bought forced him to fix it and each time it ended up costing more money than what they were worth. (That's my opinion of course.) Ron went into the shop, bought what he needed, and fixed what turned out to be a broken wire on the alternator. Didn't take him long and we were back on the road. (I guess him buying all those old trucks and working on them paid off!)

Today is November 7th. We are in Ontario, OR and just finished eating our lunch at a fast food restaurant. The restaurant was in walking distance and we both felt the exercise would do us good. This has not been the best of trips! Ron got a speeding ticket, his" VERY FIRST" after all his years of driving! We were close to the Nevada boarder when we got pulled over by a California Highway Patrol officer, (CHP). I will have to admit the CHP officer was friendly and happened to be a cat lover. Of course we had to listen to all the bragging about his two cats. He clocked us going 69 mph, but wrote the ticket for going 64 mph. He tipped us off by saying 64 mph and under, the judge is pretty lenient and most likely would reduce the fine if we sent a letter of explanation. Of course we'll have to wait to receive the ticket in the mail and then I'll send a letter back pleading our case. There is always something unexpected that comes up that you have to deal with driving truck. The worst part for us is that the ticket will stay on both of our minds until it gets resolved and we pay whatever fine is owed. I honestly don't think Ron even realized he was speeding. It was late at night, very little traffic, and he was more focused on getting us to the one and only truck stop left ahead of us. I feel bad for him.

Another irritant we're dealing with is what was a small rock chip in our windshield now has advanced to a big long crack! It really is starting to look bad and very noticeable. This would be a good reason for the DOT to pull us in when we go over their scale and do a complete vehicle inspection. We don't want that so we will get it replaced very soon. I guess these problems are to be expected when you run so many miles out on the road, but both situations will cost us nothing but money! Regardless, we still love the trucking business.

Fall is in full force, the mountains are gorgeous and there is a definite chill in the air. We have observed ranchers riding horseback herding their cattle from high ground in preparation of winter. (I took pictures because it's not that often anymore that you see real "working" cow boys.) They even had three cattle dogs herding the cattle right along with them. It was fascinating to observe the dogs. They are trained to know exactly what's expected of them and they do an outstanding job! If one cow starts to step out of line, they are right there to herd it back in with the rest of the herd! No doubt the dogs are a great help for the men on horseback. Our next stop is in Walla Walla, WA. Our route takes us over Cabbage Pass and I hope we don't run into any snow! I don't want to get out in freezing weather and help Ron throw on chains!

Now we are back in Corona, CA and it's been a few days since I have written in my journal. After we finished in Walla Walla we went to Yakima, WA, Ronan, MT, and then on to Missoula where we picked up the load we're currently under. While in Missoula waiting for our load we got our quarterly inspection done and had our cracked windshield replaced. The only snow we saw this trip was way up on the mountain tops. This meant of course that the highway was nice and dry allowing us to pour on the coal, "hammer down" and crank out the miles! There is not that much traffic on this particular route and very few "bears" so it's one piece of interstate every trucker takes advantage of. We were flying! When you travel a route often enough you get to know every bump, chuck hole, curve, where the bears hang out and you even have a pretty good idea of when to expect the "coops" to be open or closed. In addition to all that, you also have the good old CB radio! We all alert each other as to what is behind or ahead of us. Great driving for any trucker, seasoned or not!

November 18th and we are on our way home. Of course it is still a few days until we get there, but nevertheless, I'm excited to see Jason and actually be home for his birthday. We will all get together for dinner at Kim's house on Thanksgiving. No doubt the guys will occupy their time watching football while Kim and I prepare dinner. Kim also invited Ron's mom, but she declined saying she has already made plans to have family over for dinner. Actually, I'm kind of glad about that because now we will have the kids all to ourselves.

November 23rd and we made a quick trip to Montana, after stopping for a brief visit with Ron's mother when we passed through Spokane.

Now we are headed home with a load of furniture. Once in a while a dispatcher gets it right! We said we wanted to be home for Thanksgiving and it looks like a pretty sure thing now. By the way, I'm still in driver training with Ron. He is always in a hurry when we get a load so I don't drive that often, but each time I get behind the wheel it is a new experience and I always learn something. As long as I am legal, which I am, it doesn't bother me to put off the dreaded driver orientation! I still get irritated when I think about having to stay the required 10 days before they will approve me to drive with Ron. Talked to Kellie on Monday and she said little Sam is miserable with asthma again. I hope this is short term and he outgrows it. It's too bad they live so far away. Maybe when Ron and I become a team we'll get a load to Virginia. It would probably only amount to an overnight stay, but at least we would get to see each other.

There is a possibility that we might get a load to Georgia. We learned that our company is short on drivers in that area and they have a ton of freight to move. This would be a great opportunity for us to see several other states. Ron said if the rumor is true, dispatch will probably send us to Helena, MT then head us to Los Angeles to pick up the southeast load. We would be traveling on Interstate 40 the greatest amount of miles. The nice thing about I-40 is that it would get us out of the mountain snow and into warmer weather. If we do get this run, Diesel will be along with us and our neighbor could collect our mail.

November 24, 1999 and we are back at the company terminal safe and sound. It was quite a trip over Lookout Pass and Snoqualmie Pass today. It was snowing HARD on both passes and crossing over them; Snoqualmie was worse than Lookout! Visibility was poor with blizzard type snowfall. Ron had to deal with slush ruts built up on the road along with stretches covered with compact snow and ice. He did a terrific job driving through all this, but the tension and stress of keeping the truck on the road and watching out for slipping sliding four wheelers wore him out! Diesel of course, slept through the whole thing snoozing and cruising with not a care in the world. Last night we stayed in the parking lot of the Silver Dollar Bar and Restaurant in Montana. Was nice to get out of the truck, walk around their gift shop and enjoy a nice dinner.

November 26th and we had a great Thanksgiving! Mike, our son-in-law, did a great job on the turkey and dressing! Because we all don't get to see each other as often as we would like (now that Ron and I are gone all the time), we had fun opening past birthday presents that we all had saved to give each other. Kellie and Scott sent a video of Jake and Sam, and the timing could not have been better. We brought Jason a box of canned food and money for his birthday. Even though he has picked up some part time work, going to college and paying expenses doesn't leave him much left to live on. Ron surprised me when we all sat down for dinner by saying "Let's all join hands and each of us will say what we are thankful for." I think all of us were glad he came up with that suggestion.

Off again! This morning we headed out to Los Angeles, CA and have already been told by dispatch that there will be a load waiting for us when we get there. We only need to drop, hook and head right back to Washington. Tonight we are stopped in Canyonville, OR at the Seven Feathers truck stop. (This used to be called Fat Harvey's.) I know what's going to happen. Although right now the truck stop looks the same, it's just a matter of time and they're going to do a remodel or tear down. They've built a huge new casino across the interstate and I'm sure the truck stop will be their next project. No doubt whatever they do will be a big improvement but along with that we can expect a new set of rules like "no smoking". If this happens, I hope it doesn't run some of the truck driver's off! Drivers like to be around drivers, they generate a generous amount of revenue, so more likely than not, the driver's needs will be one of their top considerations before making too many fancy changes. None of us carry bow ties in our trucks or dressy clothes. Truckers come in carrying a thermos, wearing jeans and a T-shirt and that's good enough for them! We're not out to impress anyone! Before we get out of the truck and go inside to eat I want to note that the rivers are raging and have gone over their banks in some areas. One house that we saw was totally surrounded in water. Oregon must have had some real heavy rain to create this kind of mess. All I can say is that we're glad its rain not snow!

Now this is funny (odd) driving over Mt. Shasta this morning we spotted a goat! It was grazing alongside the road. I'm a farm girl at heart and what I saw was "free goat" if we could catch it! Ron of course would have nothing to do with my idea and wouldn't even consider stopping. He didn't even slow down! I do wonder how it got there because it looked like an ordinary goat that you would see on a farm. I was worried the goat might get hit by a car or truck and to that, Ron said "next time we drive over Shasta remember this spot and you can look and see if it's still there!" His remark wasn't funny and not what I wanted to hear. As

I'm writing, Ron just told me our odometer turned over to 89,000 miles. We have put a bunch of miles on this truck since buying it last May.

November 28th and all I can say is we got up while the birds were still sleeping! I cannot believe I'm sitting here awake, well at least my eyes are open! Ron loves to beat traffic and get a jump on driving, but come on; 1:15 a.m. is a little bit too early! I sat in the front seat with my coffee and looked like a zombie for at least three hours. I honestly don't know how he can do this. I would be a danger to myself and others! He always likes to get ahead of the morning commuters when he comes into Los Angeles and for that I don't blame him. When traffic gets heavy you feel like you're amongst an army of ants frantically fighting your way through a maze of other ants to get where you're going!

Thanks to Ron planning ahead he was able to get into Los Angeles, drop our trailer, pick up a loaded one and get out! We are already headed back down the grapevine. He missed all of the four wheelers before the gates opened and they busted out of the chutes! It was great, no traffic to speak of that early in the morning. We passed an orange grove just a few minutes ago and it's hard to believe that I'm seeing trees loaded with oranges this time of year. I'm used to growing seasons, and ripe fruit in November hanging on branches doesn't fit in with my thinking. This is one of the wonderful things about trucking; I'm learning so much out here. Previous to going out on the road I had never seen an orange tree. The only oranges I ever saw was in the grocery store and not near as fresh!

Wow, where did the year go! It is already the 3rd of December! We managed to get home for two days and during that time I insisted we put up Christmas lights. Ron was not too enthused when we first started, but when we were finished, I know he was quite proud of the way they looked! We also put out our light up Santa, bear and snowman family. Everything is on a timer so they'll come on at 5 p.m. and shut off at 9 p.m. in our absence. It's a little sad not to be there to enjoy the lights every night but I know the neighbors and their children will like seeing them lit up. The lights will also give the impression someone's home during our absence. (We always worry about someone breaking in to our house when we're gone.) Before leaving we even topped it off by putting a Christmas wreath on the front of our truck!

Our trip to Montana was a real challenge this time. Road conditions were bad! We had to go over four passes and three out of the four were miserable! Here we go again when I cannot believe we are out here driving through blizzard conditions hauling freight regardless of the weather! The effort and endurance a trucker puts forth while driving his rig through ice, wind, heavy snow, putting chains on in the bitter cold and then taking them off, too often is taken for granted and goes unnoticed by the general public. But, this is the reality of trucking. While we're focused on winter road conditions, making some miles and getting a load delivered on time, other people are in a world of their own. Their minds, especially this time of year, are on shopping, decorating and preparing for Christmas. Nevertheless, we chose this job and aside from bad weather and absence from home it's still a good way to earn a living.

In the past I have had a couple white knuckle (or I should say Ron) experiences while observing him challenged to the limit by suddenly finding himself forced to drive through treacherous winter weather! Today's road conditions were no exception, and believe me, I said more than one "Hail Mary"! There were moments when I thought for sure I was going to hear the dreaded word from Ron that we had to stop, pull over, chain up, or flat out get off the road and park the truck, but we didn't! He fought crappy roads all the way, delivered the load, while freezing his butt off hooking up to another trailer. Now we're off until morning or maybe even longer while waiting to get the green light from dispatch for us to go and pick up our load of paper. Nice to be parked and off the road!

We received a message over the Qualcom, (on board computer dispatch) early this morning that our load was ready. We got out of bed and while getting dressed I discovered my diamond ring missing from the night stand. We both did a desperate search but finally had to quit. It was still dark outside and after all we had a load to pick up. I could look for my ring later. No doubt in my mind "Diesel knows something about this!" If she could only talk, I would know where to look! It really upset me wondering where the ring might be or even worse, maybe she ate it!

When we arrive at the paper plant we have to drive over their scale to get an *empty* weight then go around to the back of the building to get loaded. Once we are loaded and they give us the paperwork, we drive over their scale again to get the *heavy* weight. If the total weight is over 80,000 lbs gross we cannot legally accept the load. What a headache when this happens because then we have no choice but to take the trailer and back it up to their dock again for a re-load. There is no such thing as a "light" load of paper, they are all heavy! Even after getting these weights, we still go to the nearby truck stop and weigh on a CAT scale (certified weight) and slide the axels when necessary before we ever hit the highway. Although this is a required procedure it eats up valuable driving time. To adjust a load and go through all the weighs and re-weighs after sliding axels could sometimes end up costing almost a good hour. Fortunately, this load was slightly less than 80,000 lbs and we only had to slide the axels once.

I'm still spinning my wheels waiting for daylight. Diesel, because she likes to watch all the activity going on all around us, is up front on the dash looking out the window. Whatever she did during the night with my ring she has totally forgotten about! (Later) Sure enough, as soon as I could see daylight I started once again to search for my ring. Have you ever played the game of hiding an object where you tell the other person looking for it if they were "hot" or "cold" in the areas that they were searching? That's how it was with me and the cat! She laid there watching me, totally amused and entertained by my frantic search. The only thing she couldn't tell me was if I was getting close to finding it or not. A few minutes later, finally, low and behold I discovered the ring! No doubt she batted it with her paws, knocked it on the floor, batted it around a few more times until it went under the rug. I learned my lesson and tonight when I take my ring off I'll put it away in the drawer. Darn cat anyway!

December 6th and we are not out of bad weather yet. We ran into solid compact snow and ice all the way from Dillon, MT to Idaho Falls and then we still had to deal with stretches of patchy ice through most of Utah. This is one of those loads "hurry up and wait". We had to lay over the weekend in Nevada because we couldn't deliver this load until today. Needless to say we got a room and enjoyed having showers two days in a row! When we got up this morning it was only 22 degrees but now it has warmed up to a comfortable 63 degrees. We're parked in the company driver's yard and Ron is outside washing our truck. We were hoping to get a load to Dalton, GA like I mentioned before, but the freight won't be ready until next weekend. We cannot justify hanging around here that many additional days without turning a dollar.

The driver's yard where we're at is a pig pen! It's supposed to be a place for drivers to park their tractor and relax while waiting for a load, but it also houses a "repair" shop. Everywhere you walk you get grease on the bottom of your shoes. They even have a building for drivers with a complete kitchen, laundry facilities, recreation room and showers. BUT, sadly, it's in pretty bad shape from driver abuse! What I have come to learn out here is that not all truck drivers respect other people's property and some are downright slobs!

The company even provided a nice little grassy area with tables and a BBQ to further accommodate drivers. Now all this has been ruined by inconsiderate drivers who bring their dogs inside the gated area! The dogs have pooped, urinated and dug holes in the grass. (Nice aroma when you're trying to eat dinner!) Some of the drivers tie their dog up on the inside of the fence and allow them to incessantly bark, while others let them run around jumping on people. (No doubt the reason they bring their dog inside the fence is because "they" are too lazy to take to their own dog for a much needed walk!) Having their dog confined inside a gated area allows them to sit and shoot the bull with other drivers without having to worry about their dog running off.

The BBQ grills are layered with grime and not fit to use (at least for most of us drivers) because they've never been cleaned and are coated with old burnt tracings of meat. The building itself has showers, TV lounge, laundry, a room with a couple beds and a kitchen. It sounds nice that the company would set up such a facility for drivers. Unfortunately, inside the building it is just as bad! I would call it filthy!" No fault of the company, it is the inconsiderate drivers that lack respect by not cleaning up after themselves. Often the sink is full of dirty dishes; not to mention the spills on the stove that were never cleaned up or the abandoned cartons of fast food deliveries left on tables. Makes you wonder what some of these drivers homes must look like!

You can almost pick the slobs out when you're parked amongst all the other trucks. It's the ones with dog slobber all over their windows (too lazy to clean up after them) and the dash of their truck is jammed full of garbage that I suspect. Well anyway, I think I've painted a pretty good picture of what happens when you have some, (not all) drivers that display flagrant disregard for company property. They should be held accountable!

We left Auburn, WA with a load to Helena, MT last Wednesday and of the four passes we had to go over, only Lookout was a mess. It was dark, snowing and windy by the time we got there. We were driving over what is called a "broken snow floor". Ron geared down and took it pretty slow going up and over the other side. Other trucker's were doing the same. It's not the kind of conditions that you want to take for granted and get cutesy! We were glad when we finally reached the bottom of the pass. Another driver was not so lucky! We saw his badly damaged trailer at the weigh station entering Montana giving evidence to what must have been a roll over. It was ugly, probably totaled, and as we passed over the scale I snapped a quick picture of it. (Some of my pictures I have sent to the truck driving school I attended to be shared with other students.) Later when we pulled into one of the truck stops in Missoula, we saw the other half; the cab of the semi had been towed there. It also had heavy damage and quite possibly the driver was injured. Driving during the winter requires a whole new set of rules to follow. You can get yourself in trouble real quick just by making the tiniest of mistakes. Ron always said if you're not sure of the road surface, (like maybe black ice) stop, get out and test it for yourself!

From Helena, MT dispatch sent us to Great Falls for a load of flour. Once again we ran into bad roads all the way from Dillon to Idaho Falls. Monida Pass was horrible!! We had black ice and blowing, drifting snow. At times we were in "white outs"! Believe me, that's white knuckle driving! You cannot see ANYTHING but WHITE! There is no way you can see the road in front of you, much less if there is another vehicle up there. I said a bunch of prayers and I meant every word of them! I was so glad to be riding along with Ron even if it only meant keeping him company. Times like this you earn your pay and it's certainly not a job for whimps!

We are in Fontana, CA delivering the load of flour. It is sunny and about 70 degrees. It's hard to believe all the stress we went through getting here. I have quickly learned to love dry pavement! Kim called to check in on us, which we appreciate. She loves her new job. Today she is home baking Christmas cookies and said she was up to her elbows in cookie dough. After talking with Kim, I gave Kellie a call. It is easier to talk when we're parked and the engine is shut off. Kellie said Jake loved the coin books I sent him. He calls them his "monies".

Next load is carpet and we'll take it to Washington Oh, joy! Three more snow covered passes to go over just to get someone's carpet delivered before Christmas! Once again little do the "receivers" of ALL these goods hauled 24/7 by truckers, realize what drivers must go through in order to get the load there! This thought probably never crosses their mind, they just want their stuff!

It is now December 22nd and only three days before Christmas. At a rest area in Weed, CA I had time to stretch my legs and walk around the truck. I like to grab a paper towel, wipe down head lights, turn signal lights, and trailer lights doing my own little inspection. Diesel lays up on the dash and watches me. (I guess I'm good entertainment for her.) Anyway, while walking around the truck, I discovered a "low" drive tire. I pointed it out to Ron when he returned and he took a closer look. He said he found a nail embedded in the tire but the puncture was a "slow' leak and presented no immediate problem. We went on to Redding where he was finally able to stop long enough to add more air in the tire. Nevertheless, I know the problem will bug him until he's able to get it fixed.

Wow! Ron just said the odometer hit 100,000 miles going through Corning! No wonder we have tire problems! Won't be long and we will have to replace "all" of them. No doubt it will cost us a chunk of money. (Like about three or four thousand dollars!) If we were company drivers we wouldn't have to worry about the money, but we're not. As I mentioned before we pay for everything! We are small business owners paying Federal and State road tax, insurance, (not only on our truck, but on the company trailer we're hooked to as well) license fees, toll fees, fuel, cost to scale, all repairs, (major or minor), routine preventive maintenance, tires, and not to mention the cost of eating out on the road! All of these costs get paid before we ever see "the bottom line" and frankly, sometimes it doesn't amount to much for the long hours we put in! Sometimes we wonder if it's worth the effort. This is the price we pay for what we consider freedom; managing our own destiny and striving for the American dream!

Christmas morning and we are in Canyonville, OR looking out the window at heavy dense fog. I should be sad, but I'm not. I'm thankful Ron and I are together and I'm thankful for having wonderful kids and grandsons. I guess if I wanted to be sad it would be for all the other truck drivers sitting in their trucks away from family. There are thousands of drivers out here today throughout the United States that won't be home for Christmas. There is no such word as "HOLIDAY" in a truck driver's dictionary. If you're under a load and it happens to be a holiday, so what, you're expected to stay out and deliver it!

It's December 30th and we're passing through Garrison Jct. which is 49miles west of Butte, MT. The temperature this morning is "0"! I'm so glad we're warm inside our truck. The sunrise is beautiful as we both watch it slowly rising driving along the highway. It has changed from almost a dark red color to pink and now is turning gold. Ron just told me the temperature has dropped to -2 below zero making it pretty darn cold out here. The foothills surrounding us are covered with a light layer of snow and the trees along the road are all covered with sparkling white frost. Steam is coming up off the river that follows the road beside us. Truly a winter wonderland that we are seeing and it's "post card" picture perfect!

CHAPTER 4

YEAR OF "HAMMER DOWN" DRIVING

Happy New Year 2000! (Actually, it's New Year's Eve) We just parked the truck at Whiskey Pete's casino in Primm, Nevada and will start our new year by spending the night in one of their rooms. We're are both excited about getting out of the truck and able to enjoy the luxury of hot showers, a big bed to stretch out in and a nice hot meal! Ron looked at the odometer and since we started in May, we have run 103,560 miles! Makes me wonder how many miles we'll rack up driving a full 12 months. The weather is sunny but only 59 degrees. Diesel should be just fine staying in the truck during our absence.

There is so much hype going on over the new millennium. Sometimes I think we get too much information sitting in this truck for hours listening to the radio. You would not believe some of the far out predictions we've heard; like major power outages and computers crashing worldwide! We have never experienced a year ending in 00! Some so called experts even claim that people will go crazy; of course I "really" doubt that! I have a hunch everything will go on as usual, but even having said that, we will be watching television when the clock strikes 12 to make sure the world remains unchanged! Well after all that speculation, nothing happened last night. We all have to go back to work!

It is now eight days later and what a trip this one has been so far! Our first day out we had a delivery in Mead, WA. Because we were so close to Spokane, we dropped the trailer and bob tailed up to spend the night with Ron's mother. It was dark when he pulled into her snow covered driveway. For some reason, Ron suddenly changed his mind and decided to back out, turn the truck around and then back in so he would be facing the street. (Ron may have grown up on this property, but he forgot the big rocks and shrubs!) Just as Ron was making a swing out on the street the lower part of the bumper caught on a big overgrown shrub! We instantly heard a loud crunching sound! Ron jumped out of the truck to see what damage had been done. He climbed back in, slammed the door and said "Great! Half of our bumper just got torn off!" He was not very happy; totally irritated at himself, and said we should have stayed parked! I have a hunch; this is not going to be a cheap repair. I'll bet we have to buy a new bumper!

We got up this morning at 4:30 a.m. in Spokane and headed for Helena, MT. Not surprising, the mountain passes had patchy snow in places like we expected and all was going well, at least until we hit Mc Donald pass! The road was fine climbing up, but when we headed down, it was an entirely different story! The highway levels out on top and then when you head down, you're headed down!! The minute I saw the solid packed ice on the road, all I could say to myself was" Oh my God" here we go! I could just picture us flying off the road and up in the air like Santa in his sleigh! I held my breath, but I didn't say a word as I watched Ron grab a lower gear. Driving down a hill in a big rig on icy surface leaves no margin for mistakes! One wrong move like Ron hitting the brakes a bit too hard would instantly put us into a jack knife situation! Worse yet, under icy conditions like this we could easily be thrown into an uncontrollable slide and wind up landing in the bottom of the canyon below us! Remember back when I said "trucking would be the best of both worlds?" I must have had rose colored glasses on because I obviously forgot to consider winter weather! I even had a moment of questioning our own sanity for risking our lives out here for so many others. Ron as usual drove with extreme caution and had his four ways on all the way down. When he reached the bottom of the pass he said o.k. Billie you can pry your ass off the seat now! I know he was trying to be funny and make me laugh but he had to be just as relieved as I was!

We dropped our trailer in Helena and then drove to Dillon, MT to pick up a load of talc. We thought for sure we would be driving on snow and ice when we went over Monida Pass but as it turned out, the wind had blown the snow off the road. A couple times blowing snow blinded our vision but it didn't last long. We spent the night in Idaho Falls, ID. It got VERY cold and Ron had me turn on our bunk heater before we went to bed. (The heater is a pad that you place on top of the mattress with a cord that you plug into a cigarette lighter socket.) It's amazing how quickly it warms up and you have a nice heated bed to crawl into! Sleeping all night in a warm bed allows us to save fuel by turning off the truck. Must say though it's downright freezing inside the cab when you crawl out of bed in the morning! The windows are covered with ice and cold jeans don't set well with either of us! Needless to say we don't waste any time getting dressed!

When we got up we were greeted with snow falling. We did our usual, Ron doing his vehicle inspection and updating his log while I ran in and got a thermos of coffee. The snow continued off and on as we rolled down the road. We were almost to Nephi, UT where we planned to fuel when Ron suddenly said "Oh, No!" "Something is wrong with the clutch, it feels like mush!" This put me instantly into a major stress level! Words I did not want to hear! It wasn't long and Ron lost "ALL" USE of the CLUTCH! (I thought to myself, why do things always go wrong when you are in the middle of nowhere?) It's not only the fact that he's fighting the clutch trying to get it to work, but he also has to watch out for the "four wheelers" hitting their brakes and darting around us. He had his hands full! Little did any passerby know at the time what was going on inside the cab of our black Volvo. Ron started shouting telling me to get out the "Dealer Directory" and call the nearest shop! When he raises his voice like that it makes matters worse and my hands start shaking, but despite my "self" created handicap, I quickly found the book! When I located the nearest dealer I was almost afraid to tell him the location for fear of another explosive reaction. There was no convenient grace period that would allow me to prepare him for what I was about to say. Under stress, Ron expects an answer just about as soon as he asks the question so I broke the news and blurted it out! I told him our closest dealer was in Las Vegas, NV and he instantly shouted "dam it!" "That's at least six hours away from here!"

By the time we got to the truck stop in Nephi, UT Ron was shifting "without a clutch" watching his RPM's each time he shifted into another gear. We pulled in and Ron kept the truck running while fueling and I ran inside and grabbed us another thermos of coffee. At this point Ron was feeling a bit more confident that he could get us to Las Vegas, even knowing full well what was up ahead. He even said he was sorry for yelling at me. It was a bit embarrassing when we pulled away from the pumps because other drivers parked were watching us. They couldn't help but notice our truck jump, jerk and rock as he fought to get it in gear. Ron has an ego, like most males and he takes pride in his smooth shifting. I know he was thinking that the audience watching him thought he was a "rookie" and that didn't set too well with him. Once we were away from the truck stop and out on the interstate Ron settled down. He was gaining more confidence by the mile as each shift fell into place and was pretty sure that we would make it to Vegas.

Things went pretty well without the clutch and Ron was able to grab the gear he needed over and over again when it was required. Watching him handle each situation impressed me because there are so many long winding hills that require a driver to "down shift" the further you climb towards the top. About six hours later we were approaching Las Vegas and the traffic increased dramatically to a steady flow in all lanes. (In Nevada the speed limit is 75 mph so you can just imaging the traffic in front, back and both sides of our truck. Everyone is in a hurry to get to the casinos or get through the traffic and out of town as quickly as possible. Once again our stress levels were maxed!

Just our luck, Exit 49 that we needed to take was under partial construction so there was only one lane when we merged off the interstate and on to the off ramp. Exiting traffic was backed up clear to the interstate. Ron was in pure hell behind the wheel at this point from all the pressure! It was one of those situations where you move a car length, stop, wait and repeat this pattern until you inch your way to the stop light at the top of the ramp. He shifted more on the ramp than he did in the last six hours! When we finally made it to the top, we were forced to sit and wait for a chance to pull out into the intersection. Impatient four wheelers kept forcing their way by blocking the intersection while the light was amber. So we had no choice but to sit there and wait for a chance to move forward. This predicament only made matters worse for Ron and I know he was at the end of his rope! He was about to explode!

When we were finally able to get a chance to move, our truck decided to buck, jump and stall out on us! If that wasn't enough, would you believe at that very same moment the four wheelers behind us started honking their horns and pulling out around us? Ron flipped every one of them off and I'm glad he did! For once I had to agree with him, they were all a bunch of inpatient asses! They all knew darn well we were having problems because they followed behind us coming up the ramp. I swear we would still be sitting there today if it had not been for another observant truck driver coming the other way that saw we were having problems. He pulled his 18 wheeler out into the intersection, (now that's blocking traffic" and allowed only enough room for Ron to move forward and make his right turn. What a great driver and I hope someday my book will fall upon his hands! He will know who I'm talking about. He was there; he saw it all and didn't hesitate to jump in and help a fellow trucker. Thank you brother!

The Volvo dealer is within blocks of the freeway and boy was I relieved when we pulled into their parking lot. A great shop to do business with! Within two hours and $125 later we were back on the road! So many hours we endured driving from Nephi, Utah under constant stress and anticipation only to find out we had a sheared off bolt that held the clutch slave cylinder. Who would ever guess a simple "bolt" could cause us so much pain and grief!

Today things are going great! I'm wearing the new tee shirt Kim brought back for me from her trip to Maui. When we got up this morning it was a chilly 22 degrees, but now the temperature has climbed to a sunny 65; much warmer! We're actually down for the night in Santa Nella, CA under a new load that we picked up earlier and are headed back to Washington. I'm glad we're parked because it's hard to write in my journal when Ron is driving because every time he hits a bump my pen jumps! Diesel is up on the dash watching trucks pull in and out of the truck stop. You would think she would be frightened with all the noise they make, but she isn't. However, for some reason she gets spooked anytime she sees a flat bedder pull in. Ron is sitting up front doing his log and I think now I'll relax, turn on the TV and watch the news.

January 10, 2000 and today we arrived in Kent, WA after getting up at 4 a.m. this morning in Oregon. They're unloading carpet rolls out of the trailer and when they are finished we'll head home for a short over night stay. I'm not complaining. We at least will be able to do a quick check to make sure no one broke into our home during our absence. After that, I will be just as anxious to hit the road again tomorrow morning. This is a great time of year for us to be driving truck. There's not much to do now around the house except eat, watch TV and stare at each other. Roll on Big Momma! I'm spinning my wheels waiting for the next call from dispatch!

We didn't have to wait long, January 11th and we are backed up to a dock in Longview, WA getting loaded with rolls of paper to take to Montana. We already know from listening to the CB radio that all the mountain passes are in a terrible mess! Dispatchers always like you to commit to them an estimated time for delivery. Too bad, because this time they're not going to get it! Ron sent them a message and basically said "we'll get there when we get there"! No promises because of the anticipated weather ahead!

Dispatchers don't like getting answers like that, but who's driving the truck! It's the professional driver, and ONLY that driver who is qualified to assess whether it's safe to drive or not under adverse winter conditions. Further, there is no way for a driver to know starting out if the pass ahead will be open or closed by the time he gets there! This is especially true when the state decides to do "avalanche control". They blast the snow with dynamite, it covers the highway and then they get the plows out to clean it up. This can create lengthy "down time" for truckers. Chances are, using up even more of a driver's time, when they reopen the interstate they'll slap on a chain requirement! This is why it would be impossible to estimate for a dispatcher how long it will take for us to get our load delivered, especially if we run into these kinds of delays. We don't mind if we have to pull off on the shoulder and wait with other truckers; it goes with the job. There's plenty of food on board, the heater works, and we have constant conversation going on between other drivers over the CB radio to entertain us!

I have been out here so long now with Ron on the road I can pretty much guess the load we're going to get before we even get it! Today, January 14th is no exception. We have another heavy, "suck up the fuel" load out of Montana! The roads today are fine, but yesterday it was miserable for Ron. For three hours straight he had to drive on compact snow and ice. Once in a while he would see a dry spot of pavement and switch lanes to get the tires on solid ground for traction. Unfortunately these spots didn't last long before we were right back in the skating rink! The temperature was 7 below zero going through all this! We stayed in Nephi, UT last night and the buffet was pretty good. (I don't know why we pay for me to have the buffet because by the time I'm done with the soup and salad I'm full.) The buffet also includes a nice variety of desserts. Ron always seems to save just enough room for a piece of cake or a scoop of ice cream to satisfy his sweet tooth before declaring himself stuffed!

Last night while I was updating my own log, I laid the rubber band down which I use to keep the log book pages secured to the clip board. Sneaky Diesel was lying on the bed watching my every move and when she thought I wasn't looking, (which I wasn't) she snatched it up! Her action caught my eye when she started batting it around. I remember the veterinarian when she had some previous x-rays. He spotted a rubber band in her stomach and told us this could create a serious problem for her and to keep things like that away. I tried to grab it away, but easier said than done! That cat is quick! The minute she saw me turn and look at her, she grabbed it up in her mouth! Oh, great! Now I'm probably going to have a sick cat to deal with, or maybe a dead one! I don't know how serious this is. So far she has a smug, squint eye look on her face as if to say "I won, you didn't!" I'm not sure if she swallowed it or not so I'm going to keep an eye on her to see if she spits it out.

Here we are, sitting in Three Forks, MT on the 20th of January. When I say "sitting" I mean it! We have been here since 9 a.m. this morning waiting for a load of talc, (which was the time of our appointment.) Now, it's 1 p.m. and Ron just learned that the load will not be ready until 4:30 p.m.! Times like this you want to get the dispatcher out of their secure little comfort zone, warm office, snacks on their desk, couple breaks a day, lunch and have them SIT in our truck for hours on end! Some, but not all dispatchers, can relate to what a driver has to deal with once they dispatch them a load. But, today there seems to be too many of them that are unable to see beyond the building they work in! This just cost us an entire day of driving! Ron called dispatch and complained, but not surprising, it didn't do any good. He got the "Oh well; you'll just have to wait"! (See what I mean, total insensitivity!) This delay ruined our plans to get back home in time for Ron's birthday and to see Jason in Bellingham. Now I'm going to have to tell Jason we can't make it. I'm really upset because I was counting on our visit. (Not every day goes smooth in the trucking business and today is a prime example.) Ron said we'll be lucky to make it to Butte, MT tonight. (You burn up hours when you're on duty and not driving.) Next time we'll be a little smarter and call ahead to the plant and find out for ourselves when the load is ready.

January 28th and after being out 10 days on the road we are looking forward to a weekend at home. We owe Jason a visit and plan to stop by and see Kim and Mike as well. I have not driven our truck in several weeks because the roads have been so bad. Frankly, I was plain too "chicken" and could not get up enough courage to drive on them! While traveling through California I finally decided that I had better get behind the wheel before I forgot everything I had learned. Admittedly, I allowed myself to become complacent and "vacationed" while Ron did all the work.

In all truthfulness, I had lost the confidence level I once had. I was a scared, doubted my ability and had to give myself a real pep talk! Ron was very patient and obviously "read" my reluctance. He reassured me by saying "It's just like riding a bike; once you learn, you never forget." At the time I wish I could have believed him, but I didn't. I forced myself to get my courage up, get behind the wheel and take my turn driving. I pulled out of the rest area and drove for the next few hours. Along the way, I missed a few gears, but it didn't seem to bother Ron like it has in the past.

At one point, when highway traffic started picking up and I knew I was getting close to Stockton, CA, I blurted out to Ron that I didn't want to drive through it or Sacramento! I asked him if there would be a place ahead where we could stop and change drivers. He raised his voice and said, "What are you going to do, bale out!" His sarcastic comment did not sit well with me! In fact I resented what he said and thought to myself, o.k. Ron I'll show you, I'm not a "quitter" I'll drive through both cities! I continued on without saying a word driving through Stockton and then through Sacramento without encountering any problems. Ron was very proud of me and said the only thing I lack is my "own" self confidence. I suppose he's right, but driving a big rig safely takes "constant" awareness of your surroundings. You cannot let your guard down for one second, especially in heavy city traffic. I drove as far as Corning, CA to a truck stop and Ron had me pull right up to the fuel island. Pulling up next to a fuel pump was another "first" for me and I did just fine. I breathed a sigh of relief knowing I did a pretty good job and equally glad my driving session was over for the rest of the day. I set the brakes, got back in my seat and proceeded to update my log. After fueling, Ron climbed back in the cab, put the truck in gear and we were off again!

Everything was going fine until we got to the Oregon P.O.E., (Port of Entry). As Ron drove over the scales the red light came on! Dam, we didn't need this to happen! Ron stopped on the scale and a D.O.T. officer came out and told Ron to pull around to door #2 for a "complete" inspection! This is not the first inspection we've gone through, but it doesn't matter. Anytime you're "red lighted" you don't know what to expect from them! Wouldn't you know, luck of the draw, we got a "green horn" D.O.T. woman assigned to do our inspection! I just knew we were going to be held up there a long time. I'm sure her performance was going to be judged and by her looks, clip board in hand; she wasn't about to miss one detail of her inspection. I was right on with that assessment! She proceeded very SLOWLY making sure she examined and checked off her list each and everything item she looked at. She had Ron do the usual by having him follow each of her commands while she checked out lights, turn signals, brakes and so on. She asked to see both of our logs and Ron handed them to her. I thought she would NEVER give them back to us! Although we knew our logs were up to date, we both sat there and looked at each other, no doubt thinking the same thing; what is she looking at, why does she keep flipping the pages back and forth, why does she put one log down, look at it and then pick up the one she just went over? We didn't know what to expect, but at this point we both started feeling a little bit stressed and intimidated. Her examination of our logs went on way too long. She finally flipped the pages back and handed both log books back to Ron; apparently satisfied that our log entries were accurate.

We were confined inside their building for almost a full hour when she finally climbed up and put an Oregon D.O.T. inspection sticker on our window. She then walked over to the door, pushed the button to open it and waved us out. She had the personality of an ice cube! With that attitude, she will never win the D.O.T.'s most friendly inspector award, at least if it were up to truckers! I've yet to be red lighted but when that time comes, I'll probably freak out!

Today is the 6th of February. This time out so far has been pretty good with no problems. The truck is running great and for the most part going over mountain passes hasn't been too bad. Lookout pass had freezing rain which slowed us down, but that didn't last long. We spotted more Bald Eagles in Montana. I'm getting now where I know where they are at and I watch for them. The orchards in California are starting to blossom and I'm sure next time we pass through they will be in full bloom. I'm looking forward to seeing them. I'll try to get a picture, but it becomes a challenge when I stick my arms out the window, try to steady the camera and everything is whizzing by you! (I'm always surprised to see when I get film developed that I have taken more pictures of our big side mirror or bill boards than the object I thought I was aiming at!)

Last week we made it to Bellingham to see Jason and while Ron used his computer, Jason and I went shopping to buy him a dresser. We also stopped by Mike and Kim's for dinner. Both visits were fun, not long enough, but the road ahead is waiting for us. A day off is a day lost when it comes to earning money!

Earlier today Ron asked me to take over the wheel to give him a short break. I just drove from Vancouver, WA to the rest stop outside of Olympia. I did some perfect "down shifts" more than once. Ron coached me in advance and it worked. I also did a good job pulling into the parking lot at the truck stop. I got out and was pleased to see that I was nicely centered between both parking stripes. When I have a day like today, that's when I have to remind myself of ALL the hours of work I've put in to learn this job and now the training is starting to pay off! It really does make me feel good when I'm able to give Ron an occasional break; he can trust me to drive while he relaxes and takes a short nap. If anything, he knows I'm overly cautious and won't do anything stupid while he's sleeping.

February 20th and we are down for the night in Medford, OR. Played with Diesel for a few minutes because I think she is too fat and needs the exercise. (Besides, I enjoy interrupting her daily "Life of Riley" routine. She sleeps way too much!) I have a toy that looks like a fishing pole. It has feathers attached to the end of the string. (Well, there used to be a bunch of feathers there!) That cat is quick! More often than not, when I swing the feathers back and forth, she makes a mighty jump and grabs one and pulls it off!

Ron and I both have not been feeling very well and are a bit under the weather with what we think are viral infections. Each of us has the same symptoms, sore throat, cough, and chest congestion. This is another prime example of one of the draw backs living out here on the road. There is not much we can do but endure the misery. We did buy a couple over the counter cold and flu remedies, but that's it! There are strict laws for commercial truck drivers when it comes to taking any medications and you have to be very careful; like not taking anything that makes you drowsy. If we were home, it would be a different story and one of us probably would have gone to the doctor for a prescription. We also would be able to lie down, sit in the recliner, drink chicken noodle soup, get the vaporizer out and take care of ourselves. But, this is trucking and those comforts are not available out here. You drive no matter how you feel, unless of course, you have something real serious and if that's the case, you have no business being out here!

There was snow going through Ashland, OR and even over "Shasta" California this morning. It's the 3rd of February and you would think we should be seeing the tail end of winter driving. The "chains required" sign was on about 20 miles before we got to Ashland, but by the time we got there the road was wet and slushy so we never had to stop and chain up. (We were both dreading the thought of it!) I'm sure it must have snowed hard earlier because there was a about 6" on the ground when we passed through.

March 10th and we are back on the road after having a glorious three days at home! Ron and I both concentrated on spring yard work. (That's about the only physical exercise we get anymore!) Ron also cleaned up our truck inside and did his usual maintenance on it. While he was doing that I took a pitch fork and turned over compost in the garden. After finishing up with the compost project, I went ahead and planted the early vegetables. I love gardening; it's very therapeutic for me after so many days of being out on the road.

The morning before we left home I got a call from our dispatcher telling us he had a load of beer ready for pick up in Olympia. Before I even hung up the phone, Ron was instantly ticked off and said "dam it, here we go again, they're giving us another heavy load!" We pay for our own fuel and Ron considers these loads to be all "fuel" burners! I hate it when he gets in a bad mood before we even leave the driveway! Even if I understand his frustration, what can you do? You pretty much take what is dispatched out to you. I suppose we could argue because we are owner operators, but it probably wouldn't do any good and most likely make matters worse. We are well aware of the rumors that if you turn down a load; you get put down to the bottom of the dispatcher's list. The penalty for refusing could mean sitting for two or three days while the dispatcher takes his/her own sweet time finding you another one! Sitting parked without a load doesn't make us a dollar, so obviously we're going taking it.

We packed the truck, chased Diesel around until Ron caught her and headed out. When we got to the plant Ron checked in with the office. As he headed back towards our truck I could tell by his brisk walk and the look on his face, he was steaming! (This isn't going to be a good day!) Sure enough, Ron climbed into the truck and announced that the load would not be ready for at least another four and a half hours! Now why on earth would they dispatch us out so early, knowing we were at home and the load wasn't even ready for us to pick up? Now "I'm" angry right along with him! We could have enjoyed a few more hours at home! Now we're going to have to sit, and sit until it's ready.

The longer we sat parked, the more irritated Ron became. Suddenly, much to my surprise he picked up the phone and called dispatcher "Joe". Ron proceeded to give him an ear full! I thought to myself, o.k. Mr." hot head" husband, now you really got us into trouble! (This is one disadvantage of having a cell phone. If Ron had to "walk" to a phone booth like the old days, he would have had enough time to cool off, rethink his decision over in his head and not do it! To top it off, wouldn't you know within minutes after he hung up the phone, the load was suddenly ready! I thought again, "Ron if you only had just a little more patience, BUT, that's not his personality. Typically, Ron gets upset, reacts instantly and then gets over it just as quick! I myself tend to dwell on things that upset me for a LONG, LONG time. In fact some disappointments I've had in my past I still dwell on and probably will for years to come! I must carry a grudge! Ron is so predictable, he just called dispatcher Joe and explained to him why he was so upset. I hope his call smoothed things over for us. (BUT, even if it didn't, Ron will remain satisfied, always remembering how he was able to make his point before calming down and somewhat apologizing. We're now out on the interstate and plan to pull into a truck stop located a few miles down the road. We're pushing 80,000 gross and need to scale. No doubt we'll be sliding axels!

We are at a dead stop! It's March 11th and we're sitting in a traffic jam that's as far as the eye can see. We are about 30 miles south of Sacramento; drivers coming in the other direction keep giving us reports that there is a bad accident ahead. Needless to say we will be sitting here for awhile. What we heard over the CB is that a car rear ended a pickup truck then rolled over several times resulting in serious injuries to the occupants. Drivers are reporting that there are two ambulances, fire truck and several CHP officers on the scene. I figure as long as we are sitting here waiting for traffic to move, I'll make use of my time by climbing up on the top bunk and getting clothes out of our suitcases for tomorrow morning. (Almost an hour later, we are slowly starting to roll!) Because of the long backup, by the time we reached the scene of the accident it was all cleaned up. Other than one remaining officer and a few small pieces of metal and glass you wouldn't know there was ever an accident.

I took over the wheel in Redding, CA and drove to the Weed rest stop. While I was driving Ron was able to enjoy seeing Lake Shasta and all the beauty that surrounds it. It's always a pretty drive going over Shasta, no matter what time of year. There are many up hills and down hills on this route that will not allow a driver to just sit and steer. So when you're driving and not the passenger, you've got to pay attention! Along with curves, impatient four wheelers, slow moving trucks you come upon that suddenly require you to down shift, you're also kept busy continually matching gears to handle the grades you're driving over. I dealt with all of these elements without any problem. Ron gave me a star for the day. Life is good!

What a morning! We woke up to a dead battery! Not only that, it is only 35 degrees outside! There is nothing worse than getting out of a warm bed and then having to slide your legs into cold jeans! (Enjoy American public; we're doing this for you!) Ron got dressed first, started the truck, turned the heater on and promptly went in to get us a thermos of coffee. While he was inside the store he was able to borrow their battery charger. (Isn't it interesting that they just happened to have one? Gee, maybe we're not the only truckers out here that have ever had to ask to borrow a battery charger.) It's the second time this has happened to us and we're not going to go through it again! I'm going to insist we cough up money for new ones. Ron told me our batteries should have been good for two or three years, well it's evident to me ours are shot!

March 19th and it is only 15 degrees this morning! "Icicles" are hanging off the visor outside the front window and all over the rest of the truck. To top it off, the brakes were locked up, frozen on the trailer! (He forgot and "set" the trailer brakes last night, which is always a no, no in freezing weather.) After a few "pulls" and rocking the trailer, Ron was able to get the wheels rolling. The sky is a beautiful blue and it's sunny so it should be a good day of driving for us as we continue on to Helena, MT. Yesterday we were in a snow storm in Utah with winds gusting up to 60 mph! Ron had to fight the strong wind gusts for several miles. Looks like this morning we had about 3 or 4 inches of snow fall over night. When you're driving truck it's amazing; one day you freeze your butt off and the next day you're out of it and enjoying a nice warm 74 degrees!

Last trip home Ron had the time to take a good look at the batteries. He discovered a cable that was loose and needed to be tightened. We have not had any problems since, but I still don't trust them! Ron remains in conflict with Joe, the dispatcher. (See what I was talking about. You don't want to get on their wrong side!) I talked to Joe on the phone before leaving home last week. Although he is decent in his conversations with me, he told me to tell Ron "I'm tired of dealing with him, and the next time he comes to Auburn I'm going to send him EAST! (Wonder if he meant the east coast or did he mean "east' to Idaho or Montana.) Guess we'll find out!

Talked with Kellie and she told me she is going back to work part time at a local hospital. She will be taking Jake and Sam to daycare. She expects Sam to cry because he is a real momma's boy. I remember when I had to take Jason to the daycare and I don't know who cried more, him or me! I also managed to get a phone call in to Kim and Jason. In my conversation with Jason he told me he bought Marje a VCR, and would bring it out to us next time we are home so we can take it to her.

March 30th and what a trip this has been so far! We left home last Tuesday with a "sealed load". After scaling we found out the trailer was overweight and we would have to slide the axels. With me in the front seat, Ron watched as I backed the trailer up to the hole where he wanted to set the trailer axels. We repeated this procedure several times and each time we set the trailer we would re-weigh. No matter how hard we tried, we ended up 200 pounds overweight! The load delivers in San Pedro, CA and there are a whole lot of coops between here and there! This overweight situation we're in creates a constant worry for both of us. We don't want a ticket!

Unfortunately, the company sees this as "our" problem, not theirs, and it would be out of the question for us to refuse the load at this stage. (Besides, we're already in hot water with the dispatcher.) Our luck ran out with one weigh station and they red lighted us. The officer announced over the loud speaker to circle around and re-weigh. We thought for sure they were going to nail us! When we pulled back on the scale we stopped and sat, (which seemed like an eternity), then finally after looking us over they let us go; apparently waving off the extra pounds of weight, (which I know they were very well aware of)!

We got up at 3:30 a.m. in order to beat the heavy traffic you get when driving into LA County. We have never delivered a load to this customer before and had to rely on the directions I received from them over the phone. When we arrived at the address in San Pedro, much to our surprise we discovered the address numbers were on a "vacant" building! I went over the directions with Ron and rechecked the address and could not see where we had done anything wrong. It was too early in the morning to call the customer because we were way ahead of the delivery time. Ron decided vacant building or not, he was sure we were at the right address and we would just wait and see if anyone shows up. About an hour later, a guy walked up to our truck and said he was expecting our load. (The building was an old gas station and he said he was going to open a flooring business in it.) Of course, there are no loading docks at gas stations so Ron had to get out and help unload. Not fun! It would have been nice if we had been warned by the dispatcher to look for a vacant building. It may seem like a small request, but to a driver it's a big help.

As I write, we are parked in a service bay stall located inside one of truck repair shops outside Los Angeles. We are waiting for an alternator belt and so far we have been here "FOUR" hours! They didn't have a belt in stock so they sent one of their employees to get one. He's been gone so long now I think the guy stopped for lunch! He only had to drive to Bakersfield and the town is not that far away. Not only are we grounded, but they're charging us $50 for his trip! (In my opinion, the belt should have been part of their inventory.) But, as I always say, when you're out on the road, you have to accept what is available. We are at their mercy! The belt was on its last leg pulling up the Grapevine and Ron kept his fingers crossed that we would make it to the shop before it gave out completely. (This is unbelievable, NOW they're doing a SHIFT change!) The mechanic we had, left and went home! They told us their only other mechanic doesn't come on shift until midnight! Never in my wildest dreams would I have ever imagined that Ron and I would be forced to stay inside our truck and have to sleep over night in a repair shop! That's exactly what we did!

What a night we had! All during the night, (they're open 24hrs. a day), we were awakened by the noise of other trucks pulling into the bays getting work done on their rigs. Just when I would drift off to sleep I would wake up to the scream of a "power wrench" removing lug bolts! Plus, the workers had a loud radio station on playing music in another language! What about Diesel? That poor cat must have thought she was being punished! She hates it anytime we pull inside a building and this one is no exception! She has been hiding way up high in a cabinet and she is not about to get out! I challenge anyone to try sleeping through all this! The next day, and it may sound hard to believe, but we continued to sit inside the shop until 4:30 p.m. before they finally completed the job!

We had plenty of time to observe employees and none of them got in a hurry to do anything! I would fire the entire crew! This is no joke and certainly NOT the wonderful world of trucking I expected!

April 5th and we are waiting our turn to get loaded up with a bunch of office supplies. Ron wanted dispatch to give us a load closer to home, but they didn't. A couple other drivers waiting, (who also work for the same company) came over to talk to Ron. Drivers, when they have the chance, like to compare notes with each other on how things are going out on the road as well as exchanging any new gossip about the company they work for. When Ron got back in the truck he told me the wife of one of our team drivers is home for at least three months recovering from some type of colon cancer. Apparently her type of cancer is not life threatening and that's good news. But, nevertheless her husband will have to run alone without her. This team has been with the company for years and has an outstanding reputation of getting the job done. They run hard and are admired and respected by all of us!

April 6th and we're driving under "severe" wind conditions causing us and other truckers out here a good chance of getting blown over! We are considered high profile; putting us at even a much greater risk! We heard from another driver on the CB that the interstate is closed ahead due to the severity of the storm. As I write, I feel a desperate need for us to get off the road! (Of course, once you're out on the interstate, you just can't take your monster rig, pull over to the side and simply stop!) You've got to find a spot with enough room, and we sure as hell won't choose the shoulder on this road! We can feel the entire truck and trailer as it rocks and sways back and forth relentlessly each time we get hit with another strong gust. It's a pretty scary, eerie and insecure feeling of helplessness. These are my thoughts of course, and I know Ron has no intention of stopping! He's strong willed, bull headed and stubborn! At this point he has tuned me out and is solely concentrating on keeping the tires rolling on pavement! I have no vote but to trust his gut feelings that we'll be alright. It is a bit tense inside the cab. Ron has his hands full keeping us on the road and very little is being said between the two of us. He continued to drive and in short time we were detoured off the interstate due to road construction. It put us miles out of route and took another 45 minutes to get back on the highway. The wind has calmed down and I'm wondering if the reported road closure causing me so much grief was actually due to the construction not the wind!

April 7th and dispatch has been sending us nagging messages over the Qualcomm that we need to get our quarterly inspection done. Our route took us through Montana so Ron decided to stop at one of the company shops and take the time to get it done. Wrong thing to do! They put our truck "out of service"! Amazing, our trailer is full, a customer is waiting and now the load will be late and they don't seem give a dam! The mechanic doing the inspection found about three problems. Only one deserves pushing their panic button and even at that Ron said it wasn't critical. Nevertheless, when they put you out of service you're dead in the water until you get fixed whatever they're complaining about. In this case, it was our low air pressure alarm itself. (Actual air pressure was fine.) We promptly left their garage and went to the nearby repair shop. Now we are sitting and no telling how long this will take. When they are finished, we'll return to the company and show proof of repairs and then hook back up to our trailer. This delay throws everything off in getting our load delivered on time. Bet we won't go to bed until midnight!

Home four days with the flu! Ron came down with it first, and as I have always done, I babied "him", (while all the while I was thinking "glad it's him and not me.") I really felt that "I" was home free! Not! Two days later, I got sicker than a dog! Fortunately Ron was starting to feel better so he turned around and took care of me. What a wasted four days off! While I was moaning and groaning Ron worked on our pickup truck and got it running again. He put in a new battery, cables, and starter. Nothing that we usually do when we're home got accomplished. Today both of us are feeling much better. Before we left I called all three kids and wished them a happy Easter. Come Sunday, we'll be somewhere alone eating at a truck stop. The weather is nice and it's supposed to stay that way as we head south to California.

April 27th and last night we stayed at Ron's mom's house. Her niece Penny was there and as usual enjoyed a nice dinner. I don't know Penny that well, but she is a fun person to visit with. I saw my first wild turkey this morning going over Mc Donald pass. The turkey took its own sweet time crossing the road. Ron slowed down and I got a good look at it. Tonight we've already got a load of paper to pick up in Missoula. Kellie called us and said she changed her mind. She is only going to work 1 day a week and bagged the idea of daycare for Jake and Sam. (Out here on the road, truckers like us still have family and I'm realizing more and more that the only way to hold us all together requires frequent phone calls.) Keeping in touch is important and I will do whatever it takes regardless of the phone bill!

April 28th and stuck in a huge back up! It started as we approached Provo, UT. Apparently there is an accident ahead of us. We have been at a VERY slow crawl for more than an hour now. Truckers are griping over the CB and trying to get updates from drivers headed in the opposite direction. The only good part, if there is any, is that we're going so slow I can look into all the backyards of houses. There are several lilac bushes in bloom with all shades of purple. I saw one house that had a horse and several, "deer" inside their fence. (I thought it's against the law to confine and raise wild animals.) We just passed the accident and it is amazing how a simple fender bender can back up traffic for hours! It's not us truckers causing the hold up; it's all the lookie looks! One thing for sure, "Fat Daddy" will get back to trucking and off the CB! I thought if I heard him say, "Breaker One Nine" even one more time I was going to scream. You get drivers like this one that want to monopolize the air time and not let other drivers get a word in. Ron is worn out, who cares, me! His arm is about to fall off from shifting. He told me he will push to get us to the truck stop in Nephi, but that's it! He's done driving!

April 29th and we only thought winter was behind us. We got up early as usual. It was cloudy and cold but as we traveled further down the highway the weather changed to a full blown snow storm! We have a long day ahead of us and so far it's not off to a good start. Each night before going to bed I set out clean clothes for both of us in the morning. As I write, I'm laughing my head off! I put out two red T-shirts and when Ron got up this morning he grabbed one of them and put it on. He is driving down the road very uncomfortable wearing MINE! He said "Billie, when we stop I'm going to have to change shirts because this one is too small." He then tells me his shirt must have shrunk last time we did laundry because no way could he have gained that much weight! I checked my shirt and sure enough we were wearing each other's! If this isn't enough before you've even finished your coffee, Ron is driving down the road with one shoe off! He said he discovered a rash on his foot and it really itches. (Here we go again, no doctor in this truck and no meds either so he'll have to endure.) I'm not exempt from my own problems. I have to be real careful this trip because last time home I pulled an old filling out flossing. I have a temporary crown and if I don't watch what I chew, it will come off. (My little flossing accident costs us almost 800 dollars!)

May 11ᵗʰ and it's been a very long week. We were parked in Canyonville, OR when I received a phone call from my sister letting me know our father had just passed away. (This was on May 3ʳᵈ a day before our 27ᵗʰ wedding anniversary.) She said he passed away at home with a Hospice nurse and his wife by his side. (He was 84 years old, didn't believe in doctors and flatly refused to go to a hospital.)

My father loved all of his five kids from a distance. My parents were divorced so we didn't see him that often, but when he did show up, (always a surprise visit) we were all excited upon his arrival. The one thing all of us kids will remember is his "stories". He was a big man, a logger, and to listen to him he made himself out to be the toughest man on earth! In all of the stories he told to us, "he always came out being the hero!"

I was not surprised when I got the news because I knew from a previous trip that Ron and I made to see him that his health was going downhill. Still, learning the news brought tears to my eyes and guilt for not making a better effort to visit more often than I did. I could go on with my memories, but it makes me feel sad. Besides, this is my journal about truck driving, not family history!

Today is the 14ᵗʰ of May and its Mother's day. Ron called his mom last night because he thought if he waited until today the lines might be jammed with everyone else in the world calling their mother. I know she enjoyed hearing from him. I expect a call from our kids as well. It's funny, but Kim, Kellie and Jason will want to know if they were the "first" one to call me.

We are in Helena, MT after leaving Nephi, UT early this morning. We dropped the trailer and are now waiting for dispatch to give us a new load. Earlier today we saw several ranchers herding their cattle to higher pasture for the summer months. When the snow returns they will herd them back down. It's always refreshing to see real cowboys on horseback with boots, spurs and western hats on working the herd with their dogs. Many of the cattle had baby calves; each one running trying to keep up with their mother. It's spring and what an enjoyable sight!

It is now the 25ᵗʰ of May and Ron and I made it home last weekend. We had a nice visit from my brother John, his wife and son. John brought me a shadow box incased with a picture of my dad. The box included two of dad's fishing lures mounted inside the display. It not only was creative of him to add the fishing lures as a personal touch to remember my dad's favorite pastime, but the fact that my brother made it himself makes his gift that much more precious.

CHAPTER 5

ROOKIE MAKES "TEAM" STATUS

Today is Father's Day and all three kids called Ron. We are in Santa Nella, CA for the night and the temperature is 97 degrees. It has been quite a few days since I've written in my journal and the last time we were here in Santa Nella, Ron surprised me with a beautiful windmill music box. I love his spur of the moment surprises because I never expect them! There is one exception to what I just said. When we have extra time at a truck stop once in a while Ron will stop and try to win me a stuffed animal. Unfortunately, it's not as easy as it looks! Needless to say he has lost many quarters; but has also won a few as well. Having access to all these games at truck stops is just another way to conveniently take the truckers money. That's my opinion of course!

We took the last seven days off and here it is already the 13th of July. Would you believe with all that time off we were only able to spend one of those days at home. This is what happens having only a brief window of opportunity to squeeze in family visits. We not only went to Bellingham to see Jason and then on to Sumas to see dad's grave, we also were able to spend time with Kim and have a great visit with my brother John and his family. We covered visits with everyone (at least those that wanted to see us) still living on the west side of the state!

The rest of our week off, we packed up and headed to Eastern Washington to visit Ron's mom and do as much work for her as we could. When we are at her house she expects us to WORK! I mean from sun up to sun down! I'm not kidding or exaggerating. She loves our help and will flat out say "Stay put, don't go anywhere, just keep working and I'll run errands!" Mostly what she wants is for us to do yard work, and we don't mind doing it. We need the physical exercise; which is grossly lacking for days at a time confined inside the truck. Like Ron always told our kids "A hard day's work is worth a good night's sleep!" (The kids didn't think he was so funny at the time!) Before leaving, we managed to make a quick trip to Deer Park to see our old house and hopefully run into some old but not forgotten friends. It was a bit depressing to learn some of them had passed away while others had since moved. We still felt the trip was worthwhile and enjoyed the drive.

We're parked in Olympia, WA waiting for a load of beer. So far we have been waiting over four hours! I know Ron is tempted to call dispatch and give them an ear full, but I don't think after his last experience that he's that eager to do it again! Ron is complaining, with rightful justification, and thinks the company should throw in a little detention pay. I could not agree more, we're burning up driving time, but chances are if we asked, it would end up in another debate. We don't want to rile up the dispatcher again so we'll play in smart and keep our mouths shut!

We just fueled and diesel prices are sky high! The cost keeps going up and the surcharge we receive is not high enough to offset the increase. Our settlements in the past few months have increasingly gotten a lot smaller. Ron met with a company manager yesterday and spoke on behalf of ourselves and the other truckers who also are leased on with them. He felt that he was heard and was promised they would increase the amount of surcharge paid to owner operators in the near future. He even learned they're considering giving us a bonus around Christmas, and maybe even reimbursement for the $48 we have to pay every single time we drive through Oregon. Other than these three changes, the manager would not commit to anything else, (like raising our rate per mile), which would have helped increase our revenue. Ron said "We have no choice now but for me to go through company orientation so we can drive as a team." "It is the only way we will be able to increase our earnings." Teams always are given trips that have plenty of miles and of course, that is how we are paid; it's by the miles driven, not by the long hours we put in. So, while we were in Montana I went in and signed up for orientation. I will check in next week and stay there while Ron and Diesel run without me. Not looking forward to this, but I'll do it! When I'm finished, Ron told me the company will expect us to drive 20,000 miles a month, but assured me it won't be as hard as it sounds. (We'll see!)

September 28th and we are in Laurel, MT just outside of Billings. Well, so much for starting orientation next week! We spent our last two and a half days sitting parked waiting to get dispatched. We were told we had a load of flour yesterday out of Helena to deliver in California. When we got there, the trailer, plum full of flour stacked on pallets was "Red" tagged and could not be moved until repaired. The only trip available was one to Cleveland, OH so Ron and I took it! Two and a half days of sitting might not sound too serious, but it is for the amount of money we lost! I had to reschedule my date for orientation by upping it two weeks. I'm not real sad about that because this trip will give us plenty of miles and we will get to see country that neither of us has ever seen before. Actually, I guess you could say we are really happy how things turned out! We're off to Ohio!

Wow! It is the first of October and so far venturing off from our beaten path, this trip has been great! We had sunshine all the way. We have seen several beautiful farms along the way. This morning we went through Chicago and it was not as bad as we had anticipated and had worried about for so many miles. We both loved driving through Wisconsin and tonight we'll stay in Toledo, OH. This whole trip is virgin territory for us and we love it!

Now we are in Rutledge, TN, we are backed up to a dock getting unloaded and the weather is nice but a bit too warm, (90 degrees). The humidity is high and we both feel like we're sitting in a sauna. (We've never been in a sauna, but I'm sure this is how it feels.) Kentucky and Tennessee were also beautiful states to drive through. We saw tobacco hanging in barns for the first time in our life and then there was one field that had the tobacco stacked like "teepees". I assume this is another way to dry out the tobacco leaves. We are driving through what the locals call mountains; we call them rolling hills. The trees are pine, mixed in with oak and other hardwood varieties. Leaves are turning into a variety of brilliant fall colors and are beautiful to see. Now this is truly what I previously vision as the "best of both worlds!" We're out here driving tuck for a living and enjoying the scenery! I realize more than ever now how important it is for me to go through orientation. This will be the only way to consistently get "long runs" like this one.

October 7th and we saw our first snowflakes driving through Iowa. We are stopped at a truck stop just outside Omaha, NE and while Ron is fueling, I'm going to run in real quick to pick up some snacks and fill the thermos. We thought when we left Montana we were only going to Ohio and would get a return trip back to the West Coast. We were surprised each time we delivered a load that our next dispatch would send us farther east! (Sometimes it's nice to be wrong!) The speed limit is 75 miles per hour in this state and that includes all the eighteen wheelers as well! I know I'm not ready to drive that fast and neither is Ron!

October 8th and our trip so far has taken us to Cleveland, OH, Rutledge, TN and then on to Dalton, GA. But I'm not done yet, from Dalton, GA dispatch sent us to Edison, NJ and from there to Salt lake City, UT. (I can't help but wonder if "dispatcher Joe" didn't have something to do with this! After all, he DID say he was going to send Ron EAST!) If he is responsible and considered this to be his revenge or punishment, he failed to realize what a favor he was actually doing by sending us so far away. We've made nothing but money because of the miles. We just entered Wyoming and it is my turn to drive. Ron had to get out of the truck at the POE, (Port of Entry) and show the DOT our lease agreement and BOL. (Bill of Lading) That's the first time this has ever happened! Wyoming is pretty flat with rolling hills, at least where we are at. I was surprised to see so many oil wells. One thing for sure, from this recent experience of driving across the United States we have been baptized "long haul" truckers! We're running with the big dogs!

Here it is the 12th of October and I'm getting a bit lax in making entries in my journal. Tomorrow is the day my mom passed away at Swedish Hospital in Seattle. I wish I were home to put flowers on her grave. So many of us take life for granted and it seems like it takes loosing someone dear to you before you really appreciate how precious that person was. I won't stray too far off on this subject, but I am overwhelmed with pride for all that my mother had to go through in raising all five of us kids alone and without any help. (Maybe someday I'll write a book about her!)

I drove from Redding, CA to Grants Pass, OR today. I came down the Ashland grade and let that "jake" brake (engine compression) roar! I love the loud noise and kids do too. When their parents pass by they always look up at us and give a hand sign wanting us to make more noise by blowing the air horn! Both stacks were smoke'n as I proceeded down the mountain! Look out everyone, "Sparrow" is at the wheel! (My CB handle!) By the way, Ron goes by "Diamond Back" and he wanted me to use the name of "Momma Snake" as my CB handle. I of course would have nothing to do with it! I also drove over the scale for the very first time! The scale master knew I was a "rookie". He smiled and waved as

I went through and if I could have jumped out and hugged him I would have! That guy had no idea how scared I was thinking he might red light me. In all truth, I was so nervous, as I approached, stopped, and then got the green light to move forward, I couldn't get back into first gear. Ron was sitting up front and reached over and put it in gear for me. I know darn well the scale master saw it all! I was a little embarrassed, but swallowed my pride feeling more relieved that Ron came to my rescue! I thought to myself this could have been a worse "FIRST TIME" for me driving over the scale. The officer could have decided to axel weigh me or even worse pull me in for an inspection! Thank God he didn't!

We are in Oregon tonight and tomorrow we will drop our trailer in Kent, WA. Ron and I will have one night at home together and then he will go trucking, (with Diesel our cat). I will take my car and drive to Montana to attend the orientation. (Guess who will have more fun for the next 10 days?) I don't have to be there until Monday morning so I plan to drive as far as Spokane and then spend the night with Ron's mom. At least she's good company and will keep my mind off of missing Ron! I'm already hoping that Ron gets a load to Montana because he might just be able to stop by passing through and have dinner with me.

November 17th and I had no time or desire to write in my journal. My experience of spending ten days going through orientation is something I will NEVER forget! I'm no dummy and in short time I couldn't help but feel that the instructors appeared more comfortable working with the other male recruits than me. Each day we had "class" and then we would split up in groups of four and go driving with an instructor. The instructor would sit up front with one of the recruits driving while the rest of us would sit crammed in the back bunk and wait our turn.

In my group, I was the only woman and along with me was Roger, Shorty, Tyrell and a wimpy guy. (For the life of me, I cannot remember his name.) Roger was my favorite! He was always upbeat, funny, gave Shorty more than his share of ribbing but could also become very serious offering his support and encouragement to me as well as the other drivers. Shorty on the other hand was a bluff and really displayed an "ego" problem! He was "short", but when he walked he made you think he was 10 feet tall! He would take big strides and always have a serious, manly look on his face. When it was his turn to drive, he would buzz down his window, stick his elbow out and steer with one hand. (That was only after he slid the seat forward and raised it up so he could see out the window!) It's interesting that the instructor never said anything to him and I know Shorty was trying to give all of us the impression that driving was a piece of cake! I couldn't help but laugh more than once when Shorty would shift gears and grind the hell out of them. He got into a bad habit of forcing the gear into place by putting pressure on it until the gear finally went in. The instructor would say "The pile is getting bigger!"

Tyrell was more of a quiet person but I could tell he enjoyed talking with me on breaks. He was from the south, had a wife and two children at home. This was his first trip out to the West Coast. Tyrell never got in a hurry to do anything, and I swear he would have been late for class everyday if it were not for me giving him a ride from our motel. The other nameless recruit with us, (I knew from my past exposure to trucking), would NEVER make it! He was way too nice, too naive and obviously grew up in a sheltered environment! When he told me he was going to buy a "pogo" stick and use it for exercise when he parks at a truck stop, I about choked! Drivers can be unmerciful! They sit in their trucks and watch other drivers walk around the lot. If they spotted some guy hopping up and down in the parking lot on a pogo stick, they would bust their gut laughing; get on the CB and tell other drivers to take a look. I had to tell him that was NOT a good idea!

We all were strangers to each other when we first met and it's interesting how the five of us bonded together during orientation. We leaned on each other for support and became friends. I suppose I had a soft spot not only for Roger, but Tyrell as well. (Roger also has a family at home missing him, he had gone through serious on the job injuries in the past; was unemployed and looking for a new career.) When I saw Roger eating "packaged soup" for dinner more than once, I decided I would take him and Tyrell out for a REAL meal! My offer was quickly accepted! There were no restaurants in walking distance so having my own car came in handy. We went to an "All You Can Eat" restaurant that was suggested to us by other drivers going through orientation. Boy, were they right! By the time we left we were all stuffed! It was fun for all of us to sit, relax, eat and swap opinions on what we thought about all the instructors and if any of us were getting anything out of this whole ordeal. In my particular group, each of us had our CDL so it's wasn't as if any of us needed to go through driver training all over again. However, the company obviously felt likewise.

Monday through Friday we were expected to show up for class at 8 a.m. and stay there until 5 p.m. with a few breaks and lunch. (By the way, this place is nothing to write home about. The yard is full of mud!) Admittedly, I probably could have performed better, but I have a hard time when I'm with strangers, under pressure and being watched! I didn't mind the rest of the guys riding along, but it's hard to get relaxed when you know your every move is being observed and judged by the instructor sitting up front. Compared to Shorty, my shifts were excellent and in fact, one time the instructor accused me of NOT using the clutch because the shifts were so smooth!

While I was there I also made friends with a gal near my age and although I heard great things about her efforts in learning to drive, she was always scared to death of not passing the driver portion of the exam. She really put herself through days of her own self inflicted hell by worrying so much. I was so happy for her when the day came and she passed her driving test! I also met her husband who is a well seasoned truck driver. The two invited me to join them for a beer after class at the local truck stop casino. What I learned from this experience is that my new friend enjoys slot machines as much as I do! It wasn't much of a visit before each of us parted ways in favor of playing the slots!

I also met another very nice woman going through orientation and one day when I was standing outside on a break I saw her pull in with the instructor. I don't know what happened but I felt so bad for her. She was sobbing when she climbed down out of the truck and was quickly consoled by the rest of us. From my personal experience and observation I cannot help but believe the company was much more lenient on male recruits. I witnessed more than once the instructor overlooking simple mistakes, (like Shorty made frequently), but would instantly bring to MY attention the least little thing! Unnecessary comments like "Did you see where that car went behind you? Did you see the sign you just passed?" My mind would say "Hell no, I don't know where the car disappeared to! I'm driving forward not backwards!" As far as seeing a sign, I have the dam signs memorized! (Now that I think back, in all fairness, the instructors were only doing their job!)

On the ninth day of orientation my counterparts were all excited wondering what truck they would be assigned and they all hoped it would be a newer model. That thought never crossed my mind because we have our own truck. At this point all of us were plain relieved knowing that the ten day stay was almost over. We all anxiously looked forward to leaving, start earning some money and go on with our lives! The next day when I arrived we were all hugging each other and promising to keep in touch no matter where we were. These were my friends that I spent ten days of my life with. I went to class and listened while each of my friends was assigned a company truck. They were handed the keys and one by one they left the room. I was the last one sitting. At that point, I was asked to meet in the manager's office. I had a strange feeling this was not going to be a pleasant visit. Sure enough, I was asked to spend another three days and work on my down shifting and backups. So while all my friends had something to celebrate, I went back to my motel room alone.

I called Ron on the cell phone and cried. Ron encouraged me to play their little game and stay the extra three days. He eventually convinced me. I showed up next morning feeling tense and stressed. No more classroom sessions I was told, we're just going to drive. I was really wearing down at this point and no doubt feeling sorry for myself. I absolutely felt I was being picked on! The instructor took his own sweet time while I waited for over an hour, just sitting there. Finally he came into where I was sitting and told me to go out to the lot, get in this specific truck, start it and wait for him. We went through the usual checks and then off down the road. I could feel the tenseness between the two of us. We went out on the interstate and then took an off ramp that led into the busy downtown area. I felt he was nit picking; it wasn't my shifting, using turn signals, and watching for directional signs, it was his little subtle remarks like "you could have done this or you could have done that," By the time I got through traffic and was on the other side of town, I had it! I turned my head towards him and said "you win! I told him I was driving us back to the terminal, dropping him off and I was going to get in my car and head home! You know what his response was, "Billie you are so close, and I wish you wouldn't do that." Bullshit! I was tired of being patronized and I thought to myself, I'll just continue to drive with Ron like I have been doing all along!

I parked the truck, gave him the keys, headed straight for my car, then went back to the motel and checked out. I didn't even take time to call Ron! The further I drove the better I felt! As I passed through Spokane I thought about stopping to spend the night with Ron's mother but given more thought, I wasn't ready for her to interrogate me on my reasons for not sticking it out. By the time I went through Moses Lake, WA I had to stop and fill the gas tank. It felt good to get out of the car and stretch my legs. I bought myself a sandwich and headed back out on the highway. I frequently thought about Ron and tried to imagine what his reaction would be when I told him what I had just done. Each time I consoled myself, knowing even if he was disappointed, he would be very supportive of my decision. The drive from Montana to Spanaway, WA is healthy 400 miles and when I pulled into our driveway I was dead tired. When I entered the house the message light was blinking on the phone. It was a message from Ron saying he was at his mother's house and on his way to Montana! I instantly remembered my decision "not" to stop at her house and if I had only done the opposite, I would have been able to see him! Ron already knew I was headed home because he called the motel and they told him I had checked out. Ron was, as I suspected he would be, was very understanding. He was totally pissed off at the way I claimed to be treated for the past two weeks and promptly made it known to the General Manager! The manager agreed to hear Ron out when he stops by tomorrow. (I hated the thought of having Ron speak up for me, but he's a good husband, and that's probably what most husbands would do to defend their wife.)

Ron met with the GM and was able to get a load back to Washington. Two days later Ron and I were in the big truck headed back to Montana for another go around. Ron had convinced me that my appearance back at the terminal would be treated entirely different. Sure enough, everyone was all smiles! Ron and I met with the GM and his Director of Driver Operations and Safety. It was agreed that I would go with the director, along with Ron and use "our" truck for a test drive. Much more relaxed, and about an hour later of putting me through the paces; I passed! From this day forward all paper work will be changed to "TEAM" status! This is my story, but I'm sure there are other drivers out there, men and women, who have gone through similar frustrations with whatever company they hired on to.

November 20th and just like I said, "Teams" get the miles! We are in Atlanta, GA unloading at our second drop. Ron has done all the driving. The places I could have driven would have been risky for me because it snowed all the way from Missoula to Iowa. (I have yet to drive a big rig in the snow.) Going through South Dakota I saw several deer in the fields eating hay along with the cattle. The pastures were covered with deep snow and the temperature was only 11 degrees. I'm sure the deer in order to survive, had no choice but to invite themselves to dinner. We also spotted a raccoon sitting up in a tree; what an unlikely place to see one!

We stayed in Missouri one night at a so, so truck stop. (When I say this; picture big chuck holes in the parking lot, buildings that show wear and lack of maintenance, and the rest rooms left a lot to be desired!) However, it turned out to be one of the friendliest places we have ever stopped at! This place not only has a restaurant and store it also has a big antique barn and a western store on the premises. Ron and I looked in the antique store and what a fun place to browse around in. It had tons of books, dishes, pictures and even old coins for sale. We thoroughly enjoyed being there and I know we'll probably stop again. Hopefully by then we'll have more time and money!

Jason will be 26 years old in just a few days. We won't be home to celebrate his birthday and the same goes for Thanksgiving. We both feel bad, but this line of work requires us to be out on the road. I hope in the upcoming year, we'll make more money and be able to take more time off.

Ever since we became a team we have pushed hard putting in the miles, but skyrocketing fuel prices and maintenance on this truck has eaten away most of our profit. We are a bit discouraged. If teaming doesn't work, we'll have no choice but to sell the truck. Ron would then have to go back as a company driver where they pay all expenses BUT, he sure doesn't want to do that! We both love our freedom and independence of being owner/operators. Ron as I write is in the bunk sound asleep while we are being unloaded. When you're a trucker, no matter the noise; if you're dead tired, you'll sleep no matter how much loud banging and bumping is going on around you! Ron works hard and I know he's worn out from the relentless driving and irregular hours of sleep. He rarely complains and when he does it's more than justified. Every muscle in his body aches from being so tensed up going to all these unfamiliar places that neither of us have ever been before. Sometimes I wonder if he took on the extra miles just to make me happy. I hope not, but I'm sure that's part of the reason. One thing for sure, I know he appreciates what little relief I'm able to give him when I take over the wheel.

November 23rd and it is Thanksgiving Day. I know families everywhere are getting together at grandma's house to share a traditional turkey dinner, give thanks and count their blessings. It's the one time of year when we all look forward to a good old fashion reunion with friends and relatives. Unfortunately, if there's a truck driver in the family, chances are one chair at the table will remain empty. It's the way it is out here. I know in my heart the kids will be thinking of us and wondering if we'll find a nice place to stop for dinner. We got up at 5:30 a.m. this morning in Dalton, GA and will be taking this load to Modesto, CA. It's only 35 degrees, but a beautiful sunny day. Who knows where we'll stop tonight. We may end up eating hot dogs!

November 29th, we are just outside Sacramento, CA and down to a SLOW crawl. All the "four wheelers" are on their way to work; the morning commute is in full swing! Ron shut the CB off because so many truckers are griping about the heavy traffic and he's trying not to rear end any of them! He is especially on guard for the cars that suddenly decide to slam on their brakes! Diesel is up on the dash observing all the traffic; it's almost as if she assigned herself a duty of riding "shot gun" with Ron. Oh well, three sets of eyes watching for dumb moves made by four wheelers, (other truckers included), is better than two! When traffic is this heavy anything can happen!

Yesterday I drove a little over three hours which was a nice break for Ron and we ended our day by staying overnight in Santa Nella. We went over to the restaurant where Andy works to see him, but he was not there. Rosa, another employee that we have made friends with was working. Rosa is a single parent raising her two year old son by herself. Before we left, Ron went to the gift shop, (I thought he left to go use the bathroom) and purchased a little dog that barks and walks with a remote control. He came back and presented it to Rosa. He said "Take this home to your son for Christmas". "Tell him it's a gift from two trucker friends". Rosa was not only surprised; she was thrilled with the gift for her son. (I know Ron so well, and I wish others did. He comes across "grumpy old man", but he really does have a soft side!

December 10th and we came home to a burned fence! Some punks in the neighborhood apparently built a fire next to it; the fire got out of hand, and burned several boards on our fence. We both were amazed that the fire burned itself out. We were even more amazed that the smoke went ignored by neighbors. It will cost us $375 to replace the boards. This wasn't the only bad news; the post office lost two week's worth of our mail! Ron thinks they gave our mail to someone else and whoever received it, instead of returning the mail to their postman, threw it away! I keep copies of statements in the truck so at least I'll be able to make payments over the phone while we're out on the road. Dispatch called with a load to Montana. and from there we picked up another load headed for Vonore, TN. There is snow all around us, but the roads are dry. Hope they stay that way!

December 10th and we are now about 150 miles from Rapid City, SD. It is 2:30 p.m. and I just turned the wheel back over to Ron! Miserable weather! The road was getting very hard for me to see. It's foggy, snowing hard with strong wind blowing snow through the air creating white outs! I endured as long as I could! Ron was sitting up front and was well aware of conditions and finally said "do you want me to take over"? Hell yes! I couldn't answer "YES" fast enough! In all reality, I should have asked for his help sooner, but my pride wouldn't let me. The current temperature is three below zero and we heard on the radio that blizzard conditions are expected. (I think we are already in them!) Won't surprise us if the highway ahead is shut down in Wyoming! Of course, luck of the draw, our route takes us right through that state! Wyoming is known for STRONG winds and frequent blizzard conditions this time of year. So far all of our deliveries have been on time, but this just might be our first "late" one!

December 11th and you won't believe this! The temperature outside is "seventeen" below zero (Kodaka, SD) and with the wind chill factor it's much colder than that! What are we doing out here in "No Man's Land"? Are we stupid or what! Now again, this is when I cannot help but think about all the people in their warm cozy homes safe and sound while we are out here fighting the elements just to get their goods delivered! I really wish, and it would make me feel better, if I really thought all our efforts were appreciated. It's amazing what drivers endure! The job is not easy; we are grubby, tired, and hungry for a hot meal. Our line of work leaves no choice but to keep on trucking; just like all the rest of the drivers out here today! At least Ron and I have each other to console. Other drivers don't! They're out here by themselves! They too are fighting the same roads and awful weather that we are, but don't have anyone to listen to their frustrations. (Ron frequently will get on the CB and offer support to a fellow trucker, especially when he sees one that appears to be all stressed out. His words of encouragement are eagerly accepted; instantly putting the other driver a bit more at ease. I'm telling you, it's not all roses out here! If nothing else, it makes you tough and if you can't handle the challenge, you better find another job!

December 25th and it is Christmas morning. We stayed at a Flying-J truck stop last night when the road became so bad it was way too risky to even try to drive further. Ron and I were both stressed to the max! It's strange, but even if you don't have the physical exercise, every muscle in your body aches from the unending, relentless tension that builds up for hours and hours of driving. We had heavy freezing fog which made the highway a "sheet" of ice! It's a different world for four wheelers, but WE are pulling a 53' trailer through all this! Today is not much better. Ron is driving through freezing fog and rain. The temperature has come up to a whopping 24 degrees! Not enough to help us. The news reports this morning said a winter storm watch is on for the next two days and we can expect another 10" of snow. We'll be right smack in it!

This is another Christmas without family and we both are feeling bad. The years went by too fast when the kids were young and still living at home. I always felt I had to work and this took me away from them five days a week. Now when I look back, I feel somewhat cheated on not being able to have spent more time with them individually. At the time I thought I was doing right by supplementing our income, but in reality, we all probably would have survived without the extra money. We called all three kids. Jason is at Kim's house and wouldn't you know they all are trying to get over the flu! Jake and Sam are having a great time while dad is putting together an electric train for them. We have a wonderful family!

Ron's mom is alone for Christmas as well, but she claims it doesn't bother her. She turned down an invitation from the rest of her family, so maybe she really doesn't mind. A few days ago she told me she fell and broke some ribs. I think she's getting too old to live by herself, but what can we do? We would love to be with her more often but we are not ready to retire and even if we could, at this point it would be financially impossible.

Today we had to get off the interstate! We're parked in Oklahoma City, OK because we ran into a severe ice storm! There is ice everywhere making it way too dangerous for us to even be out there! The highway is solid ice and so is the lot where we're parked; not to mention the coat of ice layered on all the trucks around us! We saw several accidents including one jacked knifed rig, plus numerous "slide offs". Diesel of course has slept through everything! I was really worried about all the power lines we drove under because they were heavily weighted down with a solid coat of ice. They drooped so low over the freeway I thought for sure one would snap and fall down right on top of us! The CB radio is blaring with driver stories on how they finally made it to the truck stop and all the freight that's now going to be late! These are you're

White Line Warriors folks! They'll get back on the road as soon as weather allows!

Our responsibility for Ron's mother is always on our minds. Five days later we made it a point to stop by and check in on her. She is doing fine and seemed no worse for the wear with her complaint of having broken ribs. While we were there we stacked several loads of fire wood by her backdoor making it easier for her to carry inside. (Nice little workout for both of us!)

When we got to Snoqualmie Pass the "chains required" sign lit up. We had to get out and put chains on every single tire; including the trailer! The shoulder of the highway was jammed packed with 18 wheelers and all of us were doing the same thing! (Times like this, it gets real annoying putting on chains when inconsiderate four wheelers whiz by too close and throw icy cold slush on your back!) Not fun, and believe me it happens all too often! I see no reason for this; they could stay out in the passing lane or at *least* slow down! Once we got back out on the highway we kept watching for "the previous reported D.O.T. warning of heavy accumulations of snow ahead", (justifying their chain requirement), but never ran into any. We did ALL that work, plus lost driving time just to have to stop and take the chains back off on the other side of the mountain! What was the DOT thinking? Guess they thought all of us drivers out here needed a little "warm up" throwing chains on to prepare us for the next few months!

We will be home soon and looking forward to having dinner with Mike and Kim. They are having prime rib and Dungeness crab and I know darn well they are doing this "special" dinner just for us! We will all share another belated Christmas together. Unfortunately Jason won't be there. He made plans to go snow boarding with friends and of course, Kellie and her family are in Virginia. I always wish, especially this time of year that our whole family could be together.

It is now January 7th and our first run for the year of 2001 was out of Helena, MT. Our mileage starting out the New Year read 247, 205 miles on the odometer! It's not hard to rack up miles when you're a team considering we often drive 1,000 miles a day! We actually took time off and stayed home until the 5th of January before we finally decided to get off our rear ends and deadhead to Helena for a load. Freight really slows down this time of year in the trucking industry and we were just glad to have the load!

January 13th and our trailer is loaded to the back doors with cases of beer. We picked it up after dropping our empty trailer at the shipper's yard in Olympia, WA. We knew instantly the load was extremely heavy and both doubted if we would legally be able to clear the several weigh stations ahead us! We drove to the nearest scale and sure enough we were well over 80,000 pounds gross weight! NOT good! We had no choice at this point but to drive to a terminal in Oregon, show them the axel weights from the certified scale receipt and ask them to readjust the pallets. (The load we're under is considered "ours" when you hook to the trailer and accept the paperwork. If there's a problem with weight, it's up to the driver to solve it!) You cannot return the load back to the shipper.

When we arrived at the terminal in Oregon, would you believe their only solution to our being overweight was to UNLOAD every pallet of beer into a lighter trailer! This was beyond belief! We were further shocked when they told Ron he would have to run the forklift and do ALL the work himself! (This isn't trucking! I never heard one time in training that part of a driver's job was to unload and load his own freight! I consider this to be a warehouseman's job!)

It took Ron almost two hours to unload the beer and put it in the lighter weight trailer. (All this extra time and work would wear any driver out before they even get started!) Even after all that time and effort, we scaled again and found ourselves still overweight on one of the axels. We ran out of options! The load had to be hauled regardless of weight! It was totally out of the question to return to the shipper and have them remove a couple pallets. At this point, we had no choice but to leave and head for North Carolina. We could only hope that with so many weigh stations ahead of us we wouldn't be red lighted by the D.O.T. I called our dispatcher and notified her of our dilemma. I wish her response would have been of more concern for us, but that's not the case. The reply I got was more like "thanks for the information and drive safe"! The load delivers in Eden, NC so needless to say we have a whole bunch of miles ahead of us to worry about!

Our luck ran out crossing the scale coming into Illinois. The red light came on and we were instructed to pull around and bring all paperwork into the office. We just knew we were going to get a ticket! Ron went in and a few minutes later he came back and got our original "Cat Scale" receipt. He didn't say a word to me, just gave me a stressed "oh, no worried look" and returned to the office! When he came back he said the officer was going to give him a chance to slide the axels and reweigh. (Unknown to us our load had shifted when Ron had to hit his brakes hard to avoid a four wheeler in Kansas City, MO last night.) I got behind the wheel to assist Ron in sliding the axels. Our second weigh did the trick! Although we still remained over weight on one axe, the officer let us go with a warning ticket! We both were so relieved and glad to get out of there! There are more scales ahead and I hope we don't get pulled in again!

It's been a while since I've written in my journal. The beer load is now behind us and we didn't get into anymore trouble with the D.O.T. along the way. My turn at the wheel and wouldn't you know it had to be driving through Wyoming when the weather went sour on us! The weather in Wyoming is tricky because you can be on dry road, then you see a few snowflakes, which you ignore, and then you drive a little further and all hell breaks loose! The road turned ugly with compact snow and ice; not to mention the wind gusts! We were way out in baron country, "no man's land" so there is no place to pull off and change drivers; I had to drive whether I liked it or not! I've never come upon so many over turned vehicles in the snow and I had no choice but to weave my way through all of them! There was no way I could stop the truck on ice; I had to power down and keep our 18 wheeler rolling! It's a wonder I didn't cut off my own circulation as tight of a grip I had on the steering wheel! These extremely hazardous driving conditions I suddenly found myself up against left no room for driver errors! Ron sat up in the passenger seat with me the whole time helping watch for more spin outs in front of us. Talk about a new driver getting their feet wet! I continued on and finally a few miles later I was out of the worst of it and able to pull over and let Ron drive! What a relief! That little obstacle course put me through the paces and maxed out my driving skills! I don't think I've ever been so glad to do a driver change!

January 27th and we are parked at the Petro truck stop in Wheeler Ridge, CA waiting for the "Grapevine" to open. It has been "closed" since 2 p.m. "yesterday" due to, if you can believe it, snow! This is supposed to be sunny California! We are upset to say the least! We have a load waiting for us in Santa Fe Springs that is supposed to deliver in Chicago on Monday. This delay has put us so far behind I cannot even imagine getting the load delivered on time!

We got up at 6 a.m. this morning, it is now 10:30 a.m. and we just heard from other drivers, "gates are open"! Now it's the mad rush of four wheelers and truckers to get back out on the interstate. The push is on and what a mess this is going to be! Los Angeles traffic is ALWAYS bad, but this will even be worse! We fought massive traffic all the way in to our delivery, did a drop and hook and we're on our way to Chicago. The good news is that the dispatcher upped our deliver to Tuesday. We headed out about 1 p.m. and drove to Kingman, AZ before stopping for the night. The push is on, so we'll be getting up about 3 a.m., hit the road and drive hard for hours and hours pulling the load behind us late into the evening January 28th and we no more than merged onto the interstate when we heard over the CB radio that I-40 was "closed" ahead of us, "shut down" at the New Mexico border. The closure was due to compact ice on the road, strong winds causing whiteout conditions from blowing snow, and massive snow drifts; too risky to plow through! Here we go again with another delay! We should have just stayed put! From this point forward we'll keep the CB radio on in hope of learning news from another trucker that the interstate is finally back open. In the meantime, we have no choice but to take the next exit, cross over the interstate and go back to the truck stop we just passed and wait the storm out! This is so defeating when we're under a load and expected to deliver it on time.

We made it through New Mexico and just inside the Texas boarder we have come to a dead stop! The backup is 25 miles long and I'm not exaggerating! The CB is screaming with truckers totally pissed off saying they should have shut the highway down a long time ago! Now we're all stuck out here in this line up for who knows how long! The road is solid ice! It's a skating rink! I know, here I go again, but at a time like this, I not only envy all the people at home in their warm houses, I also envy the "cow" I see in a pasture standing upright on all fours! I would fall on my butt if I put one foot on the ground outside this truck! I think I'll get rid of my rose colored glasses and accept the fact that "trucking is not a vacation"! We've never seen anything like this and I'm just glad we have plenty of food, water and a porta potty on board! This closure could very well end up by having us spend the night out here; parked on the interstate with several other truckers in a 25 mile backup! If this happens, there will be no way to expect hot coffee in the morning! By the way, I was the one driving that steered us right into this mess! Fortunately, when we slowed down to a crawl I was able to pull over on the shoulder and let Ron take over.

We actually did make it to Amarillo, TX without getting into an accident; many others, including big rigs, were not so fortunate. I swear this must be the storm of the century! We had a terrible time trying to find a place to park. To even think about parking at a truck stop, (there are several in Amarillo) would be a joke! They were all packed like sardines; "every" single one of them! At this point Ron and I are feeling very fatigued and worn out. We don't even care about eating, we just want to get off the interstate and park this truck! We both kept watching for a place, any place that would accommodate a big rig. All of the on/off ramps were full of parked big rigs, bumper to bumper, clear back to the interstate! Even the shopping centers were full of 18 wheelers. There was virtually no room left to squeeze in another 18 wheeler!

As a last glimmer of hope, we exited off I-40 and drove up and down the side streets. It was a sight to behold seeing 18 wheelers parked in every nook and cranny they could find. We were almost at the point of giving up knowing we had no choice but to get back on the freeway and continue driving. (It was almost 2 a.m. and the thought of that at this late hour was very depressing.) We were just about to "throw in the towel" when Ron spotted a restaurant that looked like it had enough space behind it where we could pull in and park. Yippee! What a find! I never dreamed I would ever be this happy! Tears actually filled my eyes just knowing we now found a place to spend the rest of the night! Eating dinner at this point was NOT even a consideration, besides it's almost

3:30 a.m. everything is closed! What a relief, and if someone doesn't come out and make us move in the middle of the night we should be able to sleep a few hours! It's still cold, windy with blowing snow, but we're safe and right now that's all I can ask for.

We crawled through the mess in Texas and now we're in Chicago waiting to unload a few rolls of carpet off the back of the trailer. Our next stop is near Detroit, MI and the roads continue to be a challenge. Light snow fell last night, and it is not about to melt, so we can look forward to having another day of tense driving.

I'm really irritated with the dentist I had to go to when I lost my filling at home. His temporary replacement was just that! TEMPORARY! It fell out and I almost swallowed it! Now I look like a carved Halloween pumpkin when I smile! It also annoys me that Ron thinks it's no big deal. (He would if it was his tooth!) If I was home, I would be sitting in the dentist's office getting it fixed, but I'm not, I'm in Chicago and I'm going to have to live with this ugly problem for several more days. (My dental problem is just another example of what drivers go through out here living the better part of our lives inside the cab of a truck.)

April 25, 2001 and we have been off two months. On February 11th we were parked in the driver's yard in California; it was POURING rain, and Ron got up to go to the bathroom. He slipped stepping down from the truck, (probably because he was half asleep) and fell breaking his ankle! He was in "extreme" pain, but decided to get back in bed until morning. The first thing I did when I got up was to find someone to take us to a 24hr clinic to have his ankle x-rayed. (Some of the drivers have cars that they leave parked so they have transportation when they are laid over waiting for a load.) Tom and Norma, team drivers, were there and did not hesitate in offering to take us to the clinic. Sure enough he fractured his ankle and did it up good! He broke it in *three* places! The doctor put him in a walking cast and told him he needed to see a surgeon as soon as he got home.

After returning to the yard, all of a sudden it dawned on me the consequences of his accident and the reality hit me like a ton of bricks! It would be impossible to even think Ron could drive! Now I'm the only one left and I would be "EXPECTED" to do "ALL" the driving! I'm still a greenhorn! Oh, my God! Even experienced drivers hate Los Angeles traffic and now I, me, little old Billie, was going to take over "full" responsibility and get us out in the thick of it! I was sick to my stomach at the thought! There would be several cities, towns and mountain passes ahead that I would have to drive. This thought frightened me, and I honestly didn't know for sure if I could even do it! So many times sitting up front just watching all the LA traffic while Ron cautiously drove through it, used to get me all tensed up. Running with the "big dogs" is a bunch of bullshit, I thought to myself! They can have it! I'll stay on the porch!

We spent the rest of the day in the yard. Ron was feeling much better after taking medication for the pain and spent most of the day hopping around on crutches, visiting with other drivers or sitting in our truck. (I almost think he enjoyed all the attention he was getting from other drivers!) Our load was supposed to be ready sometime after midnight. During this time I received plenty of encouragement and advice from other drivers, including Ron. By the time we went to bed I had conceded to the fact if we were going to get home, I had to buck up my courage and do it! After all, what could I do; I had no choice but to drive us both back to Washington and take him to an orthopedic surgeon.

We set the alarm for midnight, got up, dressed and then called the night supervisor at the terminal. He said our load was almost ready. It was pitch dark and the sky was black with a heavy continuous downpour of rain. Overnight Ron's injury worsened. I knew he was really hurting and at this point his ankle had swelled to the size of a football! I felt sorry for him and at the same time I even felt a little anger. I was mad that he broke his ankle and put me in this position. Fortunately, I did not allow myself to dwell on this thought; I didn't have time, I knew it was all up to me to get us home. I started the truck put it in gear and said to myself "Billie you can do this." I pulled into the terminal lot, parked the truck and went in and got the paperwork. The next challenge in the dark was backing up to the trailer and connecting the air hoses. (Ron actually insisted on helping, pouring rain at that!) I went around back to secure the trailer doors and had a heck of a time getting them to close. We were loaded to the tail! By the time I climbed back in the truck I was shivering. My hair and clothes were totally drenched from rain pouring down on me. We sat there and completed our logs. I took a deep breath, said a quick "Hail Mary" and headed out the driveway! Ron remained up front and assured me he would help me get through all the necessary highway changes, plus watch traffic. I absolutely know Ron felt bad for me, but what could he do other than be supportive. He was "out of service"; disabled!

Traffic very well could have been worse, but that early in the morning, I'll have to admit it was not that bad. Things were going pretty good until we got close to the grapevine and we learned from another driver the pass ahead was closed due to snow! Ron had me pull over on the shoulder and said we'll park here for awhile and maybe they'll open it back up. About a half hour of sitting, Ron suddenly said, "Start the truck Billie, back up and pull out on the road, I know another route we can take." I was not keen on his idea at all, but did what he told me to do. He said the route would take us through Palmdale, Mohave and Bakersfield, but what he didn't say until later; I would also be going over "Tahatchipe" and driving down a long STEEP grade! (Ron knows me too well and deliberately didn't tell me what I would be facing until we were only a few miles away. He knew I would panic at the thought!)

The one thing I have to admit is once we got to Tahatchipe, Ron with all his pain, continued to sit in the passenger seat and coach me on what to expect and I prepared me for it! I headed down the steep grade after "gearing down" and had to grab another lower gear before we reached the valley below. The more I drove, the more confident I became in my own abilities. I couldn't help but be pleased with the fact I actually DID drive through LA traffic, (which is something I said I would never do) and I made it down the mountain without driving over a cliff!! With all this apprehension of the unknown behind me now, I actually started to relax! It was evident by Ron's grin that I had earned his confidence. He could now sit back, "smooth sailing" for several miles and all he had to do was sit back and enjoy the ride!

This trip was a "forced" driving lesson for me but worth its weight in gold! I performed every task expected of any professional driver and did it with personal satisfaction! I went over mountain passes, stopped at weigh stations, pulled into rest stops and parked at truck stops without problems. Ron's pain, (regardless of pain pills), was none stop. When I parked for the night, I would go into the restaurant get our food and bring it back to him. A few stops along the way he had no choice but to climb down out of the truck, endure the intense pain and use the restroom. The short walk alone would wear him out and he would immediately go to the bunk and lay down the minute he returned. Driving an 18 wheeler for a living gets tough at times to say the least, especially when unexpected problems arise like ours. Men and women are out here by themselves and have no choice but to make the best out of the worst situation. We can only depend on ourselves; we're miles from home.

When we arrived at the terminal to drop the trailer it had to be backed up to the dock. There were several other trailers also parked at the dock and only one narrow space remaining. In order to back up to the dock you also have to pull out on the road and block oncoming traffic. This was not a "doable" for me and Ron knew it. So, with his broken ankle, he got behind the wheel and did it for me! This experience is one neither of us will ever forget, but we made it! Ron went to see a doctor and they put a cast on from his foot clear up to his knee! We are now grounded at home for the next several weeks!

Even though we're back on the road, I have not made an entry in my journal since we left home. It's now late April and I wish I would be more consistent updating my journal. Every single day out here something happens that I should write about. It's sunny this morning, but only 23 degrees. Ron has been doing fine since his accident but still wears an elastic support bandage around his ankle. (By the way, have you ever seen what someone's skin looks like when they remove a cast? Yuk! Gross! I could NEVER be a nurse!) The load we're hauling today delivers in North Carolina. It's another trailer full of talc that we picked up last night in Montana. Dad passed away a year ago today and tomorrow is our 28th wedding anniversary. We won't be home to put flowers on his grave and we won't be celebrating our anniversary either. But, as always, there is nothing we can do about it. We drive truck for a living!

It is the 16th of May and we are on our way to Myrtle, MS with a load of carpet. We just passed through Needles, CA and Ron said the temperature outside is 103 degrees! When the weather is this hot, it's really hard on the engine, especially pulling steep grades. Ron will be watching the gages no doubt. All three kids called me on Mother's Day. Out here on the interstate, so many miles away; a simple phone call, hearing their voices, means more to me than they will ever know.

We stopped last night in Sayre, OK just in time to get parked before we got hit with a huge hail storm! It decided to blow right over the top of us! I'm glad we were sitting in our truck. I must say it was pretty funny watching other drivers! They all scrambled across the parking lot making a mad dash to their truck to avoid getting beaten to death by the large hail stones! We of course have seen hail at home, but nothing like these whoppers! They were the size of ping pong balls and when you get hit by them it hurts like hell! Large hail has been known to severely damage vehicles, break windows and cause all sorts of problems. Sitting in the cab observing the hail relentlessly pounding down on us made me worry about what damage we might end up with ourselves. It didn't take long; the storm passed over and the entire truck stop was covered in a layer of white! Ron got out, brushed ice off the hood, and as far as he could tell there were no dents.

We blew a trailer tire about 30 miles outside Little Rock, AR earlier today. When this happens we have to call the company, (it's their trailer) and have them tell us where to go to get it fixed. If the company approves purchase of a new tire, they want you to save the old one; put it in the back of your trailer and then the next time you pass by one of their terminals, they want you to drop it off. This of course is extra work for the driver but for no extra pay. The company even expects you to pick up the pieces off the highway and save them if it is not too risky. Ron had to drive with the blown tire another 30 miles to reach North Little Rock, which apparently was the closest repair shop. He kept the "four ways" on and drove slow. (Having your "four ways" on out on the interstate sends a big "flashy" invitation to the bears!) Pick me, pick me! I need to get pulled over, get a ticket and lose more time driving! Fortunately, we had already gone through the scale when the tire blew and we made it to the shop without experiencing any additional problems. We are supposed to be in Myrtle, MS tonight, but we might just wait and get up real early to avoid Friday night traffic going through Memphis, TN. Ron is feeling worn out anyway and needs the night off.

May 21st and last night we were rocking and rolling with high winds, (56 mph gusts) along with blowing and drifting snow we had to fight all the way through Nebraska and into Wyoming. The further we drove, the weather got worse! We experienced "white outs" where we couldn't even see the highway in front of the hood! It was way too dangerous to continue driving so using common sense we grabbed the very next truck stop and got off the heck off the highway. We usually have a heavy load that we're hauling, but this trip we're pretty light. A heavy load pulls better under these conditions and you get less trailer sway. As much as we complain about heavy freight, this is one trip where we wish we had it. One time a wind gust hit the side of the trailer so hard that it "lifted it up in the air!" This is about as "close" as you can come to a "blow over" and it put Ron over the edge! This is when he said "we're getting the hell off the road and park this sucker!" "If we stay out here, we're either going to wreck the truck and destroy the freight or worse yet, kill ourselves!" He said, it's not worth it, and the load will just have to be late!"

We were not the only truckers out here last night that got off that miserable highway! When we pulled into the truck stop, we got lucky and found the only spot left and we barely squeezed into it. Several truckers shared their stories over the CB about what they went through before they decided it was too dangerous to continue and decided to bail out; Ron included! I must say, when you're alone, away from home and you've had a bad day driving; the one thing you can count on is the understanding you get from other drivers. Times like this we lean on each other for support, encouragement and understanding.

Unless you experience the moment "first hand" the cold reality and stress that all of these drivers frequently go through, you won't be able to fully appreciate the pain! We are out here doing this for you, your family, and your business. You, the American public, are the ones we proudly serve! We are the drivers that you totally rely on, the ones who you depend on to deliver your goods in every city and town across the United States, 24 hours a day, 365 days a year! (Beyond a trucker's family, friends and the company they work for; I often wonder if my book will make a difference in educating others so they realize how important truckers are to their personal survival.)

We are in San Diego, CA today, backed up to a dock waiting for workers to unload the trailer. Quite frankly, we're both just sitting here having a donut and milk while enjoying the sun! We did manage to get a couple days off at home and as always made good use of our time. Kim came out and gave us her old computer and my brother John came over and got it all set up for us. We were very glad to have the computer because being self employed as we are; there is a whole bunch of record keeping that goes along with it. Everyone stayed for grilled hamburgers and of course hung around to listen to my trucking stories. We had a great time!

We've been out on the road for seven days now. It is the 16th of June and yesterday we were in Edison, NJ delivering a load. Today we are headed for Myrtle, MS to pick up a load of furniture. Right now we are outside Knoxville, TN. It's amazing how we can talk to someone in the morning and by evening our location is at least three to five states! I love long haul trucking, at least for today! It's sunny and one of those days where I'm sitting up front knitting and Ron is on the CB shooting the bull with another driver.

Diesel is in her usual position, cruising, listening to country music and laying upside down on our bed in the back. Life on the road is good for her too! It won't be until we shut down tonight that she will expect me to entertain her. I have a paper bag, so while I'm doing my log, (she has a tendency to walk on my pages); I think I'll get it out for her. She likes to crawl inside of it and that will keep her occupied while I record my day of driving.

Almost forgot to mention, but last week in Missouri we were sound asleep, parked at a truck stop when we heard loud bangs on the side door of our truck. (Three o'clock in the morning!) The relentless pounding kept up, so finally Ron put his jeans on, pulled the drapes, and much to his surprise, it was security! We were told to immediately start the truck and move to higher ground! We were in a torrential rain storm and she said the back end of our trailer was starting to float! I heard all this and quickly threw on some clothes! Sure enough, you could "not" see the tires on the back of our trailer! The front tires were in about a foot of water and Ron wasn't so sure we could even move! We were in a "rushing" river and no doubt had to get the hell out of it! Had we not moved and the trailer remained, there was a good chance it would have floated right smack against the trailer beside us! Who knows what amount of damage it may have caused not only to our trailer, but the one we hit as well! It took a couple tries before Ron could get the truck to move forward. When the tires finally took hold, pulling out of the water was the weirdest out of control sensation I have ever felt! It was like a being in a boat drifting after the motor conks out on you! Rain in Missouri is nothing to take lightly, (play on words)! But, when it rains it comes down in buckets! It is very common for traffic to pull over alongside the road here and wait the storm out. Windshield wipers cannot keep up with the volume of water.

Last trip home our timing was perfect to go with Kim and watch Jason run a seven and a half mile race. It's an annual run held in Tacoma, WA. I've never watched one before except when Jason was very young. He did well way back then and just as well again in this race. I could tell he was very happy to see me and Kim cheering him on to the finish line! (I'm a people watcher and during the race, one young man running, suddenly came to an abrupt stop right in front of us!) The crowd became silent, like myself; totally surprised by his actions. We all just stood there like dummies wondering what he was going to do next. The kid was ghost white! He suddenly turned his head towards the crowd, smiled then turned his head back and proceeded to cough out a heavy load of vomit! When he finished coughing out the vomit, he looked at the crowd, smiled, waved and began to run again! The crowd came back with a roaring applause! From what I've learned from Jason, what we witnessed was not unusual; runners frequently vomit. He also informed us it's not uncommon for runners to wet their pants! I'm sure the runner I saw had what I call the old "No Guts No Glory" attitude! He was determined to finish the race!

Ron's stamina and determination never ceases to amaze me! We got a load out of Los Angeles, CA that was considered "hot"! It HAD to be delivered in two and a half days to New Jersey. (Clear across the United States in 2 ½ days!) When Ron sets his mind on something he becomes "Mission Impossible" and takes the challenge "head on"! He did the majority of the driving and I stayed awake sitting up front the entire trip. When you get a load like this it's pretty much none stop driving with only time to refuel, fill the thermos and pick up some kind of prepared food to eat along the way. The truck engine is NEVER shut off even when fueling! The night before we made it to New Jersey, we only managed to grab a few hours sleep before getting back up to deliver the load on time. It was a killer run, but "Mission" accomplished!

The old saying "too tired to eat" is true and we're not alone. Other drivers do the same thing. The entire trip was nerve wracking, especially when you're on the push! We had to deal with several delays caused by road construction, heavy traffic and once a back up of traffic due to an accident. All of these events contribute to lost driving time; especially when you are dead stopped on the highway waiting for the road to open after an accident. The wait could be significant while crews clean up the mess! Sometimes this could mean an hour or several hours before you're able to start rolling again; costing drivers valuable driving time. In our case, it was more stressful than usual knowing the deadline given for delivering our load. Regardless of our setbacks, we made it, the pressure was off, and only hoped the company would appreciated the extra effort we had to put into this! The company had sent three trucks with the same delivery requirement. Two of us made it, but we never did see the third truck. This of course will not make the company very happy because the customer was told three trucks full of freight would be delivered to them on the date and time promised.

We spent last night in Spokane, WA and we had just enough time to weed gardens and mow the lawn for Ron's mom. It is June 25th and we are in Portland, OR getting a load to deliver in Auburn, WA. After that we will be able to run home, stay the night and leave again the following morning. The day before yesterday I was driving through Montana and that's one state where we are constantly watching for deer! I spotted one ahead of me standing in the median. I was probably doing about 65 mph at the time. The closer I got, I was trying to anticipate what the deer was going to do, but it didn't do anything, it just continued to stand there. When I was within close distance, the deer suddenly bolted, jumped out, and headed straight for the truck! I jumped on the accelerator, and it's a good thing I did! The deer ran right into the back end of the trailer! It all happened in a matter of seconds, and if I had not speeded up, no doubt, it would have smashed right into the side of our truck. Yes, I do feel sorry for the deer. I hope it had instant death and went to "Deer Heaven"! I know I'm not the first one to ever hit a deer out here on the interstate, but you cannot help but feel guilty and I hope it never happens again!

All three kids called Ron on Father's Day which made him feel good. Jake and Sam also got to say "hello" to grandpa. Ron passed me the phone so I could talk to them as well. I love hearing their little voices. As I've mentioned before, it's too bad Kellie lives so far away. I would love to spend time with my only grandsons. When your job is trucking and especially when you're self employed like we are, you rarely get enough time off for trips to see family.

Today is the June 25th and we are in Phoenix, AZ getting a load that we will deliver in Dublin, GA. I am driving more often now than ever before. I actually look forward to when it's my turn. Ron frequently goes back to the bunk and takes a nap while I'm behind the wheel. There was a time not long ago when I would have panicked having him out of sight, but now I tell him "I will yell" if I need help. (So far that has not been necessary.) I usually turn the satellite radio on down low, put a couple snacks up on the dash and I'm good for the next few hours of driving. Ron has run hard for so many months, he's relieved letting me take over the wheel knowing I'll be fine and he can rest. Diesel always takes a nap with him which makes me happy because I don't want her up on the dash when I'm driving.

CHAPTER 6

GUT WRENCHING FEAR AND TERROR

One of those days! The 1st of July and we lost our air conditioning while driving through Nebraska! The temperature is pushing the 99 degrees mark and it's very windy. Inside the cab feels like an oven and we're both downright miserable! Sweat keeps rolling down our faces and I have repeatedly had to pass Ron a paper towel to prevent the salty streams from getting in his eye glasses. We stopped at two different places in Wyoming to buy a simple fan belt, but no luck! We are driving with the windows down and the vents open but it's not doing much good because the air is so hot outside. Diesel is panting and I feel sorry for her but there is nothing we can do. It's a bit depressing. Seems no matter how hard we try there are always unexpected expenses that eat up the profit! This is just another one.

We had to live without air conditioning, two weeks before we were finally able to get home and take the truck to a shop. For some reason we had a sneaking hunch there would be more to our air conditioning problem than a fan belt. Sure enough, when we picked the truck up the bill was $1,084.00!! That was a healthy chunk of money just to keep us cool in hot weather! Nevertheless, I won't forget either how awful it was not having it! On a more positive note, the countryside we have been able to see traveling through so many other states, is priceless!

As I write, we are stopped on a scale and Ron's log is being checked by a female D.O.T. officer. This check is different than the usual "red light" we get instructing us to drive our rig around to the bay area for an inspection. We got "stopped" right in front of the coop's window when crossing over the scale! The D.O.T. officer came out and asked Ron a few questions, like "what are you hauling?" and "where are you headed?" and then she asked to see his log book. (At the time, I wasn't sure of her motive.) This experience was a "first" one for me, but Ron said it's actually a pretty routine procedure for them to do "spot checks" on drivers going over their scales. No problems were found with his log or the answers he gave and she waved us on. I looked in the rear mirror as we left the scale and I could see she was checking ALL the trucks behind us. The load we're on today is bird seed! A whole trailer full and it's heavy! We are taking it to Ponchatoula, LA and from there we'll go to Myrtle, MS to pick up a load of furniture. We are both looking forward to Louisiana with all its mysterious swamps and trees laden with gray layers of moss hanging from every limb. CREEPY to say the least and no doubt, I'll be watching for alligators!

It is the 25th of July and we have been out here making our home inside the truck for over four weeks now. Finally we were able to work our way west and pick up a load in Helena, MT that delivers in Auburn, WA. We both are looking forward to having a few days off at home. We have run out of clean clothes and the truck needs a good cleaning. We'll probably have a ton of mail to go through, not to mention the weeds choking out the vegetables in the garden! We'll have our work cut out for us. I drove quite a bit this trip and Ron had no problem turning the wheel over to me. I drove through Council Bluffs, Sioux City, IA and Kansas City, MO. I have come a long way and each time I drive I gain more confidence. It is not that easy, (at least at my stage of driving) to repeatedly match required gears to the driving situations you encounter for so many miles. You don't put a big rig in "D" and cruise up and down the hills. Shifting requires matching each gear to a specific range of RPM's in order for it to slide smoothly into place. Believe me, if your RPM's are too high or too low, you'll know it! It makes a God awful sound and you'll swear you just tore out the entire transmission! However, this trip, I did great!

I missed a few days writing in my journal and for no other reason but being plain lazy! I selfishly enjoy sitting up front where I can see all the action. Documenting our daily events in my journal became mute in my mind. Anyway, now it is the 5th of August. We are in Darlington, SC waiting to unload pressboard. So far our trip has been uneventful and we enjoyed the ride. We parked way in the back row of a truck stop in Indiana the other night. Ron "nosed" in so we could enjoy the view of a huge soy bean field in front of us. Much to our surprise, as it started to get dark, we noticed tiny sparkles all over the soy crop. I can only describe the flashes like when you hold your head down too long then stand up quickly and you see bright twinkling stars flashing all around you. I had this happen to me once or twice, but I never passed out! What we observed that night, were fire flies! We have heard about fire flies, but neither of us had ever seen any. We both watched them until it was time to go to bed. This is just another advantage of driving truck. Chances are if we stayed home we never would have seen these amazing little insects. The Smokey Mountains were beautiful but we ran into pouring rain before we ever got halfway through them. This is the first rain we've had the entire trip and chances are more is on the way. We heard that there is a bad storm coming in our direction off the coast of Florida. So far the storm has dumped 8" of rain bringing with it strong wind gusts of 70 mph! I hope it weakens before it catches up with us.

Last night we stopped at a Petro Truck Stop just outside Little Rock, AR and met some very interesting "local" people while eating dinner. We have found that people living in the south are very friendly and receptive to strangers. (At least the ones we have talked to are always friendly with us.) We of course are fascinated with their southern accents and love to get them to tell us their stories; which they don't hesitate to offer! I usually am the one to "start" the conversation and I must admit sometimes Ron wishes I would keep my mouth shut, but I don't! I'm fascinated with learning about other people who have grown up living in a state that I know nothing about. I usually start by saying, "Do you live here?" and when they answer "yes", I continue by saying "Your state is beautiful, but I wouldn't want to live here because the south has so many dangerous critters!" That's all it takes! They get a big chuckle out of my comment and eagerly proceed to tell us about their "personal" encounters dealing with creepy crawlers in their state. This particular conversation that I had was with a husband and wife. Once they started talking it was almost like they were trying to outdo each other; telling the biggest whopper! When one would finish with a story, the other quickly jumped in saying; "That's nothing, wait until you hear this one, it's even better!" I must admit they had our undivided attention and they no doubt equally were enjoying watching our reactions!

The husband shared a previous fishing experience where he took the wife along with him and how he had to assure her he would keep an eye out for "Water Moccasin, (Cottonmouth) in the water. He said "That's one thing she don't like! Snakes always scare the living hell "outta" her!" He continued on telling us these snakes are usually found within a 100' from shore. One time while using his oars (instead of the motor), his wife suddenly screamed when she spotted a Water Moccasin dangling off the end of his oar! He wanted to make sure "we" understood the moment of danger they were in by adding how poisonous Moccasin venom can be when you get bitten by one! The results may be fatal! Getting back to his story, he said he instantly shook the dam thing off, got the hell out of there and rowed faster than his motor could have done! It scared them both half to death!

The husband chimes in again and says, "I'll tell you another true story"! One time I was fishing off the bank when I noticed a "moccasin" cruising along with its head out of the water. I swear, the snake's eyeballs were focused straight at me!" "I kept watching and all of a sudden the damn thing starts heading in my direction! It continued to move forward swaying its long body back and forth leaving small ripples in the water as it glided towards me picking up speed!" "There was no doubt in my mind I was his target, invading his territory, and was about to be attacked if I didn't get out of there! I frantically started reeling in my line, but it wasn't coming in fast enough!" Seconds counted as I continued to watch the snake while reeling as fast as I could! When the snake was only a few feet away I thought for sure it was going to jump right out of the water, fly through the air and attack me!" At that point, I threw my dam pole at the snake and ran as fast as I could! He ended by saying "I never did go back to find my pole!

Our conversation continued by them telling us about the food they hunt, catch and eat like squirrels, alligators and snapping turtles. (None of these critters would appeal to my appetite!) The wife said with they get a bunch of squirrels, they either fry the legs or make stew and dumplings out of them. I asked about the turtles and she said they only eat the legs and neck and usually just throw them in a pan and fry um' up! These were great people like so many others that we have met out here. They made our evening! Chances are, our paths will never meet again, but as strangers, we got to laugh and enjoy each other's company. (Now that I think about it, I thought all the alligators were in Florida and Louisiana.) Oh well, they told good stories!

We are in Nashville, TN and had a heck of a problem earlier this morning trying to find the location of our delivery while it was still dark outside. Fortunately, time was on our side and eventually we spotted the address we were looking for on a building. We arrived before the warehouse was even opened and had to sit for quite awhile. When one of the employees finally showed up for work, he told Ron he wasn't sure if he was supposed to unload us or not. We sat, and sat waiting to get his answer. Finally he returned and told us the load goes to another one of their warehouses and handed Ron directions on how to get there! In route, we ran into an almost impossible turn with the 53' trailer! I don't know how Ron did it, but he managed to pull the trailer around the corner without running over anything! People don't realize when they give truckers directions that we are not driving a car; we're all driving big rigs! We cannot navigate through obstacle courses which were never designed to accommodate large trucks with trailers. After they unload we'll try to find our way back to the interstate and then we're off to Dalton, GA. At least we can look forward to an overnight stay at the usual motel we stay at when we get there. We have stopped at this same motel often enough now that we are on a first name basis with the employees. It's nice to be greeted by someone that knows your name and sees more in you than just another customer.

On August 24th we left Dalton, GA with a load to Myrtle, MS. Picked up a load there and headed back to Washington. We got another load out of Lynwood, WA and took it to Jackson, MS and from there we were sent back to Myrtle, MS again where they already had a pre loaded trailer waiting for us. Once again we find ourselves headed west only this time to Helena, MT for a partial drop and then we will "final" the load in Auburn, WA. Basically, what I'm pointing out is that this nonstop trucking equates to approximately 5,000 miles a week! By the end of the month we will have 20,000 miles under our belt! Pretty much around the clock driving and just imagine we are only "one" of the "White Line Warriors"! There are many thousands of other men and women driving their life away, hammering down, delivering freight across the nation 24hrs. a day!

Driving through Livingston, MT yesterday there was a huge forest fire going on. As we passed through the smoke filled mountains, it was devastating to see so many trees in the pine forests already burned to the ground leaving only a blackened hillside to look at. More than 10,000 acres of timber went up in flames and crews were still battling smaller fires trying to put out hot spots. Our eyes are watering from smoke filled air. Makes you wonder about all the wildlife; some made it to safety and no doubt others were not so fortunate. I managed to take a few pictures to share with the rest of the family. The pictures will tell the story better than what I'm trying to describe. We are parked inside the repair shop in Helena, MT today getting our quarterly inspection done on the truck. Ron also told them to go ahead and replace the clutch fan. Here we go again with another expense!

I continue to drive more and more. In fact, now we have a little system where Ron gets up and drives the first five hours and then I get behind the wheel and drive another five. When I'm done, I turn the driving back over to him and he finishes out the rest of the day. This seems to be working quite well for us and we're not as tired at the end of the day. Even the cat likes it! She gets more attention now from Ron than ever before. He won't let her lie upside down and sleep like I do. He has to deliberately ruffle her feathers and get her are riled up! Sometimes I get very irritated with all the commotion going on behind me while I'm trying to drive. (It's like having kids in the back seat of a car punching it out while you're up front trying to ignore the distraction.) Makes me think of my mother; she wouldn't tolerate her kids fighting; especially when she was driving, and always somehow managed to swing her arm around, yell a few choice words, and smack everyone of us! From there on we were perfect little angels!

SEPTEMBER 11, 2001 AND THIS DAY WILL GO DOWN IN HISTORY AS THE WORST DISASTER FALLEN UPON

AMERICAN SOIL; OUR BELOVED "UNITED STATES FELL UNDER ATTACK BY TERRORISTS!! *THE REST OF THE WORLD WILL BE SADDENED AND SHOCKED!* (The following paragraphs reveal my personal thoughts and feelings on that dreadful day!)

We are backed up to a dock just on the outskirts of Detroit, MI and Ron just jumped into the truck and yelled at me to turn on the television! He shouted we're being attacked! I was stunned by his words. I knew by the look on his face he was dead serious! I yelled back, "What do you mean"? What are you talking about? He blurted out that a huge passenger plane just plowed into the side of one of the trade towers in New York City! He said "The news media is blaming the attack on **"terrorists",** turn on our television!"

We were in disbelief as we both sat there frozen to the TV watching this horrific "eye witnessing" disaster! The reporting news anchor lost control of her emotions and started sobbing, leaving it to her counterpart to take over broadcasting. There was an immense feeling of panic that came over me! The only thing I could think about was my kids and grandkids! I no sooner had those thoughts, and right before our eyes on television, *ANOTHER* huge plane "crashed" into the trade tower sending cold chills throughout my body; I was scared to death!! We were both so stunned we couldn't even talk. We just kept saying Oh, My God!! I have never in my entire life felt so panicky and at the same time so helpless! I immediately tried calling Kim, Kellie and Jason and it was impossible! The news was too wide spread; all the phone lines were jammed with families everywhere trying to do the same thing! I kept trying repeatedly, but again, it was impossible. I thought about Kellie living so close in Virginia. I thought about Jason living near Seattle where terrorists had targeted the Space Needle in the past and then about Kim living so close to Los Angeles. All of the kids live in such populated areas which seem to be the places where terrorists target the most! I was sick to my stomach thinking about it!

I started out this morning in a good mood and had planned to call Sam our grandson and wish him a happy birthday. Now, the poor kid will have this attack talked about for years to come each time his birthday rolls around. Not a pleasant thought for his future birthdays. I won't give up trying to get through on the phone lines because I won't be satisfied until I talk to "all" three of my kids. Ron's trying to console me and I appreciate his effort, but it's not working. Local news interrupted and announced that there have been two terrorist threats made upon the city of Detroit within the last half hour! We have also been informed by the news media that the President of the United States has now shut down "all" air traffic throughout the nation; this is a *first*! It's starting to feel very eerie as we sit here in our truck and look up at the sky. We are VERY close to the airport where we're parked and there is not one single plane in the sky! I told Ron as soon as they are done unloading us I want to leave! I will feel much safer getting out of Detroit. I didn't like hearing about the terrorist threats made upon the city we're in. The thought brought chilling reality realizing we could possibly become victims of terrorists ourselves!

I know we will spend the rest of the day listening to the radio, and we no doubt, will be sharing information over the CB with other drivers out here. God Bless "ALL" the truckers today, who like us, cannot just stop, turn around and head home to be with family! Businesses are shutting down right and left! The main roads that we can see in a distance have become almost gridlocked! All of these employees obviously left their jobs and are now out here anxiously making a desperate attempt to get through the traffic. They will make it home today; we won't!

Ron told me we're not about to leave the parking lot; it would be an exercise in futility to even think about getting this 18 wheeler out in bumper to bumper traffic. He said "we would be asking for trouble", and there's no way he would *attempt* driving until after "all" the four wheelers have cleared out! We are stuck sitting, worried, and there isn't a dam thing we can do but continue to sit for as long as it takes! Right now, delivering the next load on time is not a priority. It's the last thing on our minds! I will continue to try to get hold of the kids and sooner or later I'll get through. I'm sick to my stomach; the news continues with "more" terrorist attacks! No telling how many people are injured or much worse, lost their life! It is a tragedy beyond comprehension and I want it to end! **This is the United States of America! We don't get attacked like other countries! It's not supposed to happen here! Not in America!**

Tried again to reach the kids and the calls finally went through! All of them are fine and each of them expressed more concerned for Ron and me being in Detroit! Basically, our conversations ended up by consoling one another and giving support, encouragement, and reassurance that for right now, we all are safe from harm. At this moment, I wish I could believe that, but I can't! We're listening to live minute by minute updates on the crises from obviously shocked and frightened broadcasters reporting news as quick as they receive it! I'm saying a prayer for everyone; especially for all those people in New York caught by surprise in this outrageous attack; the inured, the dead and for ALL the grieving family and friends of these innocent people.

It is now 4 p.m. and we are on our way to Alabama leaving the city of Detroit behind us. We just heard that all oil refineries have been ordered to shut down; creating an instant shortage of fuel. With that news, in a very short period of time we couldn't help but notice gas stations were already putting up signs reading "10 Gallon Limit" and increasing their prices. We just fueled and the price has gone up 40 cents a gallon since yesterday!

Jason called, very concerned about the two of us and said he is still in shock over the surprise attack. News reports say the death of civilians will be in the thousands! These were *passenger* planes, full of travelers who innocently found themselves captive, being deliberately overtaken by radical *terrorists*! My God! I can't even imagine the fear those poor people went through up there in the sky! It is beyond belief why any human being would deliberately kill other innocent people only for reason of religious or political gain! The huge planes slammed into not just one, but "both" trade towers in New York City! Ron and I will never forget witnessing the tragedy on television as the buildings shockingly, before our eyes, fell apart and crumbled to the ground! If that wasn't enough, the terrorists didn't stop there! The next target attack was on the Pentagon building in Washington DC where several more innocent people most likely lost their life! This is the first time in my life the United States is under RED ALERT! I'm scared not knowing if there is more to come and feel a desperate urge to forget trucking, head home and prepare to defend ourselves! Unfortunately, this is not what will happen. We are states away and have no choice but to continue on as long as the interstates remain open. This is our job and this is what you're expected to do by the company you work for. Keep driving! Deliver the load!

I'm proud to be born an American and I know at this very time every branch of our military is ready to go! I'll bet they're all on standby, spinning their wheels, anxiously awaiting orders, eager to defend their homeland! God Bless our uniformed men and women! Jason said himself; he is ready to go back into the U.S. Air Force if called upon. American flags everywhere are at half mast. President Bush has promised all Americans that WE WILL FIGHT BACK!

I'm supposed to fly to Washington DC on the 4th of October to see Kellie and her family. I have learned that this is the same airport where one of the planes was hijacked! Needless to say, I'm worried about going there. I don't want to die because I have too much to live for! Jason isn't even married yet! I want to be around to enjoy all of my kids and grandkids for a long time to come.

It really bothers me when I allow my mind to wonder and can vision "what war looks like"! I recall previous news clips of wars going on in other countries and I've watched plenty of old war movies. They always showed fighting, bombing, people frantically running for shelter, dead and wounded soldiers and civilians lying in streets, along with the obvious suffering, pain and ruination of cities and towns. The recent tragedy is a "wakeup call" for all of us living here and taking our lives for granted! *What we thought would never happen in the United States just did!*

Four days have gone by and yesterday was declared a National Day of Mourning. I found a big American flag at a truck stop in Missouri and we have hung it inside our truck. Every American has been asked by President Bush to either fly or display the American flag on this day. Bells rang throughout the United States at 12 noon for five minutes for families who have lost or still have missing loved ones. This day is proclaimed the worst disaster in American history! One cannot help but wonder what lies ahead. On the brighter side, we are on our way home!

September 20th and we made it home, but only for one night. Just enough time to get mail, do laundry, pack and leave again. We have a huge American flag, and before we left, we proudly hung it on our porch. We're on our way to Fort Ogelthorp, GA. We have American flags flying now on both sides of the truck connected to our outside antennas. We are not alone; I've never seen so many American flags displayed! They are everywhere you look; mounted on trucks, homes, street lamps, hanging from overcrossings, bridges and buildings. This traumatic event has brought people together and formed "unity" that none of us have ever experienced before. For the first time, it doesn't matter if you are rich or poor, or whether your democrat or republican, people have come together sharing a common love and loyalty for our nation and each other. President Bush in his assurance to Americans said "*WE WILL SMOKE OUT THE ENEMY!*" He has called back to duty 50,000 National Guardsmen and has sent military planes along with three air craft carriers to the mid east.

September 25th and we are just outside Twin Falls, ID waiting to get the truck fixed. We ran over a bunch of garbage on the interstate and a piece flew up and broke the air line. We have learned to expect the unexpected and there doesn't seem to be any trip without something coming up that we have to deal with. So far we have been sitting here for about an hour and a half and it looks like we'll be here for awhile longer. So much for thinking our load will deliver on time! I wonder who will bitch at us first; dispatch or the customer!

The news continues daily with updates on the terrorist attack and sadly the number of fatalities continues to grow! Flags everywhere are still at half mast. It's very heartwarming to see all the cities, towns, neighborhoods, automobiles, trucks; you name it that continues to display the American flag. We all love our country! We have listened to the CB radio much more than we usually do and it's overwhelming the amount of truck drivers out here who are more than eager to stop what they're doing and reenlist! I'm especially talking about the drivers who are in their mid 60's! Many of them previously served in the military and are "spinning their wheels" for a chance to go back and defend our country once again! One driver said "I may be too old to fight, but there are a whole bunch of other things I could do to help!" "There are a lot of us "old guys" out here that have a ton of knowledge and experience that we could offer." It's interesting because usually you would expect one younger wise ass driver after hearing that to get on the CB and make a smart remark, but in this case, it never happened, not even once! We all just listened or got on the CB ourselves and thanked the driver for his service and for being so willing to return to the military and fight for our country!

We now are clear into the month of October since my last entry and in fact, it's already the 17th! I got my courage up and went to visit Kellie and her family in Virginia. While I was in Virginia, the United States military started bombing in the mid east. Newspaper headlines read; AMERICA FIGHTS BACK! So far no other significant terrorist's attacks have occurred, however "Anthrax", a bio chemical germ, has been showing up in the U.S. mail. It is reported that one person has died and several others are infected and being treated. Citizens are being warned to report any powdery substance found in their mail.

I thoroughly enjoyed my visit with Kellie, Scott, Jake and Sam. Little Sam calls me gamma! It didn't take long before both grandsons warmed up to me. Kellie was very prepared and had my entire stay well organized. We even made a trip to Washington DC so I could see firsthand the destruction caused by the plane that crashed into the Pentagon. I took pictures to show the rest of the family. The area, as expected was taped off, but we were able to see from a distance the amount of damage that had been done. While I was enjoying the visit, Ron had to run "solo" during my absence.

When I returned home, Sue, my sister-in-law picked me up from the airport. She had a spectacular seafood dinner waiting and although I had planned to drop her off and head home, I could not resist staying. Ron was anxious to see me and didn't like the delay, but understood. Over dinner I told her and John about my experience going through security at the Dulles airport. Inside and out there were plenty of policemen and National Guardsmen with guard dogs on a leash. I was safe no doubt, but it was also somewhat intimidating. I even got scanned! I was so surprised when I was asked to step aside. I couldn't help but wonder if they thought I looked suspicious! When I told Kellie, she said it is a random pick and for me not to take it personal! John and Sue agreed saying it's just the luck of the draw and my number came up. All I can say is that being scanned while other passengers are allowed to pass through is something I'm not going to forget!

What a husband I have! When I got home, Ron had a nice bubble bath set up for me, robe, pajamas, slippers set out, fresh flowers and a glass of wine sitting on the edge of the bathtub! It made me realize even more how much I appreciate all that he does for me.

Since I got back home we have already made one run down the coast to California and back. We had two days off at home and then off again. I figure by now "trucking" is in my blood! I was spinning my wheels to get back on the road after my trip to see Kellie. Diesel even seemed happy to get back in the routine of "cruising and snoozing"! What a cat! Thanksgiving is not that far away and it looks like we will try to get the time off to share it again with Kim, Mike and Jason. As usual, we'll have to see how it goes. No guarantee when you're being dispatched all over the place.

Today is the 24th of October and we are in South Dakota and currently experiencing snow flurries; first snow of the season. We already know from listening to other drivers on the CB that there is more snow, heavy snow along with strong winds ahead. We still have Wyoming to go through and we know what it's like being there! This state always has wind so when you combine snow with it, you can expect white outs! In this short time, the snow is really coming down now. It looks like blizzard conditions and we are ROCKING AND ROLLING! We don't need to put ourselves at this much risk for running off the road or getting blown over. Ron said if it gets much worse, we are getting off the interstate!

It is hours later and Ron actually persevered and got us to the Port of Entry in Wyoming. It was rough to say the least but a few Hail Mary's, white knuckle driving for him, and me not flapping my jaws giving advice or whining about the wind and snow, allowed Ron to concentrate and get the job done! NOW it's my turn to drive!

I made it to Billings, MT last night and decided I was too tired to write in my journal. I had strong wind gusts to deal with all the way through Wyoming and into Montana. I also had occasional snow flurries and some were pretty heavy at times, but I managed to plow through all of them. I even stopped to fuel in Gillette, WY and did great, given the icy road conditions coming off the exit and then getting back on the freeway after fueling. (I didn't spin a tire!) As I approached the coop, (port of entry in Montana), wouldn't you know luck of the draw, it was OPEN! I just hate it when they're open! I'm always afraid I'm going to miss a gear or kill the engine on the scale and that would really get their attention! As it turned out, I sailed right through; never missed a shift!

Ron is driving this morning and he's back into snow! It started coming down when we passed through Missoula, MT. about an hour ago. Drivers headed east are telling us to expect heavy snow driving over Lookout Pass. (So far chains are not required.) Ron said we'll have time going through Spokane later today to stop and see his mother; by then we'll need a break anyway. Well wouldn't you know, you no sooner say one thing and it no longer applies! WE just spent a half hour chaining up! Snowing and blowing and the two of us had to get out of our warm truck, freeze our butts off and put on several tire chains! My feet and hands are numb, my nose is running and that's enough to put anyone into a bad mood! We are bumping along now with the vibration of the chains and can only look forward to getting out again further down the interstate and take them all back off! I'm going to stomp on my rose colored glasses!

November 20th and what did I tell you about Thanksgiving; no guarantees. It is two days before the holiday and here we are sitting in Cincinnati, OH. There is no way we will make it home to share dinner with the kids or even for Jason's birthday on the 25th. I know they will understand, but while they're all having a nice visit and eating home cooked food, we'll be eating truck stop turkey!

I cannot believe my luck! I've only had the new bridge in my mouth a few months and it fell out! This is just what you get when you can't be choosy! I had to take a dentist, any dentist that would see me on short notice and this is what I paid $2,000 for? Sloppy work and I'm not going to take it sitting down! I will not go back and I want every penny I paid returned to me so I can get someone who knows what they're doing! I'm already wondering what kind of argument I'm going to have with them when I call and complain. I will stand my ground! This is another good example of having a problem when you're trucking out here and there's nothing you can do about it but live with the problem until you get home.

It is November 22nd and we are on our way to Denver, CO with a load of cosmetics. At least we're headed west! Last night we stayed in Columbia, MO and got a motel room. It was so nice to have a hot shower. Even having a sink with running water to brush our teeth was a real treat. Today is Thanksgiving and we plan to call Ron's mom and of course, all the kids. No telling where we will eat tonight. The road is getting way to bumpy for me to write so I'm going to set my journal aside for now.

Well, I can see from my last entry I got lazy and have not made notes for quite a few days. Today is the 12th of December! During this time we were home and I found a new dentist. He put in a temporary bridge and it looks great! I sent a certified letter to the previous dentist asking for my total payment of $2,336 returned to me immediately. (We'll see what happens.) We are in South Carolina delivering a load that we picked up a few days ago in California. Fuel prices here have dropped dramatically! We only paid (this is unheard of), 96.9 cents a gallon last night! That is the cheapest price we've ever paid in years! I don't know how long this low price will last but it makes a huge difference when you have to buy your own fuel.

We got a message from the company saying they will pay drivers an extra $400 bonus if they stay out over Christmas. Kim and Jason have already made plans and won't be home. Kellie of course is too far away in Virginia so Ron signed us up. I like the money, but I'm going to miss being home. I love decorating a tree and baking Christmas cookies. All of our gifts for everyone will be put on hold until we get home. I wonder how many other drivers working for this same company will choose to stay out, if for no other reason, just to get the extra $400. I hope the younger ones with kids will rule family over money and decide to go home! Ron called his mom and told her to keep the tree up and we'll have a late Christmas with her. She will be alone but absolutely insists it doesn't bother her. It would me!

December 19th and made it home for a quick stop and off again. We have had a steady snowfall this entire trip. You would think by now we would be use to driving in snow, but each time it's always a new experience. When the snow hits; you could be anywhere! A different highway, climbing mountains or driving through long straight stretches on the interstate. You have to drive dealing with whatever "Mother Nature" throws at you and try to stay out of trouble! We couldn't even make it over Cabbage Pass before the D.O.T. shut down the interstate forcing us and other truckers to wait it out parked in a truck stop located at the bottom of the mountain. When we were allowed to go over the pass, chains were required! It's cold miserable work putting chains on, drive over the pass and then have to get out in freezing weather and take them back off. Adding to our miserable day, when we got to Ladd

Canyon, chains were required again! Driving several miles through all this snow and ice creates enough tension and stress but, when you have to "chain up" twice in the same day, it wears you out!

Today is December 20th and yesterday as well as today snow continues to fall. We are now about 300 miles from Las Vegas so before the day is over we should be on dry roads and sunshine! The sooner the better; I'm sick and tired of this stuff! Going through La Grande, OR yesterday we saw a bull elk, mother and calf standing along a stream. What a beautiful sight with snow filled trees in the background. It would have made a great Christmas card.

It is the 22nd of December and we have a load out of California that will final in Sayreville, NJ. That is 3,093 miles away! We have seven stops along the way and the first drop will be in Denver, CO. The route takes us over several snow covered mountain passes. (Loveland Pass is 11,990 feet high!) Makes me wonder how many times I'll have to bundle up, get out, and help Ron put on more chains than I even want to think about right now. I'm really not looking forward to what's ahead of us!

Merry Christmas family! Ron and I are in North Platte, NE. It's beautiful, sunny and COLD! I know we volunteered to be out here, but we can't help but feel a bit sad and left out. So many families are celebrating Christmas together today. Houses are all lighted up, trees in their windows and no doubt the smell of turkey fills every room of the house. I can just imagine the anticipation of guests arriving, opening presents, everyone talking at once, sharing dinner with prayer and of course, everyone watching out for the "one" relative with a big mouth! So much for day dreaming! The reality is we are here with Diesel, (sleeping as usual) and we are alone out this cold highway that has become almost baron of four wheelers. It's basically your "White Line Warriors" remaining out here; still driving to get freight delivered on time. We have no gifts to give each other. If we are lucky, we will find a truck stop with a nice buffet tonight; at least that is something we both can look forward to. We will call all of the kids later, my eyes will probably tear up, and we will call that our Christmas for "2001!"

I guess if there is one consoling thought, it's that we're not alone. Many other truckers like us chose to put Christmas aside and it's not "all" about money. Every driver knows we are depended upon by millions of people to deliver their supplies. This Christmas however, will be "special"! It will be a time to reflect on September 11th and remember those unfortunate families that lost a loved one. God bless them all!

CHAPTER 7

RELENTLESS ROUTINE OF EAT,
SLEEP AND DRIVE

Today is January 1, 2002 and the start of a new year!! It amazes me how in a mere 24 hours a new year changes the attitude of so many people! It perks them up with visions and hope for a better year than the one they left behind! (I'm no exception!) We celebrated New Year's Eve last night parked at a truck stop in Acoma, NM watching beautiful fireworks lighting up the sky from a distance.

Last evening the interstate turned into packed ice along with heavy snow falling down and as a safety measure, Ron got off the road. We arrived too late for dinner and had to settle for fast food. Ron offered to get out in the cold and walk the distance across the parking lot to buy us something to eat. When he returned he said "Tacos were on special" but he had to buy "10" of them! (I had my doubts if we could eat them all.) He also brought back hot chili. Much to my surprise, I managed to gobble up three and a half before I called it quits. Ron ate six before he gave up! I had a brief moment of feeling sorry for myself knowing if we were home our menu would have been entirely different. Eating tacos was a far cry from our usual New Year's Eve dinner! For years we enjoyed this day plunked down in our recliners watching fireworks on TV, drinking a few beers and gorging ourselves eating fresh Dungeness crab! I'm glad I didn't allow myself to dwell on the thought. We were both tired from the long day of driving and I wasn't about to make Ron feel bad and start my whining. After all, by now I should be prepared and accept the fact that we can't always be home for holidays. It's the real world of trucking!

While parked last night another trucker climbed up on the step of our truck and told Ron he lost his little dog "Sammie". He said he's only had her in the truck four days. The guy was clearly upset and concerned for the dog's safety. Ron got out of the truck and offered to help look for Sammie. The truck driver told us he left the window down and she apparently jumped out of the truck. He went further by saying that he acquired the dog from an elderly woman who has terminal cancer and promised her he would take good care of Sammie. He said "I've got to find her!"

It didn't take long and guess who spotted Sammie hiding under another 18 wheeler, Ron! He motioned for me to get out of the truck to come and help him catch her. I saw the frightened little dog crouched down underneath the trailer and walked slowly towards her calling her by name. As I got closer to her, she started wagging her tail. Her little body began to wiggle, she looked at me and then all of a sudden, got up and ran straight into my arms! The poor little thing was shivering, wet with snow and at the same time obviously happy someone found her! I passed Sammie to Ron and he quickly went to find the owner. The trucker could not thank us enough and little Sammie no doubt was glad to be back with him!

We are in Arizona today as I write. It's only 17 degrees, but very sunny. We ran 149,200 miles last year. When we consider the time we took off for Ron's broken ankle, we were still able to rack up one heck of a lot of miles! The odometer reading on our truck has reached a total of 396,328 miles driven by the two of us. I wonder how many miles we'll rack up during the next twelve months!

We're on our way to California after taking a week off! We hardly had any time at home choosing to spend part of it visiting my brother Jerry and his wife Carol and then another day with Kim. We also made a trip to Spokane and devoted our entire time helping Ron's mom with several things she wanted done inside and outside of her house. Sometimes I think we are stupid! We stay out on the road for weeks at a time and then we come home and create more work for ourselves. We need to sit down and relax! All we do is work! I will say though, we ate very well at each house we visited! We saw our first pussy willows alongside the road driving home from Jerry's. Spring has finally arrived!

The thing I'm feeling good about today is that after paying an attorney $100 it looks like I'm going to get a full refund back from the dentist that did such a lousy job on my bridge. The attorney I hired sent the dentist a very strong letter on my behalf demanding a refund. A couple days later my attorney received a call from him saying he would be sending me a full refund. What a relief! His check should be in the mail when I get home.

We delivered our load in Pomona, CA, picked up another and took it to Modesto and now we are headed for Elizabeth, NJ. We anticipate running into a bunch of snow, especially going over Cabbage Pass. We've "chained up" so many times this year it's not funny! So many times, we're not even griping about it; we just get out, do it and get it over with! Kim called last night and said they were in New Port Beach, CA for a job interview. I hope she gets the job! She worked hard for her degree and now it's time she gets rewarded for her effort.

It is January 23rd and much to our surprise we did not encounter any snow all the way to New Jersey! We made the drop (trailer was full of wine) on time in Elizabeth and then went on to Burlington to pick up a load of powdered resin; (another heavy load)! What a stressful day!! Now just imagine there are two of us in this truck watching for signs and even at that, we *missed* the exits not just once, but *twice!* Ron's yelling, I'm yelling, the cat booked, (hid somewhere) and we, sitting up front, were freaked out because at this point we didn't know where we were at or where we were going! Massive traffic filled all lanes; jammed packed full of four wheelers buzzing in and out all around us like angry swarms of bees! We were wedged into traffic like sardines! (This will put a driver to the test!) At one point we somehow ended up in Delaware! I remember seeing the sign, "Welcome to Delaware" and I about choked! The stress and anxiety in the cab of the truck was getting worse by the mile!

We were totally out of route! At this point there is no way to pull out a map and figure out where you're at. You have to keep moving with the flow of traffic and watch for signs. The damdest thing about this is that unlike the four wheelers, you cannot just whip a U turn and head the other way! You have to find an off ramp with an overcrossing that you can drive up, cross over the freeway and then head back down the other side. (Momma said there would be days like this!) You have to be inside a big rig to appreciate the intense pain and frustration a driver goes through in situations like this. Drivers of four wheelers take big trucks for granted because there are so many of us out here. They actually think we know where we're going! Little do they know the driver inside is going bananas over all the traffic, watching for signs, and hitting the brakes to avoid plowing into them! We eventually found our way out of this maze and frankly we don't even remember how we did it! BUT, we didn't wreck the truck or the freight we're hauling and we didn't cause an accident! We both dislike the East Coast just for these reasons, not enough roads and way too many people! We are parked for the night at a truck stop and glad the day is over!

We got a phone call from Kim before we went to bed. She said the job interview went well, but from what she learned and what they previously told her, was a far cry from what the position actually offered. She has more interviews coming up with other companies. I'm glad she didn't get discouraged and remained optimistic.

Now it is the 2nd of February and we are in Halsey, OR after deciding for our own safety to get this truck and the load we're hauling off the road! The truck stop is PACKED with other drivers making the exact same decision. Believe me when I'm telling you, the wind here is so powerful we are steadily getting "peppered" by flying gravel and debris! We have been in strong winds before but we've never witnessed anything like this! It's so bad Ron is taking pictures! This is crazy! We're rock'n and roll'n along with the rest of the trucks parked here. Makes me wonder if we all might get blown over! I'm not exaggerating; I'm watching and witnessing pieces of garbage flying through the air, shingles being blown off roof tops next to us, and a big green garbage dumpster "free-wheeling" out of control behind the restaurant! Sooner or later that big dumpster is going to hit something and I hope it's not us! Other drivers are reporting over the CB some wind gusts in the area have been clocked up to 75 mph! Several telephone poles have fallen down and the power went out all around us. Another driver just reported that the truck stop restaurant closed, locked its doors and sent the employees home.

This is another "not so good day" for all the drivers parked here with us, but we'll all try as usual to make up for lost time tomorrow. Another truck just came in and parked beside us so chances are now we won't get blown over with wind gusts, but if we do, we don't have far to fall! I'm a little bit scared, but I'll get over it. Tonight we'll have to settle for what food we have on board! I guess if there's one good thing to be said, it's that our trailer is packed with heavy cases of beer; making it even harder for the wind to blow us over!

It is February 9th and can you believe this!! We just got out of one wild wind storm and we're right back in it! This time we are in Ontario,

CA. We have had such strong wind gusts, so bad, that it forced Ron and about another 100 trucks to pull off on the shoulder! I'm not kidding! This is for real! The wind is SO STRONG it just "sucked" the skylight out of our truck! It was mounted on the ceiling above our heads! Great! Now we have a "convertible" rig to drive around! Talk about instant air conditioning! We have glass everywhere and it is a wonder Ron, I or the cat didn't get injured! The pressure of the wind was fierce, and with our skylight already previously shattered (why it shattered we don't know, but Ron had put plastic over the skylight and ducked taped around the frame) that it sucked out the entire window! The loud sound scared the cat so bad she hid and now I don't know where she's at. What a mess! Now we have tiny pieces of glass all over the inside of the truck.

Well, here goes another day of creative cooking! No meal in a restaurant tonight! We're staying put and not about to move until the wind calms down. Ron already has the duck tape out and waiting for me to help him cover the opening with plastic. Are we having fun yet? I think every person thinking about driving a truck should be told by recruiters it isn't always a "paid vacation" out here! Sometimes things go wrong! I'm not very happy at the moment. We both need showers, need to do laundry and would really rather be sitting inside a restaurant enjoying a nice dinner. It's not going to happen tonight!

We arrived in southern California only long enough to drop and hook to another trailer. We both feel grubby but have no choice but to keep going. It's times like this when I have to remind myself this is the job we wanted and unexpected problems come with the territory. There is no reason to whine and even if we did it wouldn't change things. Our trailer is loaded with a mix of furniture and carpet. It is not very heavy and now we are wishing we had more weight like the beer for stability against the wind. This load delivers to Helena, MT and we plan to stop in Barstow on our way out of LA to see if we can get the skylight replaced. No telling what this is going to cost us!

Not even a month later and would you believe the skylight blew out again!! I think Diesel is going to stroke out over these sudden earth shaking surprises! Last time we got the window replaced she had to stay in the truck and endure a stranger (mechanic) while he vacuumed up glass and put the new skylight in. Our cat does not do well when her sleep, eat routine is disrupted; especially when an unknown person climbs inside the truck with her! She has been known to tackle someone's leg or arm and bite and we're thankful she decided to hide out the whole time instead. So, here we are today in Helena, Mt getting it fixed once again.

Kim got a job at a hospital in Newport Beach, CA. This is her first management position and she is very excited about it! Her location is not that far from where we "stage" for the next load out of there so we'll be able to see her more.

It is the 15th of April and we have been out on the road now four weeks. We are in Clearfield, UT this morning and after we get unloaded we will head home for a couple days. We have a Santa Clause size bag full of laundry, the inside of the truck needs a good vacuum and the walls are closing in! Face it, people need a little space from each other once in awhile and that includes the two of us. It's pretty amazing though after spending so many days 24/7 confined together inside the truck that we have very few arguments. Sometimes I wonder why we both are not sick more often. Personal hygiene leaves a lot to be desired and we get no exercise except when we fuel, hook to a load/unload, stop at a rest area or walk inside a truck stop for dinner. This job does not offer a healthy lifestyle for anyone!

We sit for hours on end driving down the highway and pulling into a rest stop is far and few between, (we've got a porta potty on board). When you're a "team' you're "expected" to drive hard every day and rack up hundreds of miles before stopping. You feel guilty for simply pulling into a rest stop because by the time you park, walk to the restroom and do a little walk around inspection; it could costs you around 20 minutes of lost driving time. We both think about how many miles further down the road we could have been had we not stopped and kept going.

Ron and I know before we ever start a new day of driving just how many miles we're going to drive and how long it will take to get there. Time is important and any delay along the way could throw you completely off schedule. We get up around 2:30 a.m. and drive until around 8 or 9 in the evening. LONG DAY! I guess it wouldn't be so bad if you did this for a couple days and then got to relax and get a good night's sleep. But, that's not the way long haul trucking works!

On the road again! We are about 30 miles from Burley, ID and right in the middle of one heck of a snow storm! To make matters worse, we're getting strong gusts of wind blowing snow across the interstate (creating drifts) making driving a big rig much more hazardous! At times the blowing snow is so blinding we are unable to see the road in front of us! With each "white out" Ron backs off the accelerator and waits to regain sight of the road again! The next day, (April 22nd), wind, wind, wind and more wind! We are experiencing 65 mph gusts and Ron finally got a belly full! His arms were worn out fighting the wheel trying to keep our truck and trailer on pavement! (We came so close to getting blown over!) I was so relieved when he decided to find a place to park! Believe me, it's just as stressful for me sitting up front and feeling the force of the wind against the cab while witnessing so much debris flying all around us. Dust and gravel alongside the highway is peppering our windshield like bullets. Being right here in the height of a storm is a frightening experience! Weather is one thing we have no control over and there's nothing we can do but endure the relentless pounding wind gusts slamming against the truck and trailer. We are at the mercy of this storm!

We are parked in Idaho Falls, but not after having to take a detour to get here! The sheriff's department shut down I-15 due to downed power lines and rerouted us. As we sit here our truck is rocking from side to side. Lights are flickering inside the truck stop so it's just a matter of time and they will lose all their power. It's amazing for the second time out here we are seeing shingles being ripped right off of roof tops and fly through the air! I'm glad we're sitting inside the truck and out of the wind. There is no telling what you might get hit with if we were outside. I'm not so sure that I could even stand up against the strong gusts; they would probably blow me over! There is nothing for the two of us to do now but stay safe and warm inside the truck and wait until the storm passes. We heard from another driver the wind is supposed to calm down this evening. This is lost time driving so when the wind calms down we will have to pull up the anchor, get back on the road and make up some miles; another long day for the two of us! This is the real picture of what we go through. Not every day is a fun one and sometimes it even gets downright depressing out here but, I've learned to roll with the punches!

It doesn't seem to matter what state we're in, there always seems to be stretches of highway where we encounter periods of strong winds that we have to deal with! I guarantee you; there isn't a trucker out here that enjoys driving through strong wind; especially with a light load and getting hammered on the side with it! One time I remember seeing a truck in Wyoming and the driver had painted on the back of his cab "Piss on the Wind!" I'm not kidding, and it reinforces what I just said; none of us like wind!

It is the 1st of May, we are in Clinton, OK and the temperature outside is a very hot 96 degrees! Yesterday we were in nothing but storms; hail, rain and threat of tornados. More often than not our route usually covers those states most likely to get hit by tornadoes; especially this time of year. We receive tornado alerts over the weather channel on our CB radio and take each warning serious! So far we have been able to stay out of harm's way and dodge the ones reported near our route. I think the locals call this "spring" weather!

May 4th and today is our wedding anniversary. We left Santa Fe Springs, CA this morning and we are on our way to Wisconsin for one drop and then we'll go on to Chicago, IL. Tonight we are parked at a very small Flying-J Truck Stop. This was the last truck stop to park at for the next 230 miles. Not quite the anniversary we expected. There is no restaurant here so we'll just have to be satisfied with snacks and a sandwich for dinner. Oh, well there will be another time to do something special for this day. Hold it! I just spotted a motel and restaurant in walking distance! Yippee! We will have a nice dinner after all!

Today is the 12th of May and I got a phone call from Kim, Kellie and Jason wishing me a Happy Mother's Day. It was sure good to hear from them. We stayed last night in South Dakota and drove none stop to Butte, MT. This is a 1,045 mile day! I took over the wheel at the

POE in Wyoming and drove to Butte. I ended my day by logging in 540 miles. Ron will get us to Missoula, MT and then we'll call it a day! Ron was able to actually sleep for awhile while I was driving and boy does that make a difference. He is not near as worn out like I've seen him so many times in the past. I feel good that I am able to help him out. Tomorrow we will stop for a day in Spokane. Ron's mom wants us to plant a vegetable garden for her. After spending so many days on the road confined inside the cab of our truck it will do us good to get out and get some physical exercise.

On our way to Dalton, GA and the weather is sunny and hot! Yesterday we had to shut the truck down going through Arizona. The temperature was 106 degrees, several hills to climb pulling our heavy load and with that combination it was just too hard on the engine. A very loud buzzing sound (scaring me half to death) came on, and the word **WARNING** lit up on the dash! In a matter of seconds, a second message followed with the word **STOP!** The computer was telling us if we didn't stop and shut the truck down, it would!! Ron immediately pulled the truck over on the shoulder and shut the engine off. We stayed there for about 20 minutes waiting for the engine to cool and then Ron started the truck back up. No warning light came on so we continued to drive. It might be hard to believe but just sitting there for that short period, sweat was pouring off of both of us! I think it was even harder on Diesel with all of her fur.

We were able to baby the truck by keeping the air conditioning off and finish out our day, but what a miserable way to go down the road! All we accomplished by opening vents and windows was a bunch of hot air and I don't mean from my mouth! This is the ugly part; there won't be any showers tonight for us because truck stops on this route are far and few between. We will have to rely on sponge baths and to make matters worse, we will probably have to wait another two or three days before we get a shower! This is truck driving and even though I don't like inconveniences like this one, overall it's still a great life offering independence and freedom. We don't punch a time clock and we don't have a supervisor breathing down our necks!

It seems like we have been out driving the highways forever and today, (June 23rd) we are in Missoula, MT. (This is what to expect when you're running hard as a team!) We have not been home except for one quick over night stay in almost two months. We ran out of clean clothes more than once. We even had to buy underwear and t-shirts a couple times at truck stops. We bring plenty to wear, but when you don't have time to do laundry, eventually you flat run out of clothes. Truck stops only have basic items to offer and most of their shirts are stamped with all this "guy" stuff like wolves, eagles, race cars or printed sarcasm! It makes it hard when you're a woman, at least for me, to find something that doesn't make you look like a walking billboard!

The inside of our truck smells of CAT, dirty laundry, (two big bags full) dirt and road grime! Ron and I even had a few moments where we exchanged some heated words with each other. Fortunately we both quickly got over whatever was bugging us, but this is what happens to people sometimes when you're confined together 24 hours a day, for days on end. When you think about it; at home when you have an argument with a spouse you can go outside, go to another room or take a walk. You can't do that driving down the road, so you verbally have to duke it out and get whatever it is off your chest! I know there are several "teams" out here that would say "Amen!" Eventually the walls close in and the least little thing can set the other one off on a tangent. We will be heading home from Missoula and plan to take a well deserved week off. We, the cat included, are looking forward to climbing down from the truck and planting our feet on the ground!

This morning driving I-70 just west of Green River, UT we saw a rare sighting of a Big Horn Sheep. At first when we spotted the animal from a distance we were not quite sure what it was. As we got closer we realized it was a large mountain sheep with shaggy hair and big curled horns! It was grazing on grass right alongside the road. Ron kept his eye on it as we passed by for fear, like a deer, it might suddenly dart out in front of the truck; but it didn't! Of course there was no way I could take a picture of this marvelous animal because we were moving too fast. Now that we know where to look we'll keep our eyes out for more the next time we drive through here.

We are on our way home after making a run to Baltimore, MD and for the most part, the trip was uneventful; meaning, no bad storms or mechanical problems. A couple times it got a little heated inside the cab once we arrived in Maryland! We were not familiar with this part of the country at all; took the wrong turn and became lost! From the very start we didn't feel good about the directions given to us and sure enough they were wrong! There were moments in the height of our frustration when each of us blurted out sarcastic remarks about the predicament we were in! At the same time, we somehow managed to refrain from blaming the other for ending up off the beaten path! During all the chaos, Ron was busy trying to avoid four wheelers while I was frantically watching for signs directing us back on the interstate!

I even became more upset when Ron suddenly made it my problem to find us a way out! He shouted "look at the dam map!" I can tell you, HIM asking ME to look at a "dam map" under immense pressure doesn't work! It's an exercise in futility! It's like my brain gets put on hold and I can't think straight! At this particular moment we happened to be in heavy traffic, driving over bumps, and Ron was either gassing on it, or hitting his brakes to avoid running over four wheelers! There was no way I could steady a map long enough to read the small printed street names under those conditions! Bull! One time he shouted "Dam 'it! Don't you know north from south?" I shouted back, "NO! Not when you're yelling at me!" Immediately, in my own defense, I thought he was at fault for getting us into this predicament in the first place! After all, he's the one driving and he had plenty of time the night before to study up on his route!

Somehow we get through times like this, but each time Ron vows we'll never come back for a second dose! What we experienced is another situation where I envy "local' residents; they know where they're at and where they're going; we don't! Maybe it would help if people living in these cities would pay attention to what's written on the doors of big trucks. Our door reads; "Spokane, Washington". That should be a *clue* to others, we don't live here, keep a distance; we are a long way from home and might be lost!

The big news to write about in my journal is that we bought a new Freightliner truck about two weeks ago. We love it! Our other truck had over 500,000 miles on it and no depreciation left. (Depreciation of equipment counts when you are self employed.) It did not take long for the two us to unload all of our belongings from the old truck and load everything back in the new one. Now THIS is a truck! Unlike our other one, the Freightliner is far from being plush! No leather seats that heat up for you in cold weather. Nothing too fancy, it's a real truck like you would expect! The nose sticks way out and I was wondering how I was going to handle this new distance once I got behind the wheel. As it turned out, it wasn't that bad; as long as I didn't stare down at the hood and kept my eyes looking forward. It's equipped with two loud air horns! The blast will send you straight up in the air! We have big chrome smoke stacks that glimmer in the sun and at night, the truck lights up like it was part of the Vegas strip! We both agree that this is the last truck we'll ever purchase. Putting it into Ron's words; it's our last Rodeo! When the truck wears out, we will too and hopefully by that time we'll be ready to retire.

Makes me think of a couple we passed out on the road. They were pulling a travel trailer and on the back of it was a sign that read "Someday" Finally Happened!" We ourselves have always said that "someday" when we financially are able to retire, we'll go fishing, raise a garden, get a few laying hens and raise our own beef. I guess we're no different than other drivers out here. We all have dreams and visions to occupy our minds while driving for hours on end through long stretches of desolate highway.

I have not written in the journal for a long time. It is October 14, 2002 and we are in Arizona. Since my last entry we have had a couple events take place. While traveling through our usual route in Nevada our new truck broke down just outside Primm. Smoke was pouring out under the hood and I thought for sure we were going to catch on fire! Ron didn't know what was wrong! Other drivers came on the CB telling us "Hey buddy, you've got a serious problem going on" followed by telling us where they thought the smoke was coming from. I remember thinking "No kidding!" Of course we know we've got a BIG problem going on!

Our situation worsened as the truck started making weird loud noises and began choking and bucking! A few miles later, we finally spotted an exit that that would take us up and over the freeway heading back towards Vegas. We *barley* even made it to Primm before the truck was on its last leg and we knew it! Ron pulled into the casino and was able to park before the truck gave out. At this point, we were dead in the water! The nearest repair shop from our location was in Las Vegas, which was another 40 some miles away! We had no choice but to call a wrecker and have the truck towed to a repair shop!

While waiting for the wrecker to arrive I went into the casino to get us a room. The minute I walked through door and into the lobby I spotted a sign "No Pets Allowed!" Oh great! That's just what I needed to read when we're stranded out in the hot desert! The temperature was in the 90's and now I learn they won't let me bring Diesel inside! How cruel! I made up my mind I was going to convince them otherwise.

By the time I got to the registration counter I had my preplanned speech ready! In fact, I had rehearsed it on how I was going to plead my case on behalf of Diesel! (I had time to do this because I first stopped by the ladies room to clean up a bit and make myself more presentable.) Not every clerk behind the counter is friendly, but lady luck was on my side this time and after all, I'm in a gambling state; once in a while you should expect to win! I was greeted at the registration counter by a young woman wearing a big smile that was larger than the glasses she was wearing! I instantly began to tell her my story and by the time I finished my tale of woe, she was on the verge of tears! (She was a cat lover herself and quickly related to my concern for Diesel's lodging!). (I could tell luck was holding out on my side!) Needless to say, she caved in; weakened, broke "house rules" and gave us a room with permission to bring Diesel inside! What a relief!

Getting a room was only one of the problems we had to deal with. Our trailer was full of freight that was supposed to be delivered in California. When I got back to the truck Ron was on the phone talking with a company employee explaining our problem. (Just because we're broke down doesn't mean we can forget about the freight we're hauling.) Ron hung up the phone and told me they would be sending a driver out to pick up our trailer. While the truck was still barely running, Ron had smarts enough to unhook the trailer and pull away from it! Had he not pulled away, the trailer would have remained locked on the fifth wheel creating another problem for the guy driving the wrecker.

I told Ron I was going to start packing up a suitcase while he stepped outside the truck in an attempt to pin point what went wrong. A few minutes later he returned without coming up with any possible diagnosis for the problem. Although he had his suspicions, he was baffled, upset and said a brand new truck shouldn't have any major mechanical breakdowns like this! Ron is one heck of a good backyard mechanic, but this problem was way over his head! What he did conclude is whatever happened to the engine was going to require major repairs and days of "down time"! He told me not to worry because the truck is still under full warranty, including the cost for the wrecker. By this time I had reached the point of acceptance. We were grounded, the truck would eventually get fixed and we have a room to stay in.

Diesel is a trucking cat and she very well knew something was wrong in her "kick back" routine! As expected, under abnormal circumstances, she was totally uncooperative! Ron had no tolerance for her hissing and spitting! He wanted to carry her in his arms, but because of her attitude and the likelihood of her biting and scratching him, I quickly grabbed the litter box (it has a top on it like a pet travel carrier) and I told Ron to put her in it! Once he had her inside, he turned the litter box opening around so it was against his belly and proceeded to climb down out of the truck. She howled all the way across the parking lot and no doubt was insulted that he put her in her own cat poop! Too bad if she didn't like it! The litter box became an instant cat carrier and we no longer had to worry about her jumping and running! There is nothing but miles and miles of desert surrounding the casino and there was no way we were going to chase a cat through the sand and sage brush; especially her! This is one time that Diesel didn't get her own way! Her minimal stress is nothing compared to what we just went through! I did not feel sorry for her one bit! I know that darn cat so well and I knew once she got inside the room, sniffed around a little, verified the location of her food and water, she would then kick back and enjoy being out of the truck! Diesel would instantly be on vacation, sun glasses, legs crossed, watching TV, enjoying the air conditioning and expecting us to wait on her! That's our cat!

By the way, our room was nothing to write home about, but at least it was clean! We were more relieved that Diesel was now safe inside, right there with us. We've stayed here before, but in the past, we always got a room with a view of the swimming pool surrounded with lush tropical plants. This room however, was located right next to stairs just as you come in the back door! So need I say more! The clerk obviously gave us the room of last resort, the room they couldn't "give away" to a regular customer, the only one they probably use for storage and the "only" one they would allow a cat to be in! This is s situation where you get what you get and be darn glad you got it!

Once we got settled in the room, or I should say Diesel got settled in the room, with food, water and litter box, we went back outside to wait for the wrecker. It didn't take long before it arrived; stopping right in front of our truck. The driver got out and spoke a few words with Ron and then the two of them proceeded to hook the truck up to the wrecker. (I think the guy was glad that Ron offered to help him.) When they finally finished and had it set up for tow, Ron signed off on the paperwork and the driver climbed back inside his truck. Ron stepped back giving him a wave while at the same time keeping his eye on the whole set up watching as the wheels began to turn. The scene itself left us both with disbelief and an absolute gut empty feeling of total helplessness! Not only did we find ourselves officially stranded, but our cozy little home on the road was being taken away from us right before our eyes! All of our personal belongings were stored inside the truck making me feel even more abandoned. We continued standing there like two homeless people until the wrecker disappeared in traffic then slowly turned around and headed back to our room.

We were anxious to learn how long it would take to fix whatever went wrong with the truck and remained inside our room waiting for a call from the repair shop. When the phone finally rang Ron quickly picked it up; it was the call we were waiting for! The mechanic said we "scored a sleeve", (piston and broken ring). This is a major breakdown and he told us it would be a least five days for the repair! The reality of this whole event was that we were absolutely grounded inside a casino, smack in the middle of nowhere! I felt like we were being held in bondage; forced to spend money on food and entertainment in order to maintain our sanity by paying for something to occupy our time. (This survival mode will be expensive and certainly something we didn't budget for!) But, it was either stay in our room and go crazy! We chose to pay the price! We headed down the hall, but this was not until we had gone over our finances. With a mental budget in place, we finally accepted fact we were going to be here for awhile and we might as well relax and enjoy the time off!

Four days later the phone finally rang and we were told the truck was ready. They didn't have anyone they could send out to pick us up so we were left with one more problem; trying to find our own means of transportation into Vegas! The nearest taxi service was out of Vegas and after learning it would cost $200 for them to drive out here, Ron said "No way! We'll hitchhike before we pay that kind of money"! I thought to myself, oh sure, with the cat and our luggage, I doubt it! We discussed what other options we might have at this point; like walking the parking lot and seeing if we could hitch a ride with another trucker headed in that direction. We also knew there was a shuttle bus that runs from here to Vegas. Either one of these rides would bring us into Vegas, but not to the repair shop. Most truckers, unless they have a load to deliver, stay on the interstate and would have only been able to drop us off on the shoulder of the road. The shuttle bus went straight to a downtown casino, so in either case a LONG walk would be ahead of us! We tried to think of what other possibilities we could come up with, but there were none. After further consideration, Ron's pride would not allow him to bother another trucker with our problem. (This is so typical of Ron. He would rather suffer the pain than ask someone else for help!) So our only choice left was to check out the cost of a shuttle. We also agreed it made more sense to bite the bullet, pay for another day in the hotel and leave Diesel in the room.

The fare for the shuttle was a far cry from the cost of taking a taxi! We had to sit and wait for more than two hours, but eventually, the shuttle arrived and we were able to board along with several other motivated tourist! There were only two unhappy people on the shuttle; Ron and me! The others no doubt were vacationing, full of excitement and anticipation of the Las Vegas strip; spending their day shopping, eating and visiting casinos! We of course were on a different mission; to reclaim our truck! Neither of us looked forward to the long walk ahead staring us in the face once we got off the shuttle! I felt a bit jealous as I sat silent by Ron and listened to the loud laughter and the continuous friendly chatter going on amongst all the other passengers. But, I also told myself to be thankful; no more layover, we can get back to doing what we're supposed be doing, and that's earning a living! Our truck is not a recreational vehicle! It's our work horse, it generates revenue and if it breaks down, we don't get fed!

Now wouldn't you know we just solved one problem and then another one comes up! Unbelievable! The shuttle bus blew a tire! We heard a loud bang and saw rubber flying all over the interstate! The driver instantly hit his brakes almost losing control before he was finally able to slow it down enough and come to a safe stop! He immediately got out of his seat, turned around, and with a half scared tone in his voice said, "We blew a tire and I'll call for another shuttle to come and get you." "It will probably be about one and a half hours before another shuttle arrives so you all can get out and stretch if you want." Whoop tee doo, just what we all want to do; spend our time standing alongside the highway in the hot sun! By the way, all these fun loving passengers suddenly became very upset and angry! The breakdown was cutting into their vacation and they didn't like it one bit!

It wasn't long before one passenger lost his patience and started waving down buses in a desperate attempt to get one to stop! The rest of us stood stranded like a herd of lost sheep watching as each bus whizzed by leaving him in a cloud of dust! The man was determined and continued waving his arms and it wasn't long before other passengers joined in. Believe it or not, finally one bus did pull over and stop! The bus driver got out and was quickly greeted by ours. They spoke briefly to each other and then the two men called all of us together. We were quickly informed about the ground rules in situations like this. The new driver offered to take us to Vegas, but not without a price! We were told, as if it was the "Golden Rule" to follow for breakdowns on the road, "That if another bus comes along and offers a ride, all passengers boarding are expected to give the new driver a tip!" There was a lot whining amongst us, but why not? We had already paid for our fare and it was obvious our driver was not about to give us a refund!! The only other option was to wait for the next shuttle and none of us wanted to do that! Everyone was anxious to leave, so with reluctance, each passenger one by one handed the driver money as they stepped on board his bus! Once we were all seated and heading down the highway I could still overhear other passengers complaining to each other about the extra fare and considered it to be "Highway Robbery!"

The new driver was friendly, but then why wouldn't he be, he just put some extra money in his wallet! Anyway, we climbed on board like the others and chose the first seats up front by the door. It wasn't long before Ron struck up a conversation with the bus driver by telling him all the details of our current predicament. Turned out the driver also had a heart! He told Ron "If you're willing to ride along with me while I make the rest of my stops, I can take you to the repair shop and you and your wife won't have to walk." He said after his last stop he would be done for the day and that our repair shop was located right along his return route. Ron didn't hesitate to accept the offer! With another worry off our minds we sat back, relaxed and continued on with what now became a sightseeing tour of downtown Vegas! The driver even pointed out certain casinos along the way where there was free entertainment or special things to see. It actually turned out to be a fun ride!

About an hour later, the bus driver suddenly pulled over and came to an abrupt stop right in front of the repair shop! Now I don't know if Ron was in a generous mood or what, but he reaches in his pocket and gives the bus driver another tip! At this point it really didn't matter to me; I was more thankful we made it to the shop and didn't have to walk! I instantly spotted our bright shinny truck parked in the distance. I was spinning my wheels just waiting to climb inside, fire up the engine and get going! We figure the total cost of this entire breakdown will come to at least $4,000 when we consider lost wages and the money we had to spend these past four days for food, room and entertainment by staying at a casino. Ron went inside and signed the paperwork, got the keys, fired up the truck and headed back towards the casino. I called dispatch and told them the truck was now up and running and we were ready for a load. It was good to hear they already had one waiting for us! All we needed to do was "bob tail" several miles to get it, but who cares; we get paid for doing this! We checked out of the casino, grabbed our luggage along with Diesel, (who again resented being carried in her litter box) and wasted no time in leaving! We were two happy truckers rolling down the interstate, back in business and eager to make some money! The truck purrs like a kitten!

Today we are in Arizona and on our way to Corona, CA with a trailer full of hotel supplies consisting of little bottles of shampoo, soap and hand cream. We're both extremely glad to be back on the west side of the United States! Our last trip out we had no choice but to deliver a load in Boston, Massachusetts! This is another state we've been sent to where we told the dispatcher up front "we don't go there", but the dispatcher insisted we take the load anyway! It seems our lease agreement no longer holds weight and has now become meaningless! Before signing the agreement we were asked by the company "Are there any states you will NOT drive in?" and we told them yes! We named "all" of the upper east coast states and said we wanted to stay out of them, but would haul to any of the others. They assured us there would be NO FORCED DISPATCH and would HONOR our request. Well, they did for a few years, but as time went by and new people came on board and the old ones left; our original agreement basically became worthless under new management. It's not that we didn't speak up and remind the manager, (who became involved when we turned down the trip) that we had a written lease agreement with the company; we did, but under continued pressure we caved in and accepted the load. We were actually told, "If you don't take the load, we'll keep you out of Los Angeles and give the long haul loads to other drivers who *will* go to the east coast!" At this point we really didn't have a choice; it was either *take* the load or *lose* the long haul runs and of course, that's where we make our money!

Pre planning is critical especially when you are going to unknown towns that you've never been to before. It requires studying your route, learning what truck stops are at what exits, where the coops are, checking for rest stops, getting specific directions, listening to weather reports, and then not only communicating with the dispatcher but the customer as well. The customer will give you specific details on what to expect like security check in procedures and location of loading docks, (if they have any) and any other procedures required by them before you can unload. A well planned trip will save hours of stress and that's one word you want to avoid when driving into unfamiliar territory! Your full attention should solely be placed on just getting there safely without having to worry about all the things I just mentioned. Obviously, Ron and I did plan ahead and did all that we could do to make the trip go as smooth for us as possible.

As it turned out, rural New York, Connecticut, and Massachusetts were absolutely beautiful! It was a great time of the year to travel through them. All of the trees were bursting with their autumn leaves like giant bouquets of brilliant red, gold and orange colors decorating the hillsides all around us. I'm glad we were able to see and enjoy nature's magnificent beauty this time of year. This is another one of our "someday" thinking. We both felt it would be nice after we retire to make a return visit in a motor home or a travel trailer where we could actually have the time to enjoy this part of the United States.

We continue to call Ron's mom everyday; once in the morning and again in the evening. She loves the vegetable garden we planted for her and said she is pulling carrots that are 10 to 12 inches long! (She might be exaggerating, I don't know.) She also said she is feeding an orphan fawn. Last time we were there I tried getting close to it by giving it apples. I got the fawn to come within about 8 feet of me before it became cautious and ran a few feet away. What I noticed about this little fawn was that its jaw appeared out of whack. It was very noticeable when the fawn would chew, so maybe that is why the mother abandoned it, or I don't know; maybe the mother got hit out on the road. In any case, it was a real treat to see it so close up. I talk to Kim, Kellie and Jason frequently and they always want to know what state we're in and how much longer we're staying out before heading home. Jason has run two "local" marathon races and took first place in one and second place in another. I don't how many runners signed up for these community sponsored races but it doesn't matter; we are very proud of our son!

It is October 22, 2002 and we are having our first snowfall of the year. We are not looking forward to the heavy load, sliding axels and the drive ahead of us, but we will deal with it as usual.

October came and went and now we are almost through the month of November. We spent Thanksgiving on the road eating amongst strangers at a truck stop. We are both getting tired of not being home for the holidays. From Peru, IN this morning we made it to Sayre, OK which is over 900 miles. Both of us are drained and very tired. We plan to stay out another three weeks and then we will take the rest of December off to spend Christmas at home. We won't see Kim because she is going to Virginia to visit Kellie, Scott, Jake and Sam but we at least will be able to share Christmas with Jason. With only the three of us eating Christmas dinner there will be plenty of leftovers to send Jason home with as well as plenty of turkey to make sandwiches in the truck.

I pulled a muscle lifting when I was putting our "stuffed to the brim" laundry bag back up on the top bunk this morning. The right side of my stomach, just below my ribs is a bit uncomfortable when I move, but I'll get over it. Actually I have no choice; I'm a long way from home so it either goes away or I'll have to live with it. The bag was so jammed full of dirty laundry; I could barely get the draw string tied! We actually have "two" bags smelling up the inside of the truck and I know each of them weigh at least 40 pounds! We have been running our tails off none stop because that's what we're expected to do as a team. We desperately need a little time off to catch up on laundry, have showers, clean the inside of the truck and get out and go for a walk. This is the reality of trucking and right now I feel like a bag lady! Other than that, Ron, myself and Diesel somehow are maintaining our current uncomfortable environment.

January 8, 2003 and as always we document our starting miles on the odometer for the start of a new year. We have 80,720 miles on our truck; starting to show some wear, but we still think "Barney" is beautiful with its metallic plum paint, chrome stacks and long nose! Our first run after Christmas, we picked up a load in Auburn, delivered it to Santa Fe Springs and from there we got a load that had three stops. One partial drop was in St. Louis, MO, another in Indianapolis and then a final drop in Brownstown, MI. Christmas at home was very nice, not only getting to see Jason, but we also managed visits to see my two brothers, Jerry and John.

While we had the time off, Ron got his DOT physical and CDL renewed. He barely passed his physical because his blood pressure reading was higher than normal. We both know it's time to give up the bad habit of smoking, easier said than done, but we are going to try. I chose to flat out quit and so far I'm doing good. Ron has cut down considerably to only one cigarette per hour. I also have a blood pressure problem and giving up our bad habit should help us live longer.

One of the things I do to keep busy and not smoke is take out the yarn and needles! So far I have managed to knit 21 pairs of slippers and 5 stocking caps. I plan to donate them to the House of Mercy, a charity organization that Kellie and Father Jack founded in Virginia to help the poor and homeless. I learned to knit years ago and it feels good to be able to give something to others in need; especially knowing the slippers will warm someone's cold feet and caps will cover their heads protecting them from winter weather. In addition to the hats and slippers, I've also managed to knit eight Afghans and gave most of them to family. I found knitting to be a creative way to keep myself occupied when there's nothing else to do for hours but sit!

CHAPTER 8

FIVE YEARS LATER

February 23, 2007. I did pretty good keeping up my journal and when I had filled every page with notes I didn't go out and buy a new one. That was a big mistake! I guess at the time I must have felt that I had written enough for my kids to give them a very clear picture of what life is like out here for long haul truckers. It never even occurred to me that I myself would one day need to draw upon my journal as a reference in writing my book. Darn! I wish I had stuck with it and not let so much time lapse! Believe me there were many events and situations that I should have documented. Why, after letting this entire time lapse, (because I don't know what prompted me to do it), I went out and bought another journal! But, even after doing that, writing a book was the farthest thing from my mind. Maybe I just felt I needed to continue writing down events as they occurred. I'm glad now that I did!

During this time span we sold our home in Spanaway, bought a fifth wheel trailer and parked it on Ron's mother's property in Spokane. This was only to be a temporary placement until we found some land to purchase that included acreage. Unfortunately, two years went by as we continued to drive truck, come home, look for property, spend a few days helping Ron's mom around her house and then hit the road again. His mother loved having us there, but it wasn't long before she jokingly started calling us her "slaves"! We both resented the title she gave us! She no doubt appreciated our work, but soon came to expect that each time home we would solely dedicate ourselves to the cleanup of her yard, garden and house. She always had a long list of things she wanted done to greet us upon arrival.

Ron and I did work for her from the time we got up until the time we went to bed cleaning inside her house and around the yard. She even got upset if I chose to run a short errand on my own and outright said "You stay here and work. I'll go get whatever you need!" Coming home to our trailer after weeks on the road started to become something we no longer looked forward to. We always ended up exhausted by the time our stay was over and would go down the road complaining about our aches and pains. His mom of course, while sitting on her deck watching us work, would always insist we take occasional breaks and offer lunch, ice tea or a cold drink. I don't think she ever fully understood how tired we were each time we pulled into her driveway after being gone so long. Unless you live the life of a driver, it would be hard for anyone to understand just how worn out you can get driving truck; mentally and physically. In all fairness to her though, there was no way she could possibly relate to how we felt after driving thousands of miles before pulling into her driveway. Besides that, we could have turned down the work she asked us to do, but willing chose to help her out. We always felt good after each visit knowing how much she appreciated all that we had accomplished.

When Ron's mother lost her husband several years ago, he took it upon himself to assume the responsibility of taking care of all the things she couldn't do for herself. He split and stacked wood, mowed the lawn, did repairs on the sprinkler system, replaced her deck, tilled and planted her garden, plus kept up on minor repairs inside and outside the house. Ron has a wonderful sister Kyra in California but living so far away she is only able to pitch in and help her mother when she comes to visit. His mother also has Jean, (her niece) who frequently checks in on her in our absence. Jean even takes her to doctor appointments when needed. Her help is a relief to us and always appreciated. Beyond that, the rest of the responsibility lies upon our shoulders. His mom has come to rely on us now for almost everything and when you drive truck sometimes it gets very frustrating when she calls with a problem and you're not there to solve it. It makes us both feel guilty thinking we should to be home taking care of her.

After two years of spending most of our days off staying in our fifth wheel parked at his mom's house things finally changed! We purchased 10 beautiful acres of land 25 miles north of Spokane. We were thrilled with the property! It was going to be our new home; giving us instant visions and inspiration for development! After that, each time we came home we headed out to our acreage and spent the next several months preparing a home site, (falling trees, clearing brush and building several bon fires to clean up the mess). When the clearing was done we proceeded to have a well drilled, purchased a large manufactured home and later had a shop built. Even with all the work accomplished on the property, we still managed to squeeze in enough time to get a few things done for Ron's mom before leaving.

There is no doubt that I could reflect back on even more *personal* memories, but this pretty much brings you up to date on at least what I consider to be the most significant. However, on the trucking side, there are many other unforgettable moments to recall that happened over the past five years! Each day is a new adventure for us out here driving the interstate and you learn to expect the unexpected! So hang in with me! Your ride is not over yet!!

I remember quite well one event that we're still paying for and although it's about me, I feel it belongs on the trucking side of our life. It all started in Kentucky! While Ron was doing the usual fueling I went into the truck stop, filled two thermos bottles and came out with two whopping cheese burgers along with a couple big bags of fries. I waited until we got back out on the interstate and Ron worked his way through the gears before passing him his hamburger. We both were hungry and didn't waste any time taking our first bite! About 20 minutes later when I had not quite finished eating mine, my stomach began to hurt on the right side. I didn't say anything to Ron but the pain continued to intensify. By the time we were approaching the outskirts of St. Louis, MO I finally decided to tell him about the pain I was experiencing. He said he felt fine adding "You had onions on your burger and I didn't, so maybe it's the onions!" As we drove further, the pain increased and became more severe! I told Ron I was going back to the sleeper and lay down. I was beginning to think maybe I had gotten food poisoning. The pain continued; getting more uncomfortable with each bump in the road! Ron kept turning his head around and asking me "do you feel any better?" and I would answer "Hell No!" I think at this point he finally started to take my complaint a little more serious. He said "When we get to Columbia we'll stop and maybe by then you'll be over whatever is making you sick." The truck stop he was talking about was still about 130 miles ahead of us, but what could he do? The truck needed to keep rolling, I wasn't dead yet, so there wasn't any choice for me but to stay put and endure the ride until we got there! By the time we arrived at the truck stop I began to worry. I told Ron "Trust me! "This is much more than a stomach ache; there's something else a lot more serious going on!" At the time, I remember how irritated I was with him wishing he would take my complaint of pain to a higher level of concern, but then I had to quickly remind myself he couldn't possibly know what I was going through!

While I lay in back on the bunk, in constant pain and agony, Ron proceeded to complete his daily log book along with doing mine as well. By this time the pain was almost unbearable and downright intense! My breathing changed and I was gasping in between the constant sharp, painful, stabbing stomach contractions going on in my abdomen. I was bent in half like a safety pin as I continued taking deep breaths between contractions and trying not to vomit. (When you experience this level of pain, you don't cry and chances are you'll vomit!) Finally I couldn't take it anymore and told Ron I needed to go to an emergency room and if he couldn't get me there; call a taxi! His first reaction was frustration and disbelief that I was asking him to take me to an emergency room. (It obviously had not registered in his brain the level of pain I was going through!) I again told him "this is not food poisoning, it's something else and I definitely have a BIG problem going on!"

Ron left me lying on the bunk and went inside the truck stop. In short time he returned saying "I know how to get to the hospital and they said I could leave the trailer here". Ron proceeded to unhook the trailer, get back behind the wheel and head to the hospital. Emergency entrances are not meant for big rigs and we were promptly greeted by a guard. Ron explained our situation; the guard understood and allowed Ron to escort me in. This was only after Ron's assurance to the guard that he would immediately return and move our truck.

I swear you can be on your last leg and the emergency room staff will still insist that you complete at least five pages of paperwork before receiving treatment! They always ask you on a scale of 1 to 10 how you would rate your pain? I told them "how about 100!!" I was way over the mark and in no mood for number games! Within minutes they had me on a bed getting examined by a doctor. It didn't take long! The doctor said "You are having a gallbladder attack!" and said he was going to admit me. At this point I was very relieved, but at the same time I could see the stress in Ron's face. I felt sorry for him. After a couple strong injections of pain killer, the contractions ceased and my body started to relax giving me much needed relief from the relentless pain I previously endured for hours on end.

I remained in the hospital for almost three days going through more tests than I ever imagined possible! (This is what to expect in a "teaching hospital.) The conclusion was that I needed surgery as soon as possible. I told them I would prefer to go back to Spokane and have it done there so I could recuperate at home. The surgeon respected my wishes and sent me down the road with pain pills, along with a warning that I could possibly have another attack along the way!

During my entire stay in the hospital, Ron was an angel. He apologized over and over for not taking my complaints of pain more seriously. He made phone calls to family and notified the trucking company of our current circumstance; all while I lay confined and helpless inside the hospital. The company we are leased on to was very understanding. They sent another driver out to pick up our loaded trailer and left us with an empty one. I was appreciative for all the care I received from doctors and nurses, but even more thrilled when it came time to leave! I was spinning my wheels to walk out the door, climb back inside our truck, give Diesel a hug and get back to what we're paid to do, haul freight!

We made it home and it wasn't long before I was scheduled for surgery at a local hospital. I was within minutes of going into surgery, when a technician came in and said the EKG reading was abnormal and he called off the surgery! He proceeded to tell us he was also seeking a Cardiac Surgeon's opinion. The surgeon concluded that there was nothing wrong with my heart and explained the blurp in the EKG was absolutely nothing to worry about. BUT, even at that, they continued to monitor my heart overnight *racking* up the dollars! The next day I went to surgery while Ron prepared for the long wait. Hours later they wheeled me out and when I opened my eyes, Ron was right there! I was so happy to see him! The next morning I was ready to go home and made no bones about it! I wanted out of there! I knew we were going to have a bunch of bills to pay to healthcare providers, not just for both hospital stays, but we were also going to get more bills from physicians, pathologist, anesthesiologist, radiologist and whoever else had any hand in my care! Talk about feeling broke!

Although Ron could have gone trucking alone, he chose to stay home and take care of me. It wasn't much more than a week later when I told Ron, "We need to get back out and earn a living!" It took some convincing on my part, but he finally agreed. During my last few days at home I stopped taking pain pills and was pretty sure I would be able to tolerate the not so comfortable lifestyle that goes along with trucking. Sitting around at home worrying constantly about the cost for all the care I received also weighed heavy on my mind. Our insurance coverage was lousy and the thought of all the new medical bills we were about to get bomb barded with overwhelmed me! This was probably my main reason and incentive for wanting to pack up and leave even more! The bills won't pay themselves! We had to start making money! Even when the truck was loaded, Ron still wasn't so sure it was a good idea to leave, but finally gave up because of my persistence.

I did pretty well the first few days and then all HELL broke loose! I was so confident before leaving that I had healed enough, I didn't even consider taking any of the pain medication along with me. I was behaving in the truck like nothing had ever happened. I simply proceeded to pick up where I left off; doing all the things I did before, like lifting heavy suitcases from the top bunk and tossing them back up. WRONG thing to do! The reward for my labor put me into excruciating PAIN! The severity by far was worse than the hell I went through when I had the gall bladder attack! When you experience this high of a level of pain, as I said before, you don't cry! The intensity will either give you the dry heaves or make you vomit! I was having relentless sharp stabbing muscle spasms under my ribs! Anyone observing me would have described my appearance to be like that of a football player; suddenly brought to his knees by an unexpected leg cramp; rolling back and forth in agony on the field in uncontrollable pain! The magnitude of pain I was experiencing remained *constant*! It was like someone was repeatedly sticking a knife in my abdomen; sharp, burning, jab after jab, none stop! A football player gets over it, gets up, and gets back in the game; I couldn't move!

The only meds we had on board were "over the counter" pain medication. I managed to swallow a few pills, but they didn't do any good! I desperately needed something more powerful (like the prescription I left behind) but that of course, was out of the question! We were miles away from home! Ron made an urgent call to Kim asking her advice, (because she specializes in diagnostic medical sonography and knowing her level of expertise, he trusted her judgment.) Kim suggested to Ron that he "up" the dose giving me the maximum amount allowed. Ron also checked in with Kellie a Registered Nurse, and Scott, our son-in-law, who is a practicing physician and they both agreed with Kim; up the dose!

Taking additional pills worked! In short time the sharp pain went away giving me the relief I desperately needed! I began to feel halfway comfortable telling Ron not to worry while assuring him "I would be able to tolerate all the hundreds of miles ahead of us." We left California with no plans of stopping until we delivered our load in Georgia. I was confident my pain was now at a moderate level, enough for me to be able to endure the rough ride. For the most part, I was pretty much out of commission the next few days, spending most of my time moaning and groaning in the back bunk.

After dropping the trailer in Georgia, Ron promptly bob tailed to the nearest "24hr Doc in the Box" (medical clinic). I checked in, and after what seemed to be like an exceptional amount of time to wait, my name was finally called! The doctor, (extremely overweight and a bit untidy in appearance), listened to my complaint then proceeded to check, (verify) my incision before writing out a prescription. (I must admit at the time, it crossed my mind that maybe he was thinking I might be a drug addict using a lame excuse for drugs!) I also thought this obese doctor was somewhat out of line and unprofessional when he started telling me weird stories about other females he's examined! Their problems were totally unrelated to mine and I didn't need to hear them! He gave me the creeps!

With my prescription in hand, I promptly left the exam room and headed out the door. Ron spotted me and immediately started the engine. I climbed in and we headed off to find the nearest pharmacy. By this time, much to my own shocking surprise, it was like a miracle from above, I instantly started feeling good! I told Ron, "I can't believe this"! "Right now I don't feel any pain!" "It's gone!" The only explanation I could think of for this sudden recovery was that maybe by laying down the past few days and not doing anything physical, helped my body heal. So after all that, I didn't need the prescription! However, as a safety measure, we both agreed to get it filled. The previous pain I went through was still way too fresh on my mind and I remained guarded for fear of it returning. Filling the prescription put me at ease knowing it was there for me, on standby, should the need arise. This thought alone gave me a huge relief!

There's nothing worse for truckers hauling freight down the highway when all of a sudden the unexpected happens; an overwhelming discomfort fills their physical being! I've mentioned this before, but the job of driving truck leaves few, if any, immediate options for remedy. When a driver finds himself experiencing unexplainable health related problems, he has no choice but to continue driving, live with whatever is going on inside his body and try to cope with it! Truckers are fully aware of the drawbacks when they hire on with a company. This is one of them! After all drivers are human and once in a while sickness or injury should be expected. Running into health problems out on the road is a chance drivers are willing to take; it goes with the job!

We are in California and parked at a Pilot Truck Stop. It is 4 p.m. and we just got the truck washed. We call this truck stop our staging area before going into Los Angeles. Ron had to get out and do some minor repair on the fuel gage because it stopped working. I'm glad he was able to fix it himself because we save money.

Just when we settled down to relax; log books done, clothes set out for morning and I'm watching television, I happen to look up and notice a "low life" skinny woman approaching our truck! She couldn't see me because I was sitting in back on the bunk. She appeared to be in her middle to late 40's, rough looking and poorly dressed. I continued to watch and sure enough, she did just what I thought she would do! She climbed right up on the driver side of our steps and asked Ron if she could wash his windows? What a ploy! Anyone could see we just came out of a truck wash! The truck was still wet and sparkling clean! When Ron declined, her reply to him was, "Well, is there anything else I can do for YOU?" She really emphasized "YOU"! That did it!! I heard her every word and I thought Ron was being way too nice! I flew from the back, jumped up, called her a bitch and told her to get the hell away from our truck! You should have seen the surprise look on her face when I climbed right over the top of Ron's lap to get to her! She quickly leaped backwards off the steps and looked up at me with a big smile, (displaying several missing teeth), saying "Sorry mamm, I didn't see you in there! I shouted back "Just leave bitch and stay away from us!" Ron was shocked at my behavior, but equally supportive of what I shouted out to her. She was a cheap prostitute willing to sell her body to any stranger, NO doubt in my mind!

I have zero respect or tolerance for women like this who use their physical anatomy for monetary gain, especially when I know there are many social programs available to help them. I'll bet, right here in this community there's a facility offering help for unemployed, displaced women. Apparently the women we encountered found it easier to walk the lot! This isn't our first experience having a prostitute approach Ron and it won't be the last! Some prostitutes like her totally ignore the "No Lot Lizards!" stickers clearly visible on both sides of the door windows! I ran her off, but not far enough. I know she will continue walking the lot, going from truck to truck, until she finds some driver (sucker) willing to take her up on the offer!

February 24, 2007 and both of us got up at 4 a.m. this morning to beat the Los Angeles traffic. We've already made the delivery, dropped our empty trailer and hooked on to another pre loaded trailer that delivers in Georgia. Our new trailer is stuffed like a Thanksgiving turkey! We had one heck of a time trying to slide the axels! I'll bet Ron and I spent a good half hour working on this project! Finally we conceded feeling our final axle adjustment probably did the trick. We drove a few miles to a scale and got weighed. Fortunately we did not have to make any further adjustments; we were D.O.T. legal! We were leaving Dodge! Off to Georgia!

We only thought! Already having one delay this morning, we no sooner merged out on the interstate and we ran into another surprise! Traffic was at a dead stop and backed up as far as we could see! We heard over the CB that a couple four wheelers decided to lock horns! Great! This second delay combined with the first, just burned up about two hours of driving time! Now we're going to have to drive harder than planned, none stop, for the next several hundred miles. (Sixteen hours later and we are in Rio Puerco, NM.) We both have put in a very long day of driving and it is one of those days that we have lost our appetite. Eating dinner is completely out of the question. The work day is not over when we stop. We still have to complete our daily logs and start a new page, plus get clothes set out for morning and do our usual sponge baths. We both are fatigued and all we want to do right now is climb in bed and go to sleep. Unfortunately that brief luxury will only last for a few hours and then back behind the wheel again! It's what all "team" drivers do!

I still need to make my nightly call to Ron's mom. She's getting up there in age and lately she has become pretty argumentative with me, (depending on the subject matter) and when she does this, it hurts my feelings. I know she doesn't realize how some of her comments upset me so I try not to take what she says to heart. I'm afraid as time passes though, caring for her will become more of a challenge. She will be 86 years old in August and it appears more and more evident that as she continues to age, like other seniors, she is beginning to lose her short term memory. Lately she repeats the same stories of her past over and over. I've had it! I'm just too tired to write anymore. I'll call my mother-in-law in the morning.

February 25, 2007 and we have stopped for the night in West Memphis, AR. It was another none stop, pedal to the metal day racking up another 1,000 miles driven between the two of us! Ron slept quite awhile when I was driving and didn't come up front until it was time to listen to a stock car race being broadcast live on radio. Earlier, I drove to our usual rest stop inside Arkansas and Ron drove the rest of the way here. We saw a couple not so nice semi truck accidents along the way and plenty of road kills! These critters flat out just don't have any safety awareness! We saw several turtles, possums, skunks, armadillos and a couple snakes run over, lying dead alongside, or in the middle of the interstate. When you think about it, they commit their own suicide! I wonder why their eye witness buddies don't learn from watching all this and pass the word around to their friends and family to stay off the highway! Other than that, it was a pretty good day of driving. We, not surprising, are quite tired to say the least. There is a nice restaurant here but we don't feel like walking the distance, so I'm heating up hot dogs. We'll slap a slice of bread around them, thrown on some mustard and ketchup and call it dinner! It's not much, but we'll be satisfied, sleep a few hours, fire up the wagon, and head out before daybreak.

It is now February 27th and yesterday we made the delivery as expected on time in Georgia. After dropping the trailer last night we had the luxury of checking into a motel. After having showers, we walked to a nearby steak house restaurant known for their prime rib. The well known restaurant is a short distance from the motel and it did us good to get some exercise. The meal, although expensive, (for our budget) was well worth the price and distance that we had to walk to get there!

It's not always rosy out here and we often carry the extra baggage of stress and worry with us when it comes to family. We are always thinking about our kids, Ron's mother, and our own future as well. Sometimes we wonder how long we can keep up this hard life style of driving truck for a living. Tonight my thoughts are with Kim in California and I'm sitting right here in the cab of the truck sharing her pain. She told me her arm just throbs from scanning patients after a full day's work. We also have Ron's mom on our minds. We think she's not eating right and there isn't anyone there to watch over and make sure that she dose. Like so many other jobs that take you away from home, (such as frequent lengthy business trips), we too eventually get to return home and carry on with our life. The difference with this scenario is that a trucker will spend more years of his life living inside the cab of his truck than he does at home with his family! That's the reality of driving long haul and chances are if you stick with trucking long enough, you're going to lose what friends you have back home. You will no longer enjoy weekend fishing trips, shooting pool at the local pub, back yard Bar B Q's or even the excitement of planning a hunting trip with your buddies. Your world and their five day a week jobs will become unrelated and foreign to you. "Two different worlds" and you ultimately end up having nothing in common. Driving a big rig to earn a living has its rewards, but not without, for most of us, substantial sacrifice!

It is the 28th of February and no way are we going to make any miles today! We are in South Dakota and in the middle of one powerful snow storm! There is a "No Travel" advisory out on the interstate and for good reason! We ourselves barely made it through the blinding snow and wind to get to the truck stop in Mitchell! It's snowing and blowing hard and as a matter of fact, we ourselves are flat out *stuck* in snow right here where we're parked! Ron already told me we're going to have to chain up when it comes time for us to leave. I'll get out and help him like I always do, but I'm not looking forward to it! I'm glad we're safe, but just getting here we passed several four wheelers and 18-wheelers that were not so fortunate! I attribute all these "spin outs" to poor winter driving skills. We passed by several vehicles in the median, too many to count, that had spun out, ended up buried in snow (clear over the hood) leaving them dead in the water (snow) until a wrecker arrived! Then there were other four wheelers that went flying in a different direction! They lost control, slid off the pavement and went several feet plowing through built up snow drifts before finally coming to an abrupt stop! I'm certain none of these people were hurt, but there are a lot of wet pants out there! No doubt they "ALL" will be sitting stuck in the snow for quite some time waiting for help to arrive! This stretch of South Dakota doesn't have enough wreckers to handle all this mess!

This time of year you don't know what type of weather you might run into. We had previously arranged with dispatch to do a drop and hook in Helena, MT (which would keep us rolling) and put us in Los Angeles just in time to get a southeastern load. Now, it's not going to happen from all the "down" time, BUT, that's trucking! This delay has thrown our schedule completely off and by the time we do get to LA, we'll either have to take a west coast run or sit a few days waiting for a load that gives us more miles. The CB radio is jammed with truckers wanting to buy chains; the truck stop is sold out! Like us, many trucks coming in are getting stuck just trying to park. This is one heck of a snow storm! It is only 11 a.m. and it's supposed to continue snowing throughout the day and into the evening. No telling how many inches of snow we will wake up to in the morning! It's times like this when I envy all those people sitting inside their cozy homes, watching the snow fall, feet propped up, while enjoying the comfort of a warm fire! Snow is not causing them any stress or misery; they just relax and appreciate the beauty of winter! We on the other hand, will sit here in the parking lot, confined inside the cab, and keep the truck running all night just to stay warm. I suppose I should be happy that at least we have a couple movies in the truck that we haven't seen yet. This is the life we live out here and regardless of my whining, we'll survive the storm!

It continued to snow throughout the night and this morning we are surrounded by 18 wheelers stuck in snow, spinning their wheels, rocking their trucks back and forth just trying to get out from where they are parked. I'm watching other drivers worse off, that had to get out of their truck in this cold miserable weather and fight the problem, (self inflicted), of trying to get their frozen trailer brakes to release! (Professional drivers know you don't set your trailer brakes in freezing winter weather, because chances are they're going to freeze up on you!))

We are not yet ready to leave and it's nice to see they have three pickup trucks with blades already pushing snow into big piles clearing up the parking lot for all of us. I also see "old faithful"; (the farmer with a giant tractor who seems to show up each time there's a big snow storm) always offering his help to any trucker that is stuck! What a nice guy! Ron said, "He isn't that nice Billie"! He's making a killing off of all the drivers"! "Did you think he was pulling them all out for free?" Well, it was a nice thought! In another hour we will have no choice but to head out along with the other truckers and deal with the elements of winter driving. I'm not looking forward to it! I don't know how far we'll get because we still have blowing and drifting snow with 35 mph wind gusts! The interstate is ice covered which makes driving a big rig that much more dangerous. I'm glad Ron is behind the wheel and not me!

Gradually we did work our way down the highway and got out of that miserable snowy blizzard, but not until we had driven 60 stressful miles over compact snow and ice! After that, the sky cleared up and the highway remained pretty good, at least until we got about 13 miles outside of Billings! The wind picked up, snow started coming down hard, and we found ourselves right back in another blinding storm! All hell broke loose! Once again Ron was faced with trying to keep the truck and trailer on the road, griping the wheel while cautiously steering his way through the relentless heavy, blowing, and drifting snow! The snow falling down at times created "solid white outs" blinding his vision! This is when driving gets rough and dangerous making it almost *impossible* to drive!

Just as Ron broke over the top of the mountain and started down the steep grade into Billings; we were shocked to see so many four wheelers that had slide off the icy road and were buried deep in snow! Worse than that, we quickly caught up with another big rig ahead of us. He was "hitting" his brakes trying to avoid running right over the top of a scared to death four wheeler! The frightened driver, overly cautious, was taking it very slow heading down the hill. Ron reacted instantly by gently applying pressure to the brake, but even with that cautious move, under icy road conditions, it put us and our 18 wheeler into an "out of control slide"!

Our trailer started to swing around and jackknife sideways on us! (At this point the trailer could have slammed into the side of the tractor or possibly break loose from the fifth wheel, and in either case, the results would have been ugly!) Ron looked over at me, raised his voice and shouted "Here we go"! I instantly thought we were about to die as the tractor and trailer slid helplessly towards the edge of the embankment! My mind flashed a vision of us flying off the cliff, up in the air, the truck bouncing off of hard rock, rolling it over and over, with pieces of metal flying everywhere, until it would finally come to an abrupt stop upside down in the canyon below! My life passed before my eyes! As quick as this thought flashed through my mind, Ron had the truck and trailer back under control! I thanked God over and over for saving us from this near life threatening experience!

During this wild ride, when all hell broke loose, our emergency air brake warning light came on triggering off an unbelievable steady LOUD buzzing alarm! The relentless sound made me even more frightened! Ron assured me the annoying buzzing sound would stop once the air pressure built back up and there was nothing for me to worry about. I had my doubts, but eventually the buzzing sound stopped and the warning light went off. Ron said later when we started sliding he almost did take a "dive" over the bank in order to avoid hitting, possibly injuring or killing someone else! I'm so glad that he didn't! In all the six and a half years I've been out here with him, this is the closest we have ever come to having a serious, if not deadly accident killing us both and I hope it never happens again! The trucker in front of us got on the CB and said "Sorry, there was nothing I could do"! "I had that four wheeler right in front of me!" Ron agreed and told him not to worry; he understood and knew what he was up against. Ron told him "My wife is a bit shaken, but other than that, we're fine."

It's not as if we don't have enough stress in our lives, we also have the ongoing concerns of looking after Ron's mom; today is no exception! She has called us twice already. It seems to be getting a bit more frequent where she is messing around with things inside the house that should left alone; like the thermostat! Today she told me she was pushing the buttons on the panel of her security alarm system because it was making a funny noise. Anytime she has a problem (mostly self created), she calls us! I don't know what she thinks we can do when we are not physically there. It upsets Ron and he becomes very frustrated when she presents a problem to him over the phone. She considers her son to be a "Jack of all trades" always thinking he will have the answer to her problem and immediately be able to tell her how to fix it! Tonight she seemed satisfied when I told her to leave the buttons on the panel alone and tomorrow she needs to call the security company to come out and check her system. I don't have a clue what prompted her to randomly start pushing buttons, but when I asked, she said defensively "I pushed *every* number on the box, now it's stuck on "9" and it's making a sound that *annoys* me!" I finally told her to go to bed, there's nothing she can do about the problem tonight.

It is now 6 p.m., our day is over, and I'm only wishing we were ending it in a better location. We are parked with a loaded trailer bumped up against a company loading dock. The next several hours will be "restless" sleep for both of us. Sometime during the night we will be awakened when they fire up the forklift and begin to unload 26 heavy rolls of carpet. We both know that no matter how hard we try to sleep, the loud noise, the bouncing and bumping from the forklift entering the trailer and removing these rolls will keep us awake. This is the life of a trucker out here and it makes you appreciate the times when you're at home. I lie down, close my eyes and find peacefulness by thinking about our 10 acres we left behind at home. How quiet it is with only an occasional sound from a not so far away Hoot Owl or a sudden howling of coyotes passing through. It brings serenity, closing the door and shutting out the never ending sounds of the rest of the world around us.

Yesterday, not too far from Drummond, MT, we spotted a bunch of Big Horn Sheep grazing alongside the interstate. I would say there were at least 12 to 15 of them bunched all together. The rams had huge curled horns and believe me; I wouldn't want to get rear ended by one of them! It's not very often you get to see rams because they usually stay higher up in the mountains. We also saw two Bald Eagles pecking on a dead deer. By the way, Ron's mom called and whatever was wrong with her security system, it's now fixed! She's happy as a clam and so are we!

Kim has been calling keeping me posted on the problem she's having with her arm. I know she's been working way too hard and it breaks my heart knowing she is going through so much pain. I wish as her mother, I could be there to comfort her and wipe away her tears, like I did when she was a little girl. I feel her pain, just like I always did when any of my kids were unhappy. Out here on the interstate my hands are tied. All I am able to do is offer my love and reassurance that her arm will get better in time if she would only reduce the amount of scans she does every day.

Jason has been dating for quite some time now a very nice girl named Bethany. He met her at work and told us they are planning on getting married in the fall. Ron and I are very happy for two of them and looking forward to having Bethany as our third daughter!

March 14, 2007 and we were home for four days! Ron managed to "hand dig" several holes and put in 17 fence posts, (which is only a start) in getting our entire 10 acres fenced. Ron's project is only one example of what a truck driver might be doing with minimum time off at home. Others drivers, amongst other things, come home and either work on a personal project or do maintenance and repairs around the house. Ron has a long way to go on the fence, but it's something he looks forward to each time we return. We have all sorts of wildlife on the property and the deer have become a real problem! They are conveniently helping themselves to my plants, eating the foliage down to the ground! Ron said our only solution is to buy deer fence and put it up all around the house. This time home we stayed put all four days. We decided not to do our usual routine of making the 60 mile round trip to see his mother. I let her know about Ron's project and she totally understood.

Back on the road and on our way to southern California with a heavy load of paper. We have stopped for the night in Jean, NV which is only a short distance from the California boarder. I drove part of Utah and into Arizona earlier today which gave me a work out shifting gears. On this route, (I counted) there are five long, steep grades to pull and then come down. Going up or down a hill requires the right gear and depending on the volume of traffic, you might end up making several shifts. I could complain about my right arm from shifting or my left leg from using the clutch, but I'm not. I enjoyed the drive!

Once in a while you see something crazy out here and earlier today was no exception! Right smack in the middle of nowhere Ron and I saw in the distance some guy moving forward at a rapid pace on the edge of the interstate, swinging his arms back and forth in a wild motion! After catching up with him we quickly realized, he was on roller skates and skating his legs off! We couldn't believe our eyes! The nearest town was at least 30 miles away and its 94 degrees out here! He only had on a pair of shorts, no helmet and I didn't see him carrying any water! What was he thinking? You're out here with cactus and sand you dumb bunny, it's all around you! I can't imagine anyone with brains who would do something like this. He was setting himself up for a heat stroke! We whizzed by this determined young man and only hoped he made it to wherever he was going. As long as I'm on this subject of what we've seen in our travels, I'll tell you about a couple other incidents that come to mind.

One day driving through the Texas Pan Handle we spotted a young man with long brown hair. He was dressed in a white robe; walking slowly alongside the interstate and dragging a large wooden *cross* which he had propped up over his shoulder. The message he was sending to passersby's was unmistakably clear! There was another time going through the Arizona desert I spotted a thin young man laying face down in the sand; barefoot, no shirt, only wearing army camouflage pants and not moving. The temperature was 102 degrees! I suggested to Ron that we should stop and walk back to check on him. Ron was not keen on the idea, especially knowing that the guy could possibly be spaced out on drugs! Ron said "you don't know what he might do if you tried to help him." (That was a scary thought left to my imagination and I quickly agreed!) He said, "If we spotted him, no doubt other people would do the same." "Eventually someone will stop and see if he's dead or alive." I know Ron was right, but I will always wonder how it all turned out.

Then there was the time in California when we passed by two young men hitch hiking near Mt. Shasta along the I-5 interstate. Boy, were they hilarious to watch! Both of them were dressed up in women's clothing, laughing and bouncing around deliberately trying to catch the eye of every driver on the highway! One in particular, wore a bright pink flowery printed dress and topped it off by wearing a fluffy blond wig full of dangling curls along with "bright red" high heels on his feet! I laughed when I noticed the hard time he was having managing his balance! Nice try I thought to myself; his hairy legs stood out like a sore thumb! I don't know if they really were looking to hitch a ride or not. If nothing else, it was very evident that both guys were having the greatest time of their life laughing and hamming it up for each passing motorist!

The guy in the bright pink dress kept lifting his hemline above the knee waving it back and forth, all while holding his arm out, thumb in the air, trying to catch a ride! This could only happen in California!

Diesel is sitting up on the edge of the window frame swishing her tail and enjoying her usual; watching other truckers as they drive in and out of the lot. You would think the noise from the trucks would frighten her but it doesn't. If I could speak for her right now, she is crossing her paws and wishing for another trucker to park right beside us with a dog! She LOVES to torment a new found barking neighbor! The more excited a dog gets, the longer she stays put; amused, swishing her tail back and forth and while all the time keeping her eyes focused straight on the dog (who is so willing to provide her with the entertainment she's been looking for)! This will go on for several minutes before she finally becomes bored and jumps down from the window. Just when the dog thinks he put her on the run, thus winning the window fight with her; Diesel returns! I won't speak for the dog at this point because I know what its thinking!

It is the 18th of March. This morning I spent my time going through five rolls of nickels looking for old coins to add to my collection. Out of all those rolls, I only found one keeper! However, it was well worth my time and trouble as it turned out to be a 1929 Indian Head! Unless we're on the push, Ron will usually offer to stop briefly while driving through Nevada; just long enough for me to me run into a casino, buy my nickels and jump back in the truck. Today it paid off! Currently we are sitting at the "truck wash" in Barstow, CA waiting for the crew to do their final polish job on the wheels. When we're done, we will continue on into Santa Fe Springs and park for the rest of the day. Kim called and said she will drive out to see us. We are very excited to see her. (Later that evening), Kim showed up right on time and stayed for almost three hours visiting with us. We all talked none stop catching up on each other's lives. I wish I could say the same for Diesel! The darn cat hissed at Kim the minute she entered the truck then hid until she left! Kim's family you dumb cat; she's not an intruder and she's certainly not a stranger so cool your jets next time she comes to visit!

Today is Sunday and here we sit "dead in the water" at a Petro Truck Stop in Oklahoma City, OK. The mechanic won't show up until midnight so in the meantime we're having the shop employee do the PM (preventive maintenance). At least that will be one thing out of the way that we won't have to wait for. The clutch plate broke off that goes to the clutch fan. It was making a horrible loud clunking sound like metal banging together. Ron had a pretty good hunch of what was going on and knew if he continued to drive, there was a good chance the engine computer would take over and shut us down. Driving further was no longer an option! We were not about to take the risk, especially knowing if the truck broke down, we would have to hire a wrecker. Believe me; wreckers are not cheap when it comes to towing big rigs! Ron did a whole bunch of cussing and swearing, (which is his usual reaction) and I've learned to expect him to do this when something mechanical goes wrong. Like always, I ignore the heated words; he gets over it!

No driver likes to call and inform dispatch that the load they are hauling will be late; even if it's a legitimate excuse! We have five drops on this trailer that are scheduled to deliver in Georgia on Monday and now of course, that's not about to happen! We continue to be parked inside the shop (along with other trucks getting serviced) and we still have another 8 hours before the mechanic is supposed to show up!

It's hard for either of us to keep ourselves occupied being confined hours on end sitting inside the cab of our truck. Fortunately Ron found a station broadcasting a stock car race that will at least keep his attention for a couple hours. I found something to do for awhile myself by writing a few post cards then walking across the parking lot to mail them. Diesel is not very happy either because she hates shops! I could get out and walk around the parking lot; it would be good exercise, but I won't. I don't feel like getting stared at by other drivers sitting in their trucks! So this is one of those times we just have to SIT it out! What a grueling experience we're going through! It's now 7:15 p.m. and we're still parked inside the shop! Where's the mechanic? Finally we gave up hope and accepted the fact our overnight lodging, without amenities, would be spent sleeping parked inside a greasy repair shop!

There was no way telling how long it would take to get the truck repaired once the mechanic showed up. To make matters worse; a truck pulled into the bay area next to us with a load of PIGS! Now I feel like I'm sharing the barnyard with them! I love these little "oinkers" but give me a break; I don't want to be imprisoned with them! Their presence has filled the shop with an unbearable aroma and it's enough to make you gag! It smells horrible and there's NO getting away from it! To make matters worse, the pigs don't like it either! They all stayed quiet for a few minutes, then all of a sudden, the whole bunch let loose with a chorus of high pitched LOUD ear piercing squeals!! Even worse, they started making one hell of a lot of noise by banging their bodies against the metal sides of the trailer! They sounded like a herd of wild charging elephants with their sudden sharp screams sending Diesel up in the air and flying off the dash! It's going to be a VERY long night for us! This is not a paid "vacation" like we were told it would be driving truck for a living! We're paying dearly for this day off in more ways than one; sharing it stuck inside a building with a loaded trailer full of unhappy pigs!

Because of all the hours of "down time" for repairs, Ron wanted to get a jump on making some miles. He had the truck fired up and running; wheels rolling, before it was even daylight! I remained in the sleeper knowing it was going to be a long day of hard driving and eventually, I would have my turn behind the wheel. In a very short time (because you get to know the sounds and movement of the truck) that I could tell Ron was having a problem! I'm sure he thought I was still asleep and I could have faked it, but I didn't. I knew he desperately needed my help! Somehow he missed the sign pulling out of the truck stop which would have directed him back on to the interstate. It was an unfortunate mistake, instantly putting him and our 18 wheeler into unfamiliar territory! (A move like this could be a trucker's worst nightmare!) I promptly threw on some clothes and came up front. Ron was very upset and said the directional signs were all screwed up with all the construction going on. When you're up against a problem like this, it really helps having two people up front watching for a way back to the interstate. It wasn't long and between the two of us we found a ramp leading back to I-40 and what a relief for both of us! By the way, the cost to repair the truck was $1,400 and needless to say it took all the profit out of this run!

The next load dispatched to us was out of a small town in Georgia, but was told it would not be ready until the following day. With time on hand, we did the usual and checked into the local motel. It's amazing what so many people take for granted becomes a real luxury to a trucker! The thought of having hot showers, nice dinner and a real bed to sleep in was priceless! The motel is the same one we always stay at and pets are allowed. I knew Diesel, after checking out her quarters, would enjoy watching a little TV, enjoy having more space, kick back with all four legs stretched out, and then fall asleep basking in the comfort of an air conditioned room! Our stay was all that we expected, at least up until we started eating dinner! Ron complained of feeling a bit nauseated and said we better head back to the motel. His condition progressively got worse and was up half the night vomiting. (Come to think of it, he conveniently gets sick in a motel room and when I get sick, it's out on the road!) Nevertheless, I did feel bad for him. He was still feeling quite miserable the following morning and there was no way physically, he could even consider getting back behind the wheel. He was *really* sick! I called dispatch and explained our situation. The next day he rallied around, woke up feeling good and was ready to go! We quickly gathered up our luggage, (along with Diesel), picked up our paperwork, hooked to the trailer, fueled at the truck stop and then it was all "Hammer Down" headed west!

March 29th we are back home and wouldn't you know, luck of the draw, I came down with the flu! No doubt it was the same flu that Ron had gone through back in Georgia. While I stayed in the house trying to get over the bug, Ron was outside enjoying a sunny day putting up deer fence. All I could do was stay in bed and make frequent trips to barf in the toilet! Not fun! Regardless of my condition, I was very glad to see the deer fence go up. Now I can plant anything without fear of the deer eating it!

I recovered like he did and once again we hit the road with a load to California. After delivery, we were on our way back to the driver's yard when Ron noticed a problem with one of the gages. He told me "the generator is going out"! Of course, I'm instantly stressed out by him telling me this! Los Angeles traffic is a mad house, so I just I kept praying we would make it back to the driver's yard. My prayers were answered and to our surprise the shop even had the generator we needed in stock! While waiting for the repair we used the time to wash windows, mirrors and clean the inside of the truck.

We've run into unexpected problems before while driving through LA traffic, but there's also one other event that took place that sticks out in my mind; I won't forget it! Ron was driving in the center lane, (again LA traffic) traveling about 50 mph. which at the time, happened to be during rush hour. All of a sudden, right before our eyes, several "four wheelers" ahead of us starting making wild frantic lane changes like someone poked them in the rear with a cattle prod! Cars and pickups were darting every which way! Why? There was a big 15' aluminum painter's ladder sliding out of control directly in front of us! Ron tried to avoid hitting the ladder, but without success! Within seconds he had no choice but to plow right over the top of it! An 18 wheeler cannot make lane changes as quick or as fast as a four wheeler! Impossible! This unexpected obstacle obstructing traffic proves it!

Instantly, upon impact, we heard a loud ear piercing screeching sound of metal on the pavement from the ladder now locked underneath us, being dragged down the highway, getting crunched and recycle! Sparks were flying! Ron slowed down, but at the time, that's all he was able to do! He was still blocked on all sides of the truck and trailer with fast moving traffic, preventing him from pulling over. It took about another mile of dragging the mangled ladder (which continued to draw attention of other motorists by the loud noise and sending out a constant spray of sparks), before he was finally able to pull over on the shoulder and stop! We both got out hoping not to find any damage done our truck. It took Ron more than a few minutes to untangle the mess, but eventually he cleared the debris; tossing it further off the shoulder, climbed back in and we were back on our way! We also had a similar experience when a pickup truck in Tennessee lost its tailgate and came sliding down the highway headed straight for us! In this particular case however, Ron dodged the bullet!

It's the 1st of April and after staying last night in Kingman, AZ we are now ending our day at a truck stop in Sayre, OK. Smooth sailing all day long! I had a great phone call from Kellie earlier. She has been very busy working on her and Father Jack's dream of creating a House of Mercy, a place to serve the poor in Virginia. This will be quite an accomplishment by the two of them when completed. Kellie becomes tenacious when she sets her mind set on something that she believes in! She puts her heart and soul in it. (Actually, all three of my kids are this way!) She and Father Jack make a good team, seem to work well together, and no doubt their visions of helping the less fortunate will become reality.

Tonight we're staging outside Nashville, TN for an early morning delivery. It's been another good day of smooth sailing! When we drove through Arkansas, I spotted several baby turtles, possibly enjoying their first field trip! Their tiny necks were stretched out, moving their little legs as fast as they could, trying to keep up with their mother! Some of the babies I swear were only 3" long! (The chance of be able to eye witness such adorable creatures, I consider to be one of the great benefits of driving truck cross country! How else would I have ever been able to get to see them in their natural environment?) I also saw a few Armadillos, but in most cases, the ones that I saw were run over, flattened out, and would have made good Frisbees! (They have too much faith in their coat of armor!) Ron and I had a brief argument over what to listen to on the radio earlier today; he won! I know it may sound petty for two adults to argue over what station to listen to, but we do! It's not surprising when you consider the amount of hours we spend together out here tucked inside the cab, sitting side by side for hours on end! We're four feet apart! It's a wonder we haven't had more arguments!

We both dragged ourselves out of the bunk at 2 a.m. this morning in order to beat the Nashville traffic. The load we had to deliver was located at a small distribution center located on a not so desirable city side street on the outskirts of town. We already knew it was going to be tough for Ron to maneuver the trailer into such a small unloading area. (I don't know why dispatchers send drivers pulling 53' trailers into places they have no business ever being in, but they do!) We arrived at our destination around 3:30 a.m., way ahead of schedule. Ron pulled off the street and parked our 18 wheeler alongside the front of their building. He shut the engine off and we instantly found ourselves silently alone, isolated in the quiet stillness of night, giving me a very eerie uneasy feeling! Stone cold silence! I turned more uncomfortable when Ron proceeded to turn the darn headlights off! The dark blackness of the sky was going to stay with us, blinding our vision for at least another couple hours. (A full moon would have come in handy under these circumstances!) In the meantime, we had to stay put with both doors locked, barely parked off the street, and wait until someone arrived to unload us.

I've already figured out we're in a BAD part of town and wasted no time in letting Ron know about my feelings!! We don't carry guns and you can forget any help from the cat! Our only protection is keeping our doors locked and grabbing a hammer under the seat, should we have the dreaded misfortune of encountering someone trying to harm us! The city has a few dim street lamps spaced too far apart in my opinion, shinning down out here providing minimal lighting to the street and sidewalk. We also can see Nashville lit up like the aurora lights out our front window, but neither one of these enhancements help us to see any better! Outlines of other buildings are in view, sending out haunting shadows filtered with other indescribable unknown objects in front of us, leaving a lot to ones imagination, especially mine! I'll be glad to be able to identify whatever all these darkened shapes are when it finally becomes daylight!

Within minutes after arriving, we quickly noticed a police officer whip in and park his car sideways; blocking off a side street only a short distance away. The bright flashing light bar on top of his car came on, illuminating up the entire area; making it even more visible for us to see what was going on! It quickly became apparent that earlier someone driving erratically, most likely a drunk driver, lost control and slammed into the big power pole. The pole was leaning way over, almost touching the ground being supported only by the wires attached to it. Whoever caused the problem, obviously upon impact, woke up, panicked, and took off leaving the scene! The officer stayed there until the power company arrived. We were both glad for the extra activity created by police response, but unfortunately, the police officers presence didn't last long enough. We watched as he drove away, disappearing into the darkness. We continued to watch the crew as they worked to restore the pole back to its upright position. It didn't take them long before repairs were completed and then they too left the scene, leaving us once again silently alone in the darkness!

After all this activity, it was only minutes later when we both observed two suspicious males walking slowly up the sidewalk. They were on the other side of the street and I was certain they saw us sitting there! I could not help but feel uneasy. MY heart started pounding when they got closer, suddenly crossing the street and continuing to head in our direction! Are they going to rob us or even worse, kill us? My mind was running wild with the anticipation of not knowing their intentions and left me with a huge lump in my throat! I held my breath! The shocking reality of our situation was that we were isolated, at their mercy, without a weapon to defend ourselves! I couldn't help but think these two males walking the streets in the wee hours of early morning darkness were up to something! They could easily have a gun, shoot the two of us, take our wallets, and run off! I even imagined us laying there dead until some employee showed up for work in the morning and discovered our bodies!

Within seconds the two shady characters were right at Ron's door! Ron buzzed his window down enough where he could hear what they had to say. As it turned out, they wanted money and cigarettes. He gave them each a cigarette, but told both men he didn't carry any cash; it was against company policy. Fortunately, they bought into Ron's story, took their cigarette and left!

As time went on I was amazed of how many other homeless people we observed walking the streets. It was like they were coming out of the woodwork, aimlessly walking the streets with what looked like, no particular destination in mind! We sat and watched another man in the near distance dig through a garbage can and eat something he had found. As we continued to watch, we spotted a man walk up to a building, turn on the outside faucet, bend down and drink the running water. We even observed a thin woman slowly walking alone in the dark, crossing from one side of the street to the other. Each time she reached the other side, she would pause, stand there for a minute, and then turn around and head back in the same direction she came from! I couldn't figure out what she was up to and it drove me nuts watching her! I was relieved when she (like the other homeless souls we observed) eventually went on and disappeared into the darkness. It's almost daylight now so at any moment we should be seeing an employee show up for work; pull in, park, get out of his vehicle and get us unloaded.

Unbelievable! Ron just got hit up again by another street walker! He told Ron "They just let me out of jail brother, dropped me off on the street only an hour ago." "I'm broke and I really need some money!" "Can you spare a couple bucks?" Ron politely refused telling him we don't carry any cash. The man replied, "Then can you at least give me a cigarette?" Ron gave him one and he quickly asked Ron for a light. Fortunately, after bumming the cigarette he apparently was satisfied and decided to leave. He thanked Ron as he climbed off from the step of our truck. Ron handed him another one for the road. He put the cigarette in his pocket, thanked Ron again and headed down the sidewalk! It continues to be a very uncomfortable, almost nauseating feeling being isolated out here in what seems to be a bad area. We both remain guarded and still a bit on edge, but it's almost daylight now and it won't be long before someone arrives to unload us.

Well we survived the rough side of town and are back on the road, but now we've run into a huge slow moving backup of traffic! Truckers ahead of us are reporting over the CB that the interstate is closed after the next exit due to an accident. Apparently a big rig, loaded with Hazmat materials, overturned his truck and trailer blocking all lanes. Another driver closer to the scene reports that Troopers are directing everyone off the interstate! Great! We are being forced to take an unplanned detour without the advantage of pre set directional signs guiding us off and on the freeway! This means it's up to us finding our own way back around this mess; driving on side streets until we finally spot a sign directing us back to the interstate. Oh joy! We've had enough stress for the past several hours; now this!

Here it is Friday the 13th and we've already delivered a load to Georgia, drove back across the United States, made it home for a couple days and now we are in California. When you drive truck you can expect a life like this; never being in one place too long! Yesterday outside Las Vegas we witnessed a shocking accident right before our eyes! At the speed we were traveling, we were only seconds away; destined to become part of it! Ron instantly hit his brakes as hard as he could while maintaining complete control of the truck thus preventing a possible "jackknife"! The accident was caused by a fast moving yellow Jeep traveling in the opposite direction suddenly bursting out across the median! It plowed straight into the driver's side door of the car in front of us, sending it rolling over and over down the interstate! I screamed "Oh my God!!" as I witnessed the Jeep fly high up in the air upon impact, do a complete somersault and then come crashing down landing right side up! Still out of control, the jeep whipped back and forth throwing up billows of dirt and gravel until it finally came to a stop! As the clouds of dust and dirt began to settle, we observed a young man and woman (obviously unhurt), jump out of the jeep and run over to the demolished vehicle in front of us! I could see an older woman in the driver's seat, not moving with her head down on the steering wheel. No doubt she had very serious injuries or worse yet, maybe she was dead! I could not help but instantly say a prayer for her or anyone else who might possibly be inside the car with her.

Ron got on the phone and called 911 to report the accident. Other motorists that had witnessed the same got out of their vehicle and ran to the aid of the woman who visibly remained trapped inside her car! Within a matter of a few short minutes police arrived at the scene. By this time it was obvious the woman was still alive, but it was also very clear the lower half of her body was entangled in the wreckage. It would take the "jaws of life" to get her out of there! I don't know to this day if the woman survived or not. We remained parked until finally a police officer motioned us to edge our truck and trailer around the accident.

The collision caused a huge back up as far as the eye could see! Trucks and four wheelers were stuck in grid lock for miles and miles behind us. I knew it would be some time before traffic would return to normal. Usually when you come upon a bad accident like this one, traffic is stopped; not only to allow room for the ambulance crew to come in and treat victims, but for all the other emergency response vehicles as well. Las Vegas traffic is always heavy! I'm sure that's why we were a bit surprised when an officer waved us on. I'm sure he wanted to clear out as much traffic as possible before emergency vehicles arrived blocking the interstate.

April 14, 2007 and we are finally stopped for the night! We'll enjoy 5 hours sleep, get up, fill a thermos, and get back out on the interstate. We cannot use the little time we have to enjoy a hot meal; we're tired and sleep trumps food! We started our day of driving before the sun even came up this morning and continued to drive several more miles after the sun went down! When you get this drained, you learn to appreciate finding a place to park and consider it to be your reward for a hard day of driving!

Diesel has been bugging me for the last several hours. When it gets dark, she thinks it's time to shut down the truck and pay attention to her. She has been on and off my lap walking across my log book, I don't know how many times. Every night I give her cat treats and I know that's what she's looking for! She finally won! I put the log book down and gave her treats; she's satisfied, and now she's up on the top bunk lying down. Her routine is so predictable; she will lay there until we get in bed and then come down and curl up next to Ron's chest with the three of us cramped all together!

What a day yesterday!! I had some stupid woman nearly run me off the road in Arkansas! She was a perfect example of having a "tunnel vision" mentality! I couldn't even have guessed where her mind may have been at the time, but it certainly wasn't on driving! I observed her in my mirror slowly coming up alongside me, taking her own sweet time to pass. As she continued to drive side by side with me, her car started creeping across the center line drifting into the side of my truck! I slowed down to allow her car to move ahead, but instead, she stayed right there, edging closer and closer, forcing me to steer further over towards the shoulder! If this wasn't bad enough, she didn't even look into her mirrors or use her turn signal when she abruptly gave me another surprise! The woman suddenly whipped over from the lane she was in and planted herself smack in front of my bumper! To avoid running right over the top her, I had no choice but to take a dive towards the shoulder! It amazes me out here on the highway how often we observe other drivers like her. It's so obvious, their minds are on everything but driving! They all just cruise down the road, playing their tunes, while their brain is somewhere else! They're off in la la land, "totally" oblivious of their surroundings! This is what causes accidents and that's why professional trucker's drive defensively.

We had the time and luxury of going to a large retail store today that allows for big rig parking. Our satellite radio bit the dust so we took this opportunity to buy a new one. I was also glad to have the opportunity to buy fresh produce and replenish supplies. While I shopped, I left Ron to buy the new radio with the understanding upon completion of our purchases; we would meet at a designated location within the store. I should have known better! Ron does not like to shop! I waited and waited and finally I went looking for him. I walked every isle inside the store, not once, but "twice" trying to find him. Finally, my legs wore out and it dawned on me that maybe he just purchased the radio and then went back to the truck. With this thought in mind I proceeded to push my grocery cart across the lot. As I approached the truck, sure enough, there he was! Boy did I chew him out!

The rest of the day turned out to be a major exercise in frustration. We went back to our motel and Ron proceeded to install the new radio. No matter what he tried, he could not get the radio to work. I don't know how many times he called tech support. After two more trips back to the store and more efforts on Ron's part to get the radio to operate; he finally decided to give up and got a refund. (This of course was not without a lot of cussing on Ron's part!) After spending all this time we were both worn out! Instead of eating dinner at one of the nice restaurants around here, we plopped down in our room, turned on the TV on and ordered pizza! We have a load to Spokane after midnight so it's probably just as well we stay put in our room and get some sleep.

April 25, 2007 and after spending four days at home we are back on the road. Ron was able to get quite a bit of work done building our deck. Once he's able to add the railing it will be finished, but unfortunately, his project will be on hold until we return home. This is trucking! If the wheels aren't turning, we're not earning! The load we're picking up is recycled paper and it's nothing but heavy! Once loaded, our weight will be pushing 80,000 lbs. and I know we're going to have to slid the axels and I hope we only do it once! The good news; we don't have to haul it that far before dropping it off and picking up another load that heads us south.

Sitting parked at the driver's yard tonight in California waiting for dispatch to call telling us our load is ready. It delivers in North Carolina but won't be ready until around midnight. In the meantime, we'll try to catch a few hours sleep and try to ignore the screeching loud noise in the background. Engineers are busy couple and uncoupling box cars banging them together. Before I put my journal away; I've mentioned this before, but the driver's yard here is nothing to write home about. This morning when I stepped into the women's restroom, there was a giant cockroach on the floor! I'll bet that sucker was at least two inches long! Yuk, and it wasn't dead! I swear you have to be prepared for encounters like this when your job is driving truck for a living. You have no choice but to share so many quarters daily (like public restrooms and restaurants) with total strangers and these places are not always clean!

Finally got the call we were waiting for shortly after midnight. We threw on some clothes, took time to use the facilities, made a pot of coffee, filled our thermos then drove a short distance to pick up the load. We did our usual and went as far as Kingman, AZ. This is what we usually do in setting ourselves up to leave early. We know there's plenty of wildlife in the mountains ahead and Ron prefers to have a little more daylight lessening the chance of hitting an Elk! Tonight we are in North Little Rock, AR on our way to Myrtle, MS only to learn they are going to turn us around when we get there and head us back to Spokane. I suppose that's good news because we like getting a couple days off at home. Together, we drove 1,100 miles today and needless to say, not surprisingly, worn out! We are sitting in a muddy lot full of huge chuck holes. Earlier today I picked up some pre made sandwiches. We'll eat those along with good old Beanies and Weenies and call it dinner. It's very late so I guess we should be satisfied with the food on hand and be more appreciative of finding a place to park.

Today is the 30th of April and we are in Matthews, MO. Once in a while you see something along the side of the road that takes you by surprise and you just never forget. Like the time I saw that young man dressed only in camouflage pants lying face down on the hot desert sand. I still wonder if he was dead or alive! What I saw today is on a lighter note! While driving on Interstate 55 along side of the road we spotted a dead raccoon, bloated up, lying upside down with all four legs up in the air. Someone with a sense of humor had placed a big green soda bottle between its two hands with the neck inserted inside the raccoon's mouth. It gave the impression that the raccoon gulped down the liquid and passed out! I'm sorry about the raccoon, but it was such a funny sight to see! Ron said the prank was probably created by one of the nearby road construction crew that we just passed. I'm sure he and his buddies got a good laugh out of it like we did.

April is behind us and now we are into May. We had a very nice surprise last night when we stopped at a small truck stop in Kadoka, SD. Ron was dead tired after maxing out his hours of driving so I went inside the truck stop to find us something to eat. It was obvious the cook was closing down for the night. Suddenly he spoke up and said to me "are you hungry?" He told me he was a Lakota Sioux and usually when he closes down for the night he takes the leftover food to his family. I told him "Yes, my husband and I are both hungry and we were hoping to find something hot to eat for dinner." Instantly he replied by saying "Let me package up all that is left in the case and you can have it free!" He added that his family would not miss him bringing home leftovers because they get them all the time. He was such a nice friendly person and I enjoyed visiting with him while he proceeded to pack into several boxes all of the food until he finally emptied out the entire case! With three large bags full of food in my hands I headed back to the truck, but not before I insisted he accept a generous tip from us. Ron couldn't believe it when I returned. There was no way we could eat it all! I stored what was left in our cooler knowing we would have plenty of snacks for tomorrow! We will never forget his kindness.

May 12th and we are not off to a good start! We just drove to the nearest scale and our load is 1,580 lbs. over weight! No way can we haul this! If we were to continue on, we wouldn't even make it past the first scale house before instantly getting red lighted. The thought of a ticket and all the additional time spent with a DOT officer is something Ron wanted to avoid! We have no choice now but to drive all the way back through Los Angeles traffic and have shipping remove some of the carpet. Even after all that, we will have to drive back to the scale and weigh all over again! This wears you out before you even get started! It eats up hours of time that could have been spent driving.

It's Mother's Day and tonight we're parked in Sayer, OK at truck stop that always offers a nice buffet. I did my usual earlier by giving Ron's mom a call to wish her a Happy Mother's Day. I suspect by now she's probably forgotten it. Lately it has become more and more evident to us that she is having trouble with her short term memory. We worry about her out here but when your job is driving truck long haul, there isn't much we can do. Kim, Kellie and Jason all called me today and I thoroughly enjoyed my conversations with each of them.

We drove 850 miles today instead of our usual 1,000 miles. Makes you wonder when we pass by so many people in their trailers and motor homes, just how far "they" traveled before fatigue set in and they had to get off the road. These people have no idea or are even able to appreciate how many miles a trucker racks up every day! My guess is that they probably drove about four or five hundred miles and feel very accomplished with their effort! I can just imagine the scene; the driver parks, gets out of the vehicle, stretching his arms in the air, yawns and begins bragging to anyone who will listen about the endurance it took to drive that far! Those that continue to listen will also have to hear about all the aches and pains from doing it; along with complaint of too much traffic and too many big rigs! Guess I really can't blame these folks, driving the many hours a day that we do takes some time getting used to.

May 14th and now we are parked at a truck stop about 20 miles outside Nashville, TN. Most drivers prefer and depend on truck stops for a place to park their rig. Unfortunately, they are a haven for easy pickings by scammers! We are corralled like cattle in a stockyard! This makes all of us an easy target for them to approach our trucks looking for a hand out or try to sell us something. Tonight is no exception! We had a rough looking character knock on our window and ask if he could polish our wheel s for a mere $10 each. Quick tax free money for him and a drain of 60 bucks out of Ron's wallet! Ron said thanks, but no thanks! The stranger wanted to debate the issue further, but Ron stood his ground and he finally left. The investment in their polishing business merely consists of a couple rags and a plastic bottle full of liquid cleaner. They claim the cleaner is some "special formula" they created; exclusively meant for polishing chrome wheels! To further describe this character; he had stringy, greasy long hair, some missing teeth, was dressed in cut offs, holes in his tank top and was covered in tattoos from his legs clear up to his neck! In my opinion he was a poor excuse for what a male should look like. I'll never understand why they don't clean up and get a real job!

5-16-07 and we are done for the day staying parked at the Squaw Creek truck stop which is about 25 miles outside St. Joseph, MO. The place is small, sits up on a hill, far enough off the freeway that we should expect somewhat of a quite night's sleep. We won't even bother getting out of the truck and walk to the restaurant; too much effort! Guess we'll do our final recording in our logs, put clothes out for morning, sit a few minutes watching fire flies and then go to bed. This is the way it goes sometimes out here.

Today isn't much different than yesterday. We drove 1,138 miles and made it to Belgrade, MT before calling it quits. Days like this of driving 18 hours straight are becoming more frequent for the two of us and I'm finally getting my act together! While Ron was behind the wheel, I took out the crock pot and dumped a big can of chili in it. I was tired of not having something hot to eat for dinner. Now the chili is piping hot and ready to serve. I also scrounged up what few fresh vegetables we had left and made us a small salad. Eat, Sleep, and Drive! That's what we and all the rest of the truckers do out here hauling freight back and forth across America! It's not a vacation; it's work!

We finally made it home for a long overdue week off. Ron's mother remains a primary concern for us, especially when it comes time to leave again and get back trucking. We both admire her independence of wanting to live alone in her house, but it is becoming more and more evident she could use some help in our absence. Each visit we have discovered food, unwrapped, (apparently snacks), like cheese, crackers, part of an apple, cottage cheese or a jar of jam with the lid off sitting out on her counter. Inside her refrigerator we found wilted dried out vegetables or prepared dishes (probably given to her by family or friends) left to mold. This is a good indicator that she's not eating properly. I took the time while home to find a company that caters meals to senior citizens. She's now set up to receive one hot meal delivered to her door seven days a week! We and the rest of the family are relieved and happy with the change!

While we were still at home, Ron happened to spot an old Ford pickup truck for sale on his way to the post office. He needed one to haul wood and decided to buy it. The old beater only made it three miles and quit! (See what I mean about him always buying junk!) After finalizing the sale, Ron started the engine and drove his newly found prize possession off the lot. He told me to follow behind him. I was having one heck of a good time laughing my head off as I watched him in front of me bouncing up and down like he was jumping on a pogo stick! (The front springs were shot!) He had to fight every gear, no doubt cussing with each shift, and when he hit a bump he would fly up in the air hitting his head on the headliner above! That truck was giving

Ron the rodeo ride of his life! He was having a hard time just keeping it on the road! My laughter quickly stopped when he suddenly coasted off on the grassy shoulder. Not so funny anymore! At this point, having being married to him for so long, I knew what I was in for! He got out, slammed the door and told me to wait inside the old truck while he took mine and ran home to get a chain. (We had to jump the batteries to even get it started, so I guess I shouldn't have been surprised when it just quit running.) Ron returned, hooked up the tow chain and after reminding him of our long ago established ground rules for me towing, (basically, no yelling) we headed home! Now we have a truck that we paid cash for and it doesn't even run! Ron keeps assuring me he'll get his "farm truck" back in shape in no time. We'll see!

If this self imposed headache wasn't enough, when we arrived home we were shocked to see our garden had been destroyed by a family of hungry marmots! There wasn't a pea on the vine; not even a blossom! Forget the cabbage and strawberries, they also got eaten! But, oh no, do you think the critters stopped there? They proceeded, even with what had to be a full belly, to come up on the deck and eat all the pretty flowers I had growing in my planters! We could not believe the devastation! This was serious and it instantly became Ron's mission; *destroy the monsters*! I received my orders from Captain Ron "We're going to move this up a notch Billie, go to town and buy a trap!" I followed his orders and returned with a trap designed exclusively for catching small animals. Ron proceeded to set the bait inside the cage, (cabbage) and looked for just the right location to place it. We both felt it was just a matter of time and we would nail the little suckers one by one! Two days went by and we had no luck trapping any of them! These little wise guys are smarter than we thought! At this point we ran out of time at home and had no choice but to get back trucking. Who knows how much more damage they will do during our absence. We're dealing with real outlaws!!

After hauling several loads of freight and staying out three weeks, we finally got a run bringing us back to Washington. We're not too far from home now staying tonight at a truck stop in Pasco. We are parked next to a truck that has a big black and white cat inside. When Diesel spotted the cat, her fur stood on end like a porcupine shooting out quills; she was ready for battle! The other cat had mutual feelings and both were ready to "bring it on"! You can always expect a dog inside a truck to act as a "guard dog" because they are protecting their home on the road, but many cats as well display the same attitude. Diesel's has forgotten she is a cat and considers herself human! She wants nothing to do with other felines!

The couple in the truck next to us with the black cat seems to be nice people, but not someone we would want to invite to a backyard barbeque! When the driver smiled he had the brownest teeth I have ever seen! Inside their truck is what they referred to as "their family"! In addition to the cat, they also had a Pit Bull, plus two other smaller dogs. I can just imagine what the inside of their truck must have looked and smelled like! Oh well, who am I to judge another person's life style? They appeared happy and that's what counts.

Here we go again, another argument between dispatchers! One tells you where you're supposed to deliver the load and the other dispatcher on the receiving end tells you something entirely different! Sometimes you can't help but feel like a ping pong ball! In this case, although we were instructed to drop the trailer off at the terminal, we settled the dispute by delivering the load ourselves, thus ending their disagreement.

June 10th and we are on our way to Jacksonville, Florida but at present we are dead stopped out here on the interstate. A semi truck and trailer lost it, flipped over on its side and has blocked all lanes of traffic causing a back up for miles in both directions. Several law enforcement officers, ambulances and wreckers are on the scene. It's dark out here but you can see pretty well with all the flashing lights surrounding the accident. I feel bad for the driver, but for us this means a long night with few hours sleep.

June 12th and we made it to our drop without getting lost! Florida is one state that we don't go to very often so we're always happy when we arrive at our destination on time. The downside of this particular delivery is that we are still here and quite frankly, I'm annoyed with the crew unloading our trailer. They must be paid by the hour because they're taking their own sweet time getting the freight off! We have been sitting here since 7 a.m. and will probably be here another two hours! They're slower than turtles walking backwards! Ron and I do not like sitting bumped against their dock! I tried taking a nap because we got up so early, but it's an exercise in futility! There are several railroad tracks in front of us and I have come to the conclusion that we're not very far from some sort of "switch yard"! I can hear what sounds like box cars being coupled and uncoupled making a loud noise. The Qualcom just beeped with a message from dispatch. They have another load for us to pick up at 3 p.m. today and it's another 150 miles away! Impossible! We sent them a note back declining the load letting them know we're still sitting, no telling how long we'll be, and we've been up since 2:30 a.m.! Now we'll wait to see what they have to say. When you run as a team, your clock is 24 hours regardless and constant driving is expected!

You know sometimes it's unbelievable what you see out here! I happen to notice a young suspicious male walking down the sidewalk; he stopped, starred into a patch of trees surrounded with thick, tall underbrush, and appeared to be searching for something. I continued to observe as he stepped off the sidewalk and headed straight into the forested area. His strides were slow as he cautiously moved forward, pulling branches away from his face, turning his head back and forth, going deeper and deeper into the thickness, until finally, disappearing from sight. I kept watching and now and then I could see bushes moving and shaking, so I knew he still had to be in there! It was only a short time later and again, movement of underbrush caught my eye! All of a sudden he popped out into the open, back to us, tugging hard and yanking on something! He appeared to be having one heck of a time struggling with whatever he was trying to pull out of the bushes! At this point Ron is watching right along with me, both fascinated by what we were witnessing. It wasn't long and we learned what his effort was all about! He broke loose from the tangled brush, stepping backwards pulling and tugging hard on a very heavy bouncing grocery cart! It was plum FULL of cased soft drinks! No doubt in our minds he had come to collect stolen merchandise hidden out of sight in the thick grove of trees. After going through such a hard time fighting his way through the brush and mud, he finally got the cart on solid ground! He paused, looked around and saw our truck with us sitting inside starring at him. For a moment I was frightened thinking maybe he had a gun and would shoot us for being a witness to his crime! Instead, he turned his head and proceeded to casually wheel his soft drinks down the sidewalk in the grocery cart like nothing was out of norm!

June 24th and we finally managed to get back home for a couple days. Even though we bought a trap, we still have the same critters eating our flowers and vegetables! I know darn well it's not the little bunny that shows up! The harvest is way too great for one little bunny alone to handle! We are pretty sure it's a family of marmots, free loaders that have moved in on us! This really ticks me off! So far, whatever we're dealing with has now eaten all of the broccoli, leaves off the beets, lettuce, strawberries and then added insult to injury by finishing off my flowering planters! So far the trap we bought has not caught and nailed one single marmot! In fact, to add insult to injury, the animal went inside, (the bait was wedges of cabbage) either ate or took the cabbage and left! We're not giving up! This is an ongoing battle and we aim on winning it! We will eventually outsmart and trap these invaders!

By the way, tonight we are in West Memphis, Arkansas after driving over 1,000 miles. We get up in the dark and end the day in the dark. Today is only one of several others in the past where the parents are too tired to even think about getting out of the truck and walking up to the restaurant. It's a hard life out here and I known many people would never be able to adjust to what's required in accepting a job like this. Sometimes I wonder myself how much longer we'll be able last. Trucking isn't something you can turn into a comfortable routine like so many other places of employment after being hired. Every day is like being introduced to the job all over again; always full of unknown challenges, long hours, weeks away from home and the lifestyle won't get any better! It's the cold hard truth about trucking!

Kim called today and she said a man collapsed at a restaurant where she was at. She gave him CPR but he didn't make it and died at the scene. She was very upset as you can imagine! We continue to worry about Ron's mom out here. Sometimes she sounds fine and then there are other times I question if she is o.k. or not. At times like this, I have to remind myself to give her credit for being the age she is and still able live at home by herself. She is one tough old gal! Ron just told me he's worn out, tired, and I need to put my journal away; he wants to go to bed. He's right, knowing myself we're looking at only getting four or five hours sleep. He napped earlier today and will start out in the morning. I'll try to catch a few more hours of sleep while he's driving before it's my turn.

June 25th we delivered our load in Georgia then bobtailed over to a nearby motel to get a room for the night. I lifted the wrong way getting our luggage down and now I'll be in pain for the next few days. There's no doubt in my mind I irritated the area where I had the gall bladder surgery. I'm not about to go see a doctor! Out of the question! Over the counter pain meds will dull the pain enough.

Diesel is very familiar with the parking lot at the motel and Ron always lets her out. The first thing she does is roll over on her back and wiggle back and forth upside down on the pavement. After she completes her own self prescribed physical fitness exercise, she then stands upright and proceeds to take a stroll across a grassy area sniffing and enjoying the outdoors. She deals pretty well with the confinement for so many days on end, and is always overly excited when it comes time to get out and stretch. Most of the time Ron can pick her up and put her back in the truck, but that's not always the case! She will get back in the truck when she is good and ready and sometimes it takes more patience then Ron is willing to endure!

We're having starter problems with the truck. When you turn the key off, it keeps running! Frustrating to say the least, but Ron's got it all figured out and he's able to shut the engine off. We're going to have to deal with this irritating problem until we get home when Ron will have the time to get the starter replaced. The sky above has quickly turned black, filled with dark clouds, indicating we are about to get hit with an enormous downfall of rain accompanied by strong bolts of lightning! No time to waste! We grabbed the luggage, Diesel, locked the truck and made a mad dash for our room!

July 7th we are in Rio Puerco, NM. And are right in the midst of a huge lightening storm! We are literally surrounded by loud sounds of thunder and strong bolts of jagged lighting strikes hitting on the ground! So far, thank heaven, the strikes seem to be off at a distance! It's a little scary but also very entertaining to watch! Diesel got scared, flew off the dash, and is hiding somewhere! She does not like the sound of loud thunder nor the repeated sizzling, crackling sounds made by lightening. This is a fast moving storm passing over us so I don't think it will last long. For the moment though, it's entertaining and gives us something to talk about.

We made it to Belgrade, MT before calling it a day, but of course, it was only after we racked up another 1,000 plus miles! I'm not one to complain very often, but this "team driving" is wearing us both out! I'm beginning to think "teaming up" wasn't such a good idea after all! Eat, sleep and drive and that sums up each and every day for "any" team out here! There's no time for *anything* else! Hours of driving takes its toll on your body mentally and physically. Being confined inside a truck for days on end you better have a compatible cell mate; otherwise, there's a good chance you'll end up killing each other! Maybe that's a bit extreme, but I've actually witnessed more than once, other drivers getting out of their truck, slam the door and walk away from their co-driver!

On our way home now and we've decided to try to hire someone to look in on Ron's mom during our absence. We absolutely know she won't like our idea, but it will make us feel better and we won't worry about her as much. I had Ron pull into a rest stop earlier today. I threw my back out lifting supplies down from the top bunk this morning and darn I hate it when this happens! The only remedy is stopping at a rest area and having both of us get out of the truck. He then proceeds to stand behind me wrapping his arms around tight and lifting me clear off the ground. This procedure straightens my spine and it works well! I felt fine after that and only wish I could do the same for him when his back hurts but, he's a little too heavy for me to lift!

Three whole weeks off at home and here we are back in California currently parked, until they put a new mud flap on the trailer. We're off to a very slow start! Our load was supposed to be ready at 5 a.m. but we had to wait another two hours before we could get the paperwork and hook to the trailer. When Ron did his pre trip inspection he discovered a missing mud flap! He was not very happy about the discovery knowing someone ignored the problem leaving it up to the driver to fix. Driving without a mud flap would be a D.O.T. violation and Ron was not about to let that happen. This second delay put us further behind schedule. Now we're running three hours late! We have two days to get from Los Angeles to Georgia and now we're going to have to drive even harder to make the delivery on time!

While waiting to get the mud flap replaced I watched another driver get out of his truck, tie his dog to a tree in a landscaped area bordering the parking lot and then proceed to go inside the building. The dog quickly ran to the end of his leash; stretching it out as far as it would go and promptly started barking his head off! Without warning, suddenly the automatic sprinklers came on! It took the dog by surprise and me as well! A whirling huge spray of cold water shot out; instantly drenching the barking dog! He couldn't get away; he was tied to the tree! You would think this interruption would distract the dog from barking and pulling out on the leash; but it didn't! The poor thing just kept barking; darting back and forth while trying to avoid getting hit with another blast of cold water! He was getting the shower he didn't ask for! (I wonder if the dog thought he was being punished!) Several minutes later the driver returned; shocked at what he saw, quickly untied the dog and dried him off. I'm sure he felt bad!

Now it is early evening and we made it to a truck stop just about 60 miles outside the New Mexico border. It was a very hot day today for driving and at one time it reached 110 degrees! We have a lightning storm going on with rain clouds that have totally blackened out the sky above. Besides being worn out after several hundreds of miles driving; the weather is another big factor for calling it a day. We didn't want to drive further knowing we would have to contend with the heavy downpour of rain, glare of oncoming headlights and the huge, sometimes blinding spray you get from other 18 wheelers passing by. We are running behind on our usual schedule and neither of us like it, but what do you do? The company doesn't want late deliveries, but they would like it a whole lot less if we ended up in an accident!

Well if this wasn't a sight to see! While traveling down the interstate through Arkansas we saw several prisoners dressed in large "black" and "white" stripped clothing picking up litter alongside the road. I have seen prisoners dressed in bright orange coveralls before, but never in these huge black and white stripped outfits! In Arkansas they mean business! We spotted a guard up on the overpass keeping an eye on the prisoners and believe me; he was very well armed! More guards were on the ground following behind each prisoner watching every single move they made while they slowly walked along picking up trash. The guards also had with them a couple of well trained German shepherd dogs on leashes, no doubt prepared to attack on command should any of the prisoners be foolish enough to try and escape. Got a call from dispatch and was told there's another run waiting for us when we get to Georgia. They want us to grab a pre loaded trailer and head for Indiana. Not what we expected, but that's trucking!

August 7, 07 and we are here in Georgia backed up to a dock getting unloaded. The load to Indiana was cancelled and now they are sending us to Montana. We were not too happy when we heard the news because there's not a whole lot of van freight out of this state and what we get is usually heavy! I told the dispatcher we don't want to end up stuck, sitting without a load, when we get there. She assured me there would be a pre loaded trailer waiting for us when we arrived. Much to our surprise she actually did find us another load that delivers in Spokane. That keeps us rolling and we'll be able to stop and do a quick check on Ron's mother.

August 8, 07 we are right smack in the middle of a wild hurricane like storm! The winds were so powerful we had to get off the interstate before it blew us over! Visibility was awful; we could barely see beyond the hood of our truck. Our windshield remained blurred by the heavy rain. The wipers could not swipe fast enough to keep the window clear;

in fact, I thought they might break off! The downpour of rain was bad enough, but along with lightening strikes and severe wind gusts well over 50 mph made for even more dangerous! Ron got tired of fighting the storm and decided not to push his luck in any further. He knew it would be much safer to get off from the interstate and wait it out. Good decision! So, here we are today, dead in the water, (play on words), sitting at a truck stop in Mound City, MO. The truck stop was packed when we pulled in with several other truckers that obviously made the same decision. When you run into weather conditions like this, finding a place to park an 18 wheeler becomes a challenge! I'm glad there were still a few empty spaces left! While sitting here I saw one biker wheel in on his motorcycle, park and make a mad dash for shelter inside the restaurant. He was totally drenched! I know it wasn't funny but he looked soaked to the bone and I couldn't help but laugh!

August 18th and I've missed a few days of writing in my journal. But today I feel the urge to express how I feel at this very moment. Sometimes you just want to slam on the brakes, park the truck, get out, and run away from it! For the last two hours we have been stuck in a back up of traffic coming into Albuquerque, NM! It is now 11:30 at night, we got up at 6 o'clock this morning which means that we have been out here driving for the past 17 ½ hours! The reality is; that while everyone else is sleeping, thousands of "White Line Warriors" are still running the interstates 24/7! This is the job! It's what we accept as truckers when we get behind the wheel. We see it as a responsibility to suppliers that we keep their freight moving around the clock! So, it is what it is, and I'll stop whining, but nevertheless without all these dedicated drivers how would industry or consumers ever survive!

We are still sitting in the back up, but are slowly working our way to a casino, (which is the only place ahead of us that has parking for big rigs). We will park, stay in the truck, complete our daily logs, eat a sandwich, and go to bed. We are both dead tired, feeling drained and fatigue has set in. Walking up to the casino, although fun, is the last thing on our minds! We'll just be thankful if there's still a place left for us to park when we get there.

We are driving today on I-40 and over the past seven years, "big rig" traffic has increased to the point where we all look like we're running together in a convoy! There are 18 wheelers ahead and behind us as far as the eye can see! (It's no wonder 4-wheelers don't like us!) The increased transport of freight has changed the attitudes of many drivers! Talking on the CB radio to one another used to be fun; now all we hear is sarcasm, smart remarks and negative attitudes! I honestly think sometimes drivers provoke an argument just to be heard! Face it, who else do they have to blow off steam to but a fellow trucker that will understand their frustrations! They could pick up the phone and complain to friends or relatives, but family and friends are not out here with us! They would not appreciate or understand the situation.

August 19th and it's a new day, in fact a much better day than yesterday! A few hours sleep for both of us did wonders! Earlier we had a tornado watch going on but we never saw any. We are in Russellville, AR tonight. I pulled the muscles AGAIN around my surgery! You would think I would have learned a lesson from my last experience, but I didn't. It's hard for me to sit still. I don't have the patience to wait for Ron to help me lift something. Maybe this time I'll be a bit more careful. The temperature is 93 degrees; too hot to sleep so we'll have to run the truck all night burning fuel just to keep cool Got up early and while Ron fueled, I headed inside the truck stop to fill the thermos, grab a couple snacks and use the bathroom. When I entered the stall in the women's bathroom I happened to look down and was instantly disgusted! There were two big cockroaches on the floor; very much alive and I thought for sure they were going to jump on me! They are so ugly! My thought was if they are in here, where else are they? I just lost my appetite! We are in Davenport, IA tonight and we learned today that one of our fellow drivers got blown over by strong winds in Casper, WY. Fortunately he only had minor injuries, but there was sever damage to the truck and trailer. We ourselves went through a huge lightening storm just before we got here. This was another long hectic day of team driving. We would love to wash clothes, do laundry, have a shower and hot meal but there's not enough time to spare. Our dinner consisted of a couple slices of ham, crackers and cheese. We're calling this our breakfast, lunch and dinner!

Got up very early, (what's new) and together we drove 1,157 miles entering one state and going into another before stopping! After parking, we did what all drivers do routinely when the day is done; complete the driver log and start a new page. I then proceeded to climb up and dig out clothes for morning. While I was doing that, Ron conveniently found a place to dump the porta potty, (it's only liquid). Last thing we did was get two thermoses filled with coffee because there's no time to waste when you're running this hard! Its log up, do a vehicle inspection, put the truck in gear and go! We saw an 18 wheeler today totally upside down! No doubt the driver was injured or worse yet, may have lost his life! It was a pretty ugly sight to see. It always makes us feel sad when we see a bad accident like this not only for the driver, but the grief extends to his family and the company he works for as well.

Here it is September and we are in Texas. Our air conditioning has been out for the past three days and it is 83 degrees! Sweat is running down our foreheads and pouring off both of us. Ron said we're going to have live without air conditioning until he can get home to order what he needs to fix it. Not fun!! We have not had a shower in almost a week! I never dreamed a shower would become such a treat for me, but that's entirely out of the question; no time to waste, we're under a load, we've got to keep rolling! I feel so sorry for Diesel. She likes heat, but not this kind with all the sticky humidity.

The heat continues as we sit here today staging in Olive Branch, MS. We cannot deliver our load until tomorrow. It's 92 degrees; we have the vents open, windows down and a small fan running. There is not even a breeze and I'm not so sure having the windows down does that much good! Ron must think there is some benefit, but I don't! Well I endured as long as I could and finally just couldn't take it anymore! Sweat was running off both of us. I went inside the truck stop to the women's bathroom and ran cold water over my head. It helped, but when I walked back outside I was right back in the stifling heat. Diesel is miserable, lying on the bunk upside down. She looks dead because she's so still. What little air circulation we're getting from the fan is aimed right at her giving minimal relief if any. We have a couple parked next to us that caught my attention. They appear to be older people and they both have been working crossword puzzles for the past two hours without speaking a word to each other. Their heads are still down filling in the letters. I cannot help but wonder if this is what I have to look forward to when Ron and I get up there in age. Boring!!

This is what always amazes me! You endure high temperatures one day and then the next day you freeze your butt off! Now we are in Sioux Falls, SD and we're in freezing cold weather! We'll probably have to run the truck tonight to keep warm. Our travels take us from one extreme to another. We did manage to crank out 900 miles before stopping tonight which is nothing to complain about. There's a big full moon tonight lighting up the sky and it reminds me back when Ron was a paramedic. He always told me every time there was a full moon he would have a busy night of transporting the looser of a family fight! Apparently a full moon would bring out the worst in some people!

Not the news I wanted to hear today out here on the road! Kim called and said she broke 8 ribs and punctured her lung while riding with one of her friends on an "off road quad" out in the desert. Of course this happened about a week ago, but she didn't tell me until a week later because she didn't want me to worry. Her friends managed to get her to an emergency room for treatment and now she's recuperating at home. Kim said she's still in pain and I don't doubt it with all those injuries. She's one tough little gal and I'm very proud of her. But, nevertheless, when she hurts, I hurt!

Let it snow, let it snow! Remember just a few days ago, sweat was pouring off of us? Well now all of that has changed! Ever since South Dakota and now into Montana it has remained cold. It's only the end of September but I suppose for the local folks, the snowfall is not a surprise to them! Their weather can change in a heartbeat! For us, it's a quick reminder that winter is just around the corner and it won't be long before "chain up" season arrives!

October 17th and we are in Pasco, WA after spending a few days at home. Ron's mom was glad to see us, spinning her wheels, anxious to let us in know in no uncertain terms that *she* was still in charge and *demanded* that I cancel her hot meal deliveries! I could not convince her otherwise, so I stopped the service. She insisted that the service was meant for people "confined" and "I'm not confined"! Her car had been in the shop for repairs, has it back, and once again she's feeling pretty independent. She ran errands while we were there and when she returned Ron noticed her license tabs had expired. I'm glad she made it home without getting pulled over. We of course, bought her tabs before we left. You might wonder what all this has to do with trucking. It has a whole lot to do with it because even if your miles away, truckers still carry the responsibility and concern for the family they left behind. The commitment to loved ones simply does not stop when you leave home. Speaking of family, we heard today on the news that there were at least 15 big rigs involved in a massive crash that happened inside a tunnel located in California. It was reported that several of the rigs caught fire! Just imagine how many families this will impact!

October 20th it is 10:30 p.m. and the entire drive today was stressful! We are hauling a very light load and that's not good especially when you're high profile faced with strong side winds. We were fighting off and on 50 to 60 mph gusts making it a challenge to keep the truck and trailer upright. The tension of holding on to the steering wheel for so long makes your arms and back hurt. We had to deal with this relentless condition for hours on end. Frankly, it wore us both out! You have to live our experience to appreciate the stress it causes! When I say we're worn out, I mean it! It's such a relief when the driving day is over and we can throw in the towel and call it a day! The off ramp becomes your road to heaven! The driving is done! This again is another one of those nights where we have to settle with what we find to eat inside the truck. Next month will be Jason and Bethany's wedding and Ron and I somehow will find a load that will take us back home to be there for it. We are on our way to Hickory, North Carolina and hopefully by the time we get up the wind will be gone.

It is November 3rd today and this will be out last trip out before we go to the wedding. Kim called today and said her ribs still hurt. Ron broke his ribs a long time ago, and I remember his pain lasting several months. I feel so sorry for her. Ron just told me to put my journal away. Our load is ready and we'll be headed for a town outside Birmingham, AL and then off to a final drop in Georgia. I must say they took their own sweet time in getting us loaded. We'll probably get as far as Kingman, AZ and call it a day. We like to stay at this truck stop because there's plenty of parking and good food.

Ron and I witnessed a near disaster driving I-40 on our way to Kingman, AZ earlier today. We had two big rigs ahead of us when suddenly one driver pulled out in the hammer lane and decided to pass the truck in front of him. The driver in the passing lane picked up speed, got right up alongside the other driver, neck and neck, slowed down and then proceeded to allow his rig to drift over the line edging closer and closer to the truck beside him. They were close to hitting each other! We couldn't believe our eyes watching the innocent driver being forced to run on the shoulder! Within seconds a loud shout came over the CB radio "GET OVER!!", "Damit, you're running me off the road!" His request went unanswered! Ron slowed down, afraid of what was about to happen. The huge eighteen wheelers were close, so close; they were within inches of slamming into each other! The driver in front of us, in order to avoid being side swiped, instantly took a dive leaving the pavement steering his truck over rough desert sand and rock! A huge cloud of dust flew up in the air sending out a spray of shrapnel that instantly peppered our windshield! We passed by and could see he had brought his 18 wheeler to a safe stop. Ron grabbed the CB and told the shaken driver that we saw the whole thing and if he wanted to report the jackass we would gladly be a witness! The driver didn't respond, probably because he was trying to regain his composure!

Ron sped up and got right behind the dumb ass that caused all this so I could get his license plate number. He checked his mirrors and could see that the driver that was run off the road got back on and was quickly gaining speed. A few miles further down the highway we spotted a bear parked, keeping an eye on freeway traffic. Shortly after passing him we saw the driver behind slow down and pull in next to the officer. (I love this part!) In what seemed like a matter of seconds, rocks flew, tires screeched, and the officer took off like a streak of lightening with blue lights flashing and a screaming siren blaring out! The shaken driver got back in his rig, pulled right out behind the patrol car, and joined the pursuit! (We now had a cop and a big rig speeding together after the bad guy!) The officer blew past us like we were standing still! He nailed him just like that!! Ron flipped the creep off as we passed by and he deserved it! As Ron watched in his rear view mirror he could see the driver behind us pull in behind the bear and get out of his truck. No doubt about it! That reckless driver was about to get the most severe ass chewing of his life! We ourselves have experienced close calls like this one and it's not something you like to deal with. Your only solution is to try to avoid an accident by doing whatever it takes to keep your 18 wheeler under control; even if it means pulling off on the shoulder and coming to a complete stop. There is no freight worth your life; let the inconsiderate driver go on his way. He's an accident going somewhere to happen!

We are in Barstow CA after driving through plenty of snow to get here! We had to chain up outside Pendleton, OR and then drive in snow for several miles. Jason and Bethany's wedding was beautiful with an array of Christmas decorations everywhere you looked. I told Ron I was afraid I might cry during the ceremony; I did!

December 2nd and our worst fear became a reality! Ron's mom fell as she was trying to steer a wheelbarrow full of wood across an icy pathway to her house. She was alone at the time when she fell and no doubt her body hit hard on the frozen ground! The intense pain she felt at that moment must have been almost unbearable! She's a tough old gal, 86 years old, and it was not surprising when we learned she crawled over frozen snow to get back inside her house. (She probably thought she would freeze to death if she didn't!) I can't imagine all the pain she went through with each crawling movement! After she reached the back door it took her several tries reaching up to the knob and finding enough strength to turn and push the door open. Once inside, she continued to crawl through her kitchen and into her living room and pull herself up on the sofa. I don't know how long she laid there before a repair man; (Dan) showed up to do some work on her furnace. He told me he knocked on the door several times and then finally decided to look through the window. He saw her on the sofa and she waved for him to come inside. After telling Dan what happened, he asked if she wanted him to call an ambulance, but she refused saying "You can call Billie for me". "My phone book is on the counter". Dan's assessment was that Ron's mother appeared to be in severe pain and he thought she might go into shock. I told him to call an ambulance!

Hours later I was able to talk to the Emergency Room doctor. He said your mother-in-law has fractured her pelvis and with this type of injury there's nothing we can do but transfer her to a rehab facility for a lengthy recover. She won't like that one bit! Ron and I wonder if she will ever regain her mobility. I know right now I'm totally worn out! I've have had so many phone calls talking to hospital staff and family. Here we are miles from home sitting at a truck stop in Sayer, OK and there isn't much more I can do from the cab of this truck. We are so thankful to have Jean, (her niece) that will look in on Ron's mom during our absence. I have a hunch our lives are about to change knowing we are the ones that have always taken care of her. For now at least, she's resting comfortable in the hospital. In a few days she will be transferred to a rehab facility and by then we should be home. Her confinement will allow time for us to plan ahead and make arrangements for whatever care she might require. Just one more worry for Ron and me out here on the road.

December 7th we've already been to Georgia, picked up a load to Spokane, stayed last night in Rapid City, SD and now we're down for the night in Missoula, MT. "That's Truck'n! Don't hang our hat in one place too long; especially when we have problems at home! Since my last entry, Marje was transferred to a skilled nursing facility on the 5th and I was told she would be there 6 to 8 weeks going through rehab. I'm glad we're headed home to take care of things. I got a call from the nursing facility and they gave me a list of things they need in order for them to complete her admission. They told me their goal is to get her to use a walker before she can be discharged. It amazes me how much I can accomplish from inside the cab of our truck. I even managed to get a phone hooked up for Ron's mom so she can talk to family.

December 12th we were able to stay home 3 days; long enough to take care of all the things that needed to be done. We spent most of our time either with Ron's mom at the nursing facility or going to her house, rolling up our sleeves, cleaning up the place and making it nice for her return. We even had Dan the repairman come back and finish the work on her heating system. She seems to be doing fine, likes the staff and all the attention of being waited on. Her only complaint is that she does not like leaving her room and going down the hall to eat with other residents. She understandingly is still a bit confused over the huge disruption in her life caused by the accident. I'm sure it's going to take a while before she settles in and accepts her circumstance.

I don't know how we did it, but even after spending so much time driving back and forth to Spokane every day to visit Ron's mom, we still managed to squeeze in the things we needed to do at home. Now, once again, cat on board, wheels are rolling! We picked back up from where we left off; pulling a loaded trailer headed south down the interstate. Who knows where our travels will take us this time or what new surprises we might run into along the way! This is our life, this is what we do, and whatever the future holds, we are prepared to deal with it, just like we always do! As long as we're together, hammering out the miles, we're earning a living and that's what truck driving is all about!

CHAPTER 9

THE LAST RIDE

Well, here it is January 19, 2008 and we had the luxury of having 3 weeks off at home! I would like to say the entire time was relaxing, but that's not how it was at all. There was quite a bit of discussion with family members whether to take Ron's mom back to her house (with outside help), or place her in an assisted living facility. Ron finally made the decision, ending further discussion, telling the rest of the family he would feel better if his mother was placed in 24 hour care during our absence. (This was her doctor's preference anyway.) I had my hands full finding an affordable facility, completing admission papers, phone calls to cancel some of her existing routine services, like weekly garbage removal and automatic refills of her big propane tank. I also made arrangements to disconnect and connect phone service so she would have access to a phone in her room. In addition to all this, Ron and I drove to her house and packed up several of her personal items along with books and pictures then delivered them to the assisted living facility. After carrying several heavy boxes to her room, we both proceeded to unpack everything; hanging clothes in her closet, filling bedroom and bathroom drawers with her belongings and then finally hanging up the pictures! It was a workout!

Neither of us knows what the next few months will bring, but at least for now we are at peace knowing his mother will be in good hands while we're out running the interstates. I'm not complaining, but this is quite a responsibility and we're not getting any younger ourselves. Seems like all we do is work and sometimes we wonder if our own health will hold out long enough for us to enjoy a few years of retirement. For right now there are no options. We don't have any choice but to continue earning a living hauling freight.

While waiting for our trailer to get loaded in California, I got out of the truck and visited with another team that we haven't seen for quite awhile. The wife told me she's had a lot of problems with her health and now she has to go on kidney dialysis. Following that statement, she quickly added "I have no intention of quitting my job!" She said she will be using a portable dialysis machine set up inside their truck to use when she's not driving. I admire her strength and determination; she's one tough lady trucker! Her husband has his own health issues as well. He previously went through open heart surgery and is on medication for high blood pressure. With medical bills mounting up, she felt they had no choice but to keep on trucking. They are owner/operators and have to pay for their own insurance. She said the medical insurance they paid monthly premiums for was a far cry from what they thought they had in coverage. Together, they've been driving team, racking up millions of miles over the past 20 years! I'm sure the trucking life style, with all the wear and tear on the body, has finally taken its toll on both of them. I wish the best for both.

January 28th we are in Montana. It's 11 below zero and I don't expect the temperature to change! The weather is miserable outside with continuous blowing and drifting snow. Earlier today we had moments of driving where we couldn't see beyond the hood of the truck! Climbing up and over Mc Donald Pass the temperature dropped to 20 below zero! Ron had to stop at the top of the pass and shake the ice off our wiper blades. We could barely see through the blinding accumulation of icy smears distorting our vision and coating the windshield. Days like this makes me wonder why we're even out here fighting all this, confined inside the truck, putting ourselves at risk and making very few miles! We should be off the road, staying at home and enjoying a warm fire!

Snow, snow and more snow! What a winter we're having! This is February 7th and we made it home for a couple days then headed back out on the road. (Knowing in advance there would be plenty of snow to greet us when we arrived; we called ahead and made arrangements for our driveway to get plowed out.) Unfortunately, during the two days off at home another storm moved in and we got blasted with an additional 10" of snow! Before we could even leave, Ron had to thrown chains on the tires just to get us out of the driveway! With chains on, he still had to bobtail another 7 miles over unplowed roads before reaching the highway. We have 3 ½ feet of snow at home now and more is in the forecast! We need to head south!

We turned down two loads before leaving, which dispatchers don't like, but we've learned from past experience to stay out of certain places this time of year! One of the loads offered to us picked up in St. Maries, ID which would have required driving on *back roads* to get there! No way! We know the route and its only two lanes, no shoulder and has several blind curves to deal with! Idaho has 4 feet of snow on the ground! Needless to say common sense told us to stay away; it would be insanity for us to even to consider leaving the interstate and running our 18 wheeler cross country over icy two lane roads! In our opinion, the trip would have been too risky and why set ourselves up for this kind of self imposed misery. The other load was to the "Bay Area" (San Francisco) and that's completely off limits! We've been there, done that and don't like it! Too much traffic and not enough roads! I'm sure they'll get company drivers to cover both loads because they don't have much of a choice. Their soul belongs to the company!

While still at home, Ron's mother was discharged from rehab and transported to the assisted living facility where we were standing by waiting to greet her. Both of us were anxious to see her reaction once she saw all that we had done in making her room comfortable. At the same time we remained guarded. His mother is out spoken and we knew she would either accept or reject! She actually was pleasantly surprised to see so many of her personal belongings but didn't understand why she was even there! She kept asking why she couldn't go back home and live by herself. I'm sure in time she will acclimate, adjust to a new routine and maybe even make a few new friends.

Right now we are stuck here in Missoula, MT surrounded by snow; in fact it's snowing hard as I write. We just learned over the CB radio that Lookout Pass is closed. I'm so glad we made it over the pass yesterday!

February 8th and what a grueling day of driving for Ron! Approaching Idaho Falls we ran into some nasty weather! Conditions went downhill fast as the weather continued to worsen with each mile! It was downright miserable! Within seconds the surface of the road changed from dry pavement to solid packed ice, compounded by strong gusty winds with blowing and drifting snow! We no more than got into one blinding whiteout before entering another! The run we accepted now became the trip from hell making us wonder why we took it! The trailer swayed with each blast of wind! (This again is one more time I hope whoever reads my book will learn to appreciate what truck drivers go through in order to get goods delivered!) I'm sure the D.O.T. closed the interstate shortly after we passed over it. Huge drifts of snow were building up across the highway and Ron plowed our truck right through them, too many to count! During conditions like this, I stay quiet allowing him to give his undivided attention in keeping the truck and trailer on the road! Our lives, lively hood, truck, trailer and the freight we're hauling were all in Ron's hands! His professional driving skills were challenged and did one hell of a job getting us out of harm's way!

We are in Payson, UT tonight and tomorrow won't be much different; the forecast remains the same with continued strong winds and blowing snow! I'm not looking forward to getting up in the morning knowing what's in store! Once again, Ron, not me, will be fighting the elements driving through relentless snowfall and icy road conditions that will go on several more miles before getting out of it! There is hope; we're on our way to sunny California!

We made it through all the bad weather and now we have a load with a drop in Myrtle, MS and then has a final drop in Hickory, NC. We're both glad to be headed into states that remain warmer this time of year and free from snow, including our cat! I'm sick of ice, snow, bad roads, freezing temperatures, and the stress it causes!

February 21st. More than two weeks have passed and I have not had the time or desire to write in my journal. I have been too busy with taking care of issues relating to Ron's mom, or paying attention to the relentless winter driving we thought we left behind. Tonight we are parked at a truck stop after starting out this morning on icy roads in Kentucky! Seems no matter where we go we can't get out of winter weather! Ron is worn out complaining of neck and backache, but no wonder! I would hate to count the many slide offs we saw along the way, including a couple big rigs! His entire day was spent on "defensive driving". I'm glad we're parked, but even at that, we are sitting with freezing rain coming down coating the truck with a layer of ice and everything else around us! Our truck looks like an ice cube on wheels! We have ice cycles hanging off the bumper, outside mirrors, fenders and all along the trailer. The parking lot has become a skating rink! It's only 19 degrees and we have to burn valuable fuel to keep the truck running all night long, or freeze to death! Under below freezing conditions, Ron does not set his trailer brake because too often the brakes end up frozen, locked up, until you can break them loose. Getting them to release can be a difficult task. It's a miserable job for any driver. We are in Warrenton, MO and have no intention of getting out of our warm truck and walk in the cold up to the restaurant. We won't starve; we have canned food on board!

Kim called earlier and said her arm is giving her trouble again, but at least now she's found someone to help her out. I was very glad to hear that. I continue my daily calls to Ron's mom and lately conversations are all about her demand that when we get home she wants us to move her back to her house. Her repeated insistence wears me down! Ron gets frustrated when he sits there and listens to my conversation and I don't blame him. I know it must be hard on his mother but she needs to stay put. It's not as if we all abandoned her. She has plenty of company in our absence from family and friends. I just hope in time she settles down, makes friends and starts to enjoy her new surroundings. It would make our life driving truck states away a whole lot easier.

Today we are in Oklahoma and Ron just pulled off the road into a truck stop after sizing up the sky above us. We both could see a huge storm coming in and there isn't another truck stop for miles! In Oklahoma, anything can happen when the weather turns sour, including tornadoes, especially this time of year! The sky is coal black, we have bolts of lightning strikes hitting all around us and now the rain is starting to fall. We both enjoy watching a good storm (as long as there are no tornado warnings going on), especially when we know we're safe, parked and not out there driving in it. We've lost a few hours of driving time with Ron's decision, but we'll make up tomorrow.

We, like so many other truckers out here running coast to coast have troublesome worries or unresolved issues with family or friends that we carry with us. Just because we're away from home several days or weeks at a time, doesn't let us off the hook; the problems stick with you and remain on your mind with every turn of the wheel. You can't shake them off and if you let worries get the best of you, they could ultimately affect your mental health. (One driver, not too long ago recently took his life! They found him dead inside his truck with a self inflicted gunshot wound!) If possible, it's best to get whatever issues are bothering you resolved before leaving! In our case, although we took every measure to take care of Ron's mother's needs, she continues to be unhappy. My daily phone conversations continue and the topic remains the same! Each time I hang up the phone with her, I'm left feeling very frustrated! At one point, Ron and I weakened and thought maybe we should quit driving and bring her home to live with us. Given more thought about our idea, the less appealing it became. She needs someone to be with her 24/7 and for now, we are not ready to take on this responsibility. Still, I cannot help but feel somewhat guilty wondering if we made the right decision or not.

On our last trip headed east we ran into mechanical problems when the truck broke down in Oklahoma. That was the last thing we needed to happen! We were hauling a full load of carpet, scheduled for delivery in Georgia and expected to be delivered on time. We limped into a shop and were told by the mechanic that the repairs would take at least three days! Needless to say, we called dispatch and they sent another driver to pick up our load, leaving us high and dry with an empty trailer. The truck was ready on the third day, but this little breakdown cost us $3,000, not to mention our expense for motel and meals! This is not going to be a profitable month! In addition to the cost of repairs in Oklahoma, while home, Ron had a new clutch installed. The combined repairs ended up costing us around $6,000! Needless to say all of the money earned for so many miles of driving went right back into the truck. We didn't make a dime!

Sometimes we get down and wonder if driving truck for a living is worth all the effort. It seems like we're just spinning our wheels and not making any headway. Our truck has over 900,000 miles on it now and fuel prices are outrageous! Due to increased expenses, our net profit has dropped considerably! Right now it makes you want to sit back, scratch the top of your head, and give yourself a few slaps on the face, just to wake up and figure out if driving truck for a living is sanity or insanity! When I get down like this, I see no way we will ever be able to retire. We will probably die out here behind the wheel without ever knowing what it's like to live our senior years enjoying family and doing the things we like to do.

We're back on the road with a new load and racked up several miles of driving today before stopping. We both went inside the truck stop to buy fast food for dinner. No sooner did we pay for it, when all of a sudden the power went off inside the building! The store instantly became dark and silent, creating an eerie feeling all around us. Employees quickly took position by all entrances and exits. Ron and I were glad we had already paid for our food and headed straight for the door. The employee standing there quickly unlocked it and let us out. The rumor over the CB radio is that lightening struck a transformer and blew it out. If this is the case, drivers at the fuel island in the process of fueling will be stuck there for who knows how long! (At this moment, no doubt, we have a bunch of pissed off truckers!)

It's the 1st of April and we are staging at a truck stop we've been to before outside Indianapolis, Indiana. We're waiting for our window of opportunity that will allow us to drive through the "big city" when there's the *least* amount of traffic! Actually, we're only here a few hours (we'll leave at 3 o'clock in the morning) and then pull out of the truck stop and get back on the interstate. Unfortunately the trip we're under is considered a "hot load" and there hasn't been enough time for us to even stop for a quick a shower! We both look and feel pretty grubby. I do not like these so called "hot freight" loads! I always wonder just how "hot" or is this just another way dispatchers get teams to drive harder! Our reward for all this effort is that we have a pre loaded trailer waiting for us going to Spokane! I'm also pretty happy and relieved that when I call Ron's mom lately, she is sounding very upbeat and does not mention anything about moving back home! What a relief! The change in her thinking gives me peace. Maybe now she will enjoy being there.

April 11th and not off to a good start! We were dispatched to pick up a load of whole dry peas in Spokane. The plant worker filled our trailer with 450 bags of dried peas stacked high on pallets. Each bag weighed 100 lbs. and after including the weight of the pallets, the total loaded scale weight in the trailer was 46,380 lbs.! This put us way over the allowable 80,000 lb. limit. Ron, needless to say was not very happy and was not about to move our truck off the property until we were D.O.T. legal. I called dispatch to let them know about the problem. They in turn called the shipper and a few minutes later a worker walked up to the truck and told Ron to go ahead and back up to the dock again. He said he was going to remove 10 bags of peas off the trailer. Even after all that, no matter how many times we slid the axels, we were still 380 lbs. over weight! Ron decided it would be pointless to argue further and we accepted the load, knowing full well if we ran over the scales and a picky DOT officer decided to give us a ticket, he certainly could! One of the tricks of the trade is when your total weight is too high you can reduce your overall weight by running less fuel in the tank. The only downside to this is that you have to frequently make more fuel stops along the way!

Little did we know when we left that we would end up in a farmer's field in California! We had a street address, but when we ran out of numbers on the houses we passed and the road turned to dirt, we thought for sure we were given the wrong information! You can't imagine what it is like driving an 18 wheeler through a residential area! You've got to watch for possible posted weight limits, low hanging branches on trees, drooping power lines, parked cars making the street more narrow and pedestrians crossing the street. At that particular moment, there was no way for Ron to turn the rig around; impossible, not enough room! We were sure the address had to be bogus leading us into an area that we shouldn't have gone into! We dead in the water!

Ron instantly became frustrated realizing our predicament and stopped the truck telling me to get on the phone and call the customer! Times like this it can get pretty heated inside the cab of the truck with Ron blurting out his frustrations and me firing back a few of my own, but frankly, I didn't blame him! I immediately got out the paperwork and called the customer. The lady answering the phone spoke with a heavy accent that I could barely understand. I finally figured out what she was saying after several "tell me again" requests. We actually were headed in the right direction! She told me to continue down the dirt road and when we saw a grey rail container in the field, we were to stop and wait for a crew to arrive.

Ron and I were both apprehensive about her directions, but had to give her the benefit of the doubt; after all, we had no other options! Ron put the truck in gear and proceeded to steer our 18 wheeler down the bumpy small dirt road creating a large wake of dust clouds left bellowing up in the air behind us. It wasn't long and we were forced to make a sharp left turn and when we did; at that very moment, we both spotted the container! What a relief, but there was no crew in sight; not a sole around! I called the lady again and she assured me the workers were on their way. We sat parked in the field and waited for about an hour in the hot sun until finally a crew of young men showed up. None of them spoke English, but after handing the paperwork over and me doing a few hand signs, we were able to communicate. They were all friendly and obviously eager to get the trailer unloaded so they could get back to whatever else they were doing.

The temperature was well into the upper 90's and of course there is no such thing as a loading dock out in a farmer's field; the entire trailer had to be "hand unloaded"! A couple young men climbed up inside our trailer and pulled each pallet forward out to the end of the trailer with the help of a pallet jack. The other workers stood outside and when the loaded pallet was placed within their reach, they quickly lifted, (one by one) every single 100 pound bag of peas off the pallet; stacking them inside the storage container. The sweat poured off these young men as they worked in the hot sun. There was no shade to be found and understandably, they had to take several breaks during the entire process. Because of the extreme heat, Ron wanted no part of it; was not about to volunteer, and was so glad they didn't ask for his help!

We sat in the hot sun and didn't run the truck because fuel has gone up to $4.25 a gallon! Ron and I are drenched in sweat ourselves and will be glad when it comes time to leave so we can turn on the air conditioning. Diesel likes heat, but this is too much for her. She is lying on her back stretched out as far as her body will allow trying to find her own relief. Ron is worried if diesel fuel prices continue to climb we will have to park the truck! Rates remain the same and the fuel surcharge has *not* gone up enough to offset the cost of what now seems to be a weekly spike in the price of fuel. It took about three hours for the crew to unload and we were thrilled when they finished! We were more than anxious to close the trailer doors and leave! Ron wasted no time in getting us out of there! He fired up the engine; put the air conditioning on high, made a complete "U" turn, and waved goodbye to the workers. We've delivered loads to other unusual locations before, but having to drive our 18 wheeler over dirt into an open field is one we're not likely to forget!

Last night in Santa Nella, CA we were hit up for money while parked at the truck stop and it came as no surprise. We've come to expect that some stranger sooner or later during our stay is going to hit us up for money! When I think about it, walking from truck to truck in a confined parking lot asking drivers for money becomes a much easier task for beggars versus them having to wave their signs out on a street corner! Truck drivers are captured prey, sitting ducks, easy targets, a cash cow, and gift horse in the eyes of the beggar! We willingly dig into our wallets and hand over free cash! Sometimes we do this to get rid of the stranger and other times because we believe their story. In this particular case, the man appeared clean cut and seemed sincere. He said he was asking for donations that support a local charity that helps under privileged kids in the area. I usually want to butt in and do my own interrogation, but for some reason, this time I thought he was telling the truth. Ron reached into his wallet and handed him a five dollar bill. He thanked us, with a "God Bless" and moved on to the next truck. Who knows, I don't know if we just got scammed or not!

I'm beginning to think this is a "hub" for homeless people or word got out that drivers at this particular truck stop are easy pickings! Whatever the case, the driver parked right beside us went the *extra* mile! He was approached by a homeless couple and no doubt felt sorry for them. They offered to polish his wheels, (for what price, I don't know), but he agreed to let them do it. The couple had sleeping bags, luggage and a guitar they were carrying giving more credibility of being homeless. We observed as the couple went from wheel to wheel leaving each one with a sparkling shine. No doubt the driver was pleased with the job. The sun was starting to set as the young couple finished polishing the last wheel. The driver got out of his truck to do a final inspection and much to our surprise the driver turns around, walks back to the door of his truck, opens it, and the two men proceed to load the bags, luggage and guitar inside! I said to Ron this trucker must plan to give them a ride. We continued to watch as the driver locked his door, engaged in a brief conversation with the couple and then the three of them headed across the lot towards the restaurant.

A short time later, still sitting up front in our truck, we observed the three of them return. The man and woman were each carrying a large bag which most likely was loaded full of fast food. Ron and I were witnessing a huge act of kindness shown to these homeless people by the truck driver! The driver proceeded to unlock his door and hand the man and woman their belongings. I thought this was the end of it and the couple wood look for a place nearby on the grass where they could eat their gift of food and then bed down for the night. I was so wrong!! The couple walked back to the driver's flat bed trailer, climbed up and rolled out their sleeping bags! The two of them sat down, opened up the bags of food and proceeded to eat their dinner. In my opinion, that trucker went the extra mile! He not only gave them money and a hot meal, but a place to sleep off the ground as well!

April 13th. We are in Tulsa, OK at a small truck stop. We were on toll roads most of the day; it costs extra money, but saves miles of driving. Once we left the last toll road we headed for the nearest major truck stop. Much to our *huge* disappointment, by the time we arrived, 18 wheelers had already filled every parking space! The entire lot was packed nose to nose like a freshly opened can of sardines! This is a dreaded situation no driver wants to face after a long day of driving; too many trucks and no place to park! We did of course like any other driver would do, get back out on the interstate and look for another truck stop that isn't so crowded. It's funny, but you can have a perfectly good day of driving and then it only takes something like this to put you in a bad mood, especially Ron! Fortunately, he only drove another couple miles and found this dumpy little truck stop, full of clutter and pot holes, but who cares, we're parked and off the road! We plan to stay put inside our truck tonight and eat what we have on board. We have to get up early anyway to make a drop in Arkansas and then on to Mississippi for another partial drop and then after that, we'll be off to Georgia. Tomorrow is going to be another long day of driving for the two of us. I'll be glad when the last piece of freight comes off the trailer!

I'm tired and in no mood to make my nightly phone call to Ron's mom. Lately she's gone back to her relentless request of wanting to move back to her own house. Talking to her would only make me frustrated by having to repeat myself several times over explaining why it's not possible. She has a way of making me feel guilty and I always end up feeling sorry for her. It bothers Ron listening to the conversation and each time I hang up the phone, he tries to cheer me up by saying "It's just her Billie and she doesn't even realize she's hurting your feelings." So, maybe I'm just a big softie! Aside from driving our life away trucking and barely making a profit these past few months, Ron's mother remains an ongoing concern. We've looked after her for so many years now and we're not getting any younger ourselves, so now it's becoming the *old* taking care of the *old*!

May 10th. We were home when our 35th wedding anniversary arrived. It's not that we did anything special, because we didn't, we rarely do, but at least we continue to enjoy each other's company and appreciate the short time off eating home cooked meals, our own shower and a big bed to sleep in. Our brief stay even allowed a short visit to meet up with a few old friends at the Deer Park Eagles Aries 3564 which we've been a member of for several years. In was such a refreshing change from the constant life of isolation we live by having a job that requires us to be gone so long. Sitting amongst friends, sharing a few laughs always boosts our spirits reaffirming we are still part of the community.

Who would ever think the things we took for granted in the past would become so special to us now! Driving truck makes you appreciate what you have at home and what you leave behind; each and every time you leave! Ron and I both love springtime; it's nature's renewal of life and we always find ourselves looking for the first plump little Robin to confirm it! Before leaving, the two of us managed to plant the vegetable garden and do spring clean up around the yard. I also made a trip to the doctor to have him check out two bright red streaks that showed up on my face. Each stripe was conveniently placed on both sides of my nose and continued across my cheek bones. I imagined myself looking like a football player; (except they use black under their eyes), or maybe I looked more like the Indians we used to see in the movies with bright red stripes of war paint on their faces! Of course the reality of my condition was learning that the red streaks were caused by *allergies*. Spring has sprung!

While waiting for our load out of California, we had a surprise phone call from Kim saying she would be driving out to see us. She brought both of us gifts. A parking lot is not the best place to visit family, but for a trucker it's much more common than you might think. More often than not it might be the only way to see each other. I wish Diesel our cat would appreciate having company like we do. She doesn't like Kim inside our truck or anyone else for that matter and becomes real crabby, goes into her "don't touch me attitude" if anyone tries to pet her! We just learned our load is about ready for us to pick up. Whoopee! No more sitting, we'll soon be out of here hooked up to a new load headed down the highway!

May 12th. We arrived in Georgia delivering our load on time but only after Ron drove his heart out to get us here. I helped out of course, but did not cover near the miles that he did. I'm very proud of his stamina, determination and endurance in getting the job done; this is the way he's always been. However, I've never taken his personality for granted, and continue to be impressed every time I witness him pulling off what I consider to be impossible! We have not had a shower in 7 days and although right now a shower would be wonderful, it will have to go on hold until tomorrow. We are very tired after getting up before dawn this morning. Later I will go and get us a couple hamburgers. We'll eat, and call it a day. Yesterday was Mother's Day and like clockwork, Kim, Kellie and Jason did not forget to call me. I always love hearing from them! We didn't forget to call Ron's mom either. She was happy that her two nieces came out to see her and didn't even mention anything about wanting to go home.

The price of diesel fuel continues to sky rocket! I honestly think this country is going into a recession, or even worse, maybe a depression! We are barely breaking even! In all reality, I don't know how much longer we can continue without the company paying us a higher rate per mile or at least, raising the amount of surcharge we receive. We've been forced to operate on such a slim margin that it's nearing the point where we're questioning why we're even out here! When things turn around like this and you end up "paying" to have a job, something is obviously wrong with that picture! It's not just us; other owner/operators are feeling the crunch as well! Not a day goes by that we don't hear some driver complaining over the CB radio expressing his fear of going broke! Outrageous fuel prices are impacting the cost of living across the board; boosting up prices on everything purchased by consumers. When I think about all those people only getting paid minimum wage, I wonder how in the world they're even surviving!

May 14th. What a way to start our morning! The alarm went off at 2 a.m. and we went through the usual routine of Ron getting up first and then me. When we get up this early, neither of us speaks to each other. We just go through the motions of getting dressed, which are best described to the likeness of two slow moving zombies making their way through a graveyard! (Only we're making our way from the bunk to the front seats!) We filled a thermos last night, so at least we had time to wake up and share a cup of coffee before Ron had to get out and do the routine vehicle inspection. No time to spare, he climbed back in, completed an entry in his log and just that quick, we were off and running! We will drive hard now for several more hours before stopping. Who knows what today will bring. Each day of a driver's life behind the wheel is filled with the unknown. There's no telling what lies ahead waiting to greet us; like accidents, construction, sudden weather changes, mechanical problems, freight shifting, animals suddenly darting across the road, tire blowout, or on a more personal note, coming down with an ailment or hearing about some bad news happening at home. This unique world goes unshared and exclusively applies to the driver behind the wheel; it's not a career cut out for everyone.

When we arrived at the drivers yard it was filled with several empty and loaded trailers. I knew it was going to take some time finding ours parked amongst so many others. Ron pulled up next to the old mail box conveniently located for drivers who arrive after hours to get their trip envelope stored inside. I jumped out of the truck and after sorting through several envelopes, I found ours. I read Ron the trailer number and he proceeded to drive slowly down the rows of parked trailers to look for it. A few minutes later we spotted our trailer parked tightly between two others. Ron backed up locking the king pin into the fifth wheel. He then proceeded to connect the air lines and do the usual routine inspection of the truck and trailer while I remained seated inside.

Next thing I know Ron climbs back in the truck slamming the door behind him! He was irritated as hell! He said, "You won't believe this, the trailer is Red Tagged! We are going to have to sit here until the mechanics show up for work!" I asked if he knew why they tagged the trailer and he replied, "Because the dam mud flap is shot!" Ron was in disbelief that whoever saw the mud flap earlier was too lazy to get it fixed and just dumped the problem on the driver! He said we would not pass a DOT inspection and he's not about to take the chance of getting pulled in at a scale house. Ron was fit to be tied over this and wasn't about to cool down. He said "There's no excuse why the problem wasn't fixed last night, other than pure laziness on the part of some employee. The company wants their loads delivered on time, but under a situation like this, it's going to set us back four or five hours! There are no "wings" on the trailer, we can't fly!" The reality of all this is that eventually the flap will get replaced, but the delay will cost us valuable driving time. Now we have no choice but to run even harder in order to make the delivery on time. Our day was ruined before we even got started; all over a simple repair!

May 31st. We're back in California in the driver's yard. We hauled 16 pallets of used batteries out of Spokane to Vernon, CA. We couldn't wait to get rid of the heavy load! When the driver of the fork lift pulled off the last pallet, I smiled at Ron and gave him a "thumbs up!" This load was a pain in the rear even before we left Spokane! We fought sliding the axels several times before Ron was satisfied with the weight distribution. Like any heavy load, it sucked up fuel and blew it out the stacks! Right now as far as we're concerned, the price of diesel fuel is equal to purchasing precious "GOLD"! It's our most costly expense!

Last night while sleeping in the driver's yard, I was awakened by the sound of a helicopter hovering up above us. At first I tried to go back to sleep but every time I did, the loud noise returned. I woke Ron up and he listened along with me. We both got out of bed to take a look and quickly spotted a helicopter hovering right above us. The chopper had high powered spot lights swishing back and forth over our truck and the surrounding area. Between the two of us we mutually agreed that they must be looking for some fugitive on the run! I double checked our doors to make sure they were locked and continued to watch as the helicopter made several passes over our heads. Ron finally said, "Billie we can't stay up all night". I knew he was right. Even though I was fascinated by the drama, I agreed to get back in bed. This morning we learned that the police were looking for someone involved in a drive by shooting just a short block away! We've been in some bad areas before in California, but I didn't think this area was one of them! There are several empty boxcars sitting on the other side of the cyclone fence that surrounds this property. No doubt whoever was fleeing the police had plenty of places to hide!

May 31, 2008. We took a load from Spokane to Los Angeles. After delivery, we did our usual routine of dropping off the empty trailer and bob tailing over to the driver's yard. This is where we wait until we're dispatched a new load. As we sat throughout the next day we witnessed other driver's getting their dispatch, leave the lot and be on their way. By afternoon we began to wonder if we would even get a load or not! The thought of being stuck over the weekend in the driver's yard was depressing to say the least! We finally lost patience and I called dispatch, (which I know always irritates them). They would prefer that you sit and wait for them to send you the information over the Qualcom. The person answering the phone told me "The crew is still working on your load". That was reassuring news for both of us knowing a load was in the making, so we patiently continued to sit and wait. A couple more hours went by and not a word from dispatch! The anticipation got the best of me; I had to find out what was taking them so long to load our trailer. Once again I lost patience ignoring the "Don't call us, we'll call you" policy and started calling dispatch by the hour! The answer I received was always the same, "The warehousemen are still out there working on it!" Ron and I had no choice but to stay put, remained parked, and continued to observe other drivers, one by one, get their load assignment and leave. Finally, when the sun started to set, Ron couldn't take the suspense any longer! We were the only drivers left still waiting for a load. He said "We're going to drive over there and find out for ourselves what's going on!"

Both of us at this point felt something was definitely wrong! We've never had to wait this long before for a load and couldn't help but wonder if the delay wasn't a *deliberate act* on their part! Maybe they were giving us a surprise *payback* for disagreements in the past! The upper east coast is "no man's land for big rigs" (at least as far as we're concerned) and every time they would try to send us there, we would turn the load down reminding them of our long standing agreement when we first signed on with the company. The terminal manager here is relatively new and like some of his predecessors, apparently didn't want to bother looking over previous agreements made with owner/operators! He expects a driver to accept whatever load he assigns without any argument in return; regardless of where it delivers!

We parked the truck at the terminal and the two of us proceeded to go inside and look for the warehouse supervisor. We found him at his desk and he told us they were running short of freight and "building" our load. From his office, we walked out into the warehouse. Sure enough, we observed an employee driving a fork lift buzzing around looking at sparsely stored racks of carpet, singling out rolls to load on our trailer. Ron checked the labels on the rolls as they were being loaded inside the trailer and noticed that a few went to Maryland! Having discovered the location, Ron was instantly upset and went straight to the manager! Ron told him "We don't go there!" The manager responded by saying, "Don't worry, just take it to Georgia and let them deal with it." This was Saturday evening after 6 p.m. and

the manager appeared anxious to go home. Rather than question him
further, we took his word and accepted the load. Besides, we wanted
to get out of there as much as he did!

We drove hard all the way to Georgia to get the load delivered
on time; arriving at the company terminal late in the evening. We
unhooked from the trailer then Ron walked around to the back, opened
the doors and put paperwork inside before leaving. From there, dead
tired, almost midnight, we bob tailed over to the usual motel we stay
at, checked in, carried the cat and luggage into the room, took showers
and went straight to bed. The next morning I received a phone call from
the dispatcher telling me that they had unloaded their portion of the
carpet and the few remaining pieces left were ready for us to deliver in
Maryland. Frankly, I was shocked! I couldn't believe what I just heard
and instantly informed her of the previous instructions we received
from the manager in California. The dispatcher responded by saying
she didn't care *"what"* we were told because *"we"* were expected to
deliver the entire load regardless of the location! Our debate continued,
and finally I had enough of arguing with her and said, "I'm ending this
phone conversation with you! We have a standing agreement with the
company and they know we do not go anywhere near the upper east
coast!" When I informed Ron of what she said to me he could hardly
believe it himself! I told him I stood my ground feeling very confident
that I had made myself perfectly clear; we were not going to Maryland!
I told her she needed to use one of their own local drivers to deliver the
remaining few rolls left inside the trailer. There was no way I was going
to weaken and I wasn't about to allow her to try to wear me down further
or to continue putting pressure on me! Ron agreed, but said, "I'll bet it's
not over! She will probably call back or get someone else to do it!"

Within a few minutes, sure enough the phone rang again, only this
time it was the terminal manager! I got the same insistent demand from
him as I did from her! I repeated to him our reason for not delivering
the rest of the load, while at the same time, making myself perfectly
clear; there was no way we were about to change our minds! He too was
unyielding and just as determined to force the delivery on us regardless!
He stood firm on his opinion, telling me "It was *our* load and he was
NOT about to use one of his local drivers to deliver it!" When I again
said NO we're not going to do it! He raised his voice and said "The load
is going to sit here until you do!" I ended his call by telling him sorry;
it's not going to happen!

It wasn't long before the phone rang again, only this time it was from another employee with apparent higher authority. He introduced himself and immediately said he was informed by the manager in Georgia that we had refused to take the rest of the load to Maryland and in his opinion, he considered our decision to be abandonment of the load dispatched. He told me "You accepted the load, and we expect you to deliver it!" Not waiting to hear what else he might have to say, I jumped in and said "You've got to hear *my* side of the story!" I proceeded once again to explain our position. I told him; "If you don't believe what I just told you; call the other manager in California!" I also reminded him of our lease agreement. His reply was that it didn't matter what the other manager told us, we accepted the load and it was our responsibility to complete the delivery, regardless of location! He argued further by telling me lots of other drivers go to Maryland all the time and there was no reason why we shouldn't do the same! I could see this conversation was going south! He wasn't about to let us off the hook! He was just as determined as the others in shoving the delivery down our throats! I had it! I told him there was no need for further conversation; we were NOT going to take the load! He ended the call by telling me "You're not going to get another one until you do!"

The remainder of the day was quiet, which gave Ron and me in our motel room time to digest the reality of our unexpected situation and what we planned to do about it! We did not waver on our belief that we were *right* and they were *wrong*! Tired of their bullying, we decided to stay firm on our decision and stand our ground, regardless of the consequences! Later in the day, I went down to the truck and checked the Qualcom for messages and sure enough, there was one waiting saying "your load is ready"! I considered this to be one more way of reinforcing their point! Instead of being upset by the message, I was more amused by visioning the two managers huddling together coming up with another way to keep the heat on us! Nice try, I thought to myself as I got out of the truck and went back to our room! After telling Ron about the message, he said call the manager and tell him "If we don't have a load by 10 a.m. Wednesday morning, were leaving"! I called, and his response was "Oh, we can give you a load, but not until you deliver the one sitting here!"

Ron's decision giving them a deadline, no doubt was final, but the shocking reality of our situation suddenly hit me like a ton of bricks! Our many years of dedicated service given to this company were apparently taken for granted and went unappreciated placing little value on what a team puts forth! Our trucking career had come to an abrupt halt! Together we must now face the consequences of our actions; unemployed for the first time in years! There are times in life when you must stand your ground, sticking to the principals you believed in; especially when you find yourself reaching the point where your honesty and integrity is being challenged! We could not allow this to happen, so now we are about to do the unimaginable! It's a long way home and the only way to get there is to bob tail; driving our truck without a trailer 2,300 miles across the United States! The entire cost for the trip to get us back home will be paid for out of our own pockets! This is the price we'll pay for standing up for ourselves. It's going to be a long bumpy ride without pulling a trailer all the way back to Washington, but we'll do it!

I would be lying if I said we didn't have our moments of sadness, feeling unappreciated and a little bit sorry for ourselves. Each time one of us would reflect back on our many years of service we would talk about all the employees and drivers that we had made friends with, the times we helped dispatchers out when they were in a bind or drove the extra miles to get a "hot" load delivered. Now all of these relationships have come to an end! It's only been a matter of hours and here we are alone, about to head home and no longer a part of their world. There will be no further attempts made to contact anyone by either of us; it would be pointless! We lost a family that has been a part of our life for so many years. It's sad to say the least, but we will close this chapter of our lives and together face whatever lies in store ahead.

Before leaving we went over to a nearby truck stop. While Ron fueled, I jumped out and filled a thermos with coffee. After he was done fueling Ron wasted no time getting us back out on the interstate. Together, we started our long journey home. We didn't say much to each other for the next several miles. I think we both were flat out stunned over what took place! We needed time for our minds to absorb the reality of everything that had transpired since accepting the load out of California. We were unhappy from the start knowing we had no choice but to either take the load or sit out the weekend. Now, in less than a week our entire life has changed leaving us with unknown certainty about what the future holds.

It wasn't until we stopped in Missouri to fuel did we learn that the company had cut off our fuel card! We were very surprised, considering they *owed us money* for hauling the load out, plus the fact we had a hefty deposit (required when you sign on), that stays on hold until you leave the company. This would have been plenty of money to cover the cost of fuel to get us home. We both felt that by blocking access to our fuel card, it must have been their way of telling us they had terminated our employment! I really think their decision was unnecessary because after all, it was not like we were trying to rip off the company! We honestly expected that they would deduct the fuel from our settlement; it's their routine procedure.

Even after all this, I feel no animosity whatsoever for any of the employees I dealt with during this entire ordeal. All of us, for our own personal reasons, felt strong about our position on the issue and did not waiver. Neither party involved was willing to change their minds, throw in the towel, or even entertain the thought of giving in to the other person's wishes! Let's face it; both sides were stuck in gridlock! Simple as that! There was no solution left on the table in resolving the differences we shared. Our only conclusion of being up against circumstances like this was to pack up and leave Dodge! Nevertheless, this is what took place and for the remainder of the trip we will try to enjoy our last ride and try not to worry too much about the future.

During the trip home we found ourselves pondering each other's ideas on what options we might have to continue earning a living. We also reflected back on our final morning and how quickly we were able to wrap up our stay at the motel, fuel and head home. We couldn't help but imagine the surprised look that must have been on the faces of those we left behind, especially when they realized we did exactly what we told them we would do!

We shared many thoughts as we traveled along but there's one that continued to remain locked inside both of our minds; we were out of a job, we officially joined the ranks of the unemployed! This was a very insecure feeling. Had we continued to allow ourselves to dwell on our predicament, our conversation could have ended up putting us both into a state of depression! Of course, neither one of us wanted that to happen! Ron and I agreed, we needed to keep our minds on the road, stop worrying about the unknown and stay focused on driving safe. Besides, on a much brighter note, I made Ron laugh when I told him we should be noted in some book of records for the longest "bob tail" miles ever driven by two truckers!

When I reflect back, I feel we were totally unprepared to deal with neither the reception we received nor the apparent disregard displayed by employees; giving no credence to another company manager's shipping instructions. Had we known in advance we would run into differences upon delivery, we would have called the manager in California to clear things up before our arrival. The employees I spoke with were not interested in hearing what I had to say and their only concern was getting the rest of the load delivered. It's a shame, because it's always been a good company to work for and we were always proud to be a part of it This is a good time for me to point out an ongoing problem that appears to be common with many other trucking companies and parallels with what we just went through. They hire on owner/operators but lack educating their employees who have to work with them that there's a difference between an "independent trucker" leased on with them and a "company employee". Owner/operators are independent contractors. They run their own business. Unlike a company employee who must follows a set of standards for job performance, gets paid vacation, sick pay, health benefits, retirement benefits and never has to worry about fuel prices or costly repairs; owner/operators are quite the opposite! They must come up with the money to pay for all of those perks and expenses themselves. Most often a lease agreement is negotiated up front and agreed upon between the owner/operator and the company he signs on with. In our case, we made it known there were certain areas in the United States we wanted to avoid, but dispatchers never seemed to be knowledgeable of this fact. Too often employees, (mainly dispatchers) find it difficult to differentiate between these two identities.

A first hand example would be when a dispatcher asks an owner/operator to assist jockeying several of their empty trailers from one location to another or asks them to run local deliveries. These jobs should be given to a company employee, (unless of course there was some previous agreement to do it), but I think that's doubtful. Most owner/operators would turn down the requests knowing they would have to log additional hours cutting into their total hours left to drive. A company employee wouldn't have any choice; they're expected to do what's being asked of them. I could go further with my thoughts comparing differences between owner/operator obligations versus company employee obligations to the firm they both drive truck for, but I doubt if my words would change anything.

I'm sure similar experiences like ours, other independent drivers have gone through themselves with the company they work for. Our differences were definitely not with the company as a whole, but only with those few individuals involved. Ron's employment with them started long before I came on board and then after that, the two of us gave them several more years. The lack of willingness to work out a problem cost the company a team! My only conclusion is that maybe after refusing loads to the upper east coast in the past, it was possible this time they decided not to compromise even though delivery instructions from the other company manage was made clear to them.

Soon we will be pulling into our driveway. We still have not decided what we will do next, although we are strongly considering taking some extended time off. Ron's mom, as I've mentioned so many times before, is an ongoing responsibility. We're leaning towards bringing her home to live with us. In addition to that, there are plenty of projects on our 10 acres to keep us busy. Now that we are no longer obligated to the company, maybe this will be a good opportunity in our life to pause and revaluate our priorities. There is still so much to think about and for now, after bob tailing over 2,000 miles to get here, we'll park our truck, unload and try to regroup. If Diesel could talk she would be thrilled with our decision!

To all of our fellow truckers out there, like we always say to each other in parting; "Keep the rubber side down and the shiny side up!" Your job is the most valuable component, the "clasp in the chain" that links together with thousands of other hard working people, providing whatever it takes, to keep America going! God Bless our White Line Warriors!

CONCLUSION

JANUARY 2012, THREE YEARS LATER

I couldn't leave my readers high and dry wondering what happened next! We did indeed take a leave of absence from trucking! After so many years of driving we both felt burned out! There's no other way to describe our feelings at that time.

It took a few weeks for us to settle back into an unfamiliar routine of staying put at home. But eventually we adapted spending our time working around the property or visiting with old friends. Ron's mother made no bones about it once she learned we no longer were trucking; she either wanted to be moved back to her home or live with us. After asking the advice of other family members we decided to give it a try. We knew it wouldn't be as easy as it sounded. Like the two of us, his mother is also set in her ways. We prepared her bedroom, packed up her things from the assisted living facility and brought her home. What we didn't realize with our decision was that we traded confinement inside the truck for being confined at home. His mother could not be left alone. This meant one of us had to be with her at all times. If we both wanted to go somewhere we had to take her with us.

Things went pretty well the first couple months before we started finding ourselves getting annoyed with little things she would do. It seems so petty of me now, but it used to irritate me when she daily had to pull out of her pocket this small one inch brass donkey on a string, swing it back and forth and then tell me to ask it a question! I had no interest in asking a brass donkey anything! I felt my intelligence was being challenged. She also carried a box of tissue in the basket of her walker and throughout the day I would pick up the ones she took out and dropped on the floor. A simple thing of flushing the toilet also became an issue. As the months went on we also went through periods of her having mood swings or wanting to argue with me over taking a shower. I soon found myself, Ron too, missing the independent life we once enjoyed far away from the "hands on" responsibility of caring for her. There were days I would find myself sitting on the front porch staring out at our truck parked in the driveway and my eyes would fill with tears. A year later her living with us came to a close. We decided to move her back to assisted living and go back on the road. It wasn't her choice and when it came down to it, we both felt bad.

In 2009 we leased on to another company and have been with them ever since. In hindsight, I know it was the right thing to do moving his mother back to 24 hour care. She has Dementia and it's progressively gotten worse these past few years. She's approaching 90 and requires a higher level of care now, much more than we could have offered.

As far as our trucking, we couldn't be any happier! The company we're leased on with allows more freedom of choice and we can take time off anytime we want. Having this flexibility has worked out great for us being owner/operators. No forced dispatch! We only made one adjustment; we agreed to stop teaming! We're getting our sleep, eating dinner each night, and enjoying the ride! Our lifestyle of living on the road has now become much more comfortable.

Sadly, Diesel had to be put down. She was 17 years old, lost continence and could not keep any of her food down. She was rapidly losing ground and we knew it. Taking your long time pet to a veterinarian to be euthanized is an experience I wouldn't wish on anyone! It was painfully gut wrenching on both of us! We still miss her and will always wonder if we did the right thing or not. We tearfully brought her home. Ron got out of the truck and instantly found the shovel and quickly proceeded to dig a grave and bury her with her blanket and plush toy duck in our back yard. After finding some stones and making a cross on top of the grave he slowly walked back and came inside the house. We both looked out the window at her grave, and much to our surprise, we saw a young snow white cat perched on top of it looking straight at us. We both wondered if this was some sort of message from above telling us, "Diesel would be just fine". Who knows, but we never did see the small white cat again.

Time has a way of healing and we now have another cat, Spooky. She's young, black with patches of white on her paws nose and chest. She's full of energy and loves being in the truck! With that, there's nothing left for me to share. We're going to keep on trucking, how much longer, who knows? There's no cure for "White Line Fever"! The life of being on the road has consumed both of us. Ron always says "I'll probably drive until I die and someday they'll find me with my hands frozen to the wheel!"

THANK YOU for ALL YOUR ENCOURAGEMENT

My mother-in-law, Marje

My brother Jerry and his wife, Carol

My brother John and his wife, Sue

Friends, Arnie and Judy

Fellow truck driver and close friend, Randy

TRUCKER'S DICTIONARY

BACK DOOR—Driver following behind one or more trucks watching for bears

BEAR—Officer of the law

BEAR IN THE AIR—Airplane or chopper above hovering over the interstate watching traffic

BED BUGGERS—Household movers

BULL HAULERS—Drivers that haul livestock with the exclusion of chickens

CAN HAULER—Drivers hauling freight containers

CHICKEN HAULERS—Load of chickens or turkeys

COOP—Weigh Station operated by the Department of Transportation

CREEPY CRAWLERS—D.O.T. Inspectors

FOUR WHEELERS—All other traffic running less than 18 wheels

FRONT DOOR—Truck driver up front of one or more other trucks watching for bears

GATORS—Pieces of blown tires on the interstate

HAMMER DOWN—Announcement by driver over the CB no bears in sight

HAMMER LANE—Applies to anything that might be going on in the passing lane

HANDLE—The names drivers use to identify themselves on the CB radio

LOT LIZZARDS—Prostitutes soliciting at truck stops

MEAT WAGON—Ambulance running with lights and siren on

PLAIN WHITE WRAPPER—Alert to other drivers there is an unmarked patrol car in the area

SKATE BOARDS—Flat bed trailers

TOMATO FREIGHTER—Driver hauling fresh tomatoes

WIGGLE WAGONS—Driver hooked up to more than one trailer

YARD STICK—Gives mile marker location of where driver is on the interstate

ZIPPER—Dotted center line on any road

CPSIA information can be obtained at www.ICGtesting.com
Printed in the USA
BVOW011233200213

313733BV00002B/38/P